PRAISE FOR CYNTHIA EDEN AND HER NOVELS

BROKEN

"Sexy, mysterious, and full of
heart-pounding suspense!"
Laura Kaye, *New York Times* bestselling author

"I dare you not to love a Cynthia Eden book!"
Larissa Ione, *New York Times* bestselling author

"Fast-paced, smart, sexy and emotionally
wrenching—everything I love about
a Cynthia Eden book!"
HelenKay Dimon

"Cynthia Eden writes smart, sexy and
gripping suspense. Hang on tight while
she takes you on a wild ride."
Cindy Gerard, *New York Times* bestselling author

By Cynthia Eden

The LOST series

Broken
Twisted
Shattered

CYNTHIA EDEN

SHATTERED

AVONBOOKS

An Imprint of HarperCollins*Publishers*

This is a work of fiction. Names, characters, places, and incidents are products of the author's imagination or are used fictitiously and are not to be construed as real. Any resemblance to actual events, locales, organizations, or persons, living or dead, is entirely coincidental.

AVON BOOKS
An Imprint of HarperCollins*Publishers*
195 Broadway
New York, New York 10007

ISBN 978-0-06-234966-8
www.avonromance.com

First Avon Books mass market printing: November 2015

Printed in the U.S.A.

10 9 8 7 6 5 4 3 2

This book is for my readers. For those wonderful romantic suspense readers who love to turn pages and find danger and romance and surprises. Thank you so much for your support. You have been absolutely fantastic!

Acknowledgments

As always, I want to say "Thank you!" to the amazing staff at Avon. I appreciate all of the help that you have given to me! The editors, the cover designers, the publicists—you are amazing, and it is a pleasure to work with you all.

For my husband and son . . . How can I thank you enough for your patience? When I disappear into my office and get lost in my stories, you always understand . . . and you are waiting for me when I come up for air. Thank you!

Writing this series has been a wonderful experience for me. I've loved being able to explore all of the characters. Jax was certainly a character who took me by surprise—and, confession time—he may just be my favorite all-time character to write. I really hope that you enjoy him, too!

Happy reading, everyone!

SHATTERED

PROLOGUE

IT WAS THE SCREAM THAT WOKE HER. SIX-YEAR-OLD Sarah Jacobs shot up in bed, her heart racing and the echo of that terrible scream still ringing in her ears. The room was dark, but moonlight spilled through her window and illuminated her favorite teddy bear—he was right at her side. Her daddy always put the teddy bear close to her at bedtime.

She clutched that bear to her, holding it tightly, as she slipped out of the bed. The hardwood floor creaked beneath her feet. She wanted her daddy. He made her feel better after she had a bad dream. And she must have just had a bad dream. She must—

"*Help me!*"

That terrible cry had Sarah flinching. The teddy bear fell from her hands and hit the floor. Sarah's fingers fumbled with the doorknob and it took her three tries to open that door. Then she was running down the hallway, rushing toward that sound. It had been a woman, crying for help. Sarah's mommy had cried for help once. In that car accident. She'd been trapped, and Sarah hadn't been able to help her.

The scream had died away again, but it had come from up ahead. The basement. The basement door was shut, but she could see the faint light shining behind the door. Who was in her basement? Why was the lady screaming for help?

Sarah's fingers were shaking when she reached for the door. But before she could try to turn that knob, the door opened on its own. Sarah's breath caught as fear swept over her but when she looked up—she just saw her daddy.

"Hello, sweetheart," he told her, flashing her a big smile. "Did you have a bad dream?"

Sarah rubbed her eyes. "Someone's screaming."

He bent and picked her up, carrying her easily. Her daddy was so big and strong. "No, sweetheart. No one is screaming. No one at all." He was humming as he carried her back to her room. Her daddy did that. He hummed his sweet tune and Sarah started humming with him. They went back to her room, and he tucked her in bed. He picked up her teddy bear and slid Mr. Fuzzy right in bed next to her. "Silly bear," her dad said, flashing her a grin that she could see even in the dark of her room. "Was he trying to make a break for it?"

Sarah giggled.

He kissed her forehead. "Sleep tight. You know you're safe tonight."

He always told her that. *Sleep tight. You know you're safe tonight.* And she was safe, as long as her daddy was near.

Sarah yawned. Her daddy brushed back her hair. "If you hear anything else tonight," he murmured, "don't pay it any mind. A storm's coming, and that must be what you heard. Thunder and lightning. Branches scraping against the house. Nothing more."

Sleep was already pulling at her.

"Stay warm in bed. No matter what you hear, it's just a storm."

She smiled and snuggled her bear closer.

Her daddy crept from the room.

Sleep was pulling at her, tugging harder and deeper and—

"*Help me!*"

Sarah squeezed her eyes shut. It was just the storm. Her daddy had said it was just the storm, and he never lied to her.

Two years later . . .

"THE WORLD ISN'T a safe place, sweetheart."

Sarah was twirling around in her front yard. Her daddy was beside her, staring out at the street. He sounded so serious, so she stopped spinning.

"There are bad people in the world."

Her hands were still over her head. She lowered them slowly, staring at her daddy.

"I won't let them hurt you, though, don't worry."

No, he would never let anyone hurt her. Sarah already knew that.

"I'll teach you how to be strong, how to spot the bad people."

Sarah tiptoed toward him. She was still wearing her

tutu, and it brushed against her legs. "How do I spot them?"

He tapped her on the nose. "It can be hard because they look just like you and me."

Sarah bit her lip. "What do the bad people do?"

"They lie, sweetie. They steal. They kill. You have to be ready for them. I'll make you ready."

Her breath heaved out. "Thank you, Daddy." He was always taking such good care of her.

"There are two types of people in this world. You'll see that. The hunters and the victims." His gaze held hers. His eyes were as dark as her own. "I won't ever let you be a victim."

Sarah shook her head. She didn't want to be a victim.

"That's my girl." He smiled at her. Her daddy was such a handsome man. She'd heard all those ladies say that—the ladies that were always trying to catch her daddy's attention. And when he smiled, his whole face seemed to light up. "Before I'm done with you, Sarah, you'll be the very best hunter out there."

She smiled at him, too. She wanted to be just like her daddy.

If he said she'd be the best hunter . . . then she would be.

Eight years later . . .

SOMETHING SMELLED FUNNY in the house. Sarah stood in the kitchen, her bare toes curling against the tile. It was her birthday—sweet sixteen. They were going to celebrate. Her friends were coming over for a sleepover.

But . . . something smelled funny.

Oh, jeez, it would be so embarrassing if her friends came over and they caught a whiff of that smell. They'd make fun of her! No way was that happening on her birthday. Sarah grabbed for the air freshener. She inhaled. Nearly choked. *Horrible.* And the smell was coming from . . . the basement. Her dad's workroom.

Had a pipe burst? Was there mold and water all over the place down there?

Sarah hurried forward. She opened the door, then hesitated. Her dad had told her not to go down there—his work was still out and he was worried she might mess it up.

If a pipe burst, that will mess everything up for him. I need to check.

Sarah walked forward. Her hand curled around the banister that would take her down into the basement. The smell was worse. So strong and thick. She hurried down those steps, spraying as she went.

When she reached the last stair, the smell was so intense that Sarah almost gagged. It smelled as if something had died down there. *Oh, no. Don't let me find a dead rat. Don't.*

She heard the floor creaking above her. Then she heard the faint sound of her father humming.

Oh, good, he was home. He'd gone out to pick up her cake, and he had said that he'd make it home before she did, but Sarah had beaten him. Just by minutes, it seemed. Now he could come down there and move whatever *thing* was stinking up their house.

And my friends will never know.

"Sarah?" It was her dad's voice. "Sarah, you've got to see the surprise I've got for you."

Her dad and his surprises. She glanced back up the staircase. "I'm down here, Dad!"

Silence.

She turned to stare at the darkened recesses of the basement. Her eyes narrowed as she stepped forward. There was some kind of bag down there. Big and thick. Burlap.

"Sarah, you're not supposed to be down here."

She jumped because her dad was *right behind her.* He'd moved silently down those stairs, and she hadn't even heard him. Sarah whirled around even as her heart raced in her chest. "Dad! You scared me."

He didn't smile at her. His dark eyes glinted. "I've told you before . . . you don't need to be afraid. It's the rest of the world—"

"—that has to be afraid." She shook her head. Right. He said that line to her all the time. She knew he wanted her to think she was some kind of superstar, but she wasn't. She was just a normal girl. One who'd started to get picked on at school. Not that she'd told her dad. He would just get mad if he knew that Ryan Klein had made fun of her when she'd fallen at PE the other day. Now everyone was calling her Shaky Sarah. If they didn't get the smell out of the house soon, that nickname would change to Smelly Sarah in about twenty minutes when her friends arrived.

She pointed behind her. "Dad, I think a pipe broke and got your bag wet. That smell is terrible!"

He moved forward. His steps were still silent. He could do that, move so quietly. He'd been showing her how lately, too. He'd been teaching her to shoot, to fight. To hunt.

"That's one of your presents. Though I was going to show it to you later. After your friends left."

Her present was in that stinky bag?

Sarah put down her air freshener and she crept forward.

Her dad turned on another light, and the bulb shone down on that bag. The bag wasn't just wet. Those stains on it were so dark in color.

"I heard about the trouble you had at school." His lips thinned. "Your counselor called me . . . told me all about that boy . . ."

Her cheeks burned. "It's nothing, Dad. I can handle him."

"He has a history of picking on other kids. Bullying them. He's older, so he should know better."

He was older. Eighteen. A senior while she was just a sophomore.

"I can handle him," she said again.

Her dad smiled. "You don't have to."

Then he opened the bag for her.

Sarah stared into that bag and she heard screaming. Screaming that she remembered from so long ago . . . wild, desperate screaming—

Help me. Help me. Help me!

—but this time, that screaming was coming from her. Sarah was screaming and crying and she was on the floor. Nausea rolled through her stomach and she vomited right there.

Her dad's arms wrapped around her.

"It's all right, sweetheart. I've got you." He pressed a kiss to her temple. "Happy birthday."

Chapter 1

MONSTERS WERE REAL, AND THEY USUALLY HID beneath the skin of men.

Dr. Sarah Jacobs had spent most of her adult life hunting monsters. She'd just finished her most recent case with LOST—Last Option Search Team—a recovery group that hunted the missing. They'd stopped the bad guy, but not before he'd killed.

More innocent lives had been lost.

No one is really innocent. Her father's voice whispered through Sarah's mind, and she hurried her steps as she walked down the busy New Orleans street. A few other members of her team were still in town, tying up the last of their loose ends. Before long, though, they'd all be packing things up and heading back to the main LOST office in Atlanta.

There would be another case waiting. There always was.

Sarah's footsteps quickened even more when she caught sight of her hotel. The doorman was outside, and a relieved smile spread across her face. She'd felt a bit odd in the last few days. As if she were being watched. She'd been taught never to ignore her instincts, but Sarah knew there was no reason for anyone to be following her. *Not now.*

She hurried past the doorman, mumbling a quick hello. Then she was in the bright hotel lobby. Her high heels clicked over that gleaming floor. She didn't slow down for a little pit stop at the crowded bar. Sarah headed right for the elevator. She got lucky and was able to slip inside immediately. *Only me in here.* A quick exhale of relief escaped her as the doors started to close.

Then a hand appeared. A man's hand—strong, tan, and tattooed. Dark, swirling tattoos slid around his knuckles. He waved his hand, activating the elevator doors' sensors and causing those doors to open wide for him.

Sarah pushed back against the wall of the elevator as Jax Fontaine stepped inside. She knew him by sight. Unfortunately. She also knew the man was trouble. The local authorities generally stayed out of his way. Unless she missed her guess, they were afraid of the guy.

And I don't blame them.

The word on the street was that Jax Fontaine was a very dangerous man. An enemy that most didn't want to have.

Thanks to her last case, she was now acquainted with him—and she knew that she'd attracted some unwelcome interest from the guy.

"Hello, pretty Sarah," he said. New Orleans drawled in his voice, just a hint of Creole rising and falling there. Jax smiled at her. *Right. Dangerous. Definitely dangerous.*

The elevator doors slid closed behind him.

Jax was tall, several inches over six feet, with broad shoulders and the kind of build that told her when he wasn't up to no good in the French Quarter, he had to spend some serious time working out.

The guy looked like a fallen angel—if fallen angels spent a whole lot of time scaring the hell out of people. His hair was blond, thick, and a little too long. His face—that face of his was eerily perfect. Almost too handsome. A strong, hard jaw, a long blade of a nose. He had sharp cheekbones and blue eyes that seemed to see right into her soul.

And the elevator isn't moving.

Probably because he'd leaned forward and pressed the stop button. *What. The. Hell?*

"I hear you're leaving town."

Her heartbeat spiked. When she was near him, that tended to happen. Her heart raced, her breathing came a little faster, and her stomach knotted.

Jax shook his head. "Leaving . . . and you weren't even going to come and tell me good-bye?"

Laughter came from her. Not real laughter. She couldn't remember what real laughter felt like. Tight and mocking, the laughter pushed out from her. "It's not like we're friends, Jax." They'd been uneasy allies on the last case. Jax had known intel that she'd needed about the killer.

"Why just be friends? That's boring." His gaze slid over her. That light blue gaze seemed to heat as it lingered on Sarah's body. "We'd be much better lovers than we'd ever be friends."

Her hands were pressed to the wall behind her—only it wasn't a wall. A mirror. Mirrors lined that elevator. To be very clear, Sarah told him, "I don't date dangerous men."

Jax stepped toward her. He didn't move like other men. He stalked. He glided. Kind of like some big jungle cat—a beast hunting his prey. His hand lifted and his tattooed knuckles slid over her cheek.

His touch made her tense. Mostly because it seemed like an electric shock flowed straight through her body when his skin touched hers.

"Who said anything about dating?" Jax asked her. His smile flashed at her, showing his even, white teeth. "I thought we'd just spend the next seven hours fucking."

Fucking. Her chin lifted. "Start the elevator." Because she knew exactly what sort of huge mistake she'd be making if she got involved with a man like Jax. Sarah preferred to spend her time with men who were safe. *Law-abiding.* Men who didn't thrive on danger and adrenaline. Men who had no idea about all the darkness that existed in the world.

Safe men.

Jax wasn't safe. And if she wasn't careful, he'd see right through the mask she wore.

When she inhaled, she could have sworn that she actually tasted him. He was so big, easily dwarfing her in that elevator, and his scent—masculine, rich—surrounded her.

Sarah pressed back against the mirror. "Start the elevator."

His blue gaze sharpened on her. "Are you afraid of me?"

"Aren't most people?" she dodged. Most smart people?

"Yes, but they have a reason to fear me." His knuckles fell away from her. "You don't. I wouldn't ever hurt you."

Right. Like she was just supposed to take him at his word. Once Jax had been drawn into LOST's investigation, Sarah had made it a top priority to learn as much about him as she could. Only it turned out that there wasn't a whole lot to discover. Most of his past was cloaked, little more than rumors and smoke. Sure, she'd seen his criminal record, but that had been all juvie stuff. The guy had been good at covering his tracks once he'd become legal.

He'd been on the streets since he was a teenager. Somehow, he'd clawed his way—quite literally—out of the gutter and become a force to be reckoned with in the area. He owned several businesses and had connections that stretched across the county. And the local police were sure that he was a criminal. They just hadn't been able to pin any serious crimes on him.

It's hard because he has money and power. And he's smart. She could see the intelligence in his eyes. The cunning. *He won't make mistakes easily.*

"I love it when your mind starts spinning," he murmured, his voice a deep rumble. "Tell me, Dr. Jacobs, are you profiling me right now?"

Her hands lifted and she shoved against his chest. He backed up, not because she'd been uber strong and knocked him back, but because . . . dammit, she suspected he moved for her.

To make her feel in control.

But he likes power.

And, hell, she *was* profiling him. "I don't understand the point of this little meeting. Stopping a woman in the elevator is hardly an appropriate pick-up routine—"

He laughed. His laughter actually sounded real. Warm and rough, and it rolled right over her.

"How is anything about us appropriate?" Jax asked. That man's voice—so deep and rumbly—it was like pure sex. She was pretty sure, like one hundred percent so, that he normally had women tossing their panties at him on sight.

She wasn't one of those women. Or, rather, she was trying not to be one of those women.

Sarah hurried to the control panel and pressed the button to get that elevator moving again. "You're lucky security wasn't called in. You can't just stop an elevator." She was muttering. She was also not looking back at him. "Look, LOST appreciates your cooperation." Well, she didn't actually think her teammates did appreciate his cooperation. They pretty much thought Jax was trouble.

So right.

"But the case is over now," Sarah continued determinedly, "and your involvement with us . . ."

The doors opened. She breathed a fast sigh of relief and said, "That involvement is over, too." Sarah stepped out of the elevator, straightened her spine, and made herself glance at him. Then she very firmly said, "Good-bye, Jax."

He caught her right hand. "You know we'd be dynamite together. We touch, and I pretty much implode."

Her whole body was trembling, but Sarah locked her knees. "That kind of desire is dangerous."

"Aw, pretty Sarah, that kind of desire is addictive."

Her room was just a few feet away. "Let go of my hand." This madness with him had to stop. And that was exactly what it was—madness. He wasn't the right kind of man for her. Not even for a night. He pushed her, made Sarah want to let go of her control, and she couldn't do that. She already walked a fine line as it was.

His index finger slid along her inner wrist. Her pulse jerked beneath his touch. He leaned toward her and his breath blew lightly against her ear as he asked, "What are you so afraid of?"

She'd never tell. "Good-bye, Jax."

He eased back from her. "When you change your mind, come and find me."

The guy's arrogance was too much.

"Did you really think I'd just jump on you when I saw you?" Her skin still felt warm where he'd touched her.

His mouth hitched into a half smile. "A guy can only hope."

She shook her head. Then Sarah turned and marched away.

"That's not why I came tonight. Though fucking you would have been heaven."

Her steps slowed.

"I wanted to ask you about your business."

Her business? LOST?

"What makes your boss decide to take on a case?"

Curious now, she looked back at him. "Is someone missing?"

Jax just shrugged. "I did my research, too, you know."

She kept her expression still. If he'd been digging into the backgrounds of the LOST agents, then she realized that he knew all about the messed-up nightmare that was her past.

"LOST takes the cold cases, right? The ones that the cops have given up hope of solving."

Sarah inclined her head. Her boss, Gabe Spencer, had originally opened LOST because he wanted to make a difference. When his sister had vanished, the local cops had been no help. Gabe had found Amy on his own, but he'd found her too late. The man who'd been holding Amy had killed her right before Gabe got to the scene.

"There's no expiration date on your cases," he said. "Doesn't matter how much time has passed. You'll still take it?"

"We've taken cases where the person has been missing for over ten years." They were the Last Option Search Team for a reason. Most people who came to them had tried every other option that was available to them. Their other efforts had turned up nothing. Desperate, at the end of their rope—yes, that was the way families were when they finally came to the LOST office in Atlanta. "But . . ." And he needed to know this, if he was looking for someone who'd been missing. "The longer a person is gone, the greater the likelihood is that you aren't going to find a live victim."

"Right." He pushed his hand through his hair. "I don't have to worry about that."

She stepped toward him. "Jax?" He'd made her curious now.

But he was backing into the elevator and shaking his head. "Forget it. I think it was a mistake." Then he flashed his broad grin at her. What she thought of as his panty-dropping grin. "Though seeing you is always a pleasure."

He was wearing a mask, one that hid his true emotions. In that moment, she was sure of it. For an instant, he'd let her glimpse behind the mask, but that instant was over.

"Have a safe trip back home. And who knows? Maybe our paths will cross again one day."

"Maybe." She was missing something there. She hesitated, then called, "Jax?"

But the elevator doors slid closed.

Sarah took a deep breath. Okay, so that had been unexpected. Pretty much everything about Jax Fontaine was unexpected. The last time she'd seen him—just days before—he'd told her, "When you need me, come find me."

Only he'd been the one to find her. Asking questions that had put her on edge.

The carpet swallowed her footsteps as she hurried to her room, and maybe it was because she was thinking so much about Jax or maybe she was just off her game, but it took Sarah a moment too long to realize that her door was ajar. She blinked, staring at it, then she tried to hurriedly back away.

But the door was yanked open. A man stood there. A man covered from head to toe in black. She whirled away from him, but he grabbed her and yanked Sarah back against him.

"*Time to pay.*"

She opened her mouth to scream, but his gloved hand covered her lips.

NORMALLY, JAX WASN'T a coward. He feared no one and nothing. But . . .

The elevator opened. He stepped into the lobby. Glanced around. The rich and the pompous filled that place. Sure, these days he pretty much counted as rich, but he wasn't pompous, and he couldn't stand the sight of those pricks.

The marble floor of that hotel gleamed. Sarah had switched her hotels since her arrival in New Orleans. Probably because she hadn't thought the last place was secure enough.

Since I broke into her hotel room. That had been a one-time deal. He'd just needed to talk with her and he'd been . . . concerned . . . about her well-being.

There were only a handful of people in that world that he cared about. Normally, he didn't give a shit about most folks. But Sarah, with her dark, mysterious eyes—she'd gotten beneath his skin. And he'd just almost told her the biggest secret of his life.

Well, one of his top five, anyway.

He paused in the lobby. Unlike the other jerks running around that place, he was wearing jeans and a battered jacket. The concierge was frowning at him, so Jax just glared at the guy. The concierge then got *very* busy shuffling his papers.

The past doesn't matter. Why the hell did I ever come here and ask about LOST?

He strode toward the exit. The doorman hurried forward.

Only . . .

Jax glanced back. The LOST group knew their shit. He'd seen them in action. He'd read reports about their successes. If anyone could discover the truth for him, it would be LOST. And the only LOST agent who might actually push for the others to take his case?

Sarah.

"Sonofabitch," he muttered.

The doorman backed up.

Jax turned on his heel. Okay, so this time, maybe he'd even try asking *nicely*. The problem with that plan was that Jax didn't exactly know how to do anything nicely.

Maybe the sexy little profiler could show him.

So once more, he found himself riding up that elevator. Only this time, he was alone. But Jax could have sworn he caught a light, sweet scent hanging in the air. Vanilla? Yeah, that was Sarah's scent. When he'd been close to her—close enough to kiss, and he'd sure wanted to kiss her badly—that scent had teased him.

It had also aroused him.

The elevator ascended quickly, and soon he was up and high and stopping on Sarah's floor. No one was in that hallway. All the doors were shut. He knew which room was Sarah's—he could always get any intel he needed in New Orleans. A phone call had done the job for him. So he strode toward Room 3809. He lifted his hand and knocked. Rather politely, he thought.

There was a thud of sound from inside the room. As if Sarah had dropped something.

His brows climbed. Jax thought that he'd hear the pad of her footsteps coming toward him, but, other than the soft thud, there was no other sound coming from that room.

He knocked again. Harder. "Sarah, we need to talk."

She couldn't pretend he wasn't there. Jax didn't intend to leave until he'd had his say.

HER ATTACKER HAD a knife to Sarah's throat. He'd nicked the skin a moment ago, when Jax had first knocked on her door.

Jax.

Right then, he was her main hope of survival.

"Make a sound, and I will slice your throat right here and now." The man's voice was a low, lethal whisper from behind his mask.

"*Sarah, we need to talk.*" Jax sounded determined. And he was pounding on her door again—harder this time. If he kept pounding like that, he'd attract attention from some of the folks in the other rooms. That attention would be wonderful.

Her attacker pulled her back against him. The knife didn't leave its spot at her throat. He was maneuvering her, trying to get her—toward the connecting door? Yes, yes, he was. He was trying to get her to the door, and then he must think he could get her out by going through the other room. Or maybe he didn't intend to get her out of the hotel. Maybe he'd be killing her as soon as he could.

Too bad. I'm not ready to die.

She'd been trained well, after all. She knew how to survive.

So her hands slid down and when he moved another

step, she knocked the lamp off the table. Just like she'd *accidentally* tripped over that chair a few moments ago. But when that lamp hit, the crash was loud and clear.

"You bitch," her attacker snarled as he yanked her around to face him. "I'm gonna hurt you so much—"

The door crashed in. Sweet hell, *yes*.

But that knife was still too close to her. So Sarah slammed her head at her attacker. He groaned when she hit him, and the hand holding the knife jerked. She leapt back, her head pounding now, and he swiped out with his knife. The blade sliced down her arm, and Sarah cried out in pain.

Then Jax was there. He pulled her toward him, then he pushed her behind his back, shielding her. Normally, she wasn't the shielding type, but she was bleeding and scared and Jax was pretty much roaring as he shot toward her attacker.

The guy's fingers were locked tight around the knife. He lunged forward, and he brought that knife down in an arc, aiming right for Jax.

Jax's hand lifted. He blocked that attack, then swung his fist into the other man. The attacker hit the floor. In the next instant, Jax was on top of him. Punching. Driving his powerful fists at the guy again and again.

Voices rose from the hallway. Right. You couldn't exactly kick in a door and *roar* without attracting attention. Someone out there was shouting for security—a very good idea. Sarah's hand wrapped around her wound. The blood dripped right through her fingers. He'd cut her so deep. She was probably going to need stitches and—

Jax still had him on the floor. She hurried forward. Sarah touched his shoulder and Jax froze, with his hand poised to punch the guy again.

Her attacker wasn't fighting anymore. Just lying there, moaning.

Every breath that Sarah took felt icy in her lungs. "Take off his mask," she told Jax.

Jax leaned down and ripped that mask off the guy.

Evil has so many faces. Her father's voice whispered in her mind. *That's why you can't ever trust what you see.*

She was staring down at a kid, a boy who looked around eighteen. His lip was busted, bleeding, and so was his nose. Sarah didn't know if she and her head butt were responsible for his injuries or if they'd come courtesy of Jax's powerful fists, but the kid was obviously down for the count.

"Who the hell are you?" Jax demanded. "And why were you after her?"

The guy tried to talk. Blood and spittle flew from his mouth. Sarah stared at him, caught by the bright green of his eyes. His eyes were familiar to her. She knew she'd seen him somewhere before . . .

"Bitch is . . . evil . . ." the boy rasped. "Just like . . . him."

Him.

"He murdered . . . mom . . . Gwen . . ."

That name—Gwen—seemed to echo through Sarah's mind, and suddenly, an image clicked for her. Gwen Guthrie. A woman who'd had eyes *exactly* the same shade of bright green as the boy who'd attacked Sarah. *His mother?*

Yes, yes, that fit. Sarah had done research on Gwen. The woman had given birth to two children . . .

Before my father murdered her.

"Have to . . . kill Sarah. What she . . . deserves . . ."

Security pushed into the room. Goose bumps appeared on Sarah's arms. No matter how many times she tried to escape her past, it just kept chasing her down. This time, the past had come armed with a knife. A very sharp one, at that.

Jax shoved to his feet. He turned, and that gaze of his—burning with a blue fury in that moment—swept over her. When he saw her wound, he swore.

"We need to call the cops," Sarah said as the security team closed in on the boy. "He just attacked me." Her voice didn't shake. Her words didn't break. There was no emotion in them at all. She couldn't let any emotion affect her, not then. Not with all those people standing around in the hallway, whispering.

"She needs medical care," Jax snapped. "Get an ambulance here!"

"No, I—" Sarah began.

"He sliced your arm. You're going to need stitches." He was holding her hand. So carefully, as if he were afraid of hurting her.

Her head tilted back as she looked up and focused on him. He'd come to her rescue, charging inside that room and probably saving her from—what? Torture? Death? "Thank you."

His gaze searched hers. "You know who that kid is, don't you?"

She glanced back at the boy. The hotel security had

circled around him, and the guy was hunched on the floor. Crying. "I've never met him before in my life."

Those words were true. But even if they weren't, Jax wouldn't know. After all, she was a world-class liar.

Some of her father's victims had been identified over the years. She had pictures of all those victims—and she'd seen the boy's green eyes before. That particular shade of green was unusual, startling. Unforgettable. Those eyes belonged to her father's first victim.

Gwen Guthrie.

POLICE STATIONS WEREN'T his scene. Mostly because he and the cops were all too often butting heads. They wanted to toss him in a cell. He wanted to tell them to fuck off. He usually *did* tell them to fuck off.

If it hadn't been for Sarah, there was no way Jax would have been at the police station in New Orleans. But he'd stayed with her while she got stitched up, and even though she had plenty of protection around her, he was still loath to leave her.

"We've got this." His shoulders tensed at that voice—a voice he knew. He turned his head and saw another LOST agent heading toward him. Wade Monroe. The guy moved with slow, deliberate steps, and his assessing gaze quickly swept the areas. Jax already knew the guy was an ex-cop, a former detective from up in Atlanta, and like the other LOST agents, the guy wasn't exactly on Team Jax.

His mistake, of course. Team Jax was awesome.

"What the hell happened?" Wade demanded as he closed in on Jax. "What did you do to her?" And the guy actually grabbed his shirt, fisting his hands in the material.

Jax glanced down at those hands. Wade was a friend of Sarah's, he had to remember that, and all the LOST agents had worked hell hard to protect Jax's friend Emma Castille. Emma had gotten tangled in some serious shit recently, and LOST had protected her. So Jax figured he owed Wade and the others a small amount of leeway.

Very, very small.

"I saved the day," Jax drawled, deliberately letting his accent deepen. He could use or discard that accent at will. He hadn't been born in Louisiana, but he sure liked the faint drawl. "Rushed in like the hero that I am."

"Bullshit," Wade threw out.

Jax's lips curved.

"You and I both know what you did to Kevin McCormack."

He let his brows climb. "McCormack? Ah, you mean the crazy-ass FBI agent who tried to kill *your* LOST buddy Dean Bannon and my . . . friend . . . Emma."

McCormack had been one psychotic asshole. He'd kidnapped and tortured his prey, and the guy had foolishly thought that Emma would be joining that prey list. McCormack hadn't realized that Emma was family. Part of the very small family that Jax had in this world.

"You set up that hit on him, didn't you?" Wade demanded. "Got some of your buddies in jail to take him out?"

Like he hadn't already heard those accusations from the local cops. "News flash. Prisoners don't exactly like

FBI agents, and when a dirty, twisted freak like McCormack wound up in their grasp, I guess one of them just snapped." And McCormack had wound up dead. *One less problem for me.*

Wade held his stare. "What happened tonight?"

Ah, well, at least they were done talking about the dead man. "I saved Sarah." He tapped his chin. "Do you think she'll be properly appreciative? I do hope so."

Wade growled. "Don't you ever get tired of being a dick?"

"Not really."

But, over Wade's shoulder, Jax had just caught sight of Sarah. She was heading toward them, and even under those garish lights at the police station, the woman was gorgeous.

Her long dark hair tumbled over her shoulders, a perfect frame for her delicate, heart-shaped face. And delicate—yes, that was the word that kept coming to mind when he thought of her. She was small, petite, with a light build and sweet curves. Her lips were full, damn near perfectly bow-shaped. She was a package made for sin and temptation, he got that.

But it was her eyes—those incredible eyes—that were really getting to him.

Deep and dark. A man could lose his soul in eyes like that. Provided he had a soul to lose.

Yes, she looked delicate, all right. All five feet and nothing inches of her. And when he'd seen that bastard in her hotel room, seen that knife in the jerk's hand, Jax had snapped.

He stepped around Wade. Let his gaze sweep over

her. She was too pale. Her normally golden skin was pallid. Her lips were bare of color, and her gaze seemed a little too stark as she stared at him.

"Sarah!" Wade called, sounding incredibly relieved. "Finally. What the hell is going on here?"

"Oh, the usual." She pushed back her hair. "Someone broke into my hotel room, pulled a knife, said I deserved to die."

Wade swore.

"But, lucky for me," Sarah continued, "Jax was there."

Wade's stunned gaze shot to him. "Told you," Jax said, shrugging his shoulders. "I saved the day." He offered his hand to Sarah. "Now, you look as if you're about to collapse. Come home with me, and I'll tuck you into a nice, warm bed."

Wade shoved Jax's hand out of the way. "Back off, Fontaine."

Wade was going to be a problem.

"The offer . . ." Jax told Sarah softly, "will always be open." Just so they were clear.

"Get out of here!" Wade exploded at him. "When are you going to get it? Sarah isn't attracted to guys like you."

Oh, but she was. "She certainly isn't interested in you," Jax murmured.

Wade surged forward, but Sarah had already moved, too, and she put her body between theirs. "I am not in the mood for this." Her voice was low, carrying only to them. "My arm hurts, I just got grilled by the cops until I thought my head would explode, and the last thing I want right now is to deal with you two having some stupid testosterone fight."

Wade's cheeks flushed.

"Jax helped me tonight. I'm grateful to him." She looked up at Jax. "I don't . . . I don't like to think about what could have happened if you hadn't been there."

He didn't like to think of that, either. He caught her chin in his hand, holding her carefully. "Who was the guy?"

"His name is . . . Eddie Guthrie."

"Aw, hell," Wade said. "I'm sorry, Sarah."

Obviously, that guy had just made some sort of connection with the name, a connection that Jax didn't get.

"He's come after you before?" Jax guessed.

She shook her head. "No, this is . . . just one of those things." Her voice became even softer when she said, "He read an article about me in the paper—about the work LOST had done down here. He saw my picture and made the connection. It's not like I could have known he was living here. I hadn't been keeping track of him."

He was confused. "Why did he come after you?"

Her chin notched up, pulling from his grasp. "Like you haven't already been digging into my past."

He had, but—

"That kid in there—Eddie—he came after me because he's an eye-for-an-eye type." Her words were stilted, but she shivered as she stood there. Wade shrugged out of his coat and put it around her shoulders.

Annoying true-blue type. *Should have given her my damn jacket.*

"You see, my father killed his mother. Tortured her for hours before he ended her suffering."

Jax sucked in a sharp breath.

"So it seems that when Eddie found out I was in town, he thought he'd take the opportunity to strike out at my dear old dad . . . by killing me." Her smile was sad. "An eye for an eye. A life for a life."

"Sarah." Wade's hand squeezed her shoulder. "I'm sorry."

"So am I. Because now Eddie is going to jail. He looks young, but turns out he's twenty-one. No juvenile status for him." Her lips turned down in a sad frown. "I highly doubt he's going to come out in any better frame of mind."

My father killed his mother.

"Time to leave this town," Sarah said. Once more, her gaze found Jax's. "How am I supposed to repay you?"

No one should have eyes like her. "Don't worry," Jax heard himself murmur, "I'm sure I'll think of something . . ."

Chapter 2

IT WAS NEARING 3 A.M. SARAH SHOULDN'T HAVE been exiting a taxi in front of the little bar on the wrong side of the town. She should have been in her *new* hotel room. The one on club level with all the so-called great security. She should have been warm and safe in her bed.

A catcall followed her as she headed across the street and toward the entrance of Shade.

She knew she shouldn't be at that place, but . . . she was.

The past is too strong tonight. I need to escape before I go absolutely crazy.

Wade was her friend, and he'd tried to understand what she was going through, but the thing was . . . he could never really understand. No one could.

A bouncer was waiting near the door. And there was a long, snaking line that seemed to circle the bar—even at 3 A.M. Hell, she hadn't even thought that so many people would be there. If she stayed in that line, she'd never get inside. Sarah inched forward and when she looked up, the bouncer's stare was on her.

He was a huge guy, rather tanklike, with a long, twisting scar that slid over his left eye, slicing right though the eyebrow. Whatever had caused that scar, well, it was pretty amazing that the guy hadn't lost his eye.

He stood up. And Sarah looked way, way up.

"You don't belong here," he said, his gaze raking over her.

She wore jeans and a T-shirt. Tennis shoes. Her hair was loose because she hadn't wanted to waste time with it. A light jacket covered her arms so no one could see that ever-so-stylish bandage she was sporting.

Sure, this might not be her typical place. Sarah usually avoided bars, but . . . "I need to see Jax."

"Dark hair. Chocolate eyes. Fucking sex appeal." The man whistled. "Pretty Sarah."

Uh, okay.

"I know you."

He did? "And you are . . . ?"

"Carlos."

Great. So now he waved to someone else, and a slightly smaller guy took up a guard position at the bar's door.

"I was told to always let you in. Provided that you came calling . . ."

Jax had known she'd come looking for him?

The guy took her inside. Music was blaring in there. Voices were shouting, and drinks were flowing. Pumping out from the long, wooden bar. There was also a woman doing some serious gyrating on the small stage that was just a few feet away. When the chick grabbed for the pole near her, Sarah looked away.

"This way." Her guide wasn't leading her toward the bar. He was taking her to a small door on the far right side of the place. "Jax is in there." He reached for the doorknob.

Sarah grabbed his hand. "Is he alone?" Maybe she should have thought about that part before. She didn't want to burst in there and find Jax with some half-naked chick—like the one out on that stage. *He said to come and find him, but I don't want to find him with someone else.*

"Does it matter?" the man asked, his head tilting as he studied her.

"Uh, yes, it matters. A rather great deal." She looked back at the bar. There was an empty space there, and Sarah was pretty sure she could wiggle into that spot. "I think I'll just wait for him over there."

But her guide had just thrown open the door. "Jax! She's here!" That bellow was close to deafening.

Jax spun around. His eyes widened when he saw her.

"Uh, hi there, Jax," Sarah mumbled.

He was alone, thank goodness. No half-naked woman to be seen.

The door closed behind her. Her guide had sure vanished fast.

Jax was stalking toward her. "What are you doing here?"

"I—" She broke off, trying to think of a fairly believable explanation. The truth wouldn't work. *Every time I tried to close my eyes, I saw my dad's face. I heard screams. And I started to wonder if Eddie was really so wrong when he came to kill me. Because I think I'm just as much of a monster as my father ever was.*

Maybe more.

But she couldn't tell that to her friends in LOST. They wouldn't understand. Wade was already treating her with kid gloves. Her closest confidante on the team—Victoria Palmer—was still recovering from an attack on their last mission. So she sure couldn't go to her.

None of her friends had ever understood about her past. They'd sympathized, they'd told her how very sorry they were for all that she'd had to endure. But they didn't *understand.* And their pity drove her insane.

Jax's blue stare was on her. And there was no pity on his face or in his gaze.

"I shouldn't be here." There. Those were the words that finally came out of her mouth, they were so true. "You're dangerous and you're too sexy and you've got a stripper on the stage outside of this door."

His brows shot up. Then he laughed. Hard.

She kept staring at him.

"Which of those," he finally murmured, "bothers you the most?"

Sarah rubbed her arms and started pacing around that little office. "Why do you even have this bar? It's a serious hole in the wall."

He seemed to consider her question for a moment, then he said, "When I was eighteen, I was begging for money outside this place."

She stopped pacing. Sarah turned back around and stared at him.

"The owner said he had something to give me. I was starving, desperate—and he brought me around back."

She waited. The owner had helped him? He'd—

"Then he beat the shit out of me and told me to never come back and loiter in front of his business again."

That wasn't the end of the story she'd expected. Sarah shook her head and said simply, "Bastard."

Jax shoved his hands into the pockets of his jeans. "Oh, he was. But don't worry, the guy got exactly what he had coming to him."

"What was that?" Sarah was almost afraid to ask.

"I healed up. Lucky for me, someone found me and took me to the hospital."

He said the words so simply, but she knew it must have been a brutal experience for him. He'd been so young then . . .

"When I was healed up, I made a vow to never beg for another damn thing in my life." He was so close to her, less than a foot away. "I took every job I could find, and, no, all of those jobs weren't exactly what you'd call legit. I worked my way up the ladder down here, I became a fucking force to be reckoned with, and on my twenty-first birthday, I bought this bar and four others." His smile was cold. "I took the former owner out back on my move-in day. I told him that I had something for him . . ."

She wet her lips. "I think I know where this tale is going now."

"He'd just beat two of his dancers so badly they could hardly walk. I figured it was time he had some payback coming his way." Jax shrugged. "So I paid him. In full."

She glanced toward the door. Coming there had been a huge mistake.

"Sarah."

Her gaze slid back to him.

"No judgment," he murmured. "There's no anger in your eyes, no rage or disgust at me for being a cold bastard. No pity for the kid I was who got beaten in a dirty alley and left to die."

"Don't be too sure you understand what I feel."

"Why not? I actually think I understand *you* very, very well."

Sarah backed up a step.

A faint smile curved his lips. "It was there from the first time I saw you. That instant connection. Doesn't happen often. Actually, it's never happened to me before. I looked up, saw you, and thought—"

Sarah pretty much ran for the door.

But he caught her. His hands wrapped around her and Jax pulled her back against his body. His hold wasn't hard or rough. Oddly, it was infinitely tender.

"Do you know what I saw when I looked in your eyes?" he whispered into her ear.

Sarah shook her head.

"You were hurting. Trying to hide your pain, but I could still see it. I looked at you and thought—*I never want her to hurt again.*"

Tears stung her eyes. "You don't know me. Or what I've done." Jax thought his past was bad? It was nothing compared to hers. She still had nightmares that had her waking in the night, choking for breath, and begging for help.

Help that hadn't come. Not in time.

"Tell me why you came to see me tonight, Sarah."

She sucked in a quick breath and decided to go with the truth. "Because I didn't want to lie in bed and be afraid. Because I didn't want to think about the past or the future." Because she'd felt that insane connection between them, too.

The first time she'd seen him, she'd looked into his eyes and thought—

He can handle all my darkness. He won't ever be afraid of what I tell him.

Because his gaze had told her that he'd already looked into hell . . . and hadn't given a damn about the demons there.

He turned her in his arms. She made herself look up and into his eyes. He was so warm and strong against her. And he made her . . . want. Yearn for things that she'd denied herself for so very long.

Because she hadn't wanted anyone to get close. She hadn't trusted anyone with all her secrets.

She didn't trust him, either. She'd be a fool to do that. But—she did want him. And every instinct Sarah possessed screamed at her that Jax Fontaine could give her the sensual oblivion she craved.

A few hours to forget. A few hours to just pretend that I'm not the freak in the room. The monster that everyone else fears.

"What do you want from me?" Jax asked her.

Just a night. She'd be leaving New Orleans soon, flying out on a plane and heading back to her little house in the suburbs of Atlanta. They wouldn't see each other again. So no one else would know about what happened tonight. Just her.

Just him.

So she rose onto her tiptoes. Her hands curled around his neck and she pulled him toward her, and Sarah kissed him. His mouth was closed and he was stiff against her. She'd expected—more. Because of the way she felt when he was near—that tight, hot energy, flowing through her veins—she'd thought—

"Not like that, princess." His hands curled around her. He lifted her up, carried her, and sat her on the edge of his desk. Then he stepped between her legs. Jax wrapped his hands around her thighs and pulled her flush against his growing arousal. "Like this."

Then he kissed her.

His mouth was open. The kiss was deep, hot, consuming. The guy wasn't sampling with his tongue. He was taking and he was making her moan against him. Desire exploded within her. White-hot. Electrifying. So perfect because it pushed everything else aside for her. Sarah let go of her fears, and she held on to Jax as tightly as she could.

The man knew how to seduce. There was no denying that. And he sure as hell knew how to kiss. Her toes were curling, and it was a good thing she was up on that table because Sarah wasn't so sure that her legs would have held her up.

Sarah kissed him back with a wild fury. Licking, sucking that sensual lower lip of his. She loved it when he growled and held her even tighter. But she wanted more. So much more.

She couldn't hear the noise of the bar. It was so quiet in that room. Soundproofed? Maybe, she didn't really care right at that moment. Her hands pushed between them as she fumbled with his belt and—

"No." His hands closed around hers.

Sarah shook her head, certain that she'd misheard him. He hadn't . . . wait . . . had he really said no? But he was enjoying this as much as she was, right? Doubt stirred within her. "You said you wanted me."

"Oh, pretty Sarah, I do." His voice was deep and sensual, and just the sound of that low rumble had her nipples tightening more. "But not like this."

Uh, like this? Sarah blinked.

"Not here. This isn't the place for you—or our first time together."

He said that as if they'd be together plenty of times. But he was wrong. It was just one night. Not even that. Only a few hours remained before sunrise.

He stepped away from her.

Heat stained Sarah's cheeks. She'd been so wrong about him. How had she been this wrong? She'd thought for sure that he wanted her, but he was standing there, eyes glinting, body tight and—

"I made a mistake." Sarah snapped her legs together and jumped off that desk. Points for her—Sarah's knees didn't tremble and she stayed upright. "I won't be bothering you again."

He blocked her path when she headed for the door. "I have a feeling that you'll be bothering me quite a bit." He opened his right hand. Held it out to her. "Let's take a ride together."

What? She'd been *trying* to take a ride on that desk, but then he'd put on the brakes.

"You can trust me, Sarah. I told you, I'd never hurt you."

Yes, he'd said that. "I don't really trust anyone." Not even the other LOST agents, not one hundred percent. "It's a flaw I have." Always looking for hidden motives. Always holding herself back from others.

"Then don't trust me, but come with me." His hand was still open, between them. Waiting. "And before this night is over, I'll have you screaming with pleasure."

Her heart jerked in her chest. "Maybe you'll be the one who screams."

He smiled at her. "You are not what others expect, are you?"

Not at all. Her hand lifted. Her fingers were trembling as they reached for his. He caught her hand in his. Held tight.

"There's no going back now," he told her.

No, there wasn't.

Just a few hours.

He didn't take her back through the bar. They went out another door, one that led them to the alley behind the bar. She could hear voices back there. People talking. Laughing. She saw one couple against the wall of that alley, kissing and stroking each other.

She quickly looked away from them and then saw that Jax was getting on a motorcycle. It was a big, black beast of a bike. He revved the engine, and the hard, rumbling growl filled her ears. He glanced back at her. "You're not afraid of a little ride in the dark, are you?"

No. She jumped on. He put a helmet on her. "To keep you extra safe." Then he kissed her. A light, fast kiss.

In the next moment, that motorcycle was lunging through the alley, then ripping down the street. Fast, faster, until it seemed like they were flying. And it was wonderful. The motorcycle was vibrating between her legs, her arms were wrapped tightly around Jax, and Sarah heard herself laughing.

She didn't know where they were going. Right then, she didn't care. The ghosts from her past weren't chasing her—or trying to use a knife to slice open her throat. She was with Jax.

And right then, being with him was the only thing that mattered.

DR. SARAH JACOBS had gone slumming.

From the shadows, he watched as she climbed onto the motorcycle. Watched as she held her lover so tightly. When the motorcycle took off, her laughter rose above the roar of that bike.

Sarah was a woman who was so very good at pretending. Pretending to be innocent. Pretending that she wanted to help the victims of the world. But he saw right through her lies.

He recognized her for exactly what she was.

Dark and twisted. Broken on the inside. Like a mirror that had been busted, then pieced back together, cracks all along the surface. Sarah had those cracks, right beneath her skin.

Did she even realize the hell that was coming her way? Probably not. She thought she was the smart one. The woman who could figure out all the killers.

She'd never figure him out.

Tonight's little visitor—that had just been the start of what he had planned. The true games were about to begin. Then he'd see just what Sarah knew . . .

But first, he had to start with the right prey. Someone who would catch Sarah's attention. No, not just her attention, but the attention of the entire LOST group. Because Sarah just followed orders, and he needed her boss to order Sarah to stay in New Orleans.

Soon, Sarah would realize that she didn't know killers nearly as well as she thought.

And I'm coming for you, Jax. Jax Fontaine. The name whispered in New Orleans like the man was supposed to be someone. *You're nothing. You've always been nothing.*

Jax and Sarah were bound, linked, and they'd both be crashing and burning together.

It was almost perfect that Sarah and Jax had found each other.

Because it sure as hell made things easier for him.

He'd planned to take them out separately, but this—this was fucking fate. His justice. They'd come together, and it was *his* time.

His time to make them both pay.

SARAH LIKED DANGER. Jax had realized that fact when she laughed as he cut through the city on his motorcycle. She hadn't even hesitated to jump on behind him.

Sarah Jacobs . . . such a mix of contradictions. She looked so controlled on the outside, all business, but then when you looked in her eyes . . .

I see the truth.

Fire. Passion. Her eyes burned for him.

He'd driven the motorcycle to one of his newest acquisitions, a house in the Quarter, not too far from the old La Laurie mansion. He headed past the main gate and parked his bike. Sarah didn't climb off right away. Her body was pressed to his back, her hands wrapped around his stomach. He liked the way she held on to him—so tight. But he had a feeling he was going to like plenty of other things about Sarah, too.

She slowly let go and eased off the motorcycle. Sarah handed him the helmet and turned to look around.

He rose, too, and typed in a quick code to send the gate shutting behind them. He'd just started renovating the house, so it wasn't much to see. Not yet. One day, though, it would be.

Sarah was staring up at the high stone wall that circled his property. Her gaze seemed centered on the broken bottles that were placed on the top of the wall.

She glanced back at him, her brows raised.

"It's an old trick we use down here," he explained to her. "If anyone tries to scale the wall, they either get cut or they knock the bottles over—and I hear them coming."

She gave a little shake of her head. "I would have thought your security system would be all the protection you needed."

"A man can never be too safe." He turned and headed toward the house. But he didn't hear the sound of her footsteps following him. Jax glanced back. She was still staring up at the broken bottles. "You haven't changed your mind?" He was having trouble believing that she was actually there with him. *Sarah*. If the woman knew that she'd been starring in his fantasies every night since they'd met, she'd probably be trying to scale that wall, broken bottles or not. There was just something about her. The minute he'd seen her, she'd just . . . clicked for him.

"I haven't." Her voice was soft, but she'd finally started walking toward him. "I've been . . . here . . . in this area of town before. I didn't realize you lived here."

"I've got a few houses, scattered about." He shrugged. "Sometimes, it's a good thing to have more than one base for operations." No, that wasn't the truth. He liked to acquire things. It was a quirk—or an obsession. But when you grew up with nothing, well, you had a tendency to want *everything.*

He opened the door for her. A curving spiral staircase led upstairs. The staircase was one of the finished elements in the house. He fucking loved that staircase.

And I'd love fucking her on it.

"Why this place?"

He shut the door behind him. Secured the alarm system in the house. "I got a great deal on it." He gave her a tight smile. "Not everyone wanted to be so close to the massacre house."

She tensed.

"The La Laurie mansion," he explained as he propped his shoulders against the door and studied her. "It's just down the road a bit. Those haunted tours come this way several times a day, everyone so eager to get a glimpse of the place—and maybe see a ghost or two."

She rubbed her arms. "Now I know why this house seems familiar."

"Went on a tour, did you?"

Her dark eyes held his.

"Like you'd be afraid of a few ghosts." And he stalked toward her. He just had to get closer. She was standing in front of those stairs and looking so beautiful that she made him ache. "I actually wonder . . . does anything scare you?"

Her hand curled around the banister. "The man and woman who used to live in that house—the ones who hurt all of those people—*they* scare me. Real-life people always scare me more than any ghost story . . . because I know just how evil we can be."

We? He caught her hand. The sleeves of her coat came down to her wrists. He brought her left hand up to his mouth. "I don't think you're evil at all."

"Maybe you just don't know me that well."

Damn, but he liked her.

He held her hand. Stared into her eyes. And thought about all the ways he wanted to have her. His hand slid around her wrist. He could feel her pulse racing right there and—

There was a long, thick line beneath his fingertips. Frowning now, he pushed back her coat sleeve as he stared at her wrist. There was a scar there, one that appeared to slice over the veins.

"I usually do a better job of keeping that covered," Sarah said, voice soft. "Tonight, I just didn't bother. I figured you'd be able to deal with me, scars and all."

His index finger slid over that scar.

"If you use your dominant hand to make the first cut and that cut is too deep, then your other hand won't be able to slice when the time comes."

His gaze snapped back to her face.

"Just a lesson I learned."

"You tried to kill yourself." Fury pumped through him. Sarah—dead? *No.*

"I was a teenager, utterly scared out of my mind." But then she shook her head. "It wasn't the fear that did it, though. It was the guilt."

He didn't understand. "Sarah?"

"You know who I am." She stepped closer to him. And her bittersweet smile made his chest ache. "Oh, not all the specifics, because few people know those sordid details, but you know my father—"

"—was a serial killer." Yes, he knew that. Murphy Jacobs, a man convicted of murdering five people, though he'd been suspected in the deaths of at least a dozen more.

"You know and you don't look at me like I'm a freak."

"Because you're not." His finger slid over that scar again. They'd be coming back to that, later. "You're the sexiest woman I've ever met."

The smile became less bittersweet. "If that's the case, then why are we wasting time just talking? Couldn't we be doing . . . other . . . things?"

Ah, so the sharing was over. For the moment. That was fine. He knew that he'd learn more about her soon enough. When it came to Sarah, he was learning that he had a rather insatiable curiosity. "You're right," he murmured.

Her lips parted.

"So come this way." Then he turned and headed into the den. He made his way into the kitchen and found a bottle of wine. Chilled and rich, just what he thought she might enjoy. But when he turned back around, he found Sarah frowning at him.

"What?" He lifted the wine. "Not your style?"

"You don't have to wine me and dine me."

He used a corkscrew to open the wine. Jax grabbed two glasses.

"I want to fuck you, Jax. I thought I made that clear."

Fuck you. His eyes closed for a moment. "I was trying not to strip you and take you on the stairs." He turned back toward her. Offered her a glass of the wine. "I'm not sure what you've heard about me . . ." Though he could well imagine. "But I can be gentlemanly, to a degree."

She tasted the wine. Then she downed it in one gulp—like it had been a shot glass.

His lips twitched.

"I don't remember asking you to be gentlemanly."

He took his time savoring the wine, the way he planned to savor her.

"We don't have a lot of time," she said. "So, um, not to rush you or anything here but—"

Jax put down the wineglass. "We have as long as we want." Then he made his way to her. Slowly, letting his gaze sweep over every inch of her body. "There's no one here but me and you. No one to see us. No one to hear us." His hand lifted and sank into her hair. "So you don't have to pretend here with me. You can let go."

Her lips parted in surprise.

That's right, Sarah. I know who you are on the inside.

"Let go," he told her, "and go wild, for me." Then he kissed her. She'd been sweet before, so delicious, but now with the taste of that wine on her lips, she was more than enough to make him a little drunk.

Her hands curled around his shoulders and she leaned up to him. She was kissing him back with a passion that had his cock jerking and wanting to shove deep *in* her. As deep as he could go. And, as he'd told her, she could scream for him. Scream and scream and he'd be the only one to hear her.

He shoved away Sarah's jacket. It hit the floor. He yanked up her shirt and tossed it aside. She wore a light blue bra, one that lifted her breasts, pushing them up so perfectly toward him. He just had to lick them.

"I don't need foreplay," Sarah gasped, her words husky and hot. "I just want you."

But he wanted foreplay because Jaxe wanted to learn every inch of her body. He picked Sarah up, and her hands tightened around him. "My house," he told her, "my rules." He carried her back into the den. Then spread her out on the couch. He'd have her on those stairs later. Have her in his bed. But first . . . he'd taste all of her.

He stripped the rest of her clothes away. Left the thin scrap of light blue silk that covered her sex. Her nipples were tight and flushed pink and when he took one into his mouth, she nearly bolted off the couch. Such a lovely start. But he'd have much more.

His hand slid between her legs. Pressed to the silk of her panties. Sarah's hips surged up against him. Now that was nice.

"Don't play," she ordered him, her voice a sensual

temptation that shot straight to his cock. "I want you, now."

But first, he wanted her to come.

He pulled the panties down her legs. Let his fingers skim over her thighs. Sarah was delightfully bare and he loved that. Nothing in his way. He could look and touch and take.

And he did. He parted her legs and opened her sex to him. His fingers trailed lightly over the delicate flesh. A half moan slipped from Sarah when he thrust his index finger into her. So tight. She was going to feel fucking insane around him. But first—

Taste.

He put his mouth on her. Sarah's hips surged, not to get away from his lips, but to get closer. He licked her. He sucked and he realized she tasted far, far better than the wine.

His fingers stroked her even as his mouth learned all her sweetest spots. And when she stiffened beneath him, when she called out his name, he licked her even more.

Jax tasted her pleasure when she came.

In-fucking-credible.

He put on a condom. Positioned his body right between her legs. Then he waited for her gaze to find his. Because he needed to stare into her eyes when he took her.

Sarah looked up at him. Her eyes were even darker than before. He caught her hands in his, making sure to use care with her bandage so he didn't jostle her injury.

Then . . .

He took.

Jax plunged into her, driving deep in one thrust and—*heaven.* As close to it as he'd ever get, anyway. She was tight and wet and hot and he was pretty sure his head might explode at any moment. He thrust in and out, moving in a frantic rhythm because his control was shot to hell and back. Sarah was with him, arching toward his hips wildly, moaning his name, calling out to him to move—

"Harder! Faster! *Yes!*"

She was the most beautiful thing he'd ever seen. The sexiest woman he'd ever met.

She came for him again. When her sex tightened around him, squeezing along the length of his cock, he erupted.

THE REDHEAD STOOD in front of the bar, her hands twisting at her sides. The crowd was heavy around her, jostling and laughing. On Bourbon Street, the party never ended.

Never.

People of all ages were out there. Seventy-year-olds. Sixteen-year-olds.

This girl—she was older than sixteen. She barely appeared to be legal, but he knew she was past the age of twenty-one.

Some frat boys called out to her, and she tensed. She didn't speak back to them. Maybe she realized that would have just been a mistake. They would have kept talking to her. Kept flirting. Maybe wanted more.

There was plenty of "more" to be found on that street. Strip clubs waited just a few doors down. Girls were in front of those doors, too, but not girls like this one. Those girls were wearing see-through negligees and high heels. Scraps of panties and bras that just revealed instead of concealed. They were calling out to all the men and women who passed, promising them private shows.

The girl with the long red hair—hair she'd pulled back in a braid—didn't look as if she wanted to give anyone a show. Instead . . .

"Are you waiting for someone?" he asked her.

She spun around. Her eyes found his. He saw the hint of fear there and realized that he'd startled her.

Before he was done, he'd do more than just make her nervous. He'd terrify her.

"I am." Her shoulders straightened. "My brother. He said he'd meet me after my shift tonight."

Oh, but he can't, baby. Your brother is in jail. Seems he tried to attack a woman in her hotel room and got his ass tossed in a cell. He snapped his fingers together. "I knew you were Molly! Eddie is a buddy of mine. He asked me to swing by and make sure you got home all right."

But Molly backed away from him. "You don't . . . look like one of Eddie's friends."

Mostly because he *wasn't* one of Eddie's friends. Despite what the fool had thought. "He's done some work for me before." He smiled at her. "The kid has a gift with that guitar of his. I've had him do a few gigs at some of my places around town."

Her smile came then, slow, but *there.*

He offered her his hand. "My name's Jax. Jax Fontaine."

Her fingers curled around his.

She was still so hesitant. She held his hand a moment, then immediately let go. "I . . . um, thank you for coming out, but I can get home just fine by myself."

Molly wasn't one of the strippers or dancers. She didn't even tend bar. She had a job as a dishwasher at the bar across the street. She worked nights and went to the community college during the day.

"I know, Molly," he told her, as he inched a bit closer. "I know why you don't like to walk home alone and I know why your brother made me *swear* I'd see you home safely tonight."

She caught the end of her braid. Pulled a bit nervously on it.

"Your mother," he said, voice soft and sad. He thought he added just the right touch of sympathy. An amount sure to fool Molly.

She flinched.

"It's never a good idea to walk alone when so many . . ." He waved his hand to the crowd. " . . . drunk jerks are about."

She almost smiled at him then.

"How about I just take you two streets over, to where the cabs wait? Will that work?"

Her fingers were still pulling lightly at her braid, but right then, a particularly drunk SOB—drunk and fat—barreled into her. Molly would have gone flying face-first into the pavement, but he lunged out and caught her.

"Got you," he whispered to her.

She smiled at him. "I . . . I think I'd like it if you came with me."

Of course, she would.

They turned together and headed down the road. He kept his pace even with hers, and he talked easily about everything. The weather. Beignets. The LSU Tigers. And a few minutes later, when the crowd thinned because they'd left Bourbon Street and no one was watching him, he put his hand on Molly's slender shoulder.

It's time. This was the spot he'd picked.

"Do you think she suffered?" he asked Molly.

Her steps stumbled. "Wh-What?"

"Your mother. Before she died, do you think she suffered?"

Molly's body tensed. She tried to jerk away from him.

He didn't let her go.

"Let's find out," he said, and he put his hand over her mouth before she could scream. "Let's find out just what those last, horrible hours were like for her." He shoved a needle into her throat. Then he lifted her up easily, and he started to hum as he carried sweet Molly away.

Chapter 3

SARAH CRACKED OPEN ONE EYE. SHE SAW A WHITE, thick comforter about two inches from her face. She opened her other eye—and she saw a big, naked male right beside her.

Jax was sprawled across the bed, and he had one arm currently wrapped around her stomach. A naked stomach since—just like him—she wasn't wearing a stitch of clothes.

They'd moved from the den. After the best orgasm that she could remember having, she'd been limp, but they'd made it up the stairs.

Then he'd given her another mind-numbing orgasm.

Fear had been the last emotion she felt during the hours with him.

She could just see the light of dawn creeping through the shades. The night had ended, and it was time for her to go. She held her breath as she slid from the bed. Morning-after scenes weren't really her thing. Mostly because she didn't have a whole lot of them. Very carefully, she rose to her feet and tiptoed to the door. Sarah was naked when she headed down the stairs. When one stair creaked beneath her feet, she stopped, but heard no sound from above.

Her heart was racing in her chest when she reached the landing, and Sarah hurried to the den and found her clothes thrown around the room. She dressed as quickly as she could, and— Her gaze fell on the wineglasses.

You don't have to pretend here with me. You can let go. She had let go with him. All of her defenses had fallen down in the darkness.

She turned away and hurried to the little alarm box near his door. When he'd been typing in the code last night, she'd been paying careful attention. She always did. She'd been taught to watch others. Her fingers quickly flew over the keypad and she disengaged the alarm. Then Sarah rushed outside. She paused briefly near the gate, then typed in the code there, too. Before she left, she glanced back over her shoulder once more. Her gaze rose to the second floor. The blinds were open now, and she could see Jax. Standing up there, watching her.

She froze. This was it. Her last moment with him. And she was running because she didn't know what to say. Oh, Sarah understood completely why she was drawn to him. *Like a moth right to the burning flame.*

It wasn't because he was drop-dead sexy, though Jax certainly was.

It wasn't because he was strong. Fierce. It wasn't even because he'd saved her life the night before.

No, it was something even more basic than that. She looked at him, looked past the mask that he wore and she realized—

His secrets are as dark as my own. He was a man who understood the ghosts she battled every day. Her fingers trailed over the scar on her left wrist. A scar that she'd always kept hidden from her fellow LOST agents. She'd worn long-sleeved shirts or her bracelet—one she'd picked just because its large width covered the wound. She hadn't wanted anyone to know how desperate she'd been on that long-ago night.

But Jax knew. She had the feeling that Jax could learn all of her secrets.

She slipped through the gate.

And that's why I have to leave him.

"SARAH . . ." JAX put his hand against the windowpane. "You can run, but I'll find you." And she *was* running. Vanishing through that gate. Clever lady, she'd learned his alarm codes last night. He hadn't even realized that she'd been watching when he keyed them in. Now he would remember that Sarah was always focused, even when it seemed her attention was elsewhere.

He turned from the window. The room smelled of her. Sweet vanilla and sex. He'd had her, but taking Sarah hadn't ended the odd obsession that he felt for her. If anything, the obsession had intensified because now he knew what it was like to sink into her, to hear her moan, and to watch her eyes go wild with pleasure.

"You can run," Jax murmured again as he touched the pillow she'd lain on moments before, "but I like the hunt."

EVEN THOUGH IT was early, the New Orleans police station was already buzzing with activity. Uniformed officers hurried around the bullpen. Tired-looking detectives hunched over their desks. Phones rang. Voices rose.

Chaos was all around her. Luckily, Sarah was used to chaos. Squaring her shoulders, she walked toward the dark-haired detective who had just risen from his desk. He was one of the detectives she'd spoken with after her attack—Brent West. He was tall, had broad shoulders, and had a no-nonsense attitude that she'd respected. His skin was a dark cream, totally unlined, so he could be anywhere from twenty-five to forty.

He turned toward her, and she saw that his gaze looked . . . tired. As if he'd been up all night. When he saw her, a furrow appeared between his brows. "Dr. Jacobs?"

She gave him a quick smile. One that she hoped didn't look particularly nervous or desperate. "Do you have a moment to spare for me?"

The furrow deepened between his eyes. "Sure. I mean, has something happened? Are you all right?"

She waved away his concern. "I'm fine. I actually . . . I wanted to talk with you about Eddie Guthrie." She kept her voice mild and her hands stayed loose at his sides.

"Oh, ma'am, you don't have to worry about him." Brent gave a firm nod. "With the evidence we have on him, it's going to be an open-and-shut case."

Yes, right, but . . . "Is there any chance I can see him?"

The detective blinked at her. "You want to run that by me again?"

She straightened her spine. "I'm a psychiatrist, and I've interviewed literally hundreds of criminals over the years."

He waited and didn't look particularly impressed. Right. Sarah cleared her throat. "What if he just needs help?"

His sharp look questioned her sanity. "Ma'am, he attacked you. He had a knife to your throat. You're lucky he didn't slice open your jugular."

What a lovely visual. She swallowed. "My father . . . killed Eddie Guthrie's mother." Such an understatement. Her father had *tortured* Gwen Guthrie. *And I heard her screaming. I was just a kid. I heard her . . . but he told me it was nothing. He tucked me in bed. Kissed me good night, and said I was safe.*

Only Sarah hadn't realized the truth of that long-ago night, not until far too late.

"Because of what you father did, you think that makes it all right for that guy in there to come after you with a knife?"

Sleep tight. You know you're safe tonight.

Sarah shook her head. "No, no, I don't." She stared into the detective's eyes. "But I think losing a parent so violently can have a lasting impact on a person. Eddie was so incredibly young when his mother was murdered." She knew he'd just been a baby. His sister had only been a little older. "Before he's thrown in jail, I'd like to see if . . . if he needs—"

"What? Counseling?" He laughed, but the sound held little humor. "You're one of those, huh? You think you can fix everyone with some therapy."

She thought of her father. "Therapy can't fix everyone." Not even close. "I just want to talk with him, okay? Five minutes, that's all I'm asking." The detective didn't understand the guilt that tore through her whenever she thought of Eddie. "I mean, he can have a visitor, right? Put us in an interrogation room, and, if it makes you feel better, you can watch the whole scene."

He hesitated. His eyes—a dark green—swept over her. "You're with LOST, right?"

She nodded.

"Heard about all you did down here recently." His breath expelled in a rush. "So, yeah, fine, I figure we owe you five minutes considering the lives you probably saved by stopping that freak who was hunting in my city."

Her shoulders sagged. "Thank you, Detective."

He nodded. "Hell, maybe you'll even get the guy to spill a full confession. That's part of your deal, isn't it? Getting the criminals to spill their secrets to you."

That wasn't exactly how being a profiler worked.

But before she could explain that to him, he had turned away and was heading toward an interrogation room. Sarah rushed to keep up with him.

IN THE BRIGHT light of day, Eddie Guthrie didn't look particularly intimidating. In fact, he looked like a skinny, scared kid. One with acne on his chin, greasy hair, and hands that were shaking.

He's really twenty-one? He appeared so heartbreakingly young to her.

"If you'd like," the detective said to Eddie, "you can have a lawyer in here, kid."

"Don't need one," Eddie said. His eyes were on Sarah. "We all know what I did. I tried to stop a monster."

Sarah didn't flinch.

The detective moved toward the far wall. He crossed his arms over his chest and watched them.

Taking her time, Sarah advanced and then sat down across from Eddie. She stared at him a moment, letting her gaze sweep over his bloodshot eyes, his too pale skin, down to his trembling hands. Her lips curved down. "Withdrawal?" All of the signs were there. Classic.

"Bitch, you don't know a thing about me—"

"I'm sorry about your mother."

She heard the sharp inhale of his breath. Her gaze lifted back to his dark eyes, and the pain in his stare was unmistakable.

"Don't talk about her," he gritted out. "Don't you dare!"

"But she's the reason that you broke into my room, right? Because of what happened to her?" *I am so sorry, Eddie.* Because as she stared at him, he stopped being the man who'd come to kill her. And, for an instant, he was a child. One who'd lost his mother to a brutal killer. *To my father.*

"You took everything away from me," Eddie whispered.

Sarah shook her head, but . . . weren't his words true? If she'd gone for help that night, if she'd tried to get more people to believe her . . . "I'm sorry," she said again.

His fisted hands slammed into the table. "Stop saying that!"

Right. Going back wasn't always for the best. She inhaled a deep, cleansing breath and said, "What happened to your sister?"

He looked away.

"Molly, wasn't it?" As if she'd forgotten. Sarah had made a point to learn about the families of all her father's victims. "She was just a little bit older than you when . . . when your mother died." They'd both been mere babies. Sarah swallowed. "How is she now?"

"Stay the fuck away from my family!"

There was so much rage in Eddie.

"Told you," Detective West murmured as he shifted his stance a bit. "Waste of time. This kid's a drug head. He's going to get thrown in jail for years."

Fear came and went on Eddie's face.

"Is that what you want?" Sarah asked him. "To go to jail? To spend years locked away from your sister?"

Slowly, he shook his head.

"Then why did you come after me? Revenge? Was that really—"

"He told me where you were."

And Sarah's heart stopped beating. She actually felt it still in her chest, then in the next instant, it was racing, thumping far too hard in her chest. "Who told you that?"

But Eddie had clamped his lips shut.

"Eddie . . . Eddie, if someone put you up to the attack, you should tell us. Detective West can help you." She thought Eddie needed to get put in rehab and start receiving some serious therapy. She thought—

"No one can help me. Not now."

She shook her head. "That's not true. It's never too late."

He laughed. "Really? Is that the same line of bull you

give to your father? Because we both know it's too late for him. He's evil, straight to the core." His eyes turned to slits as he glared at her. "Just. Like. You."

WELL, THAT LITTLE chat certainly hadn't gone well.

Sarah stepped out of the interrogation room. Her hands wrapped around her stomach as she tried to settle her nerves.

"Who was he talking about?"

Ah, Detective West had followed her out. She should have known there would be someone watching her. *Isn't there always?*

Sarah glanced back over her shoulder. Deliberately, Sarah put her hands back at her sides.

"When Eddie said that 'he' told him where to find you. Who the hell is the guy talking about?"

"I have no idea."

"Well, I sure think you and I need to be finding that out, Dr. Jacobs. Because it sounds like the guy sent Eddie to kill you."

Before she could respond, Sarah's phone beeped. She pulled it out of her pocket and swiped her finger across the screen so she could see her text. The note was from her boss, Gabe Spencer.

Client meeting. Get to the hotel ASAP.

Since when did they have another client in New Orleans? She'd actually thought that Gabe was flying out of the city that afternoon. Hurriedly, she typed back, *On my way.* "Uh, excuse me," she murmured to the detective. "I have a work meeting that I need to attend—"

But he moved into her path. "You can't be this cold."

She blinked at him.

"You just discovered someone else out there wants you dead. Aren't you afraid?"

Absolutely, but fear changed nothing. "Have you contacted Eddie's sister?" Sarah asked, instead of responding to his question.

"I left three messages for her. She hasn't called back yet." He waved that away. "Knowing that someone might be out there, gunning for you . . . what are you going to do?"

Find that person, before he finds me. "Maybe Eddie will talk more when his sister arrives." She gave the detective her card—with her cell number. "Sometimes, people will open up more around family." Then Sarah walked away.

"And sometimes . . ." the detective called after her, "it's the family that causes the problems, isn't it?"

She knew he was talking about her father. *Murphy Jacobs.*

Or, as the press liked to call him . . . *Murphy the Monster.*

She kept walking. *Yes, family can cause the worst problems. And give you nightmares that won't end.*

GABE SPENCER WAS staying at the same hotel that Sarah was using. All the LOST members were in that hotel.

Only now we've got a new client? Just how much longer would they be staying in the Big Easy? She was ready to get home.

When the elevator opened on Gabe's floor, Sarah hurried forward. A few moments later, Sarah knocked lightly on Gabe's door.

Gabe Spencer. Ex-SEAL. All-around nice guy with a serious need to right the wrongs of the past. She'd profiled Gabe within moments of meeting him, and she'd known, from the start, that he was one of those guys that a girl could always count on. Lots of power and strength, but nothing evil in his core.

The door opened. Gabe stood there. His black hair had been swept back and his bright blue gaze sharpened when he saw her.

"Sorry it took me so long," she told him. "I, uh, made a little stop by the police station this morning."

She knew Gabe had been thoroughly briefed on last night's events.

Worry was clear on his face when he said, "You went to see Eddie Guthrie."

He was a nice, *smart* guy. She nodded.

"You'll tell me all about that," he murmured as his fingers curled around her shoulder and he pulled her into the room. "After our client meeting."

Gabe wasn't just staying in a normal hotel room. The guy was loaded, so he pretty much didn't do anything *normally.* He'd booked a massive suite, and they were in the suite's meeting space. A conference table was in the middle of the room, and the team had all gathered there. Sarah's gaze swept the room, pausing briefly on each of her friends.

The closest seat at the conference table was occupied by Victoria Palmer, their forensic anthropologist. Victoria's long red hair had been pulled back in a ponytail. Glasses perched on her nose, and, as she sat there, Victoria's gaze darted a bit nervously over toward Sarah.

Victoria had healed from her recent attack—courtesy of their last case. Or at least she'd healed on the outside. Sarah knew some wounds—the ones that were hidden the deepest—could never truly heal.

Dean Bannon was across the table from Victoria. An ex-FBI agent, Dean thrived on fieldwork. He loved the thrill of the hunt, and Sarah knew he would go to any extremes to find the missing.

Wade Monroe sat next to Victoria. Wade was a former Atlanta detective and, in general, a hard-nosed guy who would do anything to get the job done. He was currently glaring—intently. But he wasn't glaring at Sarah. His golden stare was fixed on the tall, blond man who stood with his back to them all. A man who appeared to be staring out of that massive picture window and down at the city below. A man who—

—turned toward her.

Not him. Not him.

"Hello, Sarah," Jax murmured.

She could actually feel all the blood leaving her head and flowing right down her body. No, he could *not* be there. She'd left him that morning. Wait, *why* would he be there? Her gaze jerked to Gabe. Gabe was staring at Jax.

"I think you know Jax Fontaine," Gabe murmured.

Um, biblically, yes, she did. But did the others realize that?

"He's our new client."

Sarah grabbed tight to her control. She'd already revealed too much with her rapid breathing and her startled response to Jax. It was a good thing that Dean's fiancée, Emma, wasn't there. Emma could read people so very easily. The woman had a gift—or, rather, a wickedly honed talent. Emma would see right through her act.

But Emma isn't here . . .

She stepped away from Gabe and advanced carefully toward Jax. He was dressed in a suit—*not* what she expected from him at all. He didn't look like the leader of one of the biggest motorcycle gangs in the South—which he supposedly was. Instead, he looked like a too-in-control businessman. The tattoos on his arms were covered up, and the only markings she saw were the dark tats on his fingers.

"Who is missing?" Sarah asked Jax. But she really wanted to know . . . why hadn't he told her sooner? Why waste any additional time on a case? With victims, time was always of the essence, even on cold cases.

Gabe had learned that lesson the hard way. If he'd found his sister just a little bit sooner, Amy would have been alive.

"That's the tricky part," Wade called out. His voice was mild, though, despite the frown that still pulled at his features. "Seems we have the missing, right here in this room with us."

Her head cocked as she gazed back at Jax. She wasn't sure what those words were supposed to mean. Normally, they were hired to *find* someone who'd vanished. Only once had they worked a different type of case.

Back then, a woman calling herself Eve Gray had come into the LOST offices in Atlanta. Eve had possessed no memory of her life, and she'd wanted the LOST group to help her figure out just who she was. They'd found out the truth for Eve, and along the way, Gabe had fallen for the blonde.

But Jax Fontaine wasn't suffering from any memory loss, she'd stake her life on that. Was he just trying to play some game with them?

"I was seven when I was taken," he said softly.

Goose bumps rose on her arms. Staring into his eyes, she saw how very serious he was. *This is no game.*

"I don't remember where I was before then." His voice was flat, so odd, without any emotion. "I know that the man who took me was a sadistic freak. He'd hit me, he'd threaten me, and . . ." Now his gaze seemed to see into the past. "For days, he'd lock me in a closet. He did that until I stopped begging to go home."

Helpless now, she reached out to him. "Jax . . ." Her fingers curled around his arms. No emotion was in his voice or his face, but she could feel his pain, all but hanging in the air between them.

"After a while, I learned not to ask for home." He glanced down at her hand, as it curled around his arm. "But I'm asking now. I'll pay whatever price LOST demands, but I want to know where I came from. I want to know who I was . . ." His lips twisted. " . . . before I became Jax Fontaine."

Jax . . . a man who'd been arrested over a dozen times before his eighteenth birthday.

A man rumored to be the boss of the New Orleans underworld.

A man who'd . . . been a victim?

"So tell me the price," Jax murmured, "and I'll pay it."

Her fingers tightened around his arm.

"It doesn't work like that," Gabe said, his words soft but laced with sympathy. "We don't take a case, not until we've researched it more. We have to make sure—"

"—that I'm not bullshitting you?" he asked bluntly.

"Yes." Gabe's equally blunt reply.

"I'm not." Jax's gaze dipped to Sarah's hand. "The man who became my—my *father* . . ." His lips twisted with disgust as he said the word. "He . . . took me. That I know with certainty. I was someone else before, and I need to find out who the hell that kid was." His breath heaved out. "He didn't work alone. There was a woman with him. Her name was Charlene. Charlene Fontaine." His lips curved the faintest bit. "She became my mother. She . . . loved me." He pulled away from Sarah and looked back out the window. "She used to tell me that my old mother was gone. But that she'd be better. And . . . in her way, she did take care of me." After a moment, he said, "When I was fifteen, she killed herself."

Sarah's hand fell back to her side.

"I tried to save her, but I couldn't. I figured my past died with her." His fingers pressed to the glass. "But then I learned all about the LOST group, thanks to Emma. And I realized I might just find out where I'd come from, after all."

She wanted to help him. No, more than that. Sarah *needed* to help him. She'd thought that Jax was strong, dangerous—he was. But there was so much happening beneath the surface with him.

Sarah glanced back over her shoulder. Dean had tensed at the mention of Emma's name. No big surprise there, considering that the guy was in love with Emma Castille. But, once upon a time, Emma had been involved with Jax. Intimately involved. Sarah knew Dean didn't exactly like having Jax anyplace near Emma but . . .

Don't worry, Dean. Jax has moved on. Sarah just wasn't going to get into the specifics of that whole moving-on bit right then.

Gabe's intent stare was on Jax. It was Gabe who would make the final call about the case. He'd be the one to tell them if they could go ahead or if—

Gabe nodded, a small inclination of his head. "We'll see what we can find for you."

Instead of relaxing, Jax's powerful shoulders tensed even more.

"But you should be warned," Gabe continued, "you might not like what we discover."

Jax just laughed as he turned to face them all once more. "Obviously, you don't know what my life has been like. Nothing can be much worse than what I've lived through already."

Sarah believed him.

Seven years old.

A chair leg scraped. Sarah glanced back and saw that Victoria had risen to her feet. "We'll need your DNA," Victoria said. "We should do some blood work. We'll check NamUs and see if any reports match your case."

NamUs—the National Missing and Unidentified Persons System. Yes, they could check the database and see if there was a report of a seven-year-old boy vanishing around a timeline that fit Jax's story. They could see—

"Don't bother with NamUs," Jax said, his voice close to a growl. "Did you think I hadn't already tried them? Hell, I've hired three PIs in the last two years. No one ever turns up anything." His gaze bored into Sarah's. "I want you to be different."

"We don't give up easily," she whispered.

"Good. Neither do I." There was a deeper, harder note in his last words.

She shivered.

What is he doing to me?

Sarah backed away from him.

And Jax smiled.

"WAKE UP, MOLLY."

The voice was low, rumbling, and it pierced through the heavy darkness around Molly Guthrie. She jerked, but found that her hands were tied behind her back. She was sitting on a hard wooden chair, and her feet were bound to the chair's legs.

It was pitch-black around her, and even though she strained, Molly couldn't see anything.

But he's there.

"Please," she whispered. "Let me go. I won't tell anyone about you." Her words came out slurred and rough, and she wondered what he'd used to drug her.

But he laughed. "Liar. You get out, you'll tell everyone."

She shook her head. "I—I promise."

She thought she heard the faint creak of wood. As

if he'd stepped forward, somewhere in that darkness. Somewhere . . . close.

"I'm not ready to lose you, not yet."

Then she felt something cold and hard slide up her arm. Something with a sharpened tip, like a knife.

Please, no, not a knife. Not the knife!

"Are you thinking about your mother?" he asked her. His voice was such a deep rumble and an image of his face flashed in her mind. He'd been handsome. He'd smiled. Looked . . . charming. It had seemed safe enough to walk with him.

He isn't safe.

"How long do you think she screamed for help?"

Molly didn't know. She'd tried so hard not to think about her mother over the years. Or to imagine what her last moments would have been like.

"She probably screamed for help first," he said, voice almost musing. "But then I bet . . . I bet she started begging to die."

Molly shook her head, an instinctive move.

His insidious laughter came again. "You don't think so? That's what they usually do, before the end. Because the pain gets to be too much, and by then, the only escape is death."

A tear slid down her cheek.

"We'll find out, you and I," he promised as the tip of the knife pressed into her cheek. "We'll see just how long it is before you start to beg."

Then there was a flash, bright, as if—as if he'd just taken her picture.

"Now we begin . . ."

Chapter 4

"WHY DIDN'T YOU SAY SOMETHING TO ME LAST night?"

Jax turned at Sarah's question. She'd followed him out of that hotel suite and now she was in the elevator with him. The scent of vanilla clung in the air around him, and it was so tempting to have her near. He wanted to reach out and touch her.

He didn't.

Jax knew he wouldn't stop with a touch. He wouldn't stop until he fucked her again, and while sex in an elevator—with her—would no doubt be amazing, this wasn't the time.

The doors closed, sealing them inside. "Let's see . . ." he murmured. "Did you want me to say something before we fucked? Or maybe *after* you snuck from my bed?"

Her cheeks flushed. Cute. He hadn't been sure he could make her blush. He could.

"That's why you came to see me last night, isn't it?" Sarah asked. "Because you wanted to hire LOST, not because you . . . you wanted me."

He stepped closer to her. Sarah didn't retreat. He

rather liked that about her. "Let's be clear," Jax said, his words soft. "I want you very, very much."

She swallowed.

He smiled. "Hiring LOST is totally separate from us. But, yes, I came to this hotel because I wanted to see about hiring your group. Then you had that asshole in the ski mask try to knife you, and things got a little off track."

Her eyelids flickered and she glanced over at the elevator's control panel. They were slowing now, and the doors opened. As soon as the little ding stopped sounding overhead, she tried to hurry past him.

He made sure to keep perfect pace with her as they moved into the lobby. "Do you want to tell me . . ." Jax began softly, "why you were afraid when you came into that suite earlier?"

She stopped in the middle of the lobby and turned toward him.

He stood right beside her, but he was careful not to touch her. "Tell me," he pushed, "why you're scared now." Surely she wasn't afraid of him. Hadn't he shown her that he wouldn't hurt her? If he had his way, he'd destroy anyone who ever even *thought* about hurting her. Like that jerk from last night who'd—

"I went to see Eddie Guthrie this morning."

Ah, that would be the jerk in question.

But then she shook her head. "Look, no, forget about me, okay. You're a client. I'm supposed to be interviewing you. So let's go grab some coffee and we can talk—see what you might remember about your past and go from there."

So adorable. Did she actually think he'd never *tried* to visit a shrink and unlock the memories of his life before the kidnapping? "It's not that easy."

A faint furrow appeared between her brows. "Coffee is easy, I promise."

She was good at evasion and distraction. He was better. "Eddie Guthrie made you afraid today. Even though he's locked away." He didn't like that. "Want me to take care of that problem for you?"

Sarah paled, then quickly glanced around. In the next instant, she was grabbing him. "Do not," she whispered, "threaten to kill someone in a public place!"

He laughed. Jax just couldn't help it. "Oh, princess, I didn't say anything about killing." His reputation must have preceded him, again. It happened. Sometimes, that was good, and sometimes, that was bad.

She looked as if she wanted to question him, but then she gave a hard, negative shake of her head. "Just forget Eddie, okay? I'll deal with him. After you and I are done, I'll meet with Gabe and we'll figure out the next step."

He rather liked Gabe Spencer. Jax hadn't thought he would. He genuinely liked only a handful of individuals in this world, and he respected even fewer. But he'd done his research on Gabe, and the ex-SEAL legitimately seemed to want to help others. So Jax had taken a chance and called the man today.

Then they'd had that little meet and greet in the hotel suite. Sure, a few of the LOST members—or, rather, two . . . Wade and Dean—had looked as if they'd like to slug Jax, not take his case, but he thought the whole deal had gone rather well. Or as well as he'd expected.

"You won't tell me why you're afraid?" Jax asked her. Because her fear was bothering him.

"I don't know if there is even anything to fear yet. Sometimes, people facing jail will say anything to avoid getting locked up. Sometimes, they'll act like they have intel or leverage or *something* that the cops need, hoping they can work out a deal. So the guy could just be bluffing. But I'll figure all of that out. Right now, my focus is on you." Her hold tightened on Jax. "Now, look, can we go someplace and just . . . talk? I have questions that I need to ask you before LOST can proceed."

If they proceeded. He knew her team was still trying to decide if his story was real.

It's real.

"Not in public." His voice was close to a growl so he tried to soften that, adding, "The last thing I want is some dumbass in a coffee shop overhearing about my past. We'll go back to my place, talk there."

"Right." She looked down and seemed to realize that she was holding tightly to him. Her hands immediately pulled back, as if she'd been burned. "We can take a cab."

"No need." He gave her a tiger's smile. "I brought my motorcycle."

One brow rose. "In those clothes?"

"Of course." He paused a beat. "You seemed to like the ride last night."

She bit on her lower lip.

He wanted to be the one biting that lip. "You want to hear all about my past, then come with me. I'll give you every dark detail that you want to hear." Details he'd never told to anyone else. But, as she'd slipped away from him that morning, he'd come to a decision.

It was time to know the truth. Time to finally figure out what had happened to him.

The past would be laid to rest and he could finally start focusing on the future.

"All right." Her shoulders straightened. "Let's go for that ride."

Hell, yes. Soon, he'd have Sarah exactly where he wanted her.

They headed for the revolving glass doors that would take them out of the hotel. They'd taken only about four steps when Sarah's phone gave a little beep. She paused and glanced apologetically up at him. "Sorry, I need to see"—her gaze dropped to the screen and her fingers swiped across the surface—"if it's—"

Sarah sucked in a sharp breath. "*No.*"

He leaned closer to her, craning his head so that he could see the image that had just appeared on the screen.

"Please," Sarah whispered. "*No.*" Her hand was trembling around the phone.

A photo filled the screen of her phone. A woman was in that photo—fairly young, with long red hair that was tangled around her terrified face. Blood slid from a cut on her cheek, and the woman's arms appeared to be pulled behind her—tied behind her?

"I know her," Sarah whispered. "She looks just like Gwen did." A stark pause. "That's his sister, Molly."

"What the hell?" Jax demanded. *Whose sister?*

Sarah was frantically tapping on her screen. She

called someone then—maybe the person who'd just sent that fucked-up picture to her? Sarah had the phone at her ear, and fear flashed across her face as she seemed to wait for someone to answer her call.

MOLLY'S PHONE WAS ringing. Right on time. Humming, he picked up that phone and turned on the speaker. After all, he needed to be able to hear all of this conversation—and so did Molly. He brought the phone in nice and close to Molly. In the darkness he'd created, the glow from the phone was the only light.

"Hello?" Ah, that slightly sharp and desperate voice would belong to Sarah Jacobs. *Dr.* Sarah Jacobs. "Who is this?" Sarah demanded.

With his left hand, he sliced the knife down Molly's arm. She screamed. A high-pitched, desperate cry.

"Molly?" Sarah asked. "Molly Guthrie?"

Another slice of his knife had Molly screaming again.

"*Stop!*" Now it was Sarah who yelled. "I know you're there . . ." Her voice dropped. "Why are you hurting Molly?"

He smiled. He'd been waiting for this moment for so long. When he'd seen her picture in the paper and realized that Sarah was in *his* town, he'd moved up his attack. Why go all the way to Atlanta and hunt her, when he could make her play the game right there, in his own backyard? Especially since she was already there and tangled up with Jax Fontaine. *Too perfect.*

He brought the phone to his mouth. "Hurry up," he told her. "See if you can find the girl before she dies."

"*Who is this?*"

Ah, it wouldn't be that easy. Her question was really an insult. She was the profiler. She was the one who had to figure all of this shit out.

"She's lost," he taunted, "so come and find her."

SHE'S LOST, SO come and find her. He'd hung up on her. The man's words rang in her ears as Sarah slowly lowered her phone. She knew the woman in that picture—the woman who looked so terrified was Molly Guthrie. Sarah knew because she'd been researching Eddie Guthrie online, and she'd stumbled onto the guy's social media pages. He'd had so many pictures of his sister Molly posted. Only Molly had been smiling in those photographs.

She hadn't been tied to a chair with blood sliding down her face. She sure hadn't been screaming in terror.

"What's going on?" Jax demanded. "Sarah?"

"I—I have to call the police." She'd stuttered. She tried to never stutter. Never show any weakness but . . .

Molly had been screaming.

And then Sarah could almost hear her father's voice whispering in her mind . . .

No one is screaming. No one at all.

She pushed away from Jax. Her movements were too quick and jerky, and when she looked to the left, she saw Wade stepping out of the elevator. Gabe was with him. She ran toward them, aware that Jax was right on her heels.

When he saw her rushing toward him, Wade's eyes widened. "Sarah?"

She didn't speak, not then. Fear was closing her throat. She shoved her phone toward him—her phone and the picture of a terrified Molly.

Gabe crowded in behind Wade. "What in the hell is going on?" Gabe demanded.

"That's the same thing I wanted to know," Jax said.

Her breath heaved out. "We have to find her." *Come and find her.* "Before he kills her."

As a general rule, Jax liked to avoid police stations. And cops. Cops tended to piss him off, and as for the police stations . . . well, he'd already spent more than enough time in them.

But he'd tagged along with the LOST group, driven by both curiosity and an odd urge to stay near Sarah. He didn't like it when fear flashed in Sarah's dark eyes. He rather thought he fucking hated it when her skin paled and the shadows beneath her gorgeous eyes deepened.

There had been fear in her eyes when he first saw her at the hotel room. He'd turned toward her, and the fear had been the first thing he noticed. Surely the others must have seen it, too?

And now that same fear seemed to cling to Sarah as she talked with the cops. Two detectives. Guys he'd met before, in different ways.

One guy was Detective Brent West, a fairly decent detective, even if the guy had a tendency to stick to the rules a bit too much. Jax had done a few favors for Brent over the years. Or rather, he'd done some favors for Brent's family. So now Brent knew to . . . keep him in the loop on certain cases.

The other detective was Lincoln Cross, and Jax's encounters with Cross had hardly been what he'd call positive. Especially in light of the news he'd recently gotten about the guy's activities. *You're going to be paying for that, Detective. Don't think you'll escape.*

"Let me get this straight," Cross said as he lifted his hands. The guy hadn't made direct eye contact with Jax. He kept focusing on Sarah and Gabe. They were all in a conference room down at the PD. "You're saying Molly Guthrie has been abducted? And that the man who took her called you?"

"Yes—and I've said that same thing five times!" Impatience bit through Sarah's words. "Now, we're wasting time. I came to you first because I knew the cops needed to be involved." Ah, she was definitely getting pissed by their lack of action. Jax could tell it in her sharpening voice. "But if you're not doing anything, then my team can be out there, hitting the streets! Every moment counts in an abduction case, Detectives, and you both know that."

A muscle jerked in Brent's jaw. Yeah, he knew it. Jax also thought the guy would have preferred to be out in the street, searching for the victim, right then. But Cross was the lead there. Dick that he was.

"The first forty-eight hours are the most important," Gabe said, his voice devoid of emotion. "We don't usually get involved in a case this early, and while we have the time, we damn well need to be *moving.*"

"You're involved . . ." Cross began, "because the abductor just up and called Dr. Jacobs. Odd, isn't it? I mean, I think that's odd."

Jax was surprised the guy could think.

"Odd or not, it happened." Sarah jumped from her chair. "Now are you going to do anything? Put out an APB? Go to Molly's house? Hunt for her before that guy cuts her into little pieces?"

Jax saw Brent wince. It also looked like Brent was sweating.

"We'll investigate," Cross said through gritted teeth. "I do know how to do my job."

"Do you?" Jax just couldn't resist.

He didn't think Cross's jaw could clench much harder, but the detective muttered, "I'll send a patrol over to the woman's house right now."

"And two of my men will go with that patrol," Gabe said. He inclined his head toward a watchful Wade and Dean. "After all, *we* were contacted directly, so my team will be involved throughout this investigation."

"That's not—" Cross began angrily.

"Take it up with your captain," Gabe snapped.

Cross flushed.

But at least the guy finally got moving. He stood and marched for the door. Jax moved a bit, placing himself closer to the exit so that Cross had to look his way. Disgust tightened his face. "So now you're with them?" Cross asked Jax. "What are they doing, using a criminal to catch a criminal or some twisted bull like that?"

"You'd know," Jax said, keeping his voice low so that only Cross would hear him. "Isn't that exactly what *you* do?"

Cross wasn't a cop with a spotless reputation. His flush deepened as he jerked open the door. "Excellent cooperation we have here," Gabe murmured. "Amazing."

Jax's lips almost twitched.

"We'll report back in once we get to the victim's house," Wade said.

Ah, so Wade was calling her the victim already. Based on the photo Jax had seen, the woman definitely qualified as that. He was curious to see just what the LOST agents and the cops were going to do to find her.

Because he already had his own plan of attack forming.

When Wade and Dean left the room, the door shut softly behind them. That left Sarah, Gabe, Victoria, and Detective Brent West in the room with Jax. He kept his shoulders propped up against the wall . . . and he waited.

"You want to talk to the brother, don't you?" Brent said as he rubbed a hand over his face. "But until the PD can confirm that Molly Guthrie has been abducted, I can't let you see him again. The guy has a lawyer now—court appointed—and no one but PD can see him."

Then Brent glanced over at Jax. His head inclined slightly, just the faintest of movements.

"Now," Brent murmured, "I'm going to see what I can find out about Molly Guthrie. *I'll* talk to her brother, and if I learn anything—"

"You'll let us know?" Gabe pushed.

Brent nodded. "And you let me know if you get any other calls." The cops had confiscated Sarah's phone as soon as she arrived and told her story. They'd done some tracking work and found out that Molly Guthrie's phone had actually been used to text Sarah—and that was the number Sarah had called back.

Only now Molly's phone seemed to have vanished from the grid. It wasn't pinging on any towers, at least not according to the cops.

"I want us to work together on this," Brent said, and there seemed to be sincerity in his tone. "Because I know just what your team can do, and my priority is to bring that victim back alive."

Then he was striding toward the door.

While Sarah, Victoria, and Gabe talked, Jax slipped from the room. He strolled down the hall, and then he saw Brent, standing near an office on the right. They both ducked inside that office.

"What the hell is going on?" Brent demanded as he glanced toward the door, probably trying to make sure they weren't being watched. "Since when are you working with LOST?"

Jax had plenty of eyes and ears around the city—and not all of those eyes and ears belonged to criminals. "Since I took a personal interest in them." An interest in Sarah.

"What have you stepped in here, man?" Brent demanded. He blew out a hard breath. "First that kid Guthrie goes after the sexy shrink, then, this morning, he pretty much admits someone else put him up to the attack—"

"*What?*" Jax closed in on him. "Run that by me again, nice and slow." Sarah had told him some about her little chat with Guthrie, but Jax wanted all the details.

"I—I let her back to talk with him for a few minutes. I know I shouldn't have, but, shit, maybe it's those big, dark eyes of hers. They just—they got to me, so I thought . . . what would a few minutes hurt? And she's a professional after all! Not like I'm sending in some civilian off the street."

The guy needed to hurry along his little story.

"So she gets to talking with the kid and the guy—Eddie—he's all pissed about what her dad did. Says that's why he attacked the shrink." Brent gave a low whistle. "You've heard the story, right? Her father is Murphy Jacobs! *Murphy the fucking monster Jacobs*! Do you know how many people he killed?"

From the accounts that Jax had read, no one knew, not for certain.

"The kid went after her because Murphy killed his mother. Only when he's talking, right there at the end, Eddie says, '*He told me where you were.*' "

"Who told him?" This was the part of the story that interested Jax the most. Sarah had brushed it off, trying to act as if Eddie had just been spouting bull. *But if he was spouting BS, then why did Sarah seem so afraid when she first came into the hotel room?*

"I don't know! The kid shut down after that. Even after she left, I couldn't get him to say more." Brent nodded. "But someone sent him to that hotel. He was the weapon that someone else used. Just aimed him and fired him at the shrink."

No wonder she'd been afraid. Despite her words to Jax . . . *Sarah knows someone else is after her.* Would that be the same someone who'd sent her that picture of Molly?

Brent cast another nervous glance toward the closed door. "I shouldn't be talking to you here."

Jax waved that away. "Just tell anyone who asks that you were threatening me. 'Cause we all know that shit happens all the time." Plenty of cops swore they'd be taking him down.

They hadn't.

But he'd sure sent away plenty of dirty cops.

"I want to know who sent the kid after Sarah."

Brent hesitated. "This . . . personal interest you have in LOST . . . it's her, isn't it?"

Jax just stared back at him. "You'll find out who sent the kid after her."

"I'll do my best, but if Eddie isn't talking—"

"Make him talk, or I will." So many people just didn't seem to understand how far his reach extended. They would, soon enough. "All I'd need would be five minutes alone with the guy."

Brent's Adam's apple bobbed. "You really think I could just take you right back to the guy's holding cell? Because that shit would go over so smoothly with everyone here!"

Brent wasn't getting the full picture. Maybe he needed a little help. "I'd go back to the cells, if you arrested me."

Brent frowned at him.

"Like it would be the first time that happened," Jax murmured, smiling.

Then Jax heard a knock at the door. Seconds later, that door opened and Sarah was there, edging carefully into the room. "Jax, I thought I saw you come in here—" She broke off, obviously catching sight of Brent. "Is everything all right?"

"Same shit as always," Jax told her with a shrug. "Cops warning me to stick to the straight and narrow, but that's what I do every day." He saluted the cop. "See you around, Detective."

Muttering, Brent hurried past them.

Sarah shook her head. "They love giving you a hard time, don't they?"

So sweet. It sounded as if she were worried about him. "Don't fret, princess. I can handle anything they throw at me." But he was still ready to get out of that station. He caught her hand, threaded his fingers with hers, and stalked from the room. As they made their way out of the bullpen, he was aware of the stares on him. He could hear the mutters.

He ignored them, as usual.

Then they were outside. Cars were zooming down the street up ahead, and there were plenty of tourists filling the street.

"I . . . I need to work on this case, Jax." Her voice was soft. "I promise, I will get LOST to help you find your family, but right now, Molly has to be our priority. I'm sorry."

He squeezed her fingers. "I've been waiting years to find out about my past. You think I can't spare a few more days?" Days that Molly might not have? He wasn't that much of a selfish bastard.

Her breath caught. "You . . . why did you come to the police station?" She glanced back at it. "You hate being there. You didn't have to follow with us."

"You were there," he said simply. "So that meant I needed to go, too."

Her fingers pulled away from his. Sarah shook her head. “I don’t understand you.”

Who did?

“What do you want from me?”

Everything. But he didn’t think she was ready to hear that part, not yet.

“I can help,” he told her simply.

Her gaze—so dark and deep—searched his.

“You know I have contacts that you want to use.”

He could see the struggle on her face.

“Use me,” he dared her. “Because I rather think I’d enjoy having you indebted to me.”

“*LOST* would owe you,” Sarah said carefully.

A car whizzed by them.

He moved then, standing so that he was closer to the road. His body curled near her. “You would owe me,” he told her clearly. “You, Sarah. Just you.”

She bit her lip. Did she have any clue that he found that move fucking sexy?

“Before I went in that police station, I called my friend Carlos . . . I told him to learn everything he could about Molly Guthrie.” He waited a beat. “Want to see what he’s learned? Because Carlos is very good at uncovering secrets.” Mostly because when people saw Carlos, they knew to be afraid. At six-foot-four and weighing over two hundred and fifty pounds, Carlos was a man you didn’t fuck with.

Unless you wanted to get put down.

“I have my own ways of learning secrets.” Then she backed away from him.

Sighing, he took out his phone. Called Carlos. His

friend answered on the second ring. "Hello, Carlos," Jax murmured, just loudly enough for Sarah to hear. "Where's the girl?"

Sarah glanced back at him.

"Last night, she was washing dishes on Bourbon Street," Carlos told him. "I've got her leaving work—on foot—at around 4 A.M. No one saw her after that."

"The name of the bar," Jax murmured.

"Voodoo Night."

He knew the place. Hell, he'd almost bought the joint six months ago. "What else?" Jax asked.

"No boyfriend, no angry exes. She attends the community college during the day, works at night, and, no, her neighbors have *not* seen her this morning."

Ah, trust Carlos to get there before the cops. "If you learn anything else, let me know."

"Always, boss," Carlos promised.

Jax put down his phone. Sarah was staring up at him. She even tapped her foot.

He let both of his brows rise.

"Tell me," she demanded.

"Let's take a ride on my bike."

Sarah's eyes went molten. So dark and fiery.

"I'll take you to the last place she was seen, princess. Will that help?"

She lunged toward him. "Get me on that bike."

Ah, he'd thought that would work. "Just remember," Jax murmured. "You owe me." He always collected on his debts.

VICTORIA STOOD IN the New Orleans police bullpen. Voices were buzzing around her. The cops moving so fast. Everything seemed too loud. Too rough.

But then, that was the way things had been for her in the last few days. She'd gotten out of the hospital after her abduction and attack, and she'd thought life would return to normal.

It hadn't.

But the nightmares had started. Terrible twisting dreams.

"Viki?"

At Gabe's call, she flinched. She hadn't meant to do that, dammit. She didn't want her boss knowing just how rattled she was. Victoria turned toward him, carefully schooling her features.

"Are you all right?" he asked her.

Ah, that was Gabe. Always checking on his team. His handsome face was etched with concern.

"Of course," she lied. Like she'd tell him—or anyone—that she was falling apart on the inside.

His lips thinned. "I want you heading back to Atlanta."

What?

"Take some time off. You don't have to jump right back into a case, especially not *this* one." He glanced around them, then muttered, "I have a bad feeling in my gut about this case. First the girl's brother sneaks into Sarah's hotel room, then Molly's photo gets sent to Sarah?" He shook his head. "Coincidences don't happen. Someone is playing a game with us here."

And he wanted her out of the picture because . . .

what? She was some kind of liability because she'd been caught off guard before. "You don't think I can do my job?" That hurt. Because the job was all she had.

She'd never been particularly comfortable around other people. Not like Gabe was or Dean was, anyway. She said the wrong thing. Stumbled over her words. But the dead . . . she made a difference with them. She *helped* then.

Gabe's face softened as he focused on her. "I think you can do anything." He sounded as if he meant those words. "But I also know you went through hell recently."

Hell . . . Being drugged, sealed in a body bag, and nearly murdered by a madman. Yes, that whole experience hadn't exactly been a walk in the park. *And that's why the bad dreams haunt me each night.* She'd thought about talking with Sarah. If anyone could understand her nightmares, it would be Sarah. And it wasn't just because Sarah was a psychiatrist.

I know she has nightmares, too.

"I want you to recover. Hell, I'm not letting Emma Castille work this case, either. I gave strict instructions for her to recover, too, and keeping her from joining us here at the station was damn hard."

Emma . . . Emma was Dean's new fiancée and a woman with an uncanny ability to read others. She picked up on the smallest of tells. Emma could read body language like no one Victoria had ever encountered before . . . but, like Victoria, she'd also just gotten out of the hospital.

Only Emma hadn't just been sliced with a knife. She'd been shot.

"I want you both to recover." Gabe gave a hard nod. "And we don't have a body, Viki. We can find this girl, alive. If she's just gone missing, then the odds can finally be in our favor."

And Viki didn't help with the living. Only the dead.

"I'll get your plane ticket," Gabe told her. His gaze softened as he studied her. "I can have you out of the Big Easy in hours."

One of the detectives called his name and Gabe stepped away from her. Victoria stared after him. He was right, though. The team didn't need her. They didn't have a body.

Just find the girl alive.

Chapter 5

It was only noon, but Bourbon Street was already packed with people. Men and women walked down the street, their hands wrapped around their drinks. Mimosas. Hurricanes. The folks out there were all laughing and talking.

Many of the bars were open, but Voodoo Night . . . its doors were shut.

Sarah leaned forward, nearly pressing her nose to the glass as she tried to look inside the bar. But she didn't see anyone in there. The chairs had been placed on top of the tables and the interior was dim.

"It's called Voodoo Night for a reason," Jax murmured. "The place doesn't get going until the sun sets."

And he'd known that—but still brought her there? "I don't have time to waste," Sarah said. Didn't he understand? Every moment, Molly was in danger. The man holding her had taunted Sarah, saying that she had to come and find the other woman. But what if Sarah didn't find her in time? Adrenaline pumped through her blood as she whirled from that building. "I need to get the addresses of the folks who work here. I can go to their houses and talk to them. Maybe one of them remembers seeing Molly leave last night."

Sighing, Jax stepped into her path. "Have a little faith in me, would you?" Then he walked around to the back of the building. Sarah hurried to keep up with his fast steps. When they got to the back of the bar—a place that smelled of piss and alcohol—the door there was shut, too, but Jax slammed his fist against that door. Once, twice, three times—

And the door opened.

"What the fuck?" an angry bald man snarled. "We're closed, asshole. Closed until sunset—" The guy broke off, swallowed, and squeaked out, "Jax?"

Jax smiled. "Figured you'd be here, Ron. I knew you kept your place in the back."

Ron lifted his hands. "I don't want any trouble."

Everyone seemed to expect trouble from Jax. That couldn't be good. Sarah glanced at Jax from the corner of her eye. His features were set, almost grim, and she realized then—*yes, he looks like he's here to kick ass.*

"I'm looking for a girl," Jax told him.

Ron's eyes darted toward Sarah. "Why? You've got a pretty one right here." He flashed a nervous smile at Sarah. "Hey there, sweet thing."

Jax moved, putting his body in front of Sarah's. "Molly Guthrie," Jax enunciated slowly. "The girl you've got washing dishes here at night. I need to find her."

Sarah craned so that she could see around Jax.

Ron backed up a step. "Little M? She's not here. Haven't seen her since her shift ended last night." He was sweating a bit. "Go try her house. Or the college. She's got day classes. Go look there."

But Jax shook his head. "I want to come in the bar, Ron."

"Wh-Why?"

"Because Molly is missing. You said she was here last night—"

"She left around four! I swear!"

"But Ron, you and I both know . . . you can get a little . . . rough sometimes." And an even darker note had entered Jax's voice.

Sarah moved a few steps forward and glanced between the two men. The air seemed to vibrate with tension.

"I told you what would happen," Jax continued, and she saw that his hands had fisted, "if I heard that you hurt another lady."

"I didn't hurt her, I swear!" Ron said. He was sweating buckets then. "I didn't touch Molly!"

Sarah wished that she had her phone so she could show the guy that *someone* had hurt Molly. "When she left," Sarah said, "was she by herself? Was she taking a cab? A—"

Ron snapped his fingers together. "Her brother!" He beamed at them. "That brother of hers . . . I heard her say that he was coming to meet her. Eddie always comes when she has the late shift." His lips twisted. "Something about wanting to make sure she gets home safe." He stroked his chin. "Her mom was murdered, by that sadistic fuck Murphy."

Sarah kept her gaze on him.

"So the brother walks her home when she stays late.

I know, the kid's younger than Molly. The guy probably doesn't intimidate any damn one, but he's usually around, dogging her steps at night."

Only her brother hadn't been there to walk Molly home last night. *Because he'd been in jail. He came to attack me, and got locked up . . . so Eddie wasn't there to see Molly home safely.*

And had that been just what the abductor wanted?

He told me where you'd be. Her breathing came faster. Maybe . . . maybe it had all been a diversion.

"Talk to the brother!" Ron said again, his voice growing stronger as he seemed to become more confident. "He knows everything about her." He swiped his sweaty forehead. When his hand moved like that, Sarah saw the bruises on his knuckles. "If you ask me," Ron muttered. "That creepy kid has *too* much interest in his sister, if you know what I mean." His hand started to drop down.

But Jax caught Ron's wrist. He'd obviously seen the bruises, too. "Been fighting, Ron?"

Ron tried to pull away. Jax wasn't letting him go.

"Why won't you let me in the bar?" Jax murmured.

Ron's breath was panting out. "I-It's closed!"

Jax shook his head. "I told you what would happen if I found out you'd hurt another girl . . ." His voice had turned absolutely arctic.

"Uh, Jax," Sarah began.

"You should have listened," Jax said. Then he shoved Ron back, hard enough to send the guy sprawling right onto his ass. Then Jax leapt forward, even as Sarah lunged after him.

But he was so fast. In an instant, he was crouched over Ron. His left hand had clenched around the guy's shirt, and his right was a tight fist, a fist poised to drive into Ron's face.

Sarah grabbed Jax's arm. "Stop it!" she yelled at him. "You can't do this!"

Pulling against him was like pulling against steel. There was absolutely no give in the man at all.

"I can do plenty," Jax murmured. "And I will."

"No!" Ron screamed.

And . . . the door to the right, the door marked private—flew open. A woman shot out, a woman with long red hair. A woman armed with a knife. She yelled and came right at Sarah.

But Jax pushed Sarah out of the way. He shot toward the woman and yanked the knife right out of her hand. The woman attacked him with her nails then. Hitting and punching and—

Ron was crawling for the door. He was trying to make a break for it while that woman did her best to claw into Jax.

Is that Molly? The woman's red hair hid her face. She looked to be the right size, the right age . . .

She's fighting so hard.

Only . . . Jax wasn't fighting back. He was holding the woman, but not hurting her. He was talking, saying over and over, "It's okay. He won't hurt you. It's okay."

The redhead stilled. Her head lifted and Sarah saw her face. *Not Molly.* But . . . the woman had a black eye. Bruises were on her neck. Purple, blue marks that sure looked like fingerprints against her too pale skin.

Rage poured through Sarah's body and she ran toward the door. She put her body there, blocking Ron before he could escape. "You're not going anyplace! I'm getting the cops out here!" She yanked out her phone—a backup that Gabe had given her because the cops had confiscated Sarah's original phone at the station—and she started calling 911—

"Stop!" It was the redhead's desperate voice. "No cops! Don't call them!" She wasn't fighting Jax any longer. She just stood there, looking terrified.

Ron glared up at Sarah. "Bitch, you need to get out of my way."

Sarah shook her head.

In a flash, Ron surged up toward her. His fist was clenched and—

Jax tackled him. They both hit the floor, hard, and Ron's face smashed down into the tile. He howled when he made contact, and Sarah was pretty sure he'd broken something. Maybe even a couple of somethings.

She finished calling 911. She told them to send a patrol, to contact Detective Brent West, and to get there *right away*.

When she looked up again, Ron was swinging a fist at Jax. Jax dodged the blow and delivered a sharp right hook that connected with stunning impact. When Ron went down that time, he didn't get up.

"Baby, *no*!" the redhead screamed. She ran toward Ron and cradled him in her arms. "Baby, baby, look at me!"

After a long moment, Ron's eyes opened. He spat out some blood. "When . . . when the cops get here . . . tell 'em you like rough sex."

The redhead flinched.

"Tell 'em . . ." Ron had blood on his chin. "Tell 'em you asked for it."

Very slowly, the redhead nodded.

"*You're done in this town.*" Jax's voice was lethal. "Pack your bags and run. Because if you don't . . ."

Fear flashed on Ron's face.

Jax just smiled. "You know what will happen." He straightened his shirt. Wiped dust off his pants. "This bar is mine. Everything you have is *mine.*" Then Jax looked at the redhead. "You want free of him, then you say it now. You aren't the first one he's hurt. Maybe he fed you some bull about you being special, but he's lying. If you stay with him, he'll just hurt you again."

The redhead's knuckles were white as she clung to Ron. "He . . . loves me."

"No," Sarah said, her voice soft and sad. "He doesn't."

The woman stared back down at her lover.

Sarah inched closer to Jax. His body was so tense. Fury was stamped on his face. And the way he was staring at Ron . . .

Jax looks as if he wants to kill the other man.

Ron grabbed a nearby table and heaved himself up. "C-Cops won't hold me . . ."

Jax nodded. "Then you run."

Ron's eyes darted around the room, as if already seeking an escape.

"Run fast," Jax said. "And run far."

Sarah heard the sound of a police siren.

The redhead started to cry.

THEY WERE BACK at the police station. Only this time, Jax was being arrested.

"This is insane!" Sarah said for what had to be the tenth time. "Jax was defending me! You can't lock him up!"

Detective West sighed. "Ma'am, we have procedures to follow. A witness accused Fontaine here of throwing the first punch, and with his history . . . that man isn't going anyplace but to holding right now."

She shook her head, frantic. "But I need him!"

And at her words, Jax's head snapped up. He'd been standing about five feet away from her, talking with two uniformed cops. His face was grim, his eyes narrowed, but when he looked at her, a heat seemed to light his blue eyes.

Sarah sucked in a breath because that heat was scorching. "A woman is missing, and Jax knows this city. He can help us to find her!"

"Time is of the essence," Wade said from beside Sarah. "We checked the woman's house. She wasn't there. None of her neighbors remembered seeing her, and she didn't show up for classes today. That guy—he has her, and he's hurting her, right now."

Brent glanced over at Jax.

"My lawyer is already on the way," Jax murmured. The guy didn't seem to have a care in the world. It was like he wasn't even standing there, cuffed, with cops all around him. "I'll be out within the hour. But, Detective, by all means . . ." He inclined his head toward Brent. "Do lock me up until then."

What? He *wanted* to be locked up?

"That guy is one crazy bastard," Wade muttered.

Brent hesitated, but then he reached for Jax's elbow. "Procedures," he muttered. "Sorry." And then he led Jax away.

"No!" Sarah cried out.

Jax glanced back at her. "Don't worry, Sarah. I'll be out before you know it."

But Molly needed him. Sarah needed him.

And . . . she didn't usually need anyone.

Then Jax was just . . . gone.

Sarah straightened her shoulders. Something was happening to her. Her control was splintering. It was this case. Eddie, Molly—the tie to her own past. She was remembering too much about her father and not focusing enough on *this* criminal. This man who'd abducted Molly. She needed to get into his head.

"We should talk to Eddie," Wade said as he rubbed the back of his neck. His golden eyes glinted. "Gabe is already trying to get the guy to agree to a sit-down with us, but so far, the kid won't say a word. His lawyer is stonewalling things. Maybe Gabe can use his influence with the captain here in order to make him talk."

Sarah glanced over at the captain's office. His door was shut. Gabe was in there with him. A real closed-door meeting. But with every moment that passed, the seriousness of the situation seemed to grow.

This was no prank. No ploy for attention. A woman had been abducted, and they needed to be searching the city for her.

"Dean is at the college campus, talking with Molly's friends and following up leads there," Wade said.

"He's got Emma with him. That woman refused to be benched and she's riding shotgun with him. So if there's any intel to find there, you can count on them."

Yes, she could. "I need my phone back," Sarah said.

Wade's brows shot up.

"He contacted me before. He had my number. He'll do it again." Because it was a game to the perp. A game he wanted to play with her. "The cops should be done with the phone by now. I want it back." Because when he called again, she'd be ready for him. She glanced up at Wade. "I know Gabe sent that picture back to our headquarters in Atlanta. Has the tech team found anything on it?" Because they had a guy on staff who was an absolute genius with his computers. He could enhance and enlarge photos, find the smallest specks of evidence in a picture that others had completely overlooked. Leo had a true gift at enhancements.

"No word from Leo yet."

Everything was moving too slowly. She looked back over at the door that led to holding. Jax was gone. Ron was gone, too. *Ron Tate.* He'd been dragged off to interrogation.

The redhead was slumped in a nearby chair, crying.

She's the one who said Jax threw the first punch. That woman's claim was the reason Jax had just been locked up.

Sarah strode toward her.

"Uh, Sarah . . ." Wade began. He sounded nervous, unusual for him.

Sarah slapped her hands on the desk near the woman. The redhead jumped.

"You know Molly Guthrie," Sarah said flatly.

The woman nodded.

"*Sarah*," Wade hissed out her name.

"Someone took Molly. Tied her up, and sliced her with a knife."

Fear filled the woman's big, blue eyes. *Ella Jane*. That was the woman's name. She'd heard Ron tell Ella Jane to wait for him.

No, Ella Jane, you need to get the hell away from him.

"Uh, Sarah, I don't think you're supposed to be talking with her. Witness tampering and all that," Wade said softly.

She almost rolled her eyes. Sometimes, Wade was such a cop. A rule follower. She'd learned early on that it paid to break rules. "Ella Jane here is going to tell the truth."

Ella Jane hunched back into her chair.

"Because she knows just how powerful Jax is in this city." It was something Sarah was learning. The whispers about him were true. "She knows that he can get searches organized right now—searches that the cops would never be able to conduct." Searches that would lead into the city's underworld. "And we can find Molly, before it's too late."

The bruises on Ella Jane's neck were darkening even more.

But Ella Jane wasn't speaking.

"Ron buys you something afterwards, doesn't he?" Sarah asked as her gaze slid to the pretty rings that sparkled on Ella Jane's fingers. "He's so sorry, and he wants to make it up to you." Classic.

"I . . . it was just rough sex." Ella Jane's voice was a monotone. Her eyes appeared dead. "I wanted it."

"No, you didn't." Sarah leaned toward her. "Was Ron with you last night? Or did he slip away so he could see if Molly liked a bit of rough sex, too?"

"What?" Horror flashed on Ella Jane's face. "No! H-He was with me. The whole time! I know because . . . he wouldn't let me leave his sight." She swallowed and glanced down at the rings on her fingers. "Not even for a second."

That's because he wants to control you. Ron, oh, yes, she understood him. Far too well. Her father would understand him, too. Her father would have taken Ron and— Sarah slammed the door shut on that thought. "Ella Jane . . ."

Ella glanced up at her.

"Ron is going to leave town the minute Jax gets out of this police station." She'd seen the fear in *his* eyes when the guy looked at Jax. "He's going to run, and he won't look back."

And there it was . . . the faintest flicker of hope in the other woman's stare.

"If you want to be free of Ron, then you need to tell the truth. Because Jax can help you. He can—"

"*Sarah, a word,*" Wade gritted out. Then he was carefully pulling her away from Ella Jane just as another cop approached the woman. He guided Sarah toward a small alcove. "What. The. Hell? We both know Jax Fontaine is a criminal!"

She wasn't so sure of that. He hadn't been charged with anything since his eighteenth birthday.

Maybe because he's been careful not to get caught.

"The guy is trouble, and you're selling him as some kind of hero to that poor woman? She needs therapy, you *know* that."

Sometimes, therapy isn't what fixes us.

"We can do this without that guy's help. We've done it before, and we'll do it again."

Yes, they would, of course. It was just—

I don't want Jax locked up.

Something was happening to Sarah. Something she didn't understand. She'd never actually needed anyone before, and this connection she had with Jax, it was burning right through her.

"I'll get your phone, and then we'll hit the streets," Wade said with a decisive nod. "We have to focus on the missing girl. Ella Jane, Jax—look, I know they need help, but they can't be our priority right now. Molly is the priority. We head out, and we try to retrace her steps from the moment she left that bar. Because she vanished somewhere along that path. We find the spot he took her from, and we could find her."

Sarah glanced once more toward the door that led to holding. She wanted to force the cops to release him. Wanted Ella Jane to recant. She wanted—

Jax.

Her eyes closed for a moment. *Molly. Molly is the priority. Wade is right.* Her eyes opened. She'd come back for Jax. She'd fix this mess.

"Let's go," Sarah said. She didn't look at the door to holding again.

I'm sorry, Jax. She had to leave him there.

SHE'D SCREAMED AND she'd cried and she'd bled.

He stared at Molly. Light spilled through the window, falling onto her long, tangled hair. "So now you know," he murmured.

She didn't look up at him. Her body was covered with wounds. Small slices that had been designed to make her cry out. Deep puncture marks where he'd cut into her because she tried to stop those sweet sounds of pain from escaping her lips.

"At first, you just want to live," he told her. "To escape. That's all that matters."

She was crying again.

"But soon, the pain becomes too much, doesn't it? And you just want to let go."

"Pl-Please . . ." Molly whispered. Oh, sweet Molly. She'd been fun. He'd ever so enjoyed playing with her.

"Do you think your mother gave up before you did?"

Her head sagged forward.

Frowning, he marched toward her. He reached down, intending to grab her chin with his gloved fingers. But when he leaned over her, Molly heaved, surging toward him with a strength he hadn't expected. Not after all those hours. She sent the chair toppling forward. Molly slammed into the floor, her yell spilling from her.

His head tilted. He suspected Molly had just broken some bones. Maybe even fractured that lovely face of hers. But . . .

"Not . . . ready to die," she rasped out. "You won't . . . break me!"

Interesting. "The way Murphy the Monster broke your mother?"

She twisted on the floor. Poor broken Molly.

"Is it true?" he asked her. "Was she an out-of-control junkie? Is that why the cops didn't look for her, not until it was far too late?" Molly had been so young then. Had she even realized what her mother had really been like?

"She was my mother!"

"Your brother has his mother's weakness. Slip him some drugs . . . and he'll do anything."

She was struggling against her bonds. One of the chair legs had splintered so her left leg was nearly free of the ropes.

"Are you as weak as your brother? As your mother?"

She yelled and struggled harder.

"I don't think you are," he said, pleased. That was good. He needed her to be strong. Especially for what would come. He caught a fistful of her hair and yanked her head back. "Do you remember my name?"

Tears were leaking from her eyes. "Yeah . . . you're the devil." She spat at him.

He drove the knife into her stomach. "Try again."

"J-Jax!"

He pulled the knife out. "Very good . . ."

Chapter 6

HIS LAWYER HAS BEEN HERE, SO EDDIE WILL probably be making bail soon," Brent said as he led Jax back to the cells. "You won't have much time."

"I don't need much time." He rolled his shoulders. *His* lawyer would be there any moment. "Just make sure we're not disturbed."

"I already had the guy moved to a separate holding area. I'll put you with him."

Perfect.

Jax didn't say another word. Other cops passed them, and he sure didn't want to give those guys any reason to question Brent. The guy had been too useful.

A few moments later, they were in front of a dimly lit cell. Two cots were in that cell. A toilet. And the guy who'd tried to use his knife on Sarah.

Jax stared at the man's bent head. Eddie Guthrie wasn't moving at all.

Brent unlocked the cell. Jax took his time stalking inside. When he was clear of the door, Brent slammed it shut behind him. That clang seemed to echo through the cell.

And, finally, Eddie lifted his head. His eye were bleary, confused, as he stared up at Jax.

Brent's footsteps shuffled away.

"Hello, there, Eddie," Jax murmured. "We need to talk."

He advanced. Eddie hunched back against the wall.

"I know you . . ." Eddie whispered. "You . . . you were the one with Sarah Jacobs last night."

"Yes, I'm with Sarah." He offered the boy a cold smile. "And I don't like it when people try to hurt *my* Sarah."

Eddie glanced at Jax, then at the cell's door. Fear and panic fought on his face. In a flash, the guy had lunged off that cot and toward the bars. His fingers curled tightly around them as he screamed, "Guard!"

Jax crossed his arms over his chest as he studied the younger man. Fool. "No one is going to come back here for a while. It's just you and me." Until Jax was done with his little talk.

Eddie threw a fast glance over his shoulder. "Guard!" he screamed again.

Some people just didn't listen well. Jax sighed. "There are two ways this can go down . . ."

Eddie spun around. Lunged at him.

Jax just sidestepped and the guy hit the wall.

"You can answer my questions and save yourself some energy." *And pain.* Because the guy had hit the wall pretty hard. "Or you could piss me off." He flexed his hands. *Then there will be pain.*

Eddie rose and his gaze darted to Jax's hands.

"I can help you," Jax told him. That part was true. He could help or he could hurt. "Trust me, buddy, you want my help. You don't want me as an enemy." The kid should consider himself lucky, especially after the way he'd gone after Sarah. Jax didn't normally make this offer to many people.

His gaze swept over the younger man. Eddie's body was quivering. His eyes were bloodshot, and he kept licking his lips. *Drugs.* Jax shook his head. "Your sister is missing and you are so strung out that you don't even realize what the hell is happening here!"

Eddie shook his head. "Not missing! That's a lie!"

"I've told plenty of lies." Jax kept his body relaxed and ready to attack. "And I'll tell plenty more. But this is the truth. Someone took Molly. She's tied up, and he's keeping her hidden someplace. The man's got a knife. He's already sliced into her once."

All of the color bled from Eddie's face, but he stubbornly cried out. "Lie! You're lying!" He sidled around the cell. "That asshole Detective West is lying! Molly is fine! You're all trying to trick me!"

"Molly was taken after her shift at Voodoo Night."

Eddie gaze dropped. "I walk her home," he whispered. He started to rock a bit, back and forth.

"You *usually* walk her home, don't you?"

Eddie flinched.

"But last night, you didn't. Last night, you attacked Sarah." *That won't be forgotten or forgiven any time soon.* But he'd plan for the man's punishment, later. Right then, Jax needed information.

Eddie's hands spread behind him, clutching the bars there. "She deserves to die! She's as sick as he is! Evil! She—"

"I think you'd better stop talking about Sarah." He closed in on the guy. He didn't reach out to him, not yet. He didn't touch the guy at all. "Before you say something that pushes me too far."

"*Who are you?*"

"I'm someone you want on your side right now. I'm someone you want helping you find your sister."

Eddie lifted his shaking hands to cover his face. "Can't . . . think straight . . ." He slammed the palms of his hands into his eyes, again and again.

Jax tilted his head to the side as he studied the guy. "How long you been using?"

Eddie stiffened. "Just . . . a few times last night. Only then! To help . . ."

"To help you get up the courage to kill a woman?"

Eddie lurched toward the toilet. He vomited. Once. Twice.

Jax shook his head. "Can't live with what you've done?"

"My mother . . . needed justice . . . I—I had to do it! He—he said!" Eddie slumped on the floor and swiped his hand over his mouth. "He said . . ." Eddie whispered again.

"Who said?"

Eddie's body shuddered.

The guy looked like he was pushing fast through withdrawal or . . . Jax's gaze swept over Eddie in speculation. What *if* last night had been the first time the fellow drugged up? "You're coming off a bad trip."

Eddie gave a hard nod. "Want it . . . to stop . . ." He was still shuddering.

"Tell me who sent you after Sarah, and I'll make it stop."

Eddie's eyes doubled in size. "Pr-Promise?"

"Yes."

But then Eddie hesitated. "Sarah . . . evil . . ."

Jax's jaw locked. That guy was going to push him too far soon. "The man who sent you after Sarah . . . he could be the man who has your sister. Don't you want to save Molly?"

"Molly," he repeated. A wide smile split his face. "I love Molly." Then he started . . . jerking. Not just shuddering, but convulsing.

Definitely coming off a bad trip.

Shit! Jax lunged toward him. Eddie was tremoring, his whole body twisting, and his head almost slammed into the porcelain side of the toilet. Jax grabbed him and slid him safely back. But . . .

Eddie's eyes started rolling.

"Stay with me," Jax demanded. Then he raised his voice and called, "Brent! Brent, dammit, get in here!" Knowing the cop, he figured the guy had stayed close, just out of sight, while Jax had his little chat with the other prisoner.

But Jax didn't hear the rush of footsteps coming toward the cell.

And those convulsions weren't stopping.

"Brent!" Jax bellowed. "Guard!"

But no one was coming.

Jax leaned over the guy. "Give me a name. Tell me who did this."

"D-Don't . . . know . . ."

"Tell me!"

Eddie's breath was sawing out. In and out . . . desperate gulps. Then—

"S-Said we'd . . . get her . . ." His breath was wheezing. "S-Said she'd . . . pay."

"Sarah?"

"Pay for what . . . he did . . . to us . . . me . . . him . . ."

Jax's mind raced. "Wait! You're saying this guy wants vengeance on Sarah, too? Because of some shit her father did?" He needed to know—specifically—why someone wanted vengeance on Sarah. He knew that the LOST agents had plenty of enemies because of the work they did. But someone coming after Sarah because of her psychotic father, that was a whole different nightmare.

"Yes . . ." Then Eddie was rolling on his side again. Retching and—

Footsteps thundered toward him. Jax looked up and saw Brent and a uniformed cop rushing toward the cell. *About damn time.*

"What in the hell did you do?" Brent demanded.

Jax put his hands up and backed away. "Nothing." He hadn't needed to. "Get the guy to a medic. He needs treatment, now."

Eddie let out a pain-filled moan.

"The kid's pumped up on some drug," Jax added quietly. "A bad trip, and he needs help."

Swearing, Brent unlocked the cell and hurried inside. The uniformed cop behind him just stood there, blinking.

New guy. "Go get help, asshole," Jax ordered the guy.

The uniformed cop ran.

"Did he tell you what you needed to know?" Brent whispered.

Jax stared at Eddie. The guy was barely conscious. "I think he told me all that he knew."

"And?" Brent pushed. They could hear voices, coming toward them—

"We're looking for someone else with a serious grudge against Murphy Jacobs." Someone who thought he'd hurt Sarah.

Think the fuck again.

SARAH STRODE QUICKLY down the cracked street, her gaze darting to the left and to the right. It was broad daylight, but Sarah didn't see the light. In her mind, it was night. She was trying to picture the scene as Molly had. No, not Molly . . . but her abductor.

When Sarah hunted for victims, she found them by thinking like the perps. By putting herself into the minds of abductors, of killers. *It's always too easy for me to think like them.*

So she advanced down that worn street and . . . Sarah saw the night, not the day. And when Molly had vanished, shortly after 4 A.M., there would be so many shadows out then. So many dark corners.

So many places to hide.

She and Wade had begun their search at Voodoo Night. Then they'd gone to the left, away from what Sarah knew would have been the busier clubs. From what Dean had learned at the college campus, Molly wasn't a party type. No drinking. No drugs. So she would have wanted to get away from those crowds . . . and back home as fast as possible.

Cars weren't allowed on a long stretch of Bourbon Street. So Sarah marched toward the intersection where the access to a vehicle would have first been available. She kept searching the area and . . .

"Anything yet, Sarah?" Wade asked softly.

She shook her head, but muttered, "You just need to get her away from the others. There are too many people here." For an instant, she could almost see the crowd before her. So much thicker at night. Men and women jamming the streets. The alcohol would have flowed heavily. Drunken laughter hung in the air

"Okay . . ." Wade said. "I guess we've started 'cause you're doing that 'you' thing."

Sarah ignored him.

You have to get her away. You would only stay out in the open as long as absolutely necessary. Every moment was a risk.

Sarah's gaze darted to the left and she saw the narrow opening of another street. One that branched away. She knew how Bourbon Street worked at night. Bourbon itself would be packed, overflowing, but if you went one street over—

Deserted. The surrounding streets were often completely empty, especially at 4 A.M.

She turned onto that smaller street. Stilled. "You get her alone."

"Have I ever mentioned . . ." Wade asked, "that it creeps me out when you talk to yourself like this?"

Sarah ignored him. "A vehicle would be waiting.

You'd need to get her out and away as fast as you could. So it would be close by." She hurried forward. The perp would have turned his vehicle *away* from Bourbon Street and the crowd. He'd want a spot where his vehicle could be easily accessed, but not hemmed in by anyone. He'd want—

"Here," Sarah said as she stopped near the entrance to an alley. "You get her far enough away from the others that no one would hear in case she screamed. And your car could have been stashed right here, right between these buildings. You drove it out . . . and you were home free."

"But why did she come with him?" Wade asked, sounding confused. "Dean told us that her friends at college said Molly never hooked up with strangers. She's the classic 'good girl' here, Sarah. She doesn't just wander away at night with a strange man."

Sarah thought of her father. "Even good girls wander when you tell them the right things." She looked up at him. "Her brother was supposed to pick her up, but this guy . . . he made sure her brother wasn't around for that job."

Wade whistled. "He sent the brother after you."

"A diversion." She headed into the alley. A big, green Dumpster waited to the right. "So maybe this guy showed up, and he told Molly that Eddie had sent him." *You told Molly just enough that she felt safe walking with you.*

"Why her, though? Why would he go after her?" With Wade, it was always about the victims. He identified with them, no, he wanted to *save* them. Maybe because he'd worked homicide for so long in Atlanta. By the time the cases had crossed his desk, those victims had been long past saving. Now . . . now he wanted to bring the vics home alive.

But we can't always do that.

Sarah made her way to the Dumpster. She hefted herself up. The place reeked, but if this was the scene of Molly's abduction, they might need to check for—

The Dumpster was empty. It had already been cleaned out by the city's team. Dammit.

"Sarah? Why her?" Wade pressed.

Sarah shoved away from the Dumpster. She dusted off her hands and stared around at the buildings. And *up* at them. Her gaze drifted to the upper left. "Got you," she whispered.

"What?"

Sarah pointed up. Someone had an apartment up on the second floor of that building. The balcony was covered with hanging plants, and, right at the corner of that balcony, she saw a small surveillance camera.

"Hot damn," Wade said.

Now they just needed to get the footage from the camera. She and Wade ran out of the alley. They went around to the front of the building, but even though they banged on the doors, no one answered.

She looked up. "Hello!" Sarah yelled. "Is anyone up there? *Hello!*"

Wade was still struggling with the door. If it weren't for those hanging flowers up there, she would have thought the old building was abandoned. But the flowers . . . the video camera . . .

Someone *was* there.

"There's another entrance," she said to Wade. "Has to be. Let's check the back." And, once more, they were running through that alley. Goose bumps rose on Sarah's skin as they headed to the back and . . .

A door was at the rear of the building. A big, red door.

Sarah's phone rang.

She yanked it out of her pocket, her heart racing because she thought it might be the perp calling her again. But it wasn't Molly's number. It was a number she'd never seen before.

It could be him.

Wade ran toward the door.

"Wait!" Sarah grabbed his shoulder.

Wade stared at her as if she were crazy.

She lifted the phone. *This could be him,* Sarah mouthed. She put the phone to her ear. "Hello?"

"Sarah! Where are you?" That low, growling voice—it was Jax's voice. Only . . . wasn't Jax in police custody?

"I'm with Wade," she said, staring into his golden eyes. Wade was frowning and obviously impatient as he glared at her. "We think we found a lead. A video camera, on a balcony just a few streets over from Bourbon. I think the perp took her from the alley here, and I think—"

"He's after you." Jax's voice was dark. "I want you and Wade to get back in the car, and get away from that place, do you understand?"

No, she didn't understand. Running made no sense. Not if they had a lead on Molly.

"I've got my men coming to find you now."

What? "We're going to get that video feed. It will show us what happened!" Every instinct she had screamed that *this* was the place.

"He's after you." Jax's words were grim. "Don't you see? Everything . . . it's about you."

Sarah shook her head.

Wade swore. "We're wasting time." He slipped away from her and marched for the door.

"Sarah, listen to me." There was an intensity in Jax's voice that pulled at her. "This is off. Everything—it's wrong. You think you're the only one who knows criminals? I understand them, too. I've lived with them my whole life. This guy—he knows your father."

"H-How do you know that?"

"Because Eddie told me."

He'd gotten Eddie to talk? How? When?

"This guy wants you to pay for something your father did. I think he's been watching you, Sarah. Studying you, and I think he's trying to lure you into a trap that you can't resist."

Sarah glanced over at Wade. He was reaching for the back door. That bright red door. One that was like a giant X mark on a map. She could see the knob turning easily in his hand. But why would the back door be unlocked when the front had been sealed so securely? Her gaze jerked around, rising, up, going to the left, the right, the—

More video cameras. Hidden so that you wouldn't see them on the first glance, or the second. You had to search to find them positioned so carefully. Positioned to watch the back of the house.

"Wade, no!" Sarah yelled.

"Sarah?" Jax demanded. "What's happening? Wait for my men! Wait—"

She ran toward Wade. He was pulling open the door. "No!" she screamed at him. *Because I think Jax is right. I think this scene is a trap—and we're walking straight into it!*

Wade turned toward her, his face showing his confusion. She grabbed his arm and hauled him toward her.

"Sarah, what the hell—" he began.

She started running, pulling him with her, hauling and yanking at him with all her strength.

And then the building exploded. The force of the explosion picked Sarah up and hurtled her through the air.

"SARAH?" JAX SHOUTED. "Sarah!" He'd heard her scream. Scream even as something had seemed to explode in the background.

Now the line was dead. And fear clawed at his guts.

"What's happening?" his lawyer, Ty Keith, demanded. The guy cast a nervous glance Jax's way. His hold tightened on the steering wheel.

"Floor the fucking gas," Jax snarled at him. "Get us to Bourbon Street, now."

"B-But what's on Bourbon?"

From the sounds he'd heard . . . "Look for the smoke." Smoke that the firefighters would need to battle hell hard.

Sarah—be alive.

If she wasn't, then Jax would wreak some serious fury on that city. They drove faster, faster, and rule-following Ty was sure racing through those streets.

Jax leaned forward, peering through the windshield. He dialed Carlos. His friend answered on the first ring. "Tell me you're close to her," Jax demanded. He knew he sounded desperate, but he didn't care. This was Sarah. Sarah . . . mattered to him.

There was a pause. "Boss, I see the flames."

And that was when Jax saw the smoke billowing up into the sky.

Sarah!

HE SMILED AS he stared at the monitor. Fire was shooting out of the old building. Bursting from the windows that had shattered moments before.

"Boom," he whispered as he leaned forward and touched that screen. Oh, but it had been so easy. He'd tossed a few bread crumbs, and Sarah had followed them so quickly.

The image turned to static. The explosion and the fire had finally knocked out his feeds. But he'd seen enough.

Sarah had been running toward the building. She'd been shouting, probably so sure that she was there to save the day.

But you were like a moth, coming to the flame. A moth that had burned and turned to ash.

He couldn't wait for her dear old dad to find out that his daughter was dust. If only he could see the expression on the bastard's face. *Not so smug now, are you, Murphy? Now you know what it's like to have no power. To have nothing—*

But fear and rage.

Chapter 7

"GET HIM OUT OF THERE!"

Sarah coughed.

"Bring the bastard—the fire is spreading too much!"

She cracked open her eyes. She was . . . moving? Yes, and she was upside down. Slung over someone's shoulder. Smoke was all around her and Sarah coughed, choking.

"It's okay, Doc," a man told her. He was the one carrying her like she was a sack of potatoes and running fast—so fast through that smoke. "We're taking care of you."

Another coughing fit racked her body, and Sarah realized that she hurt. Her body ached in about a dozen different places because . . .

Her memory came flooding back. "F-Fire!"

They burst out of the alley. She could hear the sound of fire trucks, and when she turned her head, she saw the flash of their lights. The firefighters always responded so fast in this city—because a fire could spread too easily on these streets. The buildings were positioned right next to each other and a fire could jump from one location to another—this fire was already spreading!

She pushed against the guy's back, trying to see more.

"Easy, easy . . ." he told her, and then Sarah's world spun as he lifted her up and sat her down on the sidewalk—the sidewalk across the street from that blaze. "Let me check you out."

She looked up and found herself staring into the dark gaze of a man who had a long, slashing scar over his left eye. Carlos.

"Don't be scared," he said. Carlos was huge—a giant and currently covered in ash, just like she was. "Jax sent me to take care of you."

She heard a groan and turned her head to the left. Two other men were there—big guys with lots of tats who'd just lowered Wade onto the sidewalk.

A fire truck roared up the street. Another followed close behind. The wail of those sirens was so loud that her ears ached. She wanted to lift her hands and slap them over her ears, but Sarah found she could hardly move at all.

Then those men—all three of them, closed in around her. Sarah stared up at them, a tendril of fear snaking through her. What was happening?

Carlos smiled at her. "Don't you worry. No one is gonna hurt you again."

They were . . . guarding her. And Wade.

"Jax," she said, her voice coming out like a croak. Probably because of all the smoke. She coughed, cleared her throat, and tried again. "Jax—he sent you?"

Because he'd told her that his men were coming.

"He's on his way," Carlos said. "And you're safe."

But she almost hadn't been. Wade started coughing and she focused on him again. He'd been pulling open that door. If Jax hadn't called and told her to get away . . .

She and Wade would have gone into that building. Then they would have been the ones blown to bits.

This doesn't make sense! We were just looking for the girl.

But the girl had only been bait, to lure them in. Sarah stared over at those flames. The firefighters were on scene then, shouting orders and spraying water at the blaze. Had Molly Guthrie been in that building? Was she burning right then?

"They need to know . . ." She coughed again. " . . . that a victim . . . could be inside."

The men looked at each other. Carlos nodded. "Tell the cops." A fellow with a long, twisting tiger tattoo around his left hand nodded, and he ran toward the cop cars that had just braked to a screeching stop a few feet away.

"Are you hurt anywhere?" Carlos asked her, his voice a low growl.

She had plenty of bruises and scrapes, but nothing that wouldn't heal on its own. "I'm all right."

"What about him?" Carlos asked, jerking his thumb toward Wade. Wade was sitting up now, but his shoulders were hunched.

"*He's . . .*" Wade managed, "fine." Wade's head tilted back and his golden stare met hers. "What in the hell happened?"

She glanced over at the burning building. "He tried to kill us." And she'd bet a month's pay that the man they were after had been watching them on those video cameras. Waiting to draw them in. To get closer and closer. He'd locked the front entrance, making sure they'd have to go in through the back. And that was where he'd rigged the explosives. Open that door and—*boom.*

"How did he know we'd even get here? That we'd . . . find her?" Wade asked.

"Because he knows us." *He knows me.* That knowledge terrified her.

She couldn't stop looking at those flames. So big, streaking up toward the sky. Red and orange. The firefighters were trying to stop that blaze from spreading, but the fire was so greedy.

Another car braked to a stop. A Benz. It was just steps away. The passenger side door opened and—

"*Sarah!*" Jax shouted her name.

"She's here, boss!" Carlos called back.

Jax's head whipped toward them. Then he was running toward her. Hs face was locked in tense, angry lines. *He sure is pissed.* That thought was immediate, and it was followed by . . . *He's going to make someone pay.* She knew it with a chilling certainty.

Jax stopped right before her. She rose on trembling legs. Sarah had actually thought that he might pull her into his arms. Hold her tight. But he didn't. He just watched her with that glittering stare.

Did I want him to hold me?

"You're bleeding." Jax snapped out those words.

"Just scratches." She felt so cold. Strange, when the heat from that fire was scorching the street.

A muscle flexed in Jax's jaw. "How close were you to the fire?"

"Uh . . ." It was a bit hard to remember that part.

Carlos stepped forward. "We found her and the guy on the ground in the back. They were both unconscious."

That tended to happen when you were tossed through the air and you slammed into the concrete.

She stood there, uncertain. Jax's gaze was slowly traveling from the tips of her toes up to her—

"*Don't scare me like that again.*"

Before she could respond, Jax pulled her against him. He held her a little too hard, his grip a little too tight, but Sarah didn't care. For just a second, she let herself sag against him. Tears stung her eyes.

I didn't get to Molly. I didn't save her. And Wade almost died, too!

So much for helping. It seemed as if—once more—she was just surrounded by death.

"I've got you," Jax said. "You're safe."

Safe. She never felt safe. Her father had taught her that safety was an illusion. "There is no safe place," Sarah whispered before she could stop herself.

His hand slid under her chin. He tipped her head back so that she had to gaze into his eyes. "Yes, princess, there is. You'll always be safe with me."

She wanted to believe his words.

He scooped her into his arms. "We're getting you checked out." He started heading toward an ambulance that had just lurched up to the scene.

Her arms wrapped around his neck. "No, I'm okay," she protested. She needed to be over there, talking with the cops. Figuring this thing out.

She looked at the building. Two firefighters had just raced into the burning building. Her breath caught. They were going in—trying to find Molly? But how could the other woman possibly survive a blaze like that? It was too hot. Too powerful.

He put her into the back of an ambulance. An EMT whirled toward them. "Check her out," Jax ordered. "Make sure she's all right."

"Just scratches and bruises," Sarah muttered. "I'm fine."

Jax braced his legs apart as he stood on the ground behind the ambulance. "Check her out," he said again, his voice heavy with an unmistakable demand.

The EMT nodded and quickly started asking Sarah questions, one right after the other. She waved him away. "Send someone to my friend Wade." She pointed to Wade. A big gash was bleeding on his forehead. "He needs more help than I do."

Another EMT hurried toward Wade.

Sarah tried to sit still as the guy examined her. She knew her injuries weren't bad. But if Jax hadn't called her, they would have been. "You saved my life," she said as she turned her head to look at him.

His face was like stone.

"How did you get Eddie to talk with you?" She'd thought the guy had been adamant about not talking with anyone.

"I'm not a cop, so I didn't play by the rules."

No, she rather thought that Jax made up his own rules.

"Ma'am," the EMT said, drawing her attention. "How many fingers am I holding up?"

She pushed his hand away. "Two. Look, I don't have a concussion. I'm bruised, but fine." Actually the shock was wearing off and she was starting to feel more in control.

"There she is," Jax murmured. "I see you coming back to me."

Sarah shook her head and kept her focus on the EMT. "What else do you need to do? Can I go now?"

The EMT glanced over at Jax as if it were his decision.

Stifling a sigh, Sarah pushed out of that ambulance. But Jax was there, wrapping his arm around her before she'd even taken a step. "I don't want you out in the open."

Because he thought that jerk was still there? No. Sarah shook his head. "He was watching from a distance, playing it safe. He's not out here." She was sure of it. Being there—even hiding in the growing crowd of onlookers—would be too risky. And this man . . . she was realizing that he was far more intelligent than she'd originally realized. This guy was no amateur. When it came to killing, he knew exactly what he was doing.

Then she caught sight of Detective West. He was talking with some of the firefighters and frowning up at the burning building. "Detective West!" Sarah called out.

He turned at her call. His eyes widened when he saw her. Then he was rushing to her.

"Molly could be in there!" Sarah called out. "This place—I think he had Molly here." Actually, she thought Molly had vanished after walking near that building. *He either took her inside or he took her away . . . in the car that had been stashed in the alley's entrance.*

"What?" Brent's brows shot up. "Here? Did you see her?"

"No, but he set that place to blow and if Molly was the bait to lure us in—"

He looked back at the fire and swore. "Then she was bait that didn't make it out alive."

Staring at those flames, Sarah shivered.

JAX HELD OPEN the car door for Sarah. She looked so shell-shocked, so pale. He just wanted to pull her into his arms and hold her as long as possible.

What if she'd gone into that building?

Rage grew within him. Someone was fucking with Sarah, and he didn't like it one bit.

No, actually, they were fucking with Sarah *and* with him. Because Jax owned that building. The building that could have blown and taken Sarah's life. He'd bought the place months ago, but hadn't done a damn thing with it. He'd heard Sarah mention that video cameras had been on the second floor—they sure as shit hadn't been there when he'd acquired the place.

The cops wouldn't know the building was his, not yet. He had plenty of corporations set up to mask his identity—plenty of businesses and buildings traced back to the corporations and not to *him,* personally.

Eventually, though, the authorities might track the place back to him. If they searched long and hard enough.

Is that what that bastard out there wants? For me to look guilty?

Jax locked his jaw. He hadn't told Sarah that he owned that place. And he wouldn't, not yet. The last thing he wanted was for Sarah to doubt him. For some reason, he wanted her to . . . trust him.

Keeping the truth from her probably wasn't the best way to build trust. But confess that inferno belonged to him? Yeah, that would be the number one way to get the cops to lock him up—for real, this time.

The cops had asked questions, dozens of them. The firefighters had battled the blaze and extinguished the flames. Now only dark tendrils of smoke drifted into the air.

Had Molly Guthrie been in that fire? The fire marshal wouldn't be able to tell them, not for a while. And, right then, Jax's focus was on Sarah, not the missing woman. Sarah looked dead on her feet. He needed to get her someplace safe. Someplace *he* could protect her.

Wade wasn't in any condition to drive Sarah. The guy had a concussion, and he'd been loaded into the back of an ambulance. Jax would have felt better if Sarah went to the hospital, too, but the woman was stubborn.

And currently covered in ash and blood.

He slammed the car door shut and then glanced over at his lawyer. "I've already called my office," his lawyer told him quickly. Ty tossed him the keys. "You take the car, and my assistant will come for me." The cops had impounded Jax's bike, but he knew Ty was already working to get the motorcycle released and delivered back to Jax's place. The guy was definitely worth the retainer Jax paid for him.

Jax's fingers fisted around the keys. "Let me know what you find out." Because he knew that Ty was staying to dig for additional information on that chaotic scene. Lawyers always had a way to get the cops to talk. "You can come get your car later."

Ty nodded and backed away. The guy kept glancing curiously at Sarah, but Ty hadn't asked Jax any specific questions about her. His lawyer knew better than to pry. Especially when a woman was involved. The sunlight glinted off his blond hair as Ty turned away.

Ty came from old Southern money. He'd been one of those silver-spoon types that Jax normally hated. He'd never wanted or needed anything, and the guy had just sailed his way through law school at Tulane.

Jax had fought his way through life, battling for every single thing he possessed.

But he and Ty . . . well, they were different, that was for sure. But he'd had Ty's back over the years, and Ty had always been there for him. Though Jax was sure that hefty retainer fee figured into the equation . . .

Still, Ty was the best criminal defense attorney in New Orleans, and the guy had always kept quiet about the secrets Jax carried. *He knows better than to share them.*

Jax glanced across the street and saw Carlos waiting. Jax gave the fellow an almost imperceptible nod. He owed Carlos—more than he'd ever be able to repay. The man had been his right hand for years, and Carlos had been a good friend, even when Jax didn't deserve it. There weren't many people that Jax actually counted on in that world, but Carlos—the man *was* family to him.

Jax walked to the car. Slid behind the seat and started to crank the engine.

But Sarah's fingers flew out and curled around his. "Wait."

He glanced over at her.

"I need to . . . see the scene. Just a little longer."

She leaned forward and stared at the building. It was just a shell now. Hollow. Black. Smoke rose in long, sweeping tendrils.

"It's destruction. Death. That's what you wanted to show me," Sarah murmured. "You wanted us to see death."

His back teeth clenched. "What the guy wanted was for you to die, Sarah. He wanted to hurt your father by hurting you." He cranked that engine. Yeah, okay, Sarah wanted to stay there and get in the killer's head. Too bad. The woman was covered with bruises and blood and maybe she was too stubborn to go to the ER, but he *would* be taking care of her.

"My father . . ." Now her voice was weary as she leaned back in the seat. "If you're talking about his enemies, they'd fill the street."

He glanced over at her. She'd turned her head away from him and was staring out of the window. "Buckle your seat belt, princess."

Her hand moved and slowly clicked the seat belt into position. "I hate him."

He pulled away from the scene. Maneuvered through the cars and the onlookers who'd gathered to watch shit burn. "The dick who did this? Don't worry, I'm sure the LOST group will be taking him down. Isn't that what you do?"

"No." She was so quiet. So unlike Sarah. Sarah, who had drawn him from the beginning because he'd sensed the fire in her. "We don't hunt killers. We look for the victims. We find them. We help them."

He risked another quick look at her. Her left hand had risen and it pressed to the window. Sarah said, "I need to find Molly. If she wasn't in that fire . . ." Her breath whispered out. "Then she's still out there, and we still have a chance to help her."

Did she seriously think she was just going to run out and hit the streets again? While she was still bleeding? "There are other team members in LOST, let them hunt."

"I called Gabe. He's going to meet Wade at the hospital. Dean is already at the police station."

He kept driving.

"Are you taking me back to the station?"

"You're still bleeding," he gritted out.

"Back to my hotel room?"

"I want to take you back to my place." Where he could lock her inside and keep her fucking safe.

"But I don't have clothes at your place. All of my stuff is in my room at the hotel.

The bastard had already been inside her hotel once. "I can get you clothes in five minutes," Jax told her. One phone call, that was all it would take. He'd snap his fingers, and the clothes would be there at his house, waiting for them, no problem.

"Jax."

He liked the way she said his name. Liked the way it sighed from her ever so softly.

"Just take me to my hotel. The staff there gave me a new room, one on the concierge floor with better security. I'll be safe."

Yes, she would be—because he'd be with her.

"I'll shower, change, and then I *will* be going back out to hunt for Molly. I will hunt until I find her."

He braked at a red light. His hands were gripping the steering wheel so tightly that his knuckles had whitened. "Why?" He just didn't understand that part. "Why are you so determined to find her? You're risking your life for someone you don't even know." Sarah had almost died. Yet she was willing to run right back out into danger. Who the hell did that?

"I'm determined because Molly needs me. She's scared and she's hurting, and she needs to know that someone is looking for her."

He glanced at her once more. Her words had just driven straight to his core, and Sarah didn't even realize it.

"He told me . . . he told me that was one of the reasons his victims broke. They realized that no one was looking. No one cared that they'd vanished. No one would look . . ." Her head tilted down as her words trailed away.

"Who told you that, Sarah?"

A car horn honked behind him. Jax gave the driver the best finger he had, then he moved forward. And, again, he asked, "Who told you that?"

"My father."

The more he learned about that guy, the more he realized just what a miracle Sarah was.

Then he remembered the words she'd whispered moments before . . . *I hate him.* And he knew that Sarah hadn't been talking about the man who took Molly.

He turned at the next light. Drove in silence to her hotel. Normally, Jax always had a line ready for any situation. A fast and sarcastic quip. But this, this was different.

This was Sarah.

He pulled into the valet line. Tossed the keys to the guy there and handed him a quick tip.

"You don't have to come in," Sarah was saying. "I can go up and—"

He shook his head. "I'm not letting you out of my sight." His hand caught hers. Curled around her delicate fingers. Held tight.

She looked down at their entwined hands. "Why are you doing this?" She sounded confused. Sarah titled back her head to stare up at him. "Why do you even care?"

Because she was making him care. Chipping at the wall of ice that normally surrounded him. His left hand brushed back her hair. He decided to give her part of the truth. "Because when I was a kid, I used to hope that someone was out there, looking for me, too."

Only there hadn't been. No one had ever come for him, and the nightmare had continued. A nightmare that he didn't think most people would ever be able to understand. But Sarah, she was different.

She's a survivor, just like me.

He'd learned, later, that no one had ever even filed a missing person's report that matched up to him. No one had ever . . . looked.

A seven-year-old boy vanished, and no one had given a damn.

Sarah's fingers squeezed his. "You're hurting."

His gaze shot up to hers.

"I can tell. You . . . you go away when you hurt."

He had no clue what that meant.

Sarah shook her head. "Now you're staring at me like I'm crazy." Her laughter held an edge of bitterness. "Like that hasn't happened before." She pulled away from him. He let her go, but he followed her, making sure to stay close as his gaze swept the hotel lobby, looking for any threat.

When the elevator doors closed, sealing him inside, he said, quite simply, "I don't think you're crazy."

Her brows rose.

"I think you're one of the smartest women that I've ever met." In so many ways, she reminded him of his friend—and former lover—Emma Castille. But there was a core difference between the two women. Emma had always been afraid—deep down—of the darkness that clung to him.

Sarah . . . Sarah was drawn to his darkness.

Her lips pressed together, as if she were trying to hold back her words, but then Sarah said, "It starts with your eyes."

He tensed.

"The emotion shines there, even when you try to

school your expression. Just a glimpse, but that little glimpse is all I need."

He waited.

"But when you hurt, all emotion vanishes. You lock yourself down. I can see it happen."

The elevator doors opened.

Sarah slipped by him. "I'm sorry that you hurt."

His eyes closed, just for a second.

Her hand squeezed his arm. His fingers lifted and caught hers once again. He followed her from that elevator. Walking behind her because he literally could not turn away from Sarah. She was drawing him in, pulling him deeper and deeper into her web. The connection between them—it was more than just her desire for danger. More than his desire to be with a woman who fucking understood the sins that he carried.

It was . . . elemental.

Instinctive.

Opposites didn't always attract. Sometimes, two people who were alike met—and the rest of the world fell away. It was like two halves of a fucking whole finally connected. *That* was what it felt like for him every single time Sarah touched him.

She inserted her key into the lock and he glanced around the floor. There was a security camera mounted on the wall near the elevator. And they'd had to use a special key card to get up to that floor. A *bit* of an improvement, security-wise, but still not enough for him. Especially since anyone who worked at that hotel could get the key card that would provide access to the concierge level. Hell, anyone there could get a key to Sarah's room. Then that key could be passed right along to any jerk with enough cash to buy it.

Sarah opened her door. It was pitch-black inside—her curtains were drawn and the darkness seemed too heavy in her room. When she walked forward, Jax made sure he was just inches behind her. And then—yeah, he searched the room.

Sarah shut the door behind him. He heard her secure all of the locks. Then she was crossing that room and pulling back the blinds and sending sunlight spilling inside. The room had a view that looked out on the river, and he could see a barge slowly making its way toward the city.

"You really don't need to stay here," Sarah said softly. "I'll shower and get fresh clothes on, then I can get a taxi to take me back to the police station."

He put his hands on his hips and just stared at her.

Sarah shook her head. "I don't understand you," Sarah told him once more.

She sounded as if that really bothered her. But then, that was her thing, right? "You have to understand everyone." He figured that was part of her profiler gig. Seeing people, breaking down their motivations, learning their secrets.

"I just . . ." She raked a hand through her hair. "Why do you want to help me?"

"Because I find that I don't like the idea of anyone hurting you." In fact, that idea really pissed him off.

Her lips parted, as if she would respond, but then Sarah turned and made her way slowly to the bathroom. Her hand lifted and curled around the door frame. With her back to him, she said, "You saved my life today."

"Yours . . . and that jerk Wade." Jax would make sure Wade realized he owed Jax a serious debt.

She looked over at him, a faint smile curving her lips and chasing a few of the shadows from her eyes. "I guess that means Wade and I *both* owe you."

"I figure it's extra motivation. Once this case is over, you'll bust ass to find my family."

Her smile slipped away and he wished he could call the words back. He wished—

"I *am* going to find your family, Jax. And I'm sorry that you're having to wait, even longer, to learn the truth about your past. I will find them. I promise, I won't give up until you have the answers that you've been looking for."

He believed her. There was too much sincerity in her eyes and in her soft voice. He took a step toward her, but Sarah disappeared into the bathroom. A few moments later, he heard the rush of water as her shower turned on.

He stared at the closed door a moment longer, then he turned and made his way back to her bed. Her suitcase was at the foot of the bed. Her computer was close by. She'd dropped her phone and purse on the chair—he'd have to thank Carlos for finding those at the scene.

The room . . . it smelled like Sarah. Sweet vanilla. Every time he caught that scene in the future, he'd think of her. Always . . . her.

He turned toward the river. The water glinted, shining and—

Had Sarah just called out for him? He whirled around, sure that he'd heard her voice. Heard her say—

"*Jax*."

The call came again. A little louder and he was across that room in an instant. His hand lifted and banged against the door. "Sarah, are you all right?"

The water was pounding down. He didn't hear her. "Sarah?"

Then . . . a muffled cry. Like a—sob?

He twisted the knob. It turned easily in his grasp and he shoved the door open as his heart raced.

Sarah was in the shower, behind the glass, and tendrils of steam drifted in the air around her. Her head had been pressed to the tile, and one hand was over her mouth, as if she were trying to muffle her cries.

"Sarah?"

She jerked away from the wall and looked up at him, and that was when he realized . . . the water on her cheeks wasn't just from the shower. Sarah was crying.

"You're hurt." Dammit, he should have insisted that she go to the hospital and get checked out. That exam in the ambulance had been a joke. He rushed across that little room and yanked open the shower door.

Sarah's arms crossed over her chest, as if she were hiding her breasts, trying to shield herself. Hell, the last thing she needed to do was shield that beautiful body from him.

He reached out and turned off the spray of water.

She watched him, her eyes stark, tears still glinting in her gaze.

"It's okay," he told her, speaking softly. "You know you're safe with me." He grabbed a towel from the rack and opened it up for her. "Always, my Sarah. Always."

He held the towel out to her even as his gaze darted over her body, looking for injuries. He could see some bruises forming. Most of the blood had been washed away, but there had to be a serious wound because Sarah was crying and she—

He wrapped the towel around her as she stepped from the shower. His arms slid over her shoulders as he pulled her against him. "You have to tell me where it hurts," he said. *So I can fix it. So I can fix you.*

"She's going to die," Sarah whispered. "Because of me."

He stiffened.

"Wade almost died . . . *because of me.* Sometimes, I think I'm cursed. That I just bring pain and death to everyone around me."

Like he hadn't thought that same shit about himself a time or twenty.

He tipped up her chin and stared down into her eyes. "Baby, you're not cursed."

Her laughter sounded more like a sob. "No, I'm just evil."

The fuck she was.

"I could have stopped all of this. I should have." A teardrop slid down her cheek. "I heard the screams, and I—I just let him tell me that they were only bad dreams. The wind. I believed everything . . . *anything* he said."

Her pain was cutting into him.

"You're supposed to love your father, right? And I did. That's what makes it even worse. I loved him, while he was killing them."

He held her tighter. "Sarah . . ."

She shuddered in his arms. She was naked and beautiful, and sex was the last thing on his mind. He wanted to hold her, take her pain away. Make her smile. Make those tears *stop.*

Her eyes squeezed shut. "I'm sorry," she whispered. "Please, just give me a minute." She tried to pull away from him. He didn't let go.

Her breath blew out lightly, rasping over him. And her arms . . . they slowly rose to wrap around him. And, for a moment—a moment that just seemed to hang in time—Jax did nothing but hold her.

He couldn't remember the last time he'd held a woman like that. Without the intent to fuck her, in the next five minutes, anyway. But Sarah *needed* him right then, and he found that he needed her, too.

What in the hell is happening to me?

She didn't cry with loud, gulping sobs. Didn't shake. Her tears were silent as they fell, as if Sarah were used to keeping her pain quiet.

"I don't fall apart . . . a lot," she finally confessed.

Her words made him smile and he turned his head. He saw their reflection in the mirror. He was big and blond, she was small and so delicate. Her wet, black hair slid down her back. His hands—with all the tats that had so many meanings—were around her. Stroking that wet hair.

Sarah looked as if she belonged with him. No, belonged *to* him.

"Thank you," she added. She pushed against him once more. This time, he eased his hold and let her go. The towel almost fell, but Sarah grabbed for it and wrapped it around her body, anchoring it between her breasts.

He stared into her eyes. The tears were gone, but he could see the tracks drying on her cheeks. "Fall apart anytime you want," he told her softly. "I'll be right here to catch you."

Her head tilted and she got that look about her—the one that told him Sarah was trying to figure him out. *Keep trying, baby. It won't happen.*

"How did you know . . . I was crying?"

He turned away from her. "Because you called my name."

"No, I . . . I didn't."

"Yes, baby, you did." When Sarah called, he had the feeling he'd always answer her. "Want to finish that shower now and—"

A phone was ringing. Her phone, from the other room. He heard her sharp inhale, and then she was rushing past him, and nearly losing that towel again in the process.

She grabbed her phone and when her expression tightened, he knew who was calling her.

She hit the button to put the call on speaker. Her fingers trembled the faintest bit as she held that phone between her and Jax. "Where's Molly?" Sarah said by way of greeting.

Laughter flowed over the line. Low and mocking, and Jax's hands clenched into fists.

"She's not a pile of ash, if that's what you're wondering."

The man's voice held no accent, but something about that voice seemed to tug at Jax's memories. *Do I know him? Do I know this bastard?*

"But *you* were almost ash, weren't you, Sarah? I was watching . . . saw you running toward the door."

"On your cameras?" Sarah's voice held no emotion, but the phone was still trembling in her grasp. "You set a trap for me."

More laughter. Jax would be stopping that laughter, permanently. There were just some people who made the world a better place . . . when they weren't in it.

"Didn't think you would actually die," the man murmured. "Not in the first room, though you did make me hope for a moment, Still, I thought you'd get some nice scars on that pretty face of yours. Scars to go show Daddy."

Jax took out his phone. He had numbers for all of the LOST members. After all, he believed in being prepared. So he sent a quick text to Gabe. *The bastard you're after just called Sarah again. She's talking to him now.*

"I don't want the cops involved, Sarah." Now anger rumbled in the guy's voice. "Molly is still alive, and if you want her back . . . I told you, you have to *find* her. That's what you do, right?"

"I don't believe she's alive." Sarah's voice was flat. "I want proof of life, and I want it now."

Silence.

"Maybe she did die in that fire," Sarah continued. He was impressed that she kept her voice so calm. "Maybe you're just jerking us around until we get the report from the fire marshal. If Molly's alive like you say, then give me proof now, or I'm hanging up the phone."

His breath rasped over the line. "She's alive, bitch."

"Prove it." Sarah was staring down at the phone, not at Jax.

A text came through from Gabe. *What is he saying?*

Jax texted back. *Sarah wants proof of life . . . he isn't giving it to her.*

Because Molly was dead?

There was only silence on the phone. No background noise at all that Jax could hear. In New Orleans, it was hard to find a place that quiet. People were everywhere. Music was always playing. Performers were in the streets. *Something* was happening.

"Do you want to hear her scream?" he finally asked Sarah. "I would have thought you'd heard enough screams when your daddy was cutting people up."

Jax's gaze snapped to Sarah's face. She'd paled even more.

"Is that what he did?" Sarah asked, voice so mild and emotionless. "Did he cut up someone you loved? A mother, like Molly?"

He laughed.

"No," Sarah said. "It couldn't be your mother because you wouldn't do this to Molly if that had been the case. You wouldn't make her relive this terror."

She was profiling him.

And the guy on the line was dead silent.

"You want to be like Murphy, don't you?" Her words came faster. "You're the one giving the pain, you're the one—"

"*I am nothing like him!*" Those words were a roar. Sarah had definitely succeeded in breaking through that guy's control.

"Aren't you?" Sarah threw right back. "*Then give me proof of life!*"

The phone went dead.

"Dammit," Sarah whispered.

Jax texted . . . *No proof. We lost—*

Her phone rang again. Same number. Molly's number?

Calling again, he texted back.

Sarah didn't answer the phone. "You told LOST what was happening, right?" Sarah asked Jax quietly. "Those are the texts you're sending?"

He nodded.

"Then they can try to get a lock on the phone. Tell Gabe I'm answering again, and I'll keep the guy talking for as long as I can."

Jax sent the text through to Gabe.

Sarah swiped her index finger over the surface of that phone. Then she hit the button for speaker—

"You bitch!" The guy blasted. "You're the one who should have died all those years ago! Murphy's daughter. Blood as tainted . . . just like him!"

"Proof of life," Sarah said. "Give it to me, or *I* hang up on *you* right now."

Silence. Then . . . the rush of footsteps. The . . . lap of water? Yes, yes, it sounded like water, lapping against a dock. The man was running and Jax could hear water. And . . .

A squeak as a door opened. The thud of footsteps, a bit distorted, as if the guy were rushing up stairs. His breath was shuddering over the line and—

"*She wants proof that you're alive.*"

A woman screamed then. Loud and long, and Sarah flinched.

The caller laughed. *Why are you laughing, asshole? Because you like hurting women?* Ah, now that was just one thing that Jax fucking hated.

Yet another reason to kill this guy.

"I just drove my knife into her, Sarah. Didn't hit an organ, that way she'll just bleed and hurt, but not die. Guess who taught me that move?"

Sarah didn't speak.

"*Who taught me that move, Sarah? Who liked to keep his prey alive while they bled and begged?*"

"Murphy."

Another long scream filled the line.

"I stabbed her again, Sarah," he said, sounding almost gleeful. "I stab—"

"How do I know that's Molly? Put her on the line. Let me talk to her. Let me know it's *her.* Because maybe you've got an accomplice who's just screaming on command. Maybe you're some dumb dick who—"

"*Help me!*" That was a woman's terror-filled voice.

"Molly?" Sarah asked. Again, she was like ice. No emotion at all in her voice. But the phone still trembled in her grasp. "I need proof that it's you. Tell me something that will—"

"I won't . . . beg . . . like her." The words were weak. "Won't go out . . . like my m-mother . . . won't beg, no matter what he says . . ."

Sarah's eyes closed. "No, Molly, don't beg, do you understand? Whatever he does, don't beg for death."

Another scream then . . .

"Happy now?" the man taunted Sarah. "You're the reason Molly bled. But then, you're the reason Molly's mother died, too, aren't you?"

Sarah sucked in a quick breath of air and her eyes opened. "You think you know my secrets."

"I know where the bodies are buried." Laughter. "*All* of them. And before I'm done, Sarah, you'll be joining them. Another body, buried in a shallow grave. A grave that the police can't ever find because they believe the lies—"

"Molly, if you can hear me, I'm coming for you," Sarah said, cutting over his words. "You're going to make it out of this alive, just don't give up. Do you understand me? *Don't give up—*"

"Molly can't talk now," he murmured. "She's too busy getting stabbed."

Molly's scream filled the air once more.

"Hurry, Sarah. Find her fast. Because if you don't, she'll always be one of the lost."

Once more, the line went dead.

Chapter 8

SARAH DROPPED HER TOWEL. IT HIT THE FLOOR and she lunged for her bag. She grabbed clothes as fast as she could, dressing in a whirlwind. *Get the lock on the phone. Get the lock on the phone.*

Bra. Panties. Jeans. T-shirt. Shoes—

Jax's phone rang. He'd been standing there, his hard gaze on her. But when it rang, he answered, saying, "Did you get it?"

Her heart stopped for a moment.

"Fuck, yes," Jax said. "We'll meet you there." Then he shoved the phone into his pocket. He inclined his head toward her. "They got it to within one mile of the location before they lost the signal. Gabe and the cops are heading down to the riverfront's warehouse district—that's where he's got her. They're going to search—"

"And so are we," Sarah said. Because this was their break.

They ran from the hotel room.

I'm coming, Molly. I'll find you.

THE NEW ORLEANS airport was filled with people. So many folks coming and going. Weary passengers. Excited kids.

Victoria held her ticket as she glanced around the terminal. Her flight was going to leave in the next thirty minutes. She'd be back in Atlanta, back in her little house, that night. Then she could lock the doors, shut the blinds, and try to forget what it was like to be sealed up in a body bag.

Her phone rang. Frowning, she glanced down. Gabe's photo and name flashed across the screen. She answered immediately. "Boss, what's up?" *Not a body. Don't have found that poor girl's dead body.* This time, this case . . . Victoria just needed a win for LOST. They were supposed to be making a difference in the world. That was why she'd joined them. They weren't supposed to just be watching the body count rise.

"Okay, first, you need to know that Wade's all right."

She nearly dropped the phone. It was *never* good to begin the conversation with words like that. Because using *first* sure implied there was going to be a *second* that might not be so good.

"He's in the hospital, St. Dominic's, and he has a concussion, but the guy is tough as nails and he'll be on his feet in no time."

That was supposed to reassure her. "What happened?"

"The guy who took Molly set a trap for Sarah and Wade. The building they were searching—it exploded."

OhmyGod. Her knees were feeling very jellylike. "They were *in* the building when it exploded?" She turned away from the terminal and began walking toward the exit. Her left hand curled around her bag.

"No, no, they hadn't gone inside yet. It was a damn near thing."

So Sarah and Wade had both *nearly* been blown to hell and back?

"But we've got a new lead on the perp. The search teams are going in now and we think we'll find the girl."

"Alive?" she forced herself to ask.

"She was alive just a few minutes ago," Gabe said, his voice flat. "And we're busting ass to get there now."

She could hear voices talking behind him. Hear the wail of sirens.

The sliding doors at the airport's exit opened for her.

"Viki, I just wanted to update you. I'll call again when I think your plane has landed."

"Forget that," she told him bluntly. "I'll be at the hospital with Wade. If you need me, you call." Because she wasn't going to run away when all hell was breaking loose on this case. She also wasn't going to leave Wade on his own. He'd been there for her when she needed him.

It was time for her to return the favor.

Gabe ended the call, promising to update her.

Victoria lifted her hand. "Taxi!"

"JUST DROP ME off at the scene," Sarah said, her gaze on the road. "I'll join Gabe and the cops on the search. You don't have to stay."

He didn't respond.

She glanced over at him. His hands were tight around

the wheel. "Thanks for all you've done," Sarah rushed to say. "And—"

"The guy wants you dead, Sarah. The last thing I'm going to do is leave you unprotected on that jerk's turf." He shook his head. "I'm not dropping and ditching you, that's for sure. Consider me your personal guard."

And he'd done it again. Surprised her. She just couldn't get a handle on him. Everything she'd read in his background said he was dangerous. A man you didn't want as an enemy. But he wasn't an enemy or any threat to her. He was . . . a protector.

"How did you even get out of jail?" Sarah asked him as her brows snapped up. In all the chaos, she hadn't even asked him. "I thought they were booking you for assault on Ron Tate."

"Well, as for that . . ." He turned right and slanted a fast glance her way. "Seems that—before my lawyer even had the chance to throw his weight around—someone got the witness to recant her statement. Ella Jane pressed charges against Ron, and she said I was her hero." His lips quirked in a faint smile. "I'm sure the cops nearly shit themselves at that, but she was singing my praises when I left the jail."

And he was a free man.

Sarah considered him. He hadn't fought the cops at all when he'd been taken back to holding. In fact, he'd almost seemed . . . pleased . . . with the situation. In his mocking I'm-Jax-Fontaine-kiss-my-ass way. "You wanted to go back to lockup, didn't you? So that you could talk with Eddie?" If she looked deep enough, she could *almost* see the layers this man possessed.

"Yeah, about that . . ." He expelled a quick breath. "What with the explosion and psycho calling, I didn't get to tell you sooner, but Eddie Guthrie is in the hospital. The guy you're looking for—I think he pumped the kid with drugs, then sent him your way."

Sarah's cheeks felt too hot, then icy cold. "I . . . I thought he was a user." Longtime, an addict.

"First-timer, unless I'm wrong. Not usually wrong, though. Not about that. I've seen too many drug heads in my time."

She wasn't usually wrong, either . . . but . . . *Did I miss this?* That wasn't like her. Her fingers fiddled with her seat belt.

"He's on a bad trip. The guy was convulsing the last time I saw him."

Her fingers stilled. "Will he make it?"

"The medics were coming in so I hope they got him stable but . . . the guy was a weapon. Drug him, aim him, and fire him—"

"At me," Sarah finished. Because that was exactly what the man out there had done. Dear old dad had sure made plenty of enemies. Enemies that wouldn't stop climbing out of the woodwork.

And the worst part was . . . she understood exactly why they hated her father. Why they hated her.

Some days, Sarah hated herself.

She looked down at her left wrist. The scar was there, a stark reminder of all the things she could never forget.

What did you do to yourself, Sarah? Her father's words whispered through her mind. She'd been in the bathroom, slumped near the toilet. Her father had come into the room, and fear—actual fear—had flashed in his eyes. Blood had pooled around her and the razor—his razor—had been on the floor near her hip. It had fallen from her shaking fingers when she'd tried to slice the veins in her right hand. *My fingers had been too weak to do the job. Because I'd cut my left wrist too deeply. Those fingers had stopped working.*

And she hadn't been able to finish the job.

I'll take care of you. He'd promised her that. *You'll be as good as new.*

But she wasn't good. She wasn't new. She'd never been the same after her sixteenth birthday. Because on that date, life had changed. She'd—

Police lights appeared on the street to the left. A fast swirl of blue.

"I guess we found the party," Jax murmured.

Yes, they had. The cop cars were rushing down the street and she knew the police would be setting up a search perimeter.

Jax braked to a stop, and they hurried to join the group. Gabe saw them, and he waved them over. Dean was with him and Dean's fiancée, Emma Castille, was at his side. Emma's long, dark, flowing hair was pulled back and her hoop earrings swayed lightly with her movements. When she saw Jax, her bright blue eyes widened. "Jax, what are you doing here?" she asked him, and Emma immediately put her hand on Jax's shoulder.

Sarah stiffened. She knew that Emma and Jax had been lovers, but that had been a long time ago. *Right?* Emma was . . . the woman was great. A wonderful new addition to LOST and a woman who actually seemed to understand Sarah.

Sarah shouldn't . . .

. . . be wanting to rip Emma's hand off Jax.

Ah, so *this* was what jealousy felt like. Sarah decided she didn't like it—and she didn't have time for it. Not then. Not when Molly was waiting.

But she *did* remove Emma's hand, and Sarah said bluntly, "He's helping on this case."

"Uh, yes, okay . . ." Emma's gaze swept from Sarah to Jax. "But it's a crime scene, and Jax doesn't exactly get along with cops."

"They need as much help on this search as they can get," Sarah said. That was sure the truth. They had a big search area, and they needed to move. "If they question us, just tell them Jax is with our team."

"Then we might all get our asses thrown out of here," Dean Bannon murmured as he cast a considering glance Jax's way. Dean and Jax didn't exactly get along. Mostly because of that whole Jax-and-Emma past thing. Right then, Sarah could understand where Dean was coming from with his jealousy but—

"A woman is hurt and she needs us." Sarah straightened her shoulders. Personal shit had to wait. "We have to find her, *now.*" Because it wasn't like the perp would miss the swarm of police out there.

Detective West and Detective Cross hurried toward them. Cross frowned at Jax, but before the detective could do anything like, oh, order Jax off the scene, Jax said, "You need to be searching the buildings that are directly beside the water."

Cross put his hands on his hips. "Is that so?"

"Yeah, it's so." Jax pointed up. "And go to the second floor. When Sarah had him on the phone, I could hear the lap of the water against the dock. Then the guy went inside and *up* one flight of stairs." He paused. "Just one flight. I counted the steps."

So had Sarah.

"Impressive," Emma murmured. "Guess you still do use a few of my tricks."

Sarah knew that Emma's father—a man who'd pretended to be psychic—had trained his daughter to be extra observant. Sarah hadn't realized that Jax had picked up some of Emma's habits. Those habits sure could come in handy.

It was Detective West who turned and gave the orders to his men so that they could fan out and search.

Cross kept staring at their group. Then he muttered, "Captain said I had to let your team in on the search. I don't like having civilians out here . . ."

Gabe was an ex-SEAL and Dean was former FBI. Those two men hardly counted as civilians. And for Sarah, well, she'd worked plenty of cases that had taken her into nightmare situations.

As for Emma and Jax . . . well, Emma was part of LOST now and Jax . . . *I think the guy can hold his own anywhere.*

"Get suited with vests," Cross said as he pointed toward the police cruisers. "No weapons. We can't give you those. So you're going in unarmed."

Then he focused on Sarah. "You're the expert here, right? The one who knows what the killer is thinking?"

Most days.

"What's he thinking now?"

She tilted her head back to stare up at the buildings. "If he's already spotted us, then he's trying to decide if he should kill Molly or if he should just run."

Cross swore. "Why not just kill her *and* run?"

"Because Molly hasn't begged to die yet."

"Uh, what?"

Sarah smiled. "If she hasn't begged, then that means we have time." She hurried toward the cruiser. The uniformed cop was already pulling out vests for her team. Sarah suited up. *We have time.* As long as Molly kept fighting.

Because this jerk is playing by my father's rules. And that scared her because . . . *I thought I was the only one who knew about the way his victims' last few moments ended.*

MOLLY HADN'T BEGGED for death. The bitch was covered in slices. He'd cut her deep, but she wouldn't beg.

He could smell the river—and her blood. The two scents mingled around him as he stared at the tip of his blade. It was a dark red now, thanks to Molly. "I can end it all for you. Just like he ended it for your mother. All you have to do . . . is ask." *Ask me nicely, Molly. Beg me to do it.*

But Molly's lips were clamped shut. She had tear tracks on her face. Her skin was ashen. And the bitch wasn't talking.

He whirled away from her. The monitors on his right were blank. After the fire, they'd shut down. He'd had that signal bouncing right to him.

And . . . *signals. Fucking signals!* He realized right then the mistake he'd made.

He grabbed for Molly's phone. He'd been so pissed to learn that Sarah had escaped. He'd called the shrink and she'd fed him bullshit about proof of life. He knew that now . . . *bullshit.* "You were tracing my signal," he muttered as he threw that phone against the wall. Stupid, *stupid* mistake. Rage had led him to that mistake. It was just . . .

Sarah should have burned. Her beautiful skin should have melted, leaving her as ugly and scarred on the outside as he knew she was on the inside, and Molly should have *begged.* They weren't following the plan. They weren't doing what they were supposed to do! He'd set everything up. Worked so hard . . .

And it was all unraveling. He put the palms of his hands against his eyes. "They're going to come now, Molly. Time's up."

"They'll . . . find you," Molly whispered.

Oh, that was cute. He turned toward her. Smiled. "No, sweetheart. They're going to find you." But that, too, had been part of his plan.

He'd just wanted to hear her beg first. She'd been supposed to beg. He was the one who was strong. She knew that. *Beg me!*

But time was running out. He stalked toward her. Put the knife right over her heart. Molly was on the floor, sprawled. Still trapped in the remnants of the chair. He'd checked her rope, made sure it was too tight for her to slip away. Molly didn't get to escape.

She had a part to play first.

"Do you want to go fast?" he asked as he tilted his head. "Or do you want to bleed out slowly?" Of course, the plan was for her to go slowly. For her to live just long enough to talk with Sarah or the cops. To tell them . . .

Who I am.

She spat on him. Right in his face. His rage exploded. He hit her, hard, punching her.

Molly screamed.

SARAH HAD JUST been about to enter Warehouse 508 when she heard the scream. Her head jerked to the left, to the building just a few feet away. All of the warehouses in this stretch were old, appearing abandoned. The businesses had closed up and the places had become virtual graveyards.

A perfect spot for a killer.

But there was so much area to cover there . . . So much . . .

"She's screaming," Sarah said as she whirled and hurried toward the building on the left—it looked like an old clothing factory. She could just make out the faded sign on the side of the building. "She's close." That scream had seemed to echo back to her. "Come on!"

Detective Brent West was running with her, and he had his gun drawn. Jax was right behind her.

"NO CHOICE?" HE demanded. He'd busted Molly's lip. Blood dripped down her chin. "How about I choose for you?" Because she had to go slowly. Had to live long enough for the great Sarah Jacobs to rush in . . .

But then an alarm sounded. A little safety measure he'd installed so that he'd know if any visitors tried to get too close to little Molly Guthrie.

"No." He backed away from Molly. Saw the red light flickering. *They're in the building.* "No!" He wasn't ready for them, not yet. He rushed to the window and looked out. Cop cars were out there, too many of them. The cops were fanning the street and searching and someone was in his building already.

Someone was coming for Molly.

Was it Sarah? Was she there? It didn't matter. He'd left some surprises around the area. Those surprises . . . oh, they'd be going off very soon. Maybe Sarah would be getting those lovely scars, after all.

Hadn't the cops and that LOST team learned anything that day? Some lessons just had to be repeated, again and again . . . until the point took root.

There were lots of buildings there. Lots of doors that could be opened.

Lots of places that would just go . . . *boom.*

"Did you choose, Molly?" he murmured. Molly had been so quiet. He turned back around.

Molly wasn't on the ground anymore. She was standing up, and she had a broken chunk of the chair in her hand. "Yeah . . . I did." She swung that wood at him.

The little bitch.

IT SOUNDED LIKE thunder. A deep, horrible rumble of thunder that made the ground shake. Sarah froze at the sound but Detective West whirled toward her. "What the hell is that?"

Jax had his hand on Sarah's shoulder. "I can smell smoke," he said.

So could Sarah.

They ran back out and Sarah saw the fire, coming from Warehouse 508. There were shouts and screams and—*fire.*

"He set another one to blow," Jax said.

Sarah's gaze darted at the row of buildings, now looking even more like cemetery headstones to her as she stared at them. "Call your men back," she ordered the detective. "He's got the buildings rigged!" Some of them? All of them? Sarah didn't know. They needed the bomb squad in there before they could search.

And that means Molly loses time. He did this . . . to stop us. So he could finish with her and escape.

Or maybe the guy had thought Sarah would be the one racing in first. And he'd done this because he just wanted to hurt her.

Fire . . . it's about fire to him.

But as far as Sarah knew, her father had never used fire on any of his victims. He'd preferred the intimate touch of a knife.

A man was burning. A cop who'd just come out of the blazing warehouse. Jax ran to the guy, tackled him, and they rolled, tumbling around until those flames were out.

Sarah couldn't see Gabe or Dean or Emma. The smoke was getting too thick. Detective West was on his radio, ordering everyone to fall back. Sarah pulled her out phone and called Gabe. *Answer, answer . . .*

Hell, now she knew exactly how Jax had felt when

he'd been trying to get her at the earlier scene.

"Sarah? What's happening? The cops—"

"He's got more explosives set. Stay back!" Sarah said.

Another cop had just run from the burning warehouse. He was staggering when he burst out of that smoke-filled interior.

Sarah spun around. Her heart was racing as chaos erupted. Molly was so close. Sarah knew she was close.

And if we wait for the bomb squad to come, Molly's dead.

HE GRABBED THE wood—looked like the arm of a chair—in his right hand. "You think you're clever, don't you?"

He yanked that wood away from Molly. She'd lost so much blood . . . she was no match for him.

"I think . . . you're the devil," Molly whispered. Then she opened her mouth and screamed. Loud and long and—

"*I'm still alive!*"

She wasn't begging for death. She should have begged. Now he'd make sure she suffered every single moment that she had left.

He drove the knife into her side.

"Not for long, you aren't," he promised her.

"*I'M STILL ALIVE!*"

That scream had been so terrifyingly close. Detective West was helping the wounded officers and Jax was pulling a man from the smoky building.

They hadn't even heard the scream. Sarah had been the only one to hear Molly.

It's a trap. She knew it. It had to be a trap but . . .

If I leave her now, she's dead.

Sarah took a tentative step toward that building on the left—the old clothing warehouse. When she got inside, it could explode on her, too.

No, sweetheart. No one is screaming. No one at all. Her father's voice seemed to creep through her mind.

"Molly is screaming," Sarah said. "I hear her." Then she took a deep breath and she ran toward that second building. Ran as fast as she could.

Because if the killer is inside, he won't have set the bombs to kill himself. It will be safe. It will be safe . . .

Maybe.

JAX HAD NEVER thought he'd see the day when he was saving a cop's life. Not just one cop, two. "Remember this shit," he muttered to the guy he'd just dragged out of the fire. "You owe me."

Then Jax looked up, searching for Sarah. He wanted to get her back in case those flames spread. But she wasn't standing near the dock. His heart slammed against his chest as he rushed forward. "Sarah?"

He turned to the left. Only saw cops scrambling.

To the right.

He saw Detective Brent West. That dick Cross had joined the guy. They had a uniformed cop between them, and they were helping the guy get clear of Warehouse 508.

Jax ran to them. "Where's Sarah?"

Brent blinked at him. "With . . . you?"

Would he be asking the damn question if she was with him?

"Where did you see her last?" Jax demanded.

But Brent just looked confused. "She was behind me . . . I think . . . but then I went to help the men out of that fire . . ."

Jax had gone into the blaze, too. Was that where Sarah was? He hoped to hell not. The place had been an inferno moments before, seemingly seconds away from the whole building collapsing. But if Sarah was in there . . .

He rushed back toward the fire.

Then . . . stopped.

Fuck. Slow down . . . think. He yanked out his phone, but the thing had *melted.* He dropped it, swearing when it singed his fingers. He'd gone into the fire before. He hadn't seen Sarah in there. He and Brent had been helping the cops.

Who went to help Molly?

Because the fire was a distraction. He recognized that. Like booby-traps in their path. And Sarah had been going to the *second* building before the explosion had rocked the dock.

The second warehouse . . . a building that hadn't been touched by the fire, not yet.

He turned toward that building.

Stared up at the second floor.

"We need to get out of here!" It was Cross who shouted at him. "We have to create a safe perimeter and get the hell back!"

But he wasn't getting back, not without Sarah. He started running toward the second warehouse.

Jax didn't get far. He was grabbed from behind.

"What are you doing?" Cross snarled. "You go in there and the whole place could blow!"

He'd noticed that the door was open there. As if someone had gone in . . . Sarah? Had she broken in or had the guy she was after left that door open? "I'm going after Sarah."

"No." Cross shook his head. "We're getting out of here. If I let a civilian burn, even an asshole like you, I'm *done*."

Like the guy really gave a shit about Jax or anyone else. Jax knew the things Cross had done . . . both before and after becoming a cop. *Some sins don't vanish. And you're already done, buddy.* "Let me go," Jax told him. It was the only warning he planned to give the guy.

"No," Cross said, his hold tightened on Jax. "You might have a death wish, but it's not happening on my watch, not again—"

"Jax?" That was Gabe, shouting and running toward them.

Cross glanced over at him.

"Jax, where's Sarah?" Gabe called out. "She said to get back . . . but I don't leave my team behind."

Sarah wasn't with Gabe. She's in the second building. She needs me!

Jax slammed his head into the cop's. Cross howled, but the guy let Jax go. Jax didn't hesitate. He ran right for that second building, the old clothing warehouse. Cross yelled after him. Telling him to come back—

But Jax just ran faster and he roared, "*Sarah!*"

SARAH'S FEET THUDDED up the stairs. The main door had been unlocked, open and ready for her, and she wished that she had a weapon. Something to use because . . .

He's in here.

She hadn't heard any other screams from up above. She prayed that didn't mean Molly was dead. Not when she was so close to the other woman. Not when she could actually save her.

Sarah burst onto the landing on the second floor. She looked to the left, to the right. When they'd been on the phone, the man had gone up to the steps, then seemed to be immediately *with* Molly.

A door was just a step away. Sarah rushed toward the door, then stopped.

Was it rigged to blow? When she opened it, would that be the end for her *and* Molly? Dammit. Her hands clenched into fists and Sarah didn't take another step forward. "Molly!" Sarah cried out. "Molly, are you there?"

Sarah could hear the crackle of flames from the building next door, but she didn't hear Molly crying out. She didn't hear the other woman at all.

"Molly?" Sarah tried again.

Nothing.

She had to get in that room. She had to—

"*Sarah!*" The bellow of her name came from downstairs. Then she heard the thud of footsteps. She knew it was Jax, rushing after her. She also knew that if he got to the top of the stairs . . .

He'll take me away from Molly. Because he would think like she did. That it was a trap.

"Stay down there!" Sarah yelled. Then she didn't go

straight to that door. "Stay back!" She rushed down the hall and there—yes!—there was another door. This one was ajar. She could peer inside and see that the room was empty. She slipped through that open doorway without so much as touching the door, and fate was definitely on her side then because the room she was inside connected to the room immediately next door.

And she could see the crumpled form of a woman, lying on the floor of that connecting room.

Sarah ran to her. "*Molly!*"

Molly was lying in a pool of blood. The woman's eyes were closed and her face was chalk white.

Sarah felt for a pulse. It was there. So weak. So incredibly thready—

"*Sarah!*" Now her name was a desperate roar. Jax was close. Her head whipped up and she stared at the door—the door she'd almost opened. And Sarah saw the bomb there. It was wired, as she'd feared. When the door opened, it would blow.

"No!" Sarah yelled back. "Don't touch the door! It's wired! Stay back!" Because if he opened that door, they were all dead.

She looked down at Molly's body. Sarah put her hands over the woman's side, trying to apply pressure and staunch that terrible flow of blood. She was bleeding out so quickly . . .

The blood stained the tiles. At first, it hurt but then . . .

Then I didn't feel anything.

"Molly, I need you to stay with me." Sarah shoved the memories of her own past away. "You're still alive. You made it, now just keep fighting a little longer, okay?"

"Sarah, how the fuck did you get in there?" Jax called out.

Molly's blood seeped through her fingers.

"The second door. Down on the right. It connects." But then Sarah shook her head. "No, Jax, don't come in! Go get help! She needs a doctor!"

"Like I'm leaving you."

Her head turned to see Jax striding toward her. He'd come through the second entrance, just like she had.

"The police have cleared out the area. Until the fire's out, no one else is getting back here." He knelt on the floor next to her and he swore. "Baby, she's not going to make it."

"Yes, she is." Sarah glared at him. "If you won't bring a doctor, then help me get her out of here!" Because Sarah was not leaving that room without Molly.

Jax stared at the other woman a moment, then gave a grim nod. He slid his hands under Molly's body and lifted her carefully.

But Molly didn't make a sound.

"Where is he, Sarah?" Jax asked.

Her breath caught. "I don't know." Molly had been the only one in that room, but there were several floors in that old building. The guy could be there, hiding.

Waiting to attack.

A muscle jerked in Jax's jaw. "You go out first," he ordered. "I swear, I'll be right behind you. I'll get her out for you."

Because Jax was protecting her. Trying to cover her back. But who would protect him?

"I'm not the target," he gritted. "*Go.*"

Didn't Jax get it? The guy that they were after obviously didn't care about collateral damage. He wanted blood. He wanted death. He wanted . . .

She heard a squeak. The sound of wood, from right outside the door. The door that was wired with a bomb.

He knows we're in here!

"Jax . . . run!" Sarah whispered.

Jax lunged forward, with Molly cradled in his arms. And Sarah made sure she was behind *him*. Covering Jax's back even as—

That wired door flew inward. Only no one was there. A long pole appeared to have been thrown into the door, sending it flying open.

He did this. He—

And a ball of fire exploded seconds later.

Chapter 9

He couldn't go down the stairs. Not with the fire shooting out of that room, but Jax had been in buildings like this one before. He knew there was always another set of stairs—some fucking place. Smoke was rising, turning the air around him dark, but he kept advancing. "Sarah!"

"Right . . . behind you."

He didn't want her behind him. He wanted her in front of him. He wanted her out of that inferno and someplace safe.

His hold tightened on the unconscious woman in his arms. One look at her wounds and he'd known just how bad off she was. If he left Molly behind, he could run with Sarah. He knew he could get himself and Sarah out of there safely, *if* he left Molly . . .

"Keep going!" Sarah said. "There's fresh air—I can feel it!"

He kept going and he didn't ease his grip on Molly. She'd been hurt, brutalized. Once upon a time, he had just been looking out for himself in the world. When you lived on the streets, you had to look out for number one. Or you died.

But that had been a long time ago.

He glanced down at Molly. She looked so damn weak. Vulnerable.

I'll get you and Sarah out. Even if he had to carry them both.

Then he saw the second set of stairs. The freak who'd taken Molly might have another booby trap down there for them. The sick bastard. Jax squared his shoulders and started down those stairs. "Put your hand on my back!" he shouted to Sarah. He needed to feel her. He had to know that she was safe, or else he couldn't go forward.

Sarah's important. Sarah matters. So much more than he'd realized.

In that inferno, he understood just how well and truly fucked he was.

He hurried down the stairs. The smoke was thick at the top, but as he neared the bottom he could actually see—and he saw the form of a man, rushing forward. Jax tensed.

"Easy . . ." Gabe Spencer said as he reached out to take Molly from Jax. "I'm here to help."

Gabe had run into a burning building for Sarah. *I don't leave my team behind.* His respect for the man notched up.

"She's . . . bad," Jax said starkly. *I don't think she's going to make it, but Sarah is desperate.*

Gabe nodded and turned toward the landing.

Jax heard a groan from up above. Oh, hell, he'd heard

a groan just like that in the other building. A sound that signaled the ceiling was going to be falling in very soon.

Gabe was rushing out with Molly in his arms. Jax turned, grabbed Sarah's hand—and they hauled ass together. They flew down the last few stairs and rushed for the door. But to get to that door, they had to go forward about thirty feet . . . and the fire was burning on the ceiling over their heads. Chunks of burning wood fell down on them. One chunk hit Jax in the back, but he didn't slow down. When Sarah stumbled, he just lifted her up into his arms and ran even faster. Faster, faster . . .

They cleared the door. The air wasn't much cleaner out there because both buildings were on fire now. Sirens were screaming. Voices were shouting. It was madness.

And the perfect time for the SOB to escape. But Jax couldn't worry about him. Not then.

Dean ran toward Gabe and helped to carry Molly. They all kept running until they were away from the fire and they were safely behind the perimeter of yellow tape that the cops had set up. Jax could feel blisters on his skin, but he didn't care. He looked down at Sarah.

"You can stop carrying me," she told him.

Screw that.

He kissed her. Kissed her right there in front of her team and half of the New Orleans Police Department. Her lips were open when his mouth touched hers, giving him the perfect access that he needed. Fear was a living, breathing beast within him, clawing at his guts, and he needed the affirmation that Sarah was safe. She was alive. She was with him.

And she kissed him back. Just as deeply, as passionately. As if she didn't care who was watching. As if he were the only one who mattered to her.

One day, I will be.

Slowly, his head lifted. He stared at her. There was so much he wanted to say to Sarah right then, but he didn't have the words. When it mattered, he never seemed to have them.

"I can stand on my own," she told him.

Yeah, he knew that. She was one of the strongest women he'd ever met. For her to survive the nightmare of her past, she'd had to be strong. Most people would have been shredded on the inside—and out—after living her life. But she'd turned the nightmare into something good. She'd become a profiler to help people.

She even made him want to be more than he fucking was.

Carefully, he lowered Sarah to her feet.

"Thank you," she whispered.

He wanted to kiss her again. No, he wanted to grab her and run away from that scene. He wanted to take her far away so that she'd always be safe.

But that wasn't Sarah. He'd already realized she wasn't the type to hide. Not from anything or anyone. So when the detectives closed in on Sarah, he backed away and let them toss their questions at her.

"How did you know where the vic was being held?" Brent wanted to know.

"Did you see the perp?" Cross demanded in the same instant.

Jax hadn't seen him. If he had, the guy wouldn't have walked away.

"Are you okay?" the soft, feminine voice came from his right. His head turned and he saw Emma Castille staring up at him. Worry was stamped on her pretty features. "When you didn't come out with the cops, I was scared."

Ah, Emma. Despite what a bastard he'd been in their shared past, she still cared for him. That was one of Emma's weaknesses . . . her soft heart. He'd always tried to protect her so that others wouldn't use that weakness against her.

Now Dean Bannon was the one guarding her. With all the ferocity of a lion.

"I couldn't leave Sarah," Jax said simply.

Her eyes widened. Once, he'd nearly gotten lost in Emma's bright eyes. But Emma had been afraid of him. She'd always pulled away from his darkness.

Sarah . . .

Sarah accepts me.

And when he looked into Sarah's eyes . . . *I am fucking lost.*

"Since when did you start playing the hero?" Emma's voice was so low that only he could hear it. "What's your angle, Jax?"

Ah, right. He was always supposed to have an angle. After all, he had a rep to maintain. His gaze slid back to Sarah. "I'm working things out." That was the truth. Mostly. He really didn't like to lie to Emma. She was one of his few friends, even if he knew that she sometimes wished he'd vanish from New Orleans.

An ambulance rushed away from the scene. He tensed. That was Molly—being taken to the hospital. He looked down and realized that her blood stained his clothes and his hands.

"Is she going to make it?" Emma asked softly.

His hands fisted. "She's young. Had her whole life ahead of her."

"Jax?"

"She was bad, Em. Real bad."

He took a step away from her. He needed to call Carlos and he also needed to let his lawyer know where the guy could pick up his car.

Because I'm not leaving this scene. Not without Sarah.

"Dean told me. About your past. Your family."

He looked back at her.

Pain flashed in Emma's eyes. "All this time . . . why didn't you come to me first? You know I would have convinced LOST to take your case."

He searched her stare. And there it was. Pity. He walked back to her. Smiled down at her. "Because I have been many things to you, Emma Castille, but I have never been a man you pitied."

Her breath caught. "No, Jax—"

"I just want to know who my mother was. My father. And why the hell I never mattered enough for them to find me."

Emma's hand curled around his arm. "You matter."

He backed away from her. "So do you, Em." And

he was glad, so very glad, that she'd found her partner in Dean. Sure, the guy was a straight-A prick in that follow-the-rules, law-abiding way, but Dean had already proved that he would lay down his life—in an instant—for Emma.

Love could make a man do some stupid shit.

He looked over at Sarah. She was still between the two detectives, but her gaze was on Jax. She looked tired. Ash coated her cheek, and, like him, Molly's blood stained her clothes and hands.

"It was a near thing," Emma said from behind him. "I saw the fire raging. Then you rushed out, carrying Sarah with you."

Leaving her hadn't been an option. Either Sarah had come out of that blaze . . .

Or I would have stayed with her.

That unsettling thought had him stiffening.

"What happened to the man who took Molly?" Emma asked.

He glanced around the scene. So many cops. So many firefighters.

"Did he burn in the blaze?"

Jax shook his head. No, the end hadn't been nearly that simple. Not for the freak they were looking for. "He's still out there." He stared at the fire. Burning so bright. "And he isn't done."

"How do you know that?" Emma's soft voice followed him.

He focused on Sarah. "Because he doesn't have what he wants, not yet." *You never will. I'll make sure you don't hurt her.*

Another attack would come. They would be ready for it.

HOSPITALS. THEY ALWAYS reminded Sarah of death. Far too much of death. She'd stayed out at that scene with the detectives, answering their questions again and again. The fires had been extinguished. The area searched. But there had been no sign of the man who abducted Molly Guthrie.

Now, exhausted, body aching, voice too husky from the flames and the smoke, Sarah was pacing in the hospital waiting room. Dean and Emma had gone to the hospital earlier. They'd been calling to give her updates.

Unfortunately, there wasn't much *to* update on.

Molly had gone into surgery. The guy's attack had been brutal. The doctors had done their best to stitch up Molly and stabilize her, but she'd lost so much blood. She was unconscious now, and the doctors were monitoring her closely. She couldn't talk to the cops or to Sarah about who'd hurt her. She couldn't even open her eyes.

So the man who'd attacked Molly could be walking down the main streets in New Orleans. He could be planning another abduction . . .

And there's nothing I can do to stop him.

"This is a win, Sarah." She jumped at the voice and turned to see Victoria standing in the doorway. Her friend's hair was pulled back in a ponytail, and the light glinted off Victoria's glasses. "You found Molly. You saved her."

Wearily, Sarah shook her head. "They don't know if she's even going to last the night." And that made her heart ache. "She survived until the end, but, Viki . . ." Sarah crossed toward her, exhaling softly. "He did a number on her." So many cuts. So much pain.

Victoria's fingers closed around Sarah's. "She made it out. You got her out."

"No." She couldn't take credit. She hadn't carried Molly through the fire and down all of those stairs. "Jax got her out. He did this."

Victoria blinked. "What?"

"There's more to him than just the stories you hear."

"There's always more," Victoria allowed. "More good and more bad. That's something you and I both know."

Yes, they did. Because Victoria's past was filled with blood and tragedy and death, too. Victoria had learned, early on, that love could be a mask for evil. A mask that hid true intent so very well.

"He knows my father," Sarah confided to Victoria. "The man who took Molly . . . he's connected to my dad."

"How?" Victoria asked her.

"I don't know." And, since she didn't know who the perp was . . . that meant only one other person could tell her. "But I will find out." She'd already talked to Gabe. He was pulling the files on the families of Murphy's victims—victims they knew about. But the cops had been able to pin only a few of the crimes on her father. Sarah knew there were other bodies out there.

If they can't find the body, then there's no crime. You

have to be smarter than the cops. Don't ever give them anything. Make them work for the job.

She swallowed as her father's words replayed in her mind. "Once I know that Molly is safe, I'm going to see him."

"Sarah, *no.*"

She hadn't seen her father in . . . *no,* she didn't want to think about the last time she'd seen him. "Maybe Molly can ID the guy. Maybe it won't matter and I—I won't have to see him." Because her father terrified her.

Not because he was a monster. She knew that, with utter certainty.

A monster who would never hurt me. But, to her father, the rest of the world was more than fair game.

No, he scared her because . . . *I hate him.* She hated the man who'd murdered and tortured so brutally. A man who'd rightfully earned the moniker of Murphy the Monster.

But . . . *I love him.* She still remembered when he taught her to ride her bike. When he lifted her up to put the star on the Christmas tree. When he would take her camping and they would eat roasted marshmallows under the stars . . .

All before she'd learned the truth.

"I want to check on Wade," Sarah said. "See how he's doing."

Victoria's hands slid away from Sarah's. "He's getting frustrated. You know, typical Wade. The guy is more than ready to bust out of here, but the docs want to keep him for observation."

Sarah and Victoria slipped from that waiting room and started walking down the hallway.

"I thought I'd have to tie him to the bed," Victoria confided with a shake of her head. "And then—" Her words ended abruptly because she'd just seen the three big, tattooed men who were waiting around the corner. Men who immediately stood when they saw Sarah.

They were her guards. Guards that Jax had *insisted* follow her to the hospital.

She'd tried to tell him she was fine, but he hadn't bought that. And with the way this case was going, Sarah hadn't exactly minded a bit of protection.

Especially protection that looked so capable.

"Victoria, this is Carlos . . ."

He inclined his head. He smiled at Victoria, and his scar rippled.

"George." Sarah pointed to the man with a buzz cut and a nose ring.

Victoria waved at him.

"And Nate."

"Ma'am," Nate said, his voice pretty much like that of a bear growling. His hands were loose at his sides, and the dark, golden tiger that curved around his left hand almost looked alive.

"Uh, hello," Victoria said. "Nice tats." Then she glanced at Sarah. "They're all with you?"

"Well . . ."

"The boss wants Ms. Sarah to have an escort," Carlos said. "Until he can get back with her. Her safety is our priority."

Victoria frowned as she studied Sarah. "You're not telling me everything." Her voice rose a bit. "You're keeping things from the team, aren't you?"

Sarah bit her lip. "I told you, he's connected with my father."

"And?"

Sarah hesitated.

"You've got a group of bodyguards—three of them!—standing right here. What aren't you telling me?"

Sarah cast a quick glance toward the men. She really hated to reveal all the shady bits of her past in front of them. "I'm his target," she said quietly. "Wade was hurt because of me. Molly was taken because of me. Because the guy out there is furious with my father and he will use anyone, do anything, in order to get to me."

Victoria took a step back. "Hurting you . . . it hurts Murphy."

"I don't think anything actually hurts him." Despite what he'd said in the past. Knowing him as she did, Sarah often doubted if he actually loved her. Psychopaths were great when it came to mimicking emotions, but actually feeling them? No, that didn't usually happen.

Her father operated without any guilt. He didn't understand remorse. He'd fooled so many people—including Sarah—into thinking he was normal because he was so very good at manipulation. When you looked at Murphy Jacobs, you saw what he wanted you to see.

"But . . ." Sarah cleared her throat. "As far as the rest of the world is concerned, I'm his daughter. He's supposed to care about me. So if you want to hurt him, you go after his family."

"Oh, Sarah." Victoria sighed. The overhead light glinted off her glasses. "What can I do?"

Stay away from me. She almost said those words. But she knew Victoria would take them the wrong way. Sarah wanted to put some distance between herself and the team because she needed to protect them. She needed to find the perp out there and stop him. If he wanted to get at Murphy so badly, then she would gladly throw those two in jail together.

Two killers, one cell. They could battle it out.

But that wasn't the way the law was supposed to work. *I'm not the law.*

"We're going to stop him," Sarah said as she straightened her shoulders. Her guards were avidly watching. "We'll find this guy and we won't let him hurt anyone else. Molly will wake up, and she'll help to ID him."

Victoria's face showed her worry. "Are you going to be all right?"

Sarah forced a smile. "With these guys?" She gestured to her silent guards. "How could I not be?" But the guards wouldn't be around forever, she knew that. "Now, let's go check on Wade . . . before he drives those nurses crazy."

EDDIE GUTHRIE WAS strapped to a table. He couldn't remember how he'd gotten on that table. He didn't know where the hell he was or what was happening.

He jerked hard, but the straps were too tight. They wouldn't give.

"Easy . . ." It was a man's voice. Right next to him. "We're trying to help you."

No, no, they weren't. They were holding him down. He was struggling, screaming.

Hard hands grabbed him. "Hold him down! Secure him!"

Eddie's mind was twisting chaos. He looked up and he saw a monster in front of him. A man with a mask over his face. He screamed again and twisted his body.

The table he was on . . . it fell. Eddie hit the floor with a crash.

"He needs to be sedated!"

Sedated . . . he struggled to think, but his mind felt so thick and confused. *Sedated* . . . did that mean they wanted to drug him?

"No!" Eddie roared. He lunged away from the floor, kicking and shoving at the straps.

"We need to know what the guy has been given!" That sounded like a woman's voice. High and sharp and scared. "He was seizing before . . . hell, the way he's looking at us, you'd think he was seeing—"

Monsters.

He swiped out and his fingers found . . . a knife? It was shiny like a knife. Sharp. But . . . it was something else. He knew the weapon had a name, but he couldn't remember it. It was so hard to remember anything right then.

"He's got a scalpel!" That shrieking woman was yelling again. "Get back!"

Footsteps scrambled back.

His eyes narrowed. He wanted to see them, but there

were shadows darting across his vision. He swiped out, trying to knock those shadows away. They were like . . . like the dark ghosts he'd seen at a haunted house once. Fabric, hanging on a wire.

"Haunted house . . ." he whispered. He took another swing at the shadows, slicing with his weapon. Maybe he could cut them down.

"That guy is insane!" a man shouted. "He's still tripping on something. Get the guards. *Guards!*"

More footsteps thudded into the room. That meant more people, right? He stopped swinging and narrowed his eyes as he tried to see them.

That was when Eddie saw the guns. Two big, hulking men had their guns aimed at him.

"Drop the scalpel, now!" one snarled.

He rubbed his forehead. He was sweating. It was so hot in there. So hot he couldn't think. "Where am I?" He had memories pushing through his mind, trying to get past the thick fog that had been weighing him down. He remembered . . .

I was in a mask.

But, no, why would he have worn a mask?

Have to kill her. A life for a life.

His body shuddered. He took a step back.

He remembered . . .

I had a knife in my hand. I put the knife to the woman's throat.

He looked down and saw the glint of the light, shining off the weapon in his hand.

Did I kill someone?

His fingers tightened around that weapon.

He remembered . . . jail. A cell. A big, blond man saying that Molly . . .

"Where's Molly?" Eddie asked, his voice rasping out. His heart was racing. His palms were sweating. Every breath he took seemed to burn his lungs. "*Where's my sister?*"

"Drop the weapon!" was the only response he got.

But if he dropped it, would they fire at him? Were they going to kill him anyway? He glanced around wildly. He didn't know these people. He'd never seen them before in his life. And his sister . . .

Molly had been . . . taken. That was what the blond man had told him.

Then Eddie had woken up, strapped down. They'd been about to drug him.

Did they take me, too? "I'm getting out of here!" He'd find his sister. He and Molly . . . they always stuck together. It was them against the world. Always had been. Through all the foster homes. Through the different schools. They'd been together.

Molly needs me. "Give me my sister!" His head was throbbing, as if a jackhammer were digging right behind his eyes.

"We have to subdue him!" It was the woman again. Yelling. Her voice made his head ache even more.

"Shut up!" he told her. "Shut up, shut up. *Shut up!*" Then he lunged toward her.

Thunder erupted. No, not thunder. It was more like fireworks. He and Molly liked to watch the fireworks on New Year's Eve.

But he didn't see any fireworks and his chest . . . hurt.

His knees sagged. He hit the floor. The knife—*scalpel*—fell from his fingers. "I . . . want Molly."

More footsteps rushed into the room. He strained to keep his eyes open.

"*What the hell?*" The shocked cry came from the guy who'd just burst into the room. A guy wearing a suit, with a badge pinned to his belt. The guy's green eyes glittered.

Wait . . . he knew that guy. He was a detective. West—

I can see them all now. So clearly.

The detective must be there to help him. Eddie tried to speak, but he only managed a groan.

Then the cop was in front of him. "Stay with me, kid," he said.

"Mol . . . ly . . ."

"We found your sister. She's in a hospital." The guy's head turned to the left. "You fucking hit him dead in the heart! Why? *Why?*"

"He was lunging with the scalpel! I told him to drop it, again and again, and he wouldn't! He wouldn't!"

Eddie felt so cold. Cold everywhere, except for his heart. It seemed to be burning right in his chest. "Mol . . . ly . . ."

"Your sister is safe, do you hear me?" The detective leaned in close to him. "We got her. She's safe."

That was good. "L-Love . . . Mol . . ."

His chest didn't burn anymore.

His eyes closed.

Chapter 10

JAX WAITED OUTSIDE OF THE POLICE STATION. HE'D gotten a call from Brent. The detective had said he needed to see Jax, right away.

Night had come. Darkness had swept over the city. In New Orleans, the darkness just meant that the real party was about to begin. This city never seemed to sleep. Vegas had nothing on the Big Easy.

He saw Brent hurry out of the station and quickly run down the steps. Jax hunched his shoulders and eased deeper into the shadows. Then he walked down the street, knowing that Brent would follow him. They wouldn't have that chat right on the doorsteps of the PD. That would be far too obvious. But the perfect spot waited just ahead.

Jax propped his shoulders against the wall of an alley. Brent came into sight again a few moments later.

"He's dead," Brent said.

Jax waited. "Tell me you're talking about the prick who took the girl."

"I'm talking about Eddie Guthrie." Brent started pacing. He jerked his hand over this face. Jax had noticed before that the guy did that whenever he was nervous or upset. "He was in the med unit, they were supposed to be taking care of him."

Hell.

"He got loose—I don't know how. Eddie grabbed a scalpel. The guards thought he was attacking a nurse, and they shot him. In the fucking heart." He stopped pacing. "Why not shoot his shoulder? His hand? Why the heart?"

Jax locked his jaw.

"His last words were for his sister. I lied to the kid. I told him she was all right." Brent swung around. "But the docs are saying she might not last until morning."

Yes, Carlos had called and told Jax the same thing.

"I have nothing to go on here," Brent continued, and his words sounded ragged. "All the evidence burned, and the guy got away scot-free." Frustration seethed in his voice. "Is he going to do it again? You've got the in with LOST. I mean, damn, it's obvious you're fucking the pretty profiler."

Ah, because of the kiss? But, yes, he had fucked her . . . and he planned to do it again, at the first opportunity.

"What does she say about this guy? Do we have one of them serial killers hunting in the city? What's happening?"

Jax pushed away from the wall. He rolled his shoulders. This was Brent's first big case, and the guy was breaking. "I'm sorry about Eddie."

"Me too." Brent shook his head. "I heard the gun blast when I was in the hall outside of the med ward.

If I'd just gotten there faster, I would have stopped it! I would have saved him."

We can't save everyone.

But Sarah was trying to do just that.

"Molly might remember her attacker," Jax said. "She's not dead yet." *So don't give up, not yet.*

Brent nodded. Then he said, "We had a deal. I'd keep you in the loop . . ."

Yes.

"But I need *you* to tell me what's happening, too," Brent pushed. In the dark, his eyes gleamed. "If LOST has intel, they aren't sharing, I have to know about it. Because it sure as shit isn't like Cross is going to be making breaks on this one. The guy can't solve his way through a crossword puzzle."

Jax inclined his head. "If the LOST group think a serial is hunting here, you can be certain that you'll know." He turned away from the cop. It was getting late, and he didn't want Sarah staying at that hospital all night.

"Wait!"

He looked back.

"I've . . . been researching Sarah Jacobs." Brent hesitated. "Is all that shit true? Her dad was killing when Sarah was just a kid?"

Jax hadn't asked Sarah for details about her past. She hadn't pressed for his, and he'd given her the same courtesy. Anything she shared . . . *she'd share.* He wouldn't dig.

"She stopped him, right? Put a gun to her own father's head and stopped him from killing that last victim?"

"If that's what the stories say . . ."

"What does that do to a person?" Brent wanted to know. "To know that your father is a twisted killer? To see what he does . . . what does that do to you?"

It makes you stronger. At least, that was what it had done for Sarah.

He started walking.

"Do you think she's like him . . . deep down?"

"No."

"How can you be sure? If she lived with him all that time, how can you be sure she's not just like Murphy the Monster? I mean, Jesus, man, when I look into her eyes, I get unnerved. She sees too much."

Too deep.

Jax kept walking.

"We don't need another serial killer hunting down here!" Brent called after him. "This city just survived one nightmare, we don't need another one."

No, they didn't. But it wasn't about what they needed. It was about what the twisted prick out there had planned.

"SARAH . . ." HER NAME was a low rumble, one that pushed through the fog of sleep that surrounded her. "Sarah, it's time to go."

She blinked and realized that she was slouched in one of the waiting room chairs. She'd fallen asleep. She hadn't meant to drift off. Sarah straightened quickly. "Is everything okay? Is Molly all right?"

Jax's hand closed around her shoulder. "Molly's condition hasn't changed. But it's time for you to come home. You're dead on your feet."

She rubbed her eyes. "I—I can't leave. Someone has to stay and make sure—" She broke off, then confessed her fear. "What if he comes back for her?" Just because they'd saved a victim, it didn't mean the case was over. They'd rescued another girl, only to have her die in a hospital. Sarah stood. "Someone has to stay here and—"

"I'm here, Sarah." That was Gabe's voice. Her head turned. He was sitting a few feet away. "I'll call you if anything happens to her."

But she didn't want to leave him, either. He had to be as tired as she was. "We can both—"

"Go, Sarah," he said firmly. "And that's an order."

She still didn't want to ditch him, but at that moment, another woman walked into the waiting room. A woman with blond hair and green eyes. A woman who focused only on Gabe.

"Eve?" Gabe demanded, sounding stunned, and he shot to his feet. "What are you doing here? I was coming home—"

"And I wanted to be with you," she said, giving him a small smile. "So I found you." Worry slid across her face. "Victoria updated me. The victim . . . she's still in ICU?"

He nodded, then he pulled Eve close to him. He just . . . held her for a moment. Sarah saw the long shudder that shook Gabe's body when he had Eve close. He pulled back, but only so that he could kiss the blonde. And, watching them, Sarah felt like an intruder because there was so much incredible tenderness in that kiss. Powerful emotion. It wasn't just about passion. With those two, it was about love.

Sarah hadn't even been sure that she believed a couple could love each other that much, not until she'd seen Eve and Gabe together.

Jax cleared his throat. "I think your boss is good," he said. "We should go."

Sarah felt her cheeks flush. With Eve around, she was sure Gabe was more than good.

"Brent sent some cops to keep watch down here, too," Jax added. "Molly is going to be safe."

Gabe's head slowly lifted. His face had softened with love as he stared down at Eve. But then he seemed to remember that he and Eve weren't alone. He looked over at Sarah.

"Why don't you and Eve go to the hotel," Sarah offered. "I can—"

Eve turned toward her. "I'm staying with Gabe. Viki told me that *you* were in the fire today. How are you even on your feet?"

Her feet—and knees—were rather wobbly.

"We've got this," Eve said, giving Sarah a faint smile. "Go and rest. And chalk this up as a win for LOST."

A win . . . the way Eve's case had been.

Jax followed Sarah toward the door.

"You'll keep her safe?" Gabe called after them.

Before Jax could answer, Sarah glanced back at him. "I can keep myself safe." Just what did he think her father had been teaching her all of those years?

How to hunt.

How to kill.

How to survive.

Jax was silent as they rode the elevator down to the

parking garage. He led her toward a big, black SUV that waited near one of the columns. Before Sarah slid up onto the seat, she asked, "You're taking me back to the hotel?"

He caught her chin in his hand. "No, Sarah."

Her breath whispered out. "My clothes—"

"—will be taken care of." He smiled at her, a smile that looked like a tiger, sharp and predatory. "So maybe you should send a text to your friends. Let them know you'll be at my place. I *will* be keeping you safe."

Oh, had that struck a nerve with him? Too bad. It was who she was.

"And we'll be fucking."

Yes, well, um, she wasn't going to include that bit in the text.

He leaned down and kissed her. Hard and deep. He made her want *more*. "You scared the hell out of me today," he muttered against her mouth.

Wait . . . she'd scared big, bad Jax Fontaine? Impossible. Nothing was supposed to scare him.

"Next time, run away from the fire," he told her. "Save yourself."

Ah, but that was what he didn't understand. She had too many sins to atone for in this world. If she didn't try to help, then . . .

What will I become?

She climbed into the vehicle. He slammed her door, then came around to the driver's side. Sarah fired off a quick text to Gabe. A few moments later, she and Jax were leaving that parking garage and heading out into the dark night. "What's their story?" he asked her, actually seeming to be curious.

Sarah glanced over at him. "You mean Gabe and Eve?" Well, technically, Eve wasn't the blonde's name. She was Jessica Montgomery. Or she had been.

"Yeah, them. Gabe looked like—"

"He could pretty much devour her." As soon as the words left her mouth, Sarah clamped her lips shut. She had to learn to watch herself around Jax. For some reason, she revealed too much with him. "They're pretty intense together," she mumbled.

"They are." His hand slid over. Squeezed her thigh. "And so are we." His touch seemed to burn right through her jeans.

She wanted him to move his fingers a little bit. To slide them inside her thigh and up to the—

"Sarah? Their story," he prompted.

Right. Coughing a bit, Sarah said, "Eve was a client. She came in the doors of LOST, and I'm pretty sure Gabe took one look at her and the guy fell . . . hard." She'd never thought the mighty Gabe would go down that fast. But he'd been nearly obsessed. So determined to stay close to Eve.

To win her heart.

"Who had gone missing from Eve's life?"

"She had." Her head turned as she stared out her window. The streets were packed with people, and, up ahead, a horse-drawn carriage was slowly meandering through the city. "Eve woke up in a hospital, with no memory of her past. She happened to see a story in a newspaper—it was a story about the Lady Killer. He was a serial killer who'd been targeting wealthy, blond women—"

"I remember that story," Jax said, his voice grim.

"Eve looked in the paper, saw the photos of the guy's victims, and she saw her own face staring back at her." The horse-drawn carriage turned. Jax sped up. "She came to LOST because she wanted us to find out if she had been a victim. She wanted us to find out *anything* we could about her." And in the end, they had. They'd stopped the Lady Killer. Eve had learned about her past . . . and Gabe had fallen in love.

"Some people get happy endings," Sarah said. "Even if they have to walk through fire first."

Silence. She closed her eyes, feeling weary all the way to her soul. "I need to speak with Detective West. I want to make sure he's told Eddie that Molly is alive." *For the moment.* But, no, she couldn't think that way. Molly would make it through the night. She'd be stronger by morning. With every moment that passed, Molly would keep fighting. She'd survive.

"Eddie . . . Eddie was shot, Sarah."

Her eyes flew open. "What?"

"Guards thought he was attacking one of the nurses that was there to check on him. One of those guards fired at him. I'm sorry, but he didn't make it."

It felt as if someone had just punched Sarah in the gut.

"Brent told me that Eddie was acting erratically, saying things that didn't make sense." He turned to the right. "It had to be the drugs, still in his system. The kid never had a chance."

No, he hadn't. Tears stung her eyes but she blinked, trying to stop them from falling. *Brent had told Jax all of this?* She was sure starting to suspect that those two were closer than they'd let on. She knew Jax supposedly had informants all over the city. Was Brent part of his network?

"Sarah . . ." His voice was a growl. "Eddie tried to kill you."

"You said yourself"—her words were hoarse—"he was just a weapon that bastard out there used. Aim and fire . . ." Only now Eddie was gone. And Molly . . .

Live, Molly, please.

SARAH THOUGHT SHE was so damn clever. Escaping from his fire. Getting the girl out.

He'd figured Sarah would leave that girl behind as soon as the bomb exploded. Why not leave her? Molly Guthrie had been dead weight—literally. But Sarah hadn't been alone. Jax Fontaine had been with her.

Jax. Did the guy even realize how he fit into the game? When he'd seen the two of them together—kissing in front of everyone—rage had consumed him. Jax knew what Sarah was. Fruit of the fucking poisoned tree. And he was going to touch her? Screw her?

Jax didn't get it. Sarah was the one screwing with him. She was a master at the mind fuck. Like her father, she showed the world only what she wanted them to see. A true manipulator, all the way to her core.

He'd underestimated her. He'd thought taking Sarah out would be easy.

He wouldn't make that mistake again.

He would show her—and Murphy—just how strong he'd become. He wasn't helpless. He wouldn't cower and beg for help any longer. Now, everyone would be begging him.

Sarah would beg.

Then she'd die.

As for Jax Fontaine . . . he smiled. Jax was a pawn that would be used. A pawn whose time had finally come.

Jax didn't know it, but he knew all of Jax's secrets. Every single one of them. He'd use those secrets.

Right now, Jax was protecting Sarah. Keeping his goons around her so that she'd never be vulnerable. But he'd get Jax to turn on Sarah. Before he was done, Jax would be serving Sarah up for death.

And Sarah would be screaming.

JAX SHUT THE door behind Sarah and secured his alarm. She stood a few feet in front of him, her shoulders slumped, her hair trailing down her back. As he watched her, Sarah moved forward a bit, and her fingers curled around the banister. "I feel safe with you." She said those words as she began to climb up the stairs. "And that's probably wrong, isn't it?"

Behind her, he shook his head. Then he stalked toward her and picked her up. Sarah gave a little gasp of surprise.

"Nothing's wrong between us," he told her. His arms tightened around her. "You need to remember that." He started carrying her up the stairs. She was so small and delicate compared to him. She almost felt too light in his arms.

She didn't struggle in his hold. Sarah curled her

hands around his neck and said, "I think you like carrying me."

Guilty. He liked holding her. Sarah . . . fit.

"Just so you know, though, you don't have to do this whole Rhett Butler routine to impress me."

He laughed. Her words were so unexpected—after everything that had happened—the laughter just spilled from him.

And Sarah smiled.

Fuck . . . *Sarah smiled.* It was a real smile, one that made her dark eyes light up. He almost lost his footing right then and nearly sent both of them tumbling down the stairs. But he steadied himself and held her even closer.

"I'm already impressed plenty," she said. "Promise."

Get her up the stairs and into bed.

He concentrated hard. One foot. The other. He really just wanted to kiss her and fuck her, but he was trying to hold on to some control. For the moment. He knew, though, that when he got Sarah naked, his control would splinter.

By some miracle, they got to the top of the stairs. His cock was swollen, his muscles tight. He marched down the hall, but he didn't take her to his bed. Not yet.

Take care of her. Sarah needed to see that he could be someone she could count on. Despite what the rumors said, he'd be more for Sarah than just a—completely unforgettable—fuck. For her, he'd be one hell of a lot more.

Always . . . her.

He took her into the bathroom. That had been one

of the first rooms he'd had redone in that place. Now marble gleamed in the room. The tub—hell, the thing was big enough for five people, so it would easily fit him and Sarah.

He lowered Sarah to her feet. Then he backed away and turned on the water, making sure it was nice and hot. "Figured you'd want to wash off this day . . ." He sure as hell did.

Jax turned his back and reached for his shirt. He tossed it over his head even as he toed out of his shoes and then—

Sarah pressed a kiss to his back. Jax's muscles went rock-hard at her touch. His hands were on the button of his pants. He eased that button open and slid the zipper down *very* carefully. As a general rule, Jax didn't bother with underwear, and he sure didn't want to hurt his overeager dick because he was frantic for Sarah.

"I like your tattoos," Sarah said as her fingers trailed down his arms. So many tattoos were there. Milestones, from his life. From the times when he'd had to crawl out of the gutter. Those tats showed others where he'd been. They told him where he was going.

Sarah eased away from him. He heard the faint rustle of clothing, and when he looked back, Sarah was naked. Naked and fucking perfect.

Unlike him, she had no tats that colored her body. The only mark on her . . . that was the scar on her wrist, and he'd noticed that Sarah covered that mark from others. *But not from me.* She stood before him, completely naked, and she was the most beautiful thing he'd ever seen.

The water kept pouring into that tub. Steam was rising lightly. Sarah slipped past him and lowered into the water.

She sank into it, sighing softly. That sigh was a lot like the sound she made when he was balls-deep *in* her. A sound of pure contentment. Pleasure.

"Aren't you coming in?" Sarah asked. She'd reached for the soap and was rubbing it on her body. The lather was over her skin. Caressing the pink of her nipples. Sliding between the heaven of her legs.

Did she even realize that he'd bought that vanilla-scented soap just for her?

He slid in beside her, sending that water sloshing. Her hands reached for him, and Sarah was . . . stroking him with her slippery hands. The lather got on him, eased over his chest and down his abs.

Then Sarah reached for his cock. Her eyes were on his as she stroked him. Once. Twice. From root to tip. And her touch was incredible. Faster, harder, she stroked him.

If she was going to play, then he figured it was only fair that he did, too. He wrapped his hands around her hips, lifted her up, and onto him.

"Jax!"

He didn't thrust his cock into her. Oh, he wanted to. But he was holding back then, for her. *Show her what you can do.* Her legs curled around his hips in that big tub, and she was straddling him as the water poured down. He had her in the perfect position. She was stroking his cock—hell, yes—and he could slip his fingers right between her spread legs. Right over her delicate folds and into her sex.

"Jax!" Her hold tightened on him, squeezing so good.

He trailed his thumb over her clit. He knew just how to stroke that button so that she'd shiver. And when Sarah pushed down against him, moving even harder, he knew that she liked what he was doing to her.

He wanted her to love it.

His fingers eased in and out of her. He kept his thumb on her clit, pushing down, rubbing harder, stroking her into a feverish pitch. And she kept her fingers wrapped around his cock. Working his erection again and again. It was a race then; he was pushing her, determined to make Sarah come first.

Come *for* him.

And she did. He felt her inner muscles clench around him as she choked out his name.

Yes . . .

He was staring into her eyes and he saw them go blind with pleasure. Her cheeks flushed a sweet pink and her lips parted as she tried to suck in air.

You belong to me. Did she realize it yet? She would, soon enough.

She sagged against him. "Jax . . ."

He rose, lifting her with him. They were both soaking wet as he took her back to the bed. He wasn't about to stop so they could dry off. He needed her too much.

He lowered her onto the bed. Her legs were spread. Her breasts glistening with those tight nipples. He climbed on top of her. Kissed Sarah. Deep and hard because he loved her taste.

She arched against him. Her hands curled around his arms and her short nails bit into him.

He pulled away from her.

"Wait, Jax—"

He pushed between her legs. Lifted her hips up and put his mouth on her. He didn't just want Sarah to come. He wanted her to break apart for him. To go insane with the pleasure. To know nothing but him and the way he could make her feel.

He licked her. He sucked her. He caressed her in and out . . . again and again, and her hips were jerking against him, but he held her easily, keeping her just where he wanted her. Where he needed her.

She shuddered when she climaxed again—and she screamed that time. Screamed for him. That was exactly what he wanted from her.

Maddened now, her taste pushing him to the edge, he grabbed for his box of condoms. He jerked one on and then plunged into her. There was no control. No holding back. There was only taking. Taking. *Taking.*

Her legs wrapped around him. He drove deeper. As deep as he could get. Faster and harder and deeper. The tension built, as the desire, the ravenous hunger he felt for Sarah, spiraled out of control. Her taste was on his lips and her sex took his cock. She was wet, hot silk around him, driving him the edge of sanity—then right fucking over that edge.

"Jax!"

He erupted when he felt her contractions. He poured into her, gutted out and consumed by the pleasure that whipped through him. Deeper and stronger than anything he'd ever felt before. The climax seemed endless, holding them both in its grip so that he knew nothing beyond the pleasure of the moment. The pleasure of . . . her.

"SARAH?" IT WAS her dad's voice, seeming to come from a distance away. "Sarah, you've got to see the surprise I've got for you."

Part of Sarah knew that the scene wasn't real. It wasn't a nightmare, either, not really. It was a memory and she was trapped. *Trapped . . .*

Sarah glanced up toward the stop of the stairs. "I'm down here, Dad!"

She saw the burlap sack, waiting in the corner. Frowning, she moved closer to it.

"Sarah, you're not supposed to be down here."

She whirled around even as her heart raced in her chest. "Dad! You scared me."

He didn't smile at her. His dark eyes glinted. "I've told you before . . . you don't need to be afraid. It's the rest of the world—"

"—that has to be afraid." He told her that line so many times. But it wasn't like she was some big, bad beast. She was Sarah Jacobs, cheerleader wannabe. "Dad, I think a pipe broke and got your bag wet. That smell is terrible!"

He moved forward. "That's one of your presents. Though I was going to show it to you later. After your friends left."

Her present was in that stinky bag?

Her dad turned on another light and the bulb shone down on that bag. The bag wasn't just wet. Those stains on it were so dark in color.

"I heard about the trouble you had at school." His lips thinned. "Your counselor called me . . . told me all about that boy . . ."

Her cheeks burned. "It's nothing, Dad. I can handle him."

"He has a history of picking on other kids. Bullying them. He's older, he should know better."

"I can handle him," she said again.

Her dad smiled. "You don't have to."

Then he opened the bag for her.

Sarah screamed because Ryan . . . Ryan Klein was in that bag! Ryan's eyes were closed. His face was ashen, and his throat had been cut . . . from ear to ear. A macabre smile that split open his neck.

Her screams wouldn't stop. Because Ryan couldn't be in that bag. This couldn't be happening! This couldn't be real!

She slapped her hand over her mouth. The nausea and the fear were rising. Sarah couldn't stop herself.

She vomited. Again and again.

Her father pulled back her hair. "It's all right, sweetheart. I've got you." He pressed a kiss to her temple. "Happy birthday."

Sarah jerked away from him. She grabbed the bag. "Ryan? Ryan!" He . . . fell out.

Tears rolled down her cheeks. "He's just a boy, Daddy." A boy who'd said something mean. Ryan was just a boy, and . . .

Sarah looked up at her father.

He was smiling at her.

Ryan was a boy, a dead boy, and her father was a monster.

A monster.

"No!" Sarah jerked up in bed, sweat covering her, her heart racing too fast in her chest. Her fingers had a death grip on the covers and—

She wasn't alone.

It was dark in the room, but she heard the squeak of wood. He was there, coming from the bathroom, coming toward her.

"Bad dream?" Jax asked as he slid into the bed and pulled her close to him. He had to feel the frantic thud of her heartbeat. That beat seemed to be shaking her whole body.

"N-Not a dream," she managed to say. Her eyes squeezed closed, but she could still see Ryan Klein's face. She'd never been able to forget that sight. "I wish it had been." Because dreams couldn't hurt you. Reality could.

He pressed a kiss to her temple. Sarah flinched. "No, don't!" She tried to jerk away from him because . . . her dad had kissed her temple. After she'd found Ryan, he'd kissed her temple and thought that she'd understand why he'd killed the boy. Her father had thought that she'd be just like him.

"Sarah." Jax said her name so softly. "Look at me, Sarah."

She forced her eyes to open. He'd turned on the bedside lamp, and a warm pool of light spilled onto the bed.

"I'm here. Not anyone from your past. Me."

He didn't get it. Sometimes, she felt like her past was always with her, no matter where she went or what she did. Like a chain, dragging her back to hell.

"The past doesn't matter."

She shook her head. They both knew that was a lie. "You want LOST to find your family. They matter, Jax. Where we come from, where we've been, it always matters." She looked into his eyes, knowing that he had to understand that truth.

"Do you think your past matters, even a little bit, to me?"

He sounded as if he meant those words. But he didn't know all that she'd done. Not many did.

"What do you want from me?" Sarah asked him as she shook her head. Their attraction had been instant and undeniable. The sex between them was hot enough to incinerate but . . . what was Jax looking for? Why was he risking his life, protecting her? "Tell me," she said, the words torn from her. "Tell me what you want from me."

"Don't you know it yet? I want everything."

She shook her head. "I don't have very much to give." He should know that. The physical connection they had—that was more than she'd given to men in the past. She'd hooked up, but always slipped away before dawn. Always slipped away . . .

Just as she'd tried to do with Jax.

Only she was back in his bed, when she'd never returned to the others.

"Sarah . . ." When he said her name that way, it

sounded like a caress. "I always get what I want. You should know that."

And she thought about the bar he owned, all of the businesses. The fortune he'd amassed. He'd pulled himself from nothing . . .

I want everything.

But why did he want it with her?

"You've never even asked me . . . about him." Others had. They'd asked with a sick curiosity. With disgust. With pity. With fear in their eyes. Different emotions, but they'd always asked.

She felt him shrug against her. "If you want me to know, you'll tell me."

Her breath came out on a ragged gasp. So simple. So . . . "I wish I didn't know."

The back of his knuckles slid over her arm. "Why? Do you think it makes any difference to me? You aren't your father."

"But that's why *he's* after me." The man who'd taken Molly. The devil in the darkness. "To punish me for my father's sins."

"No, Sarah." His knuckles slid over her skin once more in an oddly soothing caress. "He just wants to punish your father."

"I want to punish him, too." Those words tumbled out. "I wish, so many times, that I'd been strong enough to stop him."

"Sarah?"

"Eight months," she said, shuddering. "I knew what he was for eight months, and I didn't stop him."

"You were a child—"

"I'm a liar."

He stiffened.

"I first heard the screams when I was six. I let him tell me to just go back to sleep. I listened to him. There were other signs . . . other nights when I'd wake up. Things he'd say and do, but I ignored them . . . he was my father, and he loved me."

No, he didn't. He just acted as if he did. He's a psychopath. Psychopaths don't love. They mimic. She'd learned all she could about her father's condition when she'd been in school. Her father had driven her to become a profiler because by that point . . .

I already thought like a killer. So why not try to learn more and catch the other killers out there?

"I lied to myself for years. I believed my own lies as easily as I believed his." And her father had been such a genius when it came to lying. On the surface, he'd been charming. Everyone had loved him. That was why—when the truth came out—all the neighbors had been so shocked.

He was such a good man. Always willing to help out with my yard work.

He never bothered anyone. He was a widower. He took such good care of his little girl.

He never caused trouble with anyone. Quiet, courteous . . .

Lies.

"There was this boy at school . . . he'd been teasing me, calling me names." She had to swallow to clear the lump in her throat. "I hadn't even told my dad about him, but I learned—later—that one of my teachers had called Dad. She was worried about me being bullied and she was trying to follow up at home." She bit her lip. She bit it to stop the tremble.

"Stop, Sarah."

He tapped her lip.

She realized that she'd nearly drawn blood.

Sarah's tongue swiped over the lip, soothing the pain.

"I was having a sweet sixteen slumber party. My friends were coming over when I found the—the bag downstairs."

He'd gone still. As still as stone.

"Ryan was in that bag. My dad had . . . sliced his throat. From ear to ear. Ryan's blood had soaked through the bag, and my dad was there . . . *telling me happy birthday.*"

Jax swore and pulled her into his arms. He held her there, right against his heart, with a hold that was so tight and warm.

"My dad said he did it for me. To protect me." She shook her head. Jax's hold tightened on her. "I never wanted that. I never wanted him to kill *anyone.* Not for me."

"I know."

Did he? She'd seen suspicion on so many faces.

"He'd trained me to kill, for years, and I didn't realize it. I was thirteen and he was showing me people in malls . . . people who weren't paying attention to what was happening around them. People who would make easy marks. I didn't know he meant people who could be his victims!"

"What did you do?"

Sarah pulled back to stare up at him.

"When did you cut your wrist, Sarah?"

She blinked. "That night. On my birthday. I—I canceled my party. Told my friends that I was sick. And when I was alone . . . when he left to get rid of the body . . . I sliced my wrist."

"Christ." His hold was almost painful then.

"I was bleeding out on the floor. I thought I was dead, and then he came back." She'd never told anyone this part. Not the shrink she'd seen, not the cops. "He was crying when he found me. My dad told me that he couldn't live without me . . . that he needed me to keep going." He'd wrapped up her hand. He'd rushed her to the hospital. Then he'd fed the nurses a lie about her being despondent because her boyfriend had broken up with her.

The boyfriend? Ryan Klein. A guy who'd seemingly deserted everyone and left town.

"He watched me after that, so carefully. He would stare at me as if he couldn't figure me out. I think he expected me to be just like him. I wasn't though, so he kept trying to turn me into a hunter, just like he was."

"Sarah, you don't have to tell me this."

Maybe he didn't want to hear it. She pulled away, her body curving a bit as her shoulders hunched.

"Stop."

She looked up at him.

"You're hurting when you talk about him. Do you think I can't tell?" His jaw was clenched so tightly as he gritted out those words. "I wish I could take all of this pain away for you. I wish I could have stopped him."

"I did." Her chin lifted. "I'm the one . . . I finally stopped him." The night was burned in her mind. "He'd taken a woman from the city—a lady who worked at the bakery. I'd seen her dozens of times, and he had his knife to her throat. He was telling me that I had to watch. That I had to see what she'd do . . . what she'd say. That in the end, they all confessed and they all begged . . ."

She wanted to stop the words, but now that she'd started talking, it seemed like a dam had burst and she couldn't hold them back.

"I found a gun in my dad's closet. He liked to use his knives when he was . . . working . . . on the victims. Said it was more personal." In college, she'd learned that others thought just as her father did. A knife was intimate. *You got close to your victim with the knife. It sliced into the skin, cutting deep into flesh. Carving—one life, taken.* "But he had the gun . . . just in case. Just in case some burglar ever broke in, so we'd be safe."

She stopped a minute, lost by the insanity of that. Her dad had kept a gun because he wanted to keep them safe from burglars. *Who would keep us safe from you, Dad?*

"I took that gun. When he was down in that basement, making her scream, I took the gun."

She could see that scene so clearly in her mind. She'd gripped the gun in her hand. Her palm had been slick with sweat. She'd inched down the stairs, one at a time. The wood had creaked beneath her feet, but her father hadn't heard her approach. The screams had been too loud.

She'd reached the bottom. Crept right up behind him.

Daddy, stop.

"He thought I'd come to watch. To help. But I put the gun to his head. He laughed at first and said it wasn't even loaded." Every breath felt painful. "But I'd found the bullets. I told him that if he didn't let her go, I'd shoot him."

Jax was staring into her eyes.

"I meant it."

"I know." His voice was soft, gentle. There was no horror in his eyes, no pity. Just a blue stare that held her own.

"She ran out . . . I knew that she'd call the cops and I didn't move. I kept that gun to my father's head. If he'd tried to attack me, I would have pulled the trigger." Goose bumps had risen on her arms as she told him the story. "When the cops finally arrived and they took him away, do you know what he said to me?"

Jax shook his head.

Right, of course, he didn't know. Stupid question. No one knew . . . no one but her and the cop who'd been holding her father. "He said he was proud of me. That I had his killer instinct, just like he'd always wanted."

There it was. Her shame. Her horror.

Her life.

And now he knew everything.

Chapter 11

"DETECTIVE WEST?"

Brent tensed when he heard his name and he turned away from the window. Not that he'd had much of a view—the hospital's waiting room window overlooked the place's parking garage.

A young nurse, one with short, curly brown hair and dark eyes, waited a few feet away.

"The doctor wanted me to tell you that Ms. Guthrie has stabilized some. She may even be able to answer a few brief questions. Very brief," she emphasized.

Relief had him rushing across the room. "Can I see her now?"

He was aware of Gabe Spencer rising behind him. Gabe and the blond looker had been in that waiting room for most of the night. He'd heard Gabe on his phone, calling in favors left and right—and Brent knew just how important that kind of power was. When a guy could get the Feds to jump and do your bidding, then that was a man with some serious pull.

He's a man that I want on my side.

"Now," the nurse agreed, with a nod, "but only for a

few moments. And she can't be stressed. Her body has been through a terrible trauma."

Her body and her mind. And when the poor girl found out that her only remaining family member was dead, the pain would be even worse for her.

Brent turned toward Gabe. "You want in?"

"Hell, yes." Gabe pressed a quick kiss to the blonde's cheek. "Let the others know," he said to her.

She nodded, and Gabe hurried toward Brent.

Brent had done his research on the other man. He knew just what had happened to Gabe's sister, and it was some seriously messed-up shit. On paper, the guy was a tough-as-nails ex-SEAL. And in person, well, the man knew how to get the job done.

"This is my show," Brent warned him before they entered Molly's room. "I ask the questions because this is the NOPD's case."

Gabe lifted a brow. "A case we've sure as hell assisted on."

"And that's why you're here now." But he didn't want the guy stepping on his toes when he went inside that little room.

"Lead the way," Gabe murmured.

Squaring his shoulders, Brent entered the room. When he saw Molly Guthrie, he felt a fist punch into his chest. The woman looked so delicate, so damn breakable, as she lay against the stark white sheets. She had bruises on her face and arms. Her lip was busted. But that was nothing . . . nothing compared to all the bandages that covered her. The perp had sliced her, again and again.

"He tried to break her," Gabe said, his low voice carrying only to Brent. "But it didn't work. She made it out. She got away from him."

The machines around Molly were beeping in a steady chorus of sound. A doctor stood to the left of her bed. He was checking her chart and when Brent approached, the guy tensed.

"The patient shouldn't be stressed right now," the doctor began. "I need you to know—"

Brent lifted his hand. "Right, I got the spiel from the nurse." A nurse who'd followed him in. "Doc, the last thing I want to do is hurt this lady, I promise you that. I want to find the man who did this to her, and I want to throw him in jail for the rest of his life." *So he can't ever hurt anyone else like this again.*

He touched Molly's hand. She flinched and her eyes opened. Fear was in her stare. Such deep, consuming fear.

"Easy, Molly," the doctor said. "You don't need to be afraid. This gentleman is a police officer. He wants to help you."

The fear didn't ease in her eyes. If anything, it got worse.

"Hi, Molly," Brent said, working to keep his voice gentle. A tough job because he knew that, most days, his voice sounded like a growling bear. "I just need to ask you a few questions, okay?"

She stared back at him. Such big, beautiful eyes. Eyes that showed her terror.

He tried to smile for her. She seemed to relax a little. That was good.

"Where's my . . . my br-brother?" Her voice was a soft rasp of sound.

Brent tensed at her question. The last thing he wanted to do was tell her that her brother was dead. When she found out, he knew she'd shut down. A guy didn't have to be a shrink to figure that out.

"Can you tell me about the man who took you?" Brent asked her. "Molly, did you see his face?"

She gave a slow nod.

"Describe him . . . please."

"B-Big . . . like you. Wide sh-shoulders. Tall." Her brow crinkled. "He h-had . . . bl-blond hair . . ."

"Caucasian?"

She nodded.

"What color were his eyes, Molly?" He kept saying her name. He'd been told that was a tactic to create intimacy with a witness. He didn't know if the technique was working or not, but he was more than willing to try anything right then.

"Bl-Blue . . ."

"Was there anything about the man that stuck out for you, Molly? Any scars or marks on his face?"

Slowly, she shook her head.

"Molly—"

"I want . . . my brother. H-He said . . . the man said that Eddie had . . . had sent him to get me. To pick me up." A fat tear drop rolled down her cheek. "I—I went with him . . . he knew about Mom . . ."

The machines were beeping louder now, and the doc was frowning at him. Brent figured this counted as getting the patient agitated.

Molly tried to sit up, but she winced, and he saw the flash of pain on her face.

"No, Molly," the doctor ordered as he put his hands on her shoulders. "You've got too many stitches. You have to remain stationary—"

"I want . . . my br-brother . . ."

"Family should be notified," the nurse snapped. She glared at Brent as if saying . . . *Why the hell didn't you bring in her brother first?*

Brent squared his shoulders. "I'm sorry, but your brother . . ." Oh, hell. More tears were falling from her eyes. "Your brother is dead."

He'd never seen a person break before. But as he stared into Molly's eyes, he saw it happen. She just seemed to splinter right in front of him. Her face became even paler and her lips moved, but she couldn't get a sound out. She tried to talk, again, and a low, keening cry escaped from her.

Then she jerked up in bed, fighting the doctor, and trying to reach for Brent. "No! Not Eddie!" Her hands grabbed hold of him and she held tightly to Brent. "N-Not—ah!" Her face contorted in pain.

He looked down. A circle of red had appeared on her white hospital gown.

"I said not to upset the patient!" The doctor rushed over and shoved Brent back. "Leave, now!"

She was bleeding again. Crying out. Her pain seemed to cut right into Brent.

The nurse grabbed his arm and hauled him to the door.

"H-His name . . ."

He jerked away from the nurse. Molly was trying to tell him something. "What, Molly? What is it?"

"H-His name . . ." Molly rasped. The doctor was opening her gown. *So much blood.* "His n-name was J-Jax . . . Jax Fontaine . . . that's what he . . ."

The machines beeped even louder.

The nurse pushed him and Gabe all the way out of ICU.

He stood there, his hands clenched, fury twisting in him.

Jax Fontaine.

SARAH HAD BARED her soul to him. Told him things that he was sure she'd never revealed to anyone else. Now she was trembling in his arms, and all he wanted to do was take her pain away.

"Do you want to run away now?" Sarah asked him.

His fingers curled under her chin, and he made her look up at him. "I'm not the running type." He never had been. "And nothing you could say would scare me off."

Her gaze searched his. "Why? Why do you want to be with me? I'm sure there are plenty of women who'd jump at the chance to be with you."

"Plenty," he agreed as his lips twitched.

"I know you've got money, Jax. Money and power mean a lot, in this town and in so many others. So I need you to answer my question. I need to know . . . why me? Is it because you want the thrill of fucking a killer's daughter? Because I've been down that road and—"

"I can kick his ass." He could and would. "Give me a name and it's done." Some prick had used Sarah that way? He would *destroy* the guy. He would—

"Jax . . ."

He liked it when she said his name. He liked it even more when she screamed it. Or when she moaned it.

"I don't give a shit about your father." Actually, he did. Jax hated that the man had hurt Sarah so much. And he was glad the guy was far away from Sarah so that he couldn't do any more damage to her. "I'm fucking you because I look at you and I want." Simple fact. "I want you naked. I want *in* you. I want you so much that I know my control won't hold long, not when you're around. Because the desire I feel for you is too raw, too strong." Too unlike anything he'd ever felt, and, yeah, he had plenty of opportunities to hook up with others. But those other women . . . they weren't Sarah.

There was only one Sarah.

"When you look at me . . ." Now it was his turn to bare his soul. He figured it was only fair. "What do you see?"

"Strength." Her response was immediate.

"That's what I see when I look at you."

She blinked at him.

"Others . . . when they look at me, they see a criminal." She needed to hear this. "Make no mistake, Sarah, I haven't lived an easy life. I've broken laws. Done things that I regret." And things that he'd never regret. "When it's do-or-die, we all have to fight, and I'm a fighter to my core."

"I know."

Yes, she did.

"I try to follow a few rules. I never hurt a woman, no matter what the hell she's done." Because of the woman who'd raised him. Because she had loved him, and he'd loved her. He'd wanted to protect her, but that bastard who'd taken him . . . that bastard had hurt her again and again.

Until I got big enough to stop him. I wasn't going to let anyone hurt her ever again.

He brushed his knuckles over Sarah's cheeks. He felt the faint wetness of her tears. "I don't hurt innocents." He never went after the weak. When he ran his business, the people he was involved with knew the score. Always.

"The world isn't black and white." Oh, hell, no, it wasn't. "I've been operating in the gray for a long time." Until Sarah. Until she'd made him want to step out and into the light again. "I wish I could be different." He looked down at all of the tats on his hands and thought of the battles he'd faced. "But you can't change the past."

If they'd come to find me . . . if my parents had looked . . .

If anyone had looked for me . . .

But he'd always known that his real family hadn't cared. No one had ever bothered to search for him.

"You're not the only one with nightmares, pretty Sarah." He still dreamed of being trapped in that closet. Being a lost, scared kid. Calling out for his mother. Only she'd never come for him.

Then, later, the dreams had changed. He'd been a

teenager. The bastard who took him . . . he'd come swinging at Jax when he stepped in front of Charlene. Jax had swung back. He'd hit him so hard and the man had slipped, falling down those stairs . . . falling . . . falling . . .

How do I tell her that I killed a man when I was fifteen? No one knew. Charlene had helped him. They'd covered up the past.

Another secret to stay buried.

But maybe, maybe Sarah could handle—

His phone rang. Jax swore. Someone had serious shit for timing.

"It could be the hospital," Sarah said. "Gabe knew I was coming with you . . ."

He rose from the bed. He had on a pair of jogging sweats and he stalked toward the ringing phone. Jax glanced down at the screen and saw Brent West's number flash on the screen. He answered, saying, "Is Molly all right?"

"She's up and she's talking." West's voice was hushed. "Get your lawyer man, get him *fast*."

"What? Why?"

"Because I'm outside your place." Again, his words were low, as if he didn't want others to overhear him. "Molly named you. She said *you* took her."

What the hell?

"I have to bring you in," Brent said. "Procedure, shit—the captain is chomping at the bit on this one, so I have to bring you in," he told him again.

Jax strode to his window. He saw Brent's car outside, but Brent wasn't alone. A cruiser was pulling up, and was that—yes, the man standing under the street light looked like Gabe Spencer.

"Call the lawyer, then come out." Brent hung up.

Jax stared down at the phone. He quickly deleted that call from his phone list, not wanting to have that record in case anyone searched his phone.

"Jax? What is it?"

Sarah rose from the bed. She wrapped the sheet around her and it trailed over the hardwood floor as she came toward him. "Is Molly awake?"

"Yes." He kept his gaze on the swirl of blue lights.

Sarah gasped and he knew she'd seen the lights, too.

"I didn't do it, Sarah."

"Jax?"

"I didn't have anything to do with her disappearance." Now he turned toward her. "I wouldn't try to hurt you."

"I know that."

He nodded. "Good. Remember that, would you?" He grabbed for his clothes. And dressed as quickly as he could because he'd be damned if the cops hauled him out of his house half naked.

Sarah grabbed his arm. "What's happening?"

"Molly's awake, and, according to a tip I just got, she's saying that I'm the man who took her."

Her hand jerked away from him, as if she'd been burned. "That's not possible."

He pointed to the window and the swirl of blue lights. "They're here to take me in." He dialed his lawyer. The guy was on retainer, so it was no big surprise that—even in the middle of the night—Ty answered on the second ring. "Meet me at the station," Jax ordered him.

Ty swore. "What is it now?"

"If I had to guess, then I'd say the charges will be kidnapping and attempted murder." Those would just be the start.

"Holy shit . . ."

Exactly.

He heard rustling and turned to see Sarah yanking on her clothes. She was moving so fast.

And someone was pushing on the call button near his main gate. The buzzing sound echoed through the house.

"Hurry to that station," Jax told his lawyer. He shoved the phone in his pocket. Then he crossed the room to stand in front of Sarah. "I didn't do this."

"I know." Her chin lifted. "I know you didn't."

Good. Because plenty of people had doubted him over the years and if Sarah had, too . . .

He kissed her. Not wild and hard. Soft. Gentle.

She tasted so damn sweet.

But he had to pull away from her. Had to walk down those stairs and to the door. He was aware of Sarah following silently behind him. He didn't look back at her. Right then, he couldn't. Jax sucked in a deep breath before he turned off his alarm. He had to get his game face on. The face he wore with everyone but Sarah.

Then he reached for the door. He walked across the courtyard and straight toward his gate. He deactivated the security there, too. When he yanked the gate open, Jax was smiling. He looked at Detective West. At that dick Cross who was rushing to join the little party. At the uniformed cops.

"Well, well, little late for a chat, isn't it?" Jax asked.

Brent stepped forward. "You need to come with us."

"Am I under arrest?" Because he needed to be clear on that.

Brent gave a short, negative shake of his head. But it was Cross who spoke. "You're wanted for questioning, Fontaine." And he had his cuffs at the ready.

Jax felt his smile turn into a snarl. If that guy actually thought he'd cuff him . . . right on Jax's own property . . .

"He didn't do it," Sarah said from behind him. "Jax had nothing to do with Molly Guthrie's abduction."

"And how would you know about that?" Cross demanded. "Did he tell you that we were coming to arrest him—"

"I have my own intel. I know exactly what's going on."

Her voice was so cool and in control. It was hard to believe that she was the woman who'd been so vulnerable in his arms just moments before.

"Jax has been with me . . . he *was* with me. The night that Molly vanished, he and I were in bed together."

Gabe had approached, and Jax knew the guy had been close enough to overhear her confession.

"He didn't take Molly. You've got the wrong man."

Brent looked from Jax to Sarah. "We have to follow procedure," he said.

Of course, procedure was always so big with the cops.

"You'd better call a lawyer," Cross growled.

Jax smiled. "He'll show up." But before he left with them, Jax glanced back at Sarah. "Don't worry. I'll be seeing you again soon."

"You didn't do it!"

She was so convinced of his innocence. That was touching. But surely even Sarah realized that if he'd wanted to take someone—even when Sarah was curled up in bed with him—all he had to do was make a phone call.

He knew the cops realized that fact, and, based on the assessing stare in Gabe's eyes, that guy knew it, too.

He wondered . . . had the cops found out that he'd owned that building that had exploded, the little place a few minutes from Bourbon Street? He knew the fire marshal was still supposed to be studying those charred remains. Maybe the cops had finally untangled the paper trail for that building and tied it back to Jax.

"I'll prove your innocence, Jax," she said. "They won't pin this on you."

He nodded. No, they wouldn't, but it was nice to know that she was ready to protect him. "See you soon, Sarah." Then his gaze cut back to Gabe. He stalked toward the other man, moving right by the cops. "He's out there," he told Gabe. "Waiting. Watch your team." *Watch Sarah.* Jax had already given orders that his men were to keep a watch on her. But he wanted to be there, making absolutely certain she was all right. As soon as he ditched the cops . . .

I'll come back for you, Sarah.

HE WATCHED FROM across the street as Jax Fontaine was led away by the cops.

Step one . . . divide.

Step two . . . fucking conquer.

He smiled as Sarah stared after the disappearing car lights. Poor Sarah. She looked so upset. Having her lover ripped from her in the middle of the night must have been painful.

It would be *nothing* compared to the hell that he had coming her way.

Sarah and the other guy, Gabe, they got in his vehicle. Cranked it up. He waited a little bit and then he slid into his car and followed them. In the darkness, they didn't even see him. So much for being the savvy LOST agents.

How would they react when one of their own vanished and was never seen again?

"THIS IS BULLSHIT," Sarah said flatly. "Jax didn't do this. He was with me. He was—"

"The guy has a mini army at his beck and call. If he wanted one of his men to take that woman, all he had to do was snap his fingers."

No, Gabe hadn't just said that to her. She twisted in her seat so that she could better glare at him. "He wouldn't do that." Jax had rules. He had—

"You don't know him, Sarah. I get that you're having sex with him, and that's your business, but this guy . . . have you seen his juvie rap sheet? I mean, come on, he wasn't exactly playing light and easy back in those days."

She wasn't at all surprised he'd gotten access to files that *should* have been sealed. "If you were a teenager cast out on the street, I'm sure you'd break the law in order to survive, too." But Gabe hadn't been like Jax.

Gabe had been given a family that loved him. He'd been protected. He'd had a home. Food. Clothing. He'd had—

"She ID'd him, Sarah. I was there. I heard her—she described him and she said his name. I would think the woman would remember the identity of the guy who tried to kill her."

"You'd be surprised," she said as her stomach twisted in knots. "The mind can trick anyone." And so could a smart killer. "I need to talk with her."

"Yes, well that's probably not going to happen right now. She got a little . . . agitated during Detective West's questioning. She reopened her wounds, and the doctor kicked him out."

Her hands fisted in her lap. "You should have contacted me the minute she woke up. I could have helped. I could have—"

"You're the one always telling me that you're better at profiling the killers, and not at figuring out the victims."

She flinched.

"You'd barely crawled out of the fire yourself. I just wanted you to rest," he continued, his voice softer. "I sure as hell didn't realize she'd be pointing the finger at your boyfriend."

"He's not my boyfriend." The words were automatic. They were also true. He was nothing as simple as a boyfriend. A hot and intense lover. A man who broke through her defenses. A man who'd learned her secrets . . . "And he didn't do this."

"I wish I could be as certain as you are, but Sarah,

come on, you can look into that guy's eyes and see the truth."

His words made fury twist within her. "What truth is that?"

"He's got the killer instinct," Gabe said with certainty. "I saw that instinct in the eyes of SEALs. They would do whatever necessary to get the job done. No fear. No hesitation. He looks the same way, and a man like that can be very, very dangerous."

He's not a threat to me.

"Why do you trust him so much? Make me understand."

She turned her left hand over so that she could see her wrist. "He's not afraid of my darkness."

"Okay, I don't even know that the hell that means."

He was driving fast and hard down the road. And . . .

Sarah could have sworn that she heard another engine growling. One that was very close. She turned her head and looked behind them. She didn't see anyone. They'd turned onto an older road, one that was so dark. No street lights.

That growling sound came again.

"Gabe . . ." She began.

"I hear it," he snapped back. "Hold on."

He shoved down the gas and they lurched forward. There were lights up ahead, she could see them. If they got there, then whoever was hiding behind them would be revealed. *Someone is driving back there, with the headlights off so we can't see him.*

Tricky bastard.

"Maybe it's just Jax's men," Sarah offered. Keeping an eye on them. Like before—

"No, I don't think so."

She didn't really think so, either. Jax wouldn't want his men to scare her.

Gabe had rolled down his window a bit. The better to hear the growl of the other engine? "Sounds like a Mustang and he's—"

Gunfire exploded. It pounded into the back of Gabe's car. She could hear the sound of breaking glass even as Gabe yelled, "Get down!"

She ducked, getting as low as she could in the car even as they raced forward. That bastard back there was shooting at them? *What the hell?*

Then she heard the thunder of gunfire again. It was slamming into the back bumper. Driving through the chunks of glass that remained. Gabe grunted, the sound quick and pain-filled.

He's been hit!

"Gabe?"

"Gun . . . in glove box . . ."

She fumbled, trying to get to that glove box even as—

They crashed.

WHEN THEIR VEHICLE slammed into the pole, he braked his car. He was smiling as he exited and kept his gun at the ready. Had his bullets hit one of the targets? If not, he'd be sure to eliminate Gabe Spencer first. Then he'd have some nice, quality time with Sarah—

"*Get back!*" That was Sarah's yell, and he froze because Sarah didn't sound afraid. She sounded furious. "You're not the only one with a weapon!"

Sirens screamed in the distance. Someone had heard

the shots or the crash, and some damn fool good Samaritan had called 911.

"*Sarah . . .*" He called out her name. He wanted her to know—this was all about her. "Did my bullet hit your friend?" Because he could just see the guy's slumped figure in the front of the car. "That's on you, Sarah!" But he took a step back into the darkness. "Anyone between us . . . I'll take them out. You're going to be mine. You're—"

That bitch shot at him. And she *hit* him. The bullet burned across his upper arm and he jerked back.

Then she was running around the car. Coming at him. And the scream of that siren was just getting louder and louder. He jumped back into his car. Revved the engine.

Fucking bitch.

He'd be seeing her again.

HE ROARED AWAY. Sarah's finger was squeezing the trigger but he was weaving, going so fast, and she couldn't aim at him.

Dammit!

He'd shot Gabe. He was hurting everyone . . . because the guy wanted to get to her. "I'm right here!" Sarah yelled after him.

But the shriek of the sirens was the only response she got.

Sarah whirled around and ran back to the car. She yanked opened Gabe's door. When she touched his shoulder, she felt the wet warmth of his blood.

"Eve . . . is gonna freak," Gabe managed.

Her breath heaved out. *He's okay!* If he was talking about his Eve, he had to be all right.

She unhooked his seat belt and Sarah hissed out a breath because she could see his wound now. Blood was pumping from his shoulder.

"In . . . and out . . ." He shifted his body, trying to get out of the car. She pushed him right back inside. "Just . . . lost control when it . . . hit me . . ."

"Stay in there until the cops can help us!" She didn't want to risk that guy coming back. He'd just been . . . shooting at them. Right in the middle of the street. He'd followed them when they left Jax's house. That was the only explanation but that would mean . . .

He was out there the whole time. Waiting for us. Waiting for his chance to get at me. When the cops had taken Jax, he'd seen his moment to attack.

And he had.

A police cruiser rushed down the road. Sarah looked down and realized that she still had her gun. Oh, such a bad move. The last thing she wanted was to appear armed in front of the cops. She knew how that scene would go down. She put the gun on the cement, raised her hands, and yelled, "We need help!"

Two uniformed cops jumped from the vehicle.

"He's been shot! Hurry, you need to help him!" One of the cops ran forward. "There's a man who was in a—a Mustang." Gabe knew his cars. The guy had been able to identify the ride just by the growl of its engine—how wild was that? Sarah rushed to add. "He was just here! Put out an APB. You have to find him. You can—"

"Gun!" the closest cop yelled.

Sarah tensed. "I put the gun down when you arrived. He was *shooting* at us. I had to stop him from killing Gabe!" They had to listen to her. "The man who did this—he just left! Get the APB out now. We can find him!"

But they weren't grabbing for their radios. They were closing in slowly. And the man so determined to kill her—he'd just gotten away.

Again.

Chapter 12

SARAH RODE IN THE AMBULANCE WITH GABE. THE EMTs had cut his shirt away, and she could see that he'd been right. The bullet had gone in and out. It had blasted through the back of his seat, into his shoulder, then exploded into the front of the car.

The man who'd done that . . . a guy who had a thorough knowledge of explosives and was skilled enough to fire from a moving vehicle like that . . .

Military training. This guy isn't some amateur. He's deadly. He's honed his skills and he's done this before.

This wasn't some tentative killer. A guy out for revenge who was testing the waters. No, this was a guy with balls of steel who didn't hesitate to blow up buildings or shoot at his prey in the middle of a public street. He was unpredictable, and that just made him all the more dangerous.

The ambulance braked at the ER, and the back doors flew open. As Gabe was wheeled out, Sarah caught a flash of Eve's face. Eve ran toward the ambulance and grabbed Gabe's hand. His fingers curled tightly around hers, and then they vanished after passing through the automatic sliding doors.

Sarah jumped out of the ambulance. She'd told her story to the cops at the scene, but she knew there would be more questions. A uniform had followed the ambulance. She could already see the guy heading toward her.

Sarah braced her shoulders. He'd finally put out an APB, but Sarah doubted they'd find the man who did this. Not until he wanted to be found.

Not until he comes for me again.

And who would be in his way the next time? Who would he take down in order to get to her?

HE DROVE THE Mustang into the old building and killed the engine as fast as he could. His arm hurt, but the bullet had just grazed him. Sarah wasn't as good as he was with a gun.

He heard muffled cries as he approached the back of that building. "Shut the hell up," he muttered.

But the cries continued. Growling, he kicked open the door and saw the man. Tied to the chair. Eyes wild and angry. The guy was muttering behind his gag. Really pissing him off.

He stalked forward and yanked that gag out of the way.

"You can't do this!" the man yelled. "You can't—"

He shot him, right in the shoulder. The bound man howled.

He cocked his head and studied the wound critically. "Do you think she'll remember exactly where she hit me?"

"You fuckin—"

He put the gun to the guy's head. That stopped his screams.

"No, I don't think she will, either."

Then he laughed. Because he had such grand fucking plans.

INTERROGATION ROOMS SUCKED.

Jax tapped his fingers on the table. Cross was on the opposite side of the table, staring intently at him, but not saying a word. Jax figured that was supposed to be some kind of intimidation bullshit, but it was really just annoying.

If the guy wanted to waste time, that was his deal. But Jax had somewhere he needed to be.

With Sarah.

The door burst open. "Don't say a word!" Ty told him as he rushed in. The guy's face was flushed, his blond hair tousled, and he was huffing and puffing. "My client has nothing to say and unless you're arresting him—"

"He was ID'd by the victim. You'd think he would have plenty to say about that," Cross drawled.

Jax didn't move.

"ID'd?" Ty jumped on that. "There was a lineup? Why wasn't I informed? You can't do that without—"

"No lineup," Cross gritted out as his cheeks flushed. "She said his name. She described him. That's what we call a slam dunk."

Ty dropped his suitcase on the table. "That's what I call a confused, injured victim. A woman who isn't remembering straight." He nodded his head. "When she's out of the hospital, let's see if she still tells the same story, shall we?"

Cross glared. "Jax here won't give us an alibi, but his

girlfriend sure was accommodating. She was trying to say the two of you were screwing at the time of poor Molly's disappearance, right?" He leaned forward. "Is that what went down? You were screwing the sexy shrink when—"

"Don't," Jax warned him. It would be so easy to jump across the table at that guy.

But he was supposed to be playing it cool. Cross was trying to push his buttons. He got that. The guy would love to slap him with an assault charge so that he could hold Jax longer—until the cop found some additional evidence he could use against Jax.

"Don't what?" Cross taunted. "Don't ask if you were fucking her then? Because that's what *she* said. I mean, hell, you've worked some number on her. If she's willing to lie for you this way . . ."

Jax's muscles were tight. His body stiff.

"Or maybe . . . maybe what they say about her *is* true. 'Cause I did some research on her. Some folks think she's as screwed in the head as her old man. *That's* how she understands the killers. She is one of 'em. And she probably wants to screw you because . . . it's like to like, right, man? One sick, twisted freak to—"

Jax jumped to his feet, his fists ready to swing.

"No!" Ty screamed.

And the door flew open again. Brent was there. Like Ty, he seemed to be a little out of breath, as if he'd been running. His gaze immediately found Jax's. "She's okay."

What?

"Get that in your head first, okay? Sarah is all right."

Jax shoved the table out of his way.

"This isn't good," Ty muttered.

Jax stalked toward Brent. "What are you talking about?"

"There was an . . . incident."

Jax shook his head.

"She's all right," Brent rushed to say again. "But . . . some guy in a Mustang followed Sarah. He shot at her and Gabe, and they—they crashed."

He could feel all the blood draining from his head. Sarah had been in danger, and he'd just been sitting in that damn room with Cross.

"There was a gun in the car. Sarah fired back and the guy got the hell out of there. Cops are searching for him now."

Fury was making his blood boil in his veins. "He's dead." The bastard wasn't going to do this to Sarah. He wasn't going to terrorize her any longer. Wasn't going to attack her again and again. "*Dead*."

"You can't take the law into your own hands," Brent said, his face showing his worry.

"Watch me." Jax looked back at his lawyer. "Can they hold me any longer?"

Ty's mouth had dropped open. He quickly snapped it closed. "The ID . . . that's not admissible. Most of the people in this town know *of* my client. She can't just say his name like it's gold. I want the victim to actually pick his photo out of a lineup. Because I'm saying she can't do it."

Cross and Brent shared a long look.

"You know where to find me," Jax muttered. He'd

played their bullshit game. Gone into the station like a good freaking citizen. And how had that worked out?

Sarah could have been killed.

"If you don't have anything to hide . . ." Cross said, giving him a sly smile. "Then how about letting us search your homes? Your businesses?"

Was the guy serious? Jax looked at Cross and gave him a smile, too. A go-to-hell grin. "When you've got a warrant, you come try that shit. Otherwise . . ." He rolled back his shoulders and thought about how much he'd like to slug the guy. "I'll be seeing you later."

He'd discovered real fast that, no, the cops hadn't realized the first piece of property that the perp had blown up . . . well, that it actually belonged to Jax. They hadn't figured it out, and he sure wasn't going to reveal that information to them. *They'd just say I set the bomb. That I had access to that place.*

Cross's eyes were angry chips of ice.

Jax leaned in close to the guy. "And I won't be forgetting. Not what you said about Sarah and not what I *know* you've done."

He saw the fear flash—just for an instant—in Cross's eyes. That was right. The dick should be afraid of him. "You think a badge is going to keep you safe?"

"Are you threatening me?" Cross sputtered. Then, voice rising, he demanded. "Did you just hear him, Brent? This dumbass threatened a police detective!"

"No!" Ty's instant denial. "My client did no such thing. I was right here. I never heard him threaten you, but I am curious." Ty's head tilted as he studied the cop. "What have you done?"

Jax knew. So did Cross.

"Get the hell out of here while you can," Cross snarled. "Because soon, we'll have enough evidence to nail your ass. If not for this case, then for another. A guy like you only ends up in one place . . ."

"Right." Jax nodded. "On top. See you around, Detectives."

Then he brushed by Brent, making sure not to reveal any other emotion. He was already gripping the bare end of his control. He needed to get to Sarah. Right then. And make sure she was all right.

Ty was silent as they headed out of the station. Jax could feel the stares of the other officers on him. Some would be staring with fear. Some with disdain. What the hell ever.

Ty didn't speak until they were outside and well away from the station. And then he glanced at Jax with a worried shake of his head. "Tell me that I'm right. Tell me that poor woman isn't going to ID you in any kind of lineup."

"She won't. Because the only thing I did was pull her out of the fire." From hero to villain in about sixty seconds flat. That was generally the story of his life.

"You're sure?"

"I didn't do it."

Ty exhaled on a long sigh. "Good, then we'll let the ID situation play out, and in the meantime, could you *try* to stay out of trouble?"

Jax shrugged. "I don't really think that will be happening."

"What? Come on, we're talking about your life!"

"No, we're talking about Sarah's life." And Sarah was the most important thing in *his* life. "Sarah is mine." He started walking away from his lawyer. "The bastard hunting out there doesn't screw with her. No one attacks Sarah and just runs away. *No one.*"

COPS WERE BLOCKING Molly's hospital room door. Sarah stared at that door. She needed to get inside. It was vital that she talk with Molly Guthrie . . . about Jax . . . about the abduction . . . about the freak who was still loose out there.

She'd been sitting in the waiting room of that hospital. Ideas and theories had raced through her head. She'd been slowly building a profile of this perp ever since Molly had first vanished.

With every new detail that she learned, she'd revised her profile a bit. Shaping. Changing. Letting it evolve.

White male. In his thirties or early forties. Strong. Fit. Military background. Personal vendetta. He doesn't see victims, he sees tools. People he can use to accomplish what he wants.

And what he wanted—vengeance.

Not on Sarah. Not exactly. *I'm another tool for him.* He wanted vengeance on Murphy.

The guy couldn't sympathize with any of his prey. He lacked total empathy, a sign of a sociopath or a psychopath. But . . . she thought this man had been functioning in society. She thought he blended well. That he acted just like everyone else around him.

So he exhibits more traits linked with psychopathy . . .

Because he was organized. He was calculated. Sociopaths were disjointed, their attacks more random and out of control.

Not with this guy. He was a planner. Like a chess master. Every move led to another and another and . . .

His endgame.

That endgame seemed to be the destruction of Sarah's life . . . and of her friends? Because when he'd taken Molly, that move had deliberately drawn in the LOST team. At the initial explosion, just blocks from Bourbon Street, Wade had been the first one in the building.

Wade always goes in first. That was left over from his cop days. If anyone had studied Wade, they would have known that . . .

Then when they'd gone to the riverfront, searching for Molly, the bombs had been set in those buildings—buildings that Gabe and Dean had been searching.

And Gabe had been shot just hours before. She'd looked at the back of the car. All of the bullet holes had been concentrated on *his* side of the vehicle.

He's targeting my friends.

"Dr. Jacobs?"

Her head whipped up as Sarah was pulled from her thoughts.

Carlos stood in front of her. "Jax asked me to come and get you."

Get her? "I'm not leaving. I need to talk to Molly in order to *clear* Jax."

"He's not at the police station. His lawyer already took care of things there." Carlos stood with his hands loose at his sides. "He wants you to meet him at Shade.

He's on the way to that bar now." He glanced around when a nurse passed him. "He figured he'd better not show up here, not until the mess with the Guthrie woman is cleared up."

Right. Because he couldn't exactly waltz close to Molly's room without raising some serious suspicion. But she shook her head. "I'm not done here. I can't leave, not until I talk with her."

Carlos's eyes narrowed. "Most people don't refuse Jax."

"And I'm not most people." Her mind was still racing. *Two* LOST agents were in the hospital. She needed to make sure that no one else wound up hurt.

"I think that's why the boss is so interested in you," he murmured.

Right then, Molly's door opened. A young doctor came out, a guy with brown hair and a small pair of glasses perched on his nose. "Doctor!" Sarah hurried toward him. She flashed him her LOST ID, but he just frowned at it. "I need to speak with Molly."

"You're not a cop."

"Uh, no, no, I'm not, but—"

"You're family?"

"She doesn't have any family left."

The cops behind him were shifting nervously.

"Look, if you'd just let me talk to her . . ."

"Let her through, Doc."

She glanced over at that hard voice and saw Detective West marching down the hallway. His badge was clipped to his belt.

"Let her through," he said again. Detective Cross was

right behind him. So was . . . wait, was that other guy Jax's lawyer? Yes, she remembered seeing him before.

"I think she should hear this," Cross said, his face smug.

Sarah's stomach knotted. Whatever he wanted her to hear, it couldn't be good.

JAX PACED INSIDE his bar, rage still filling him. No matter what he did, there were always going to be people who thought he was nothing but a criminal. A thug straight from the streets.

He looked down at his hands. Saw the tats there. Remembered the blood that had covered his knuckles before.

Maybe he should be rotting a jail cell someplace. But he'd tried to make a difference. Tried to change.

Let me out! Daddy! Daddy!

His voice, from so long ago. He'd begged and begged, but he'd never seen his real dad again. He'd given up on Jax.

Jax grabbed the tequila. His fingers were tight around the bottle. Sarah was on her way to him. Sarah . . . Sarah believed in him. She didn't know all his secrets, but she'd still been there, defending him to the cops.

Sarah.

And that bastard is trying to kill Sarah.

He threw the bottle across the bar. It hit the mirror and shattered. No, not on his watch. No one was going to hurt Sarah.

Where the fuck is Carlos? The guy should have been back with Sarah by then. He should have . . .

Jax's phone rang. He grabbed it, but . . . he didn't know the number flashing on the screen. Jax lifted the phone to his ear. "Who the hell is this?"

"I'm the man who's going to slice your Sarah into pieces . . ."

MOLLY GUTHRIE WAS small, bruised and . . . broken. Her eyes were red, bloodshot, and tremors shook her body.

"Look at the pictures," Brent was telling her. "And I want you to point to the man who did this to you."

She was staring at the pictures. Biting her lip. Shaking her head. "H-He isn't there . . ."

Sarah saw Cross tense.

"Take your time," Brent told her softly. "Look and be very sure."

Molly glanced up at him. "I—I told you. It was Jax Fontaine." Her voice was raspy, as if she'd been crying for a very long time and her body seemed to be covered with bandages.

Jax Fontaine's picture was right in front of her. But Molly didn't recognize him.

"How do you know it was Jax? I mean, Mr. Fontaine?" Sarah asked.

Molly frowned and glanced over at her. "I . . . I know your voice."

Swallowing the lump in her throat, Sarah nodded. "Yes, I was the woman on the phone. The one who told you—"

"Not to beg . . . for death," Molly finished, whispering. She shook her head. "I didn't. He wanted me to . . . he kept stabbing me . . . but I didn't."

And Sarah realized that while Molly was battered, she was far from broken.

"Are you saying . . ." Now it was the lawyer that spoke up. Ty Keith. " . . . that you don't recognize the men in any of those pictures?"

"It was Jax! He told me! Jax Fontaine!"

Sarah stepped forward. "That was how you knew. The man who took you *said* his name was Jax Fontaine?"

Molly nodded. "M-My brother . . . that man said he knew my brother. That Eddie had played at his bars. He was supposed to take me home, but . . . but he lied."

"Yes," Sarah said definitely. "He lied." *He lied and told you his name was Jax so that the cops would pick Jax up. So that they'd tie him to the crime.* If Molly had survived . . .

The bastard had already had a backup plan in place. And that plan had been Jax Fontaine.

Why?

She didn't understand—

Sarah's breath caught.

Is he trying to frame Jax, because of me? Because she'd been with Jax? No, she was still missing something. "Can you describe the man who took you?"

"I did! He was big. Over six feet. With broad shoulders. Blond. His eyes were blue!" Molly's eyes were tearing up. "What more do you want? It was *Jax Fontaine*!"

She hated to push the woman. Sarah kept her voice soft and soothing as she asked, "What did his tattoos look like?"

"T-Tattoos?"

The room got very quiet then. The only sound was the beep of the machines to the right of Molly's bed.

"YOU'RE A DEAD man," Jax told him.

Laughter flowed over the line. "Is that so? Am I supposed to be afraid of you?"

"You should be." Something about that guy's voice was still nagging at Jax. *I've heard that voice before . . . I've heard it.*

"I'm not. You're the one who should be afraid. Afraid you'll find pieces of her. And that's going to happen. I'm going to take her away from you. I'll cut into her, slowly, and maybe I'll send you those pieces—"

"*Stay the fuck away from Sarah!*"

Silence, then . . . "Why don't you make me?"

"I will. Tell me where you are, and I'm there right now."

"I know what you've done, Jax Fontaine. You're just as much of a killer as I am. As she is . . ."

"Sarah isn't a killer!" And that was why Jax would handle this. He'd stop the bastard. "Where are you?"

"Do you still scream . . ." that man wanted to know. "Begging at night for a father that just doesn't give a shit? A father who threw you out because he knew what a freak you were?"

His heart turned to ice in his chest. How the hell did that bastard know about his past?

"Your family threw you out because they knew you were no good. Cast you out . . ." Laughter. "That's what you thought, anyway. But guess what I know? I know, I know, I know . . ."

The man's voice was driving him crazy. "Where are you?"

"I know what really happened. I can tell you . . ."

And I can kill you.

"But you have to come alone and you have to come now."

"WHEN YOUR ABDUCTOR tied you up, did you see his hands?" Sarah asked carefully.

A furrow appeared between Molly's eyes. "I did. His hands were tanned, dark . . . like he spent a lot of time outside."

"There wasn't anything unusual about his hands?" Brent pushed.

"No . . . no . . . why?" Tears were bright in Molly's eyes. "Am I saying the wrong thing? I told you who it was! I told you—"

"Jax Fontaine has tattoos on his hands and on his arms. Rather unmistakable tattoos," Ty said, sounding quite pleased. "So I don't possibly see how my client could be the man who so grievously attacked Ms. Guthrie here."

Sarah didn't think Jax was the man they were after, either, and judging by the way Brent West was watching Molly, he didn't seem to think so, either.

"But . . . but he didn't have any tats." Molly rubbed her forehead. "I didn't see any."

"Maybe they were covered with makeup," Cross said quickly. "You can do that. Cover them with makeup or long sleeves. It could still be him!"

Sarah frowned at him. Didn't he see what was happening? The man they were after was trying to set up Jax. But she wasn't going to let him take Jax down.

Sarah's attention turned back to Molly. She was so pale. "It's going to be all right," Sarah said. And as soon as those words came out of her mouth, Sarah winced. They were the words people always said when situations were grim. *It's going to be all right. Things will get better.* Little lies that were supposed to make others feel better.

Molly looked up at Sarah. "My brother's dead."

And my father killed your mother.

Sarah took a step back. She didn't want Molly to make that connection. Not then. The woman had been through too much.

"He wanted me to—to suffer . . . just like my mother."

And her mother *had* suffered.

"I'm sorry," Sarah told her.

"I don't have anything. There's nothing for me . . ." Tears were filling Molly's eyes and spilling down her cheeks.

Sarah wanted to reach out to her—

But Brent was already there. He brushed back Molly's hair. "You've got your whole life ahead of you. You beat that bastard. You got away. You're alive."

Molly stared up at him. "Why do I feel dead?"

"You're not." His face was tender as he stared down at her. "You're a fighter. You've been through hell. You lost your brother, so yes, hell, yes, you need to grieve."

The tears kept sliding down her cheeks.

"But then . . . you'll keep going. One day at a time. One step at a time. You'll live. And you'll see that there are still good things in this world."

"What if he comes after me again?" Molly whispered.

"Then he'll find me standing in his way."

Sarah swallowed and eased from the room. The soft sound of Molly's sobs followed her, tearing into Sarah with every breath that she took.

My father started this. He took Molly's mother. He put the chain of events into motion.

Sarah didn't believe that monsters were born. Not even Murphy. She thought they were made. Actions, environment, shaping and changing an individual until . . .

Either the good within triumphed.

Or the evil inside won.

"You okay?"

She looked up at Carlos's low, growling voice.

"I need to hurt someone for you?" he asked.

Sarah shook her head. "Everyone's already hurt enough." She squared her shoulders. "Jax is at his bar? Shade?"

He nodded.

"Call him." She didn't have any clue where her phone was right then. "Tell him to get to the hospital. I think Molly needs to see him." Then they could clear this up, once and for all.

Carlos pulled out his phone. Sarah waited beside him. Nervous energy filled her. She heard footsteps and glanced over to see Victoria and Wade heading her way. Wade looked tired, but otherwise back to his old self.

"Guess who got sprung?" Victoria said, a wan smile on her lips.

Sarah hugged Wade. "I'm glad you're okay," she murmured.

He squeezed her. "Can't keep me down for long." He let her go and glanced over at Carlos. A Carlos who was looking increasingly worried. "What's going on, Sarah?"

"I'm trying to get in touch with Jax."

Carlos put his phone down. "He didn't answer."

"Carlos?" She could tell, by the way he spoke, that something was wrong.

Carlos rubbed at the edge of his scar. "The boss always answers when I call."

But he wasn't answering then.

Brent came out of Molly's room. Sarah grabbed him and practically dragged the detective down the hallway and away from the others.

"Lady, what are you doing?" Brent demanded. "Are you crazy?"

She pushed him into an empty hospital room. Slammed the door. "Call Jax."

"Uh, what?"

"Call Jax." She motioned toward his phone. "I know what's going on with you two, okay? I know you're the one who tipped him off about Molly's ID, I know you're the one who gave him access to Eddie Guthrie. Look, I get it. You're on his—his payroll."

Brent stiffened. "The fuck I am. I've never taken a bribe and I never will."

"I don't care exactly *what* sort of agreement you two have going on. What matters to me right now is that . . . if you call him, Jax answers, right?" *Only he was supposed to answer Carlos, too.*

Brent didn't nod. His face didn't change expression at all.

"I'm worried something is wrong." Her guts were twisted in knots. "Just call him, okay? Please?"

Before something happens.

Chapter 13

JAX'S PHONE WAS RINGING AGAIN. HE STARED UP AT the old house, and his gaze slid over the windows. The ones on the first floor were boarded up. The windows on the second floor were covered by old, sagging shutters.

A balcony swept around the side of the place, and big, columns—columns that had once been a bright white but were now a faded gray—supported the structure.

He'd been led to this place. If he went inside, the bastard was supposed to be waiting for him. He'd been told to come without cops. Without backup of any kind.

Did the guy think he was a fool?

He looked down at his phone. Saw Brent's number this time. Frowning, he picked it up.

"Jax!" Brent's voice seemed strained. "Where are you and what the hell are you doing?"

He tilted his head back. "Five-oh-eight Dubois Street." A street with overgrown azaleas and twisted oaks. "And I'm waiting for the cops to arrive."

"*What?*"

"The man who took Molly Guthrie may be waiting

inside or . . ." Jax exhaled slowly. "Maybe he just thinks I'm a dumbass who will walk straight into a building that's probably wired to explode if I so much as breathe on the door."

"Jax, stay where you are, do you understand? I'm on my way!"

He could see police cars rushing down the road. Their sirens weren't blaring—a good thing. He'd warned them to come in silently, just in case. "Better hurry," Jax told Brent. "Looks like the show is getting started."

HE HUMMED AS he positioned his prey. Moving him a bit to the left, because he wanted this picture to be absolutely perfect. He'd sliced with his knife, a drive straight to the fool's heart. In and out.

Easy.

He wondered when the body would be found. Who would find it. Oh, but he could hardly wait to see what would come next.

His knife tapped on his victim's face. Then cut through the gag. But the guy wasn't trying to talk anymore. He wasn't doing anything.

He was stone-cold dead.

THERE WAS A line of police cruisers leading up to 508 Dubois Street. Lots of cop cars, but, thankfully, no terrible blaze rising into the air.

As soon as Brent braked his car, Sarah leapt out. She could see Carlos in the vehicle behind her. A silent guard who was still shadowing her. Sarah didn't stop to talk with him. She ran toward the cops, calling, "Jax! Jax!"

"I'm here, Sarah."

She turned.

He was leaning against the front of a patrol car. Looking like he didn't have a care in the world. His arms were crossed over his powerful chest. He had on a short-sleeved, white T-shirt, and the shirt stretched over his muscles and contrasted with the dark swirl of his tattoos.

She rushed to him and had one of those instances in which she wasn't sure if she wanted to yell at him for taking such an insane risk or if she just wanted to hug him tight.

But then, she didn't do either thing. She stumbled to a stop in front of him. Sarah glared up at Jax. "Do you have some kind of death wish?"

One blond brow rose. "Not to my knowledge."

Not to his . . . Her teeth clenched. "When a psychopath calls you, you don't run out to confront him yourself!"

He was staring over her shoulder, at the old house. "He wasn't here."

Sarah wanted to catch that guy—so badly—but she was glad he hadn't been there. "Good, that's why you're still alive."

His gaze shifted to focus on her.

"He's baiting you."

"He said he would *kill* you. That he would slice you up, Sarah." His hands closed around her shoulders. "You think I would let that happen?"

"And do you think I want anything happening to you?" *No.* "He's pulling you into this mess because of me. Because he knows that we're involved and he's using you in order to get to me—"

"He knows things that he shouldn't."

Sarah shook her head.

"About my past." Jax's voice lowered. "He knows things that I only told you and your LOST members. The bastard said that if I came here, alone, he'd tell me about my past."

"He's lying to you," she said. Couldn't Jax see that? "I don't know how he found out—maybe the jerk put a bug in Gabe's hotel room—but he wasn't going to tell you anything."

"I know that."

The bomb-sniffing dogs were running around, but they didn't appear to be catching any scents.

"And *he* knew," Jax continued roughly, "that I wasn't coming over to talk. I was coming over to kill him."

"Jax . . ."

He smiled at her. "But I changed my mind. I called the cops. I didn't come armed to send the bastard to hell."

Her heart was beating too fast.

"And do you know why I did it?"

Sarah shook her head.

"For you. Because I wanted you to think I was more than a fucking killer." His eyes darkened as he stared at her. "But now I'm wondering, hell, maybe she already thinks that. Everyone else does. What *do* you see, Sarah, when you look at me?"

She stepped closer to him. "I told you before, I see strength." Sarah wrapped her arms around him and held tight. "I see the man I want." A man she was coming to need, more and more, with every moment that passed. "I see you."

She stayed there with him, her hands linked with his, and she watched as the cops searched the scene. They didn't turn up any bombs and the man they were looking for wasn't there.

Maybe he never had been.

Maybe it was all just one of his sick games.

The sun rose, sliding higher and higher into the sky. By the time the cops gave the all-clear, it was close to noon.

And Sarah knew exactly what she had to do. "Will you . . . come with me, Jax?"

"Where?"

"Back to my past. There's someone there that I have to face." She didn't want to see him. Sarah had vowed once that she would *never* see him again, but, this time, she didn't have a choice.

It was time for Sarah to visit her dad, Murphy the Monster.

A faint furrow appeared between Jax's eyes. "But first," she told him. "We're going to need to make a little pit stop."

"ARE YOU SURE about this?" Brent asked Jax as they walked down the hospital corridor. "I mean, yeah, I get that Sarah is keen on you seeing Molly to clear up suspicion, but . . ." He grabbed Jax's hand. "How do you know that girl won't start screaming as soon as you walk into the room?"

"I know because I've never done anything to hurt her." And Sarah wanted him to go out of town with her. He couldn't fly out until the cops cleared him. So . . . time to check in with Molly Guthrie.

"I don't like this," Brent said. "I really freaking don't."

There were plenty of things that Jax didn't like right then. The big thing on his list? The crazy SOB who was trying to play games with his life.

Sarah pushed open the door to Molly's room. Jax squared his shoulders, and then he went inside. Molly was lying down, so still at first that he actually thought she was dead. But then he heard the beep of her machines and she slowly turned her head to look at him.

Her eyes widened. "I . . . remember you."

"Shit," Brent muttered. "Here we go . . ."

"You carried . . . me out." Her lips trembled. "You carried . . . me . . . *thank you.*"

Jax didn't know what he was supposed to do. Helpless, he looked Sarah. She mouthed, *Go take her hand.*

He crossed the room. Touched the slender fingers that had been reaching out to him.

"Th-Thank you . . ." Molly whispered.

He squeezed her hand. "You're the one who survived that bastard. All I did was run down some stairs."

Her lips lifted. The smile was weak, but it was there.

When he looked up a few moments later, Sarah had slipped from the room.

"YOU CAN'T BE serious," Gabe said, glaring at Sarah. "This is the worst idea I've ever heard. Don't do it."

"Damn bad, Sarah," Wade echoed. "You don't need to talk with him. We can figure this out on our own. We always do."

She'd known they wouldn't exactly be game-on about her plan to travel to her father's prison. "I think my dad knows him. He knows who this guy is."

Gabe's eyes briefly closed. He'd been stitched up, bandaged up, and then—according to Eve—he'd jumped out of the ER while the docs had their backs turned. Eve had told Sarah that was SEAL mentality. If Gabe wasn't shot in the heart or head, he wasn't staying down.

"Knows him?" Wade said. "What . . . you think they killed together?"

"No." She glanced back over her shoulder. Molly's door was still shut. She couldn't be in there with Molly without guilt eating her alive. "I think that he wants revenge on my dad. The same way that Eddie did." That was actually why she thought the perp had used Eddie. "All of my father's victims weren't found." A stark and sad truth. "I have to get him to tell me about the others because one of those victims . . . our perp is tied to one of them."

"And you think your dad is just going to offer up this information? Sarah, I know how he got arrested," Gabe said. His expression held sympathy, a sympathy that just made her feel even more uncomfortable right then. "I know what happened between you. I know—"

"I've visited him since then."

Gabe's lips parted, but he didn't speak.

"There is more that you don't know." She straightened her spine. "Jax is coming with me."

"Sarah . . ."

"I think the rest of the team should go back to Atlanta. We found Molly. Your job is done here."

Wade growled, a low sound of frustration. "And will you be coming back to Atlanta?"

"After I find the man who took Molly." Once he wasn't a threat to anyone else, then, yes, she'd be heading home, too.

Wade stepped toward her. "Sarah, we're not leaving you alone!"

"*She's not alone.*"

Sarah glanced back. She hadn't even heard that door open, but Jax was there.

"She'll be with me," Jax said.

"That is not the reassurance I wanted," Wade muttered.

"Too bad," Jax threw back. "It's what you're getting." His hand curled around Sarah's hip.

Wade's stare dropped to that hand. "Like that, huh?" He shook his head. "Sarah, do you know what you're doing?" Worry was there. Concern.

I know exactly what I'm doing. I'm protecting my team. "Go back to Atlanta," she told him and Gabe. "Take the rest of the team and just go back."

Gabe whistled. "You think he's coming after us."

He'd always been sharp. That was why she'd agreed to work for LOST.

"I think that he'll do anything to get to me. I think you've been shot and Wade nearly wound up dead." Her chin lifted. "We don't need to take any more chances. This guy—he's got a vendetta against me. I won't let you be risked."

"But—what? Jax over there can handle the risk?" Wade's face tightened. "Better than an ex-SEAL and an ex-cop? Better than men who've been trained for this shit?"

"I tend to handle myself pretty well," Jax murmured with a casual shrug. "In any situation."

"Sonofabitch," Wade snapped.

Gabe smiled. "I'm sure Jax is well accustomed to danger." His head inclined. "But I'm not accustomed to abandoning my team when the shit hits the fan."

"Gabe—"

"When you get back, I'll be eager to learn what your father had to say."

Wade was pacing now. "This is such a bad idea." He pointed at Gabe. "*You* thought it was a bad idea five minutes ago, too. Only now you're changing your mind. What? Is everyone going crazy? Everyone but me?"

"If her father knows who this man is, then she has to see him." Gabe closed the distance between them. As he gazed down at Sarah, his expression softened. "But be careful, and whatever you do, don't let that asshole get into your mind again."

Sarah nodded. She'd try. The goal, this time, was for her to get into the mind of her dear old, twisted dad.

"Be safe," Gabe told her.

Wade stopped his pacing. "Jax, you guard her with your life, understand?"

"Wade, he doesn't—" Sarah began.

"No one will hurt her," Jax promised. "Not without going through me." His words were flat and cold and scary. Sarah knew that he believed exactly what he'd just said, and, from the grudging nod that Wade gave, she knew that he believed Jax, too.

Jax Fontaine was a powerful, dangerous man.

He was also an enemy that you didn't want to have.

THE ONLY MOTEL close to Biton Penitentiary was little more than a truck stop. Small and old, the place was not exactly where Jax would have preferred to spend the night with Sarah.

But their plane had landed so late that they couldn't get in the prison then. It was nearing midnight, and this no-tell motel was their only option.

"Oh, look," Sarah said. "I think the bed vibrates."

He heard a squeak and a bounce, and he looked over to see Sarah on the bed. She'd just pushed a button and that bed was seriously moving.

"It does," Sarah said as she shook.

He dropped their bags and just watched her. Sarah was smiling up at the ceiling and she was . . . humming softly. He frowned because he thought he knew that song.

Jax walked closer to her. "Sarah, what are you humming?"

She immediately stopped. "I don't hum."

Uh, yeah. She had been. She'd been humming a tune.

And it sounded so familiar to him. Like something he'd heard when he was a kid.

She turned off the bed. Lay still. Her smile was gone. Her whole expression was just . . . empty. Like a light had been switched off inside her.

"Sarah . . ."

She sat up. Stared at him. Only she didn't look quite like his Sarah. She was different. Cold. And when she looked at him, Jax could have sworn that he saw calculation in her gaze. "I know you want something from me," she said.

Did he now? "And what's that?"

"I haven't figured it out, not exactly. But I mean, why else would you come all this way? Why take these risks? It's not as if you took one look at me and fell in love."

He stalked closer. "You seem very sure about that."

"You're not the type of man to fall in love. Not at first sight and, well . . . after what happened between you and Emma, maybe not at all."

He sat on the bed next to her. It immediately sagged beneath his weight. "I care for Emma."

"Caring and loving aren't the same."

He put his hands on either side of Sarah, caging her in place. "And you and Emma aren't the same, either."

"Why did you let her go?"

"Because she didn't really want the man I was. She was looking for a way out." They'd both been kids on the street, desperate. For a time, they'd clung to each other. "She found her way out." She'd fought for her freedom from the past. But Jax knew, every time she looked at him, she just saw darkness and pain. She remembered what it was like to have nothing.

To want everything.

"What will you do . . ." Sarah asked and her face was still too emotionless. "When you find your family? Are you going to talk with them? Or are you going—"

"To just keep living my life?" Because that was an option. Doing nothing. "I just want to know who they are."

Her gaze fell. "Maybe you're better off not knowing, did you ever think of that?"

Now it was his turn to laugh, and that laughter was bitter. "I grew up with an abuser. He spent his days hitting Charlene, because she'd get between him and me. He took me . . . he was a fucking kidnapper, and in the end, he got exactly what he deserved."

Death.

"You did it," Sarah said.

He leaned in closer to her. "You don't really want me to confess, do you? Because then you might have to tell someone about what I did."

She didn't pull away. Her hand lifted and touched his cheek. "No, I won't tell anyone. Haven't you realized it yet?" She leaned forward and kissed him. "Your secrets are safe with me." The kiss was slow, sensual. So soft. Her lips feathered over his and her tongue lightly teased him.

"And you," he growled back against her delectable mouth, "will always be safe with me."

Her hand slid up his cheek. Sank into his hair. "I will learn all of your secrets, Jax. And they won't scare me."

He kissed her. Harder, deeper than she'd kissed him. "Good." Because he wanted her to know, even if he was reluctant to say the words himself. Sarah had come into his life and she'd taught him about fear.

He'd been afraid when she'd been in the fire. Terrified that he wouldn't get to her in time.

And when he thought of her turning away from him . . . because she might come to hate him or be disgusted by him . . .

Fear.

He tumbled her back onto the bed. He'd been slow with her before. He'd savored her. She truly was a woman to be savored.

But something seemed to be happening in that room. To her. To him. To them.

Emotions were tangling out of control. The present—it was a time bomb, and he just needed—

"Fuck me, Jax."

Her. She was what he needed.

He pulled back, just enough to yank open her jeans and shove them down. She kicked off her shoes. Tossed the jeans and her underwear. Then she was straddling him. Wrapping her legs around him and bringing her sex against his crotch. His dick was long and hard because—this was Sarah. He always got turned on by Sarah.

She jerked open the snap of his jeans. Pulled down the zipper, and then her hot, soft hands were pumping him. Again and again. She swiped her thumb over the tip of his arousal, and then she brought her thumb up to her mouth and sucked it. Her eyes were on his as Sarah tasted him. She was so sexy that he thought he might explode right then.

But Sarah pushed up. Her hands closed around his shoulders as she positioned her body. And her sex brushed against him. Warm silk but . . .

"Condom," Jax gasped out. He grabbed for his pants, started to put on the condom as fast as he could—

"I'd like to feel you," Sarah said. "Skin to skin."

He stilled, his whole body locking down as a surge of primal arousal flooded him. He would like nothing more than to fuck her, skin to skin, nothing between them. Nothing at all.

"I'm clean," Jax told her, because he was fanatical about protection. He never wanted to risk having a child he didn't know about. A child out there who was wondering . . .

Where's my dad?

No, Jax slammed the door on the thought.

"So am I," Sarah said.

And an image popped into his head. A baby, with Sarah's smile. The real smile that didn't come often enough. His heart seemed to hurt.

"But I'm not on the pill," Sarah said. Her eyes looked so deeply into his.

She's different. I want to be with Sarah. But . . .

He wanted to protect her, too. Because he had plans for Sarah. Plans that lasted far longer than a few dangerous days in New Orleans. But he wouldn't be forcing her to stay with him because she was pregnant.

She'd stay because she wanted him. Just as desperately as he wanted her.

He kissed her. Heard that soft, sexy moan that she gave, and it just made him want her all the more. His hand slid between their bodies. When he touched her, Sarah was hot, but not nearly wet enough, not for him. He needed her wild, just the way he liked her.

So he stroked her.

"Jax, now!"

No, not now. Not yet. He was holding tightly to his control, for her.

He slid his index finger into her, then worked another finger into her tight sheath. She closed around him, feeling fucking fantastic, and he knew he'd explode when he drove balls-deep inside her.

His thumb pressed to her clit. He pushed and heard that moan come again. He pushed—

Her nails dug into his shoulders. "I need you." Sarah kissed a hot path down his neck. Licked. Bit lightly. "Don't make me wait, Jax. Don't."

He couldn't refuse her. Not his Sarah.

His fingers withdrew. She was nice and wet now. Ready for him to sink inside her hot core.

Jax drove into her. His hands locked around her hips, probably digging in too deeply, but Sarah just arched toward him. Faster and harder they went and he was pretty sure they were breaking that old bed.

He didn't care.

She was a tight glove around him. Every arch and glide of her body just pushed him ever closer to the edge of his control. He'd never wanted anyone the way he wanted Sarah.

No one would ever be like her.

She stiffened against him, her delicate muscles tensing, and he eased back because he liked to see the pleasure sweep over her face.

Fucking beautiful.

Then he pulled her down against him, holding her even closer, and he plunged into her. The orgasm pumped through his body, hollowing him out, and he shuddered against her. Jax pressed a kiss to her throat, right over her frantically pounding pulse. Kissing her hard there, wanting to mark her. Wanting everyone to know that Sarah was *his.*

Just as he was hers.

Brent West knew that he should go home. There was no reason for him to keep staying at the hospital. Molly Guthrie was recovering. The docs and nurses were watching her, and the captain had given approval for one of the uniformed cops to keep guard that night.

But . . .

He slipped into Molly's room. She was still hooked to machines. Their steady beeping filled the air. Her head was turned away from him and she seemed to be gazing out of the darkened window. She wasn't, of course, she was probably asleep and—

"I know it's you, Detective West."

A ripple of surprise ran though him.

"I can smell your cologne." Her head turned and she glanced over at him. He saw that Molly was very much awake.

He blinked at her response. "I . . . ah, my mom gave me that." Hell, that was a stupid damn thing to say.

He knew it was. Especially considering that it just reminded Molly that her own mother—

"Your mom has good taste."

He found himself taking a step closer to her. She looked better. Not that stark white pallor to match the sheets. She almost seemed to have a touch of color in her cheeks. The shadows were still heavy under her eyes, but . . .

"Were you there, when my brother died?"

He should have never walked into her room that night. "Yes."

"Will you tell me what happened to him?"

Brent shook his head. "You should rest tonight. You need to get your strength back."

"Please . . . tell me."

That one word pierced through him. *Please.* He knew this girl . . . no, this woman, hadn't begged her captor. But she was right there, begging him. "Don't," he said as he took another step toward her. "Don't you ever beg anyone for anything."

She licked her lips. Nodded.

Oh, hell. "He was shot. A guard . . ." A stupid, overzealous guard. "Your brother had been given some bad drugs, Molly. They messed with his mind. We didn't realize how much, not until it was too late. He grabbed a scalpel. A nurse was there and the guard . . . he . . . fired." The words seemed so cold.

Molly's hands had fisted on the covers.

He reached over and his fingers curled around hers. "He said something, there at the end."

"What?" Her voice was so hoarse.

"He said that he loved you. He knew you'd been

found. I told him you were safe, and the last thing he said was that he loved you."

Her head turned away from him. He could see her shoulders shaking. The machines were starting to get louder. He expected the nurses to rush in at any time and demand that he leave.

But he didn't want to leave Molly.

His hand curled around her shoulder. She turned back toward him, moving fast, and she reached out to him.

Hugged him.

He didn't move. The last thing he wanted was to push her away and hurt Molly. She'd been hurt enough. But . . .

"Thank you," Molly said.

She had nothing to thank him for. If he'd just gotten to the med ward two minutes faster, she wouldn't be grieving then. Her brother would be alive. Brent had been too slow.

"I loved him, too," she told him. He could hear the tears in her voice.

His hand brushed over her hair. Molly looked up at him. "Will you stay, just until I sleep?"

He nodded.

"I feel better," Molly said, "when you're here."

He pulled a chair closer to the bed. "Then I'll stay as long as you need."

She smiled at him, and Brent knew he wasn't going anyplace.

Sarah's eyes opened. The room was dark around her. A nightmare hadn't woken her, not this time. She reached out, but the bed next to her was empty.

That was why she'd woken. Because Jax wasn't there.

She sat up in bed, pulling the covers to her chest. "Jax?"

"I'm here."

Her head turned toward his voice. After a moment, her eyes adjusted to the darkness, and she saw him standing near the window. He appeared to be staring out at the night.

"Is something wrong?"

"I don't always sleep so well." He dropped the curtain and walked toward her. She could hear the sound of the floor squeaking beneath his feet. "I didn't want to keep you up."

"You didn't." She reached out for his hand. Wound her fingers through his. Then she remembered when she'd been with him before. She'd woken from her nightmare at his house, and he hadn't been in bed. "Do you want to talk about it?"

He tried to pull away. She just held his hand tighter. "I'm not asking as a shrink," she told him quickly. "I'm just asking because if you want to talk, I want to listen." He'd heard all about her darkest moments. She wanted to hear his.

"There are some things you shouldn't know."

There were some things that Sarah wished she didn't know, but those things . . . they weren't about Jax. When it came to him, she wanted to know everything.

"I'm not going to judge you." She wished that she could see his face, but it was too dark.

"No, but you just might run hell fast away from me. And that's not an option for me. I can't lose you."

"You won't." She didn't want to lose him. They had something together. Something between them that she didn't fully understand, but she wanted nonetheless. She'd never had someone who made her feel so comfortable. Someone who seemed willing to risk so much, for her.

"Don't be so sure of that, pretty Sarah."

Pretty Sarah. He'd called her that from the beginning. And she liked the way his voice roughened when he said her name.

"I've done things that might scare even you."

She shook her head. "I don't believe that."

"I've lied, stolen . . ."

That was supposed to scare her?

"I learned to use my fists far too early. When someone hurt me, I always struck back."

"Still not afraid." She wasn't.

He sat down on the bed. The mattress dipped beneath his weight. "What do you think happened to the man who took me?"

Her breath froze in her lungs.

"Do you think I just let him walk away? I always knew what he'd done. It was in the back of my head. And all those years . . . he kept hitting Charlene. Kept hurting me. Did you think I was just going to let that all go?"

She could feel her lower lip trembling. To stop that movement, Sarah caught her lower lip between her teeth. And she waited.

"One day, he slammed Charlene's head into the wall.

She didn't get up, just lay there, hurting . . . hurting so much. He was standing over her, ready to swing again, and I wasn't going to let it happen."

Her fingers were still twined with his.

"I ran at him. Hit him as hard as I could and he just . . . fell down the stairs. I heard his neck when it snapped. I knew what had happened. It's a sound I'll never forget."

Jax!

"He didn't die right away. I walked down to the bottom of the stairs. His eyes were wild, and he was trying to talk. I just stared at him because I knew there wasn't a damn thing that could be done. A few moments later, his eyes closed. He was gone."

Sarah was silent, still biting her lip.

"You're supposed to say something, Sarah." His voice roughened. "Call me a murderer. Pull away from me. Get the phone and call the cops!"

Did he really think that was what she would do? "Self-defense." An act that got out of control. "You didn't mean to push him down the stairs—"

"Didn't I? I meant to stop him, Sarah, by any means."

Her left hand came up, and, in that darkness, pressed to his face. She could feel the rough growth of stubble along his hard jawline. "And I meant to stop my father that day." Her finger had been squeezing the trigger. So ready to take that shot. If he hadn't stopped . . . "I don't really see how you and I are so different."

"We are." His head turned, and he pressed a hot kiss to her palm. "Because you didn't ditch the body and lie to the cops. I did. Charlene helped me. And then, a few weeks later, she killed herself because she couldn't stand to see what I'd become."

"No." Her denial was immediate. Absolute. "That's *not* what happened."

"You weren't there. I was. I saw her, fading away each day. She couldn't even look me in the eye, and she'd jump every time she so much as heard a creak of sound. She couldn't handle what I'd done. She couldn't handle me. I—I loved her, and she killed herself to get away from me."

"No." The denial came again, even harder this time. "I don't believe that, Jax. You saved her life. You protected her."

"Not soon enough," he said, and she heard the guilt in his voice. "She was the reason I survived that hell, and I'm the reason she died."

"Jax, you don't know what she was thinking. You don't know—"

He'd lifted her hand up higher and he pressed a kiss to the scar that slid along her inner wrist. "I never want to do anything to hurt you. Sarah, don't leave me."

Something seemed to break inside her at his words. "I'm not going anywhere." She pulled him fully down on the bed with her. And Jax just held her. He cradled her against his chest and his arms curled around her back.

Sarah had never felt more protected.

And she'd never felt as if she belonged with someone else, *to* someone else, more than she did in that moment.

His words hadn't scared her, they'd just made her understand him—and the connection they seemed to have—all the more. They'd both been through hell. Both battled their own demons, and they both weren't ever going to completely shake their pasts.

But the past didn't have to determine their future.

"Good night, Sarah," Jax whispered.

Sleep tight. You know you're safe tonight.

She closed her eyes.

Chapter 14

SARAH SAT AT THE LITTLE TABLE IN THE NARROW prison cell. The warden had granted her special permission for this little visit. She was surrounded by prison bars, and the table in front of her was about five feet long. Jax was next to her, looking as dangerous as usual. Two guards waited near the cell's door. They were both armed.

Sarah had pulled back her hair. She hoped that she looked cool and in control. *Looked* that way, because on the inside, she was a ball of nerves. She couldn't let her father see those nerves, though. He would use any weakness that he could spot.

She heard the clang of another door opening. The shuffle of footsteps. He was coming.

Her chin lifted. Her heart raced.

Jax reached over. He caught her wrist and his fingers slid over her scar in the briefest of caresses. "I'll be at your side the whole time."

She nodded. He let her wrist go and . . .

Her father came in.

He was wearing a garish orange prison jumpsuit. His

hands were shackled and his feet were in ankle cuffs. He shuffled forward, moving slowly, and when he saw Sarah, a wide smile lit his face.

Prison should have changed him. He should have lost weight. Lost his hair. Grown pale and skeletal. He *should* have aged.

But . . . he hadn't changed.

His hair was still a rich, thick black. His skin was still golden. His body was fit, probably because he spent hours working out in his cell. Her father had always been handsome—that had been part of his lure. *People have such a hard time seeing evil when it's wrapped in a nice package.*

Those had been his words.

"Sweetheart, it's been too long." He ignored the guards who shadowed his movements as he came toward the table. "You need to come and see your father more often."

He was chiding her, as if she were just a daughter who hadn't visited her dear old dad often enough. Like any father would say to his daughter. But he wasn't any father. And she sure wasn't just any daughter.

"Hello, Dad," Sarah said softly. She didn't let emotion enter her voice. With him, she couldn't.

His smile stretched a little more.

The guards eased him into the seat across from her, and Sarah watched silently as they secured his restraints. Then the guards stepped back. They wouldn't leave the room, that wasn't a possibility, not with Murphy the Monster. Sure, he might look all well-behaved right then, but he could turn in an instant. Could, and *had* in the past. After one of her earlier visits, he'd gotten particularly violent. She'd learned that a guard had been hospitalized for three weeks after that encounter.

Everyone took extra care now. *Everyone.*

"And who is this, sweetheart?" Her father asked as his gaze slid to Jax. Her father's stare was even darker than Sarah's own. That stare of his was assessing as it slid over Jax. Jax just looked back, his face stoic. His body seemingly relaxed. "Well, well . . ." her father murmured. "Isn't this interesting." But his face . . . hardened . . . as he looked at Jax. A flash of what could have been anger appeared in his eyes. "Very interesting."

It was then that Sarah realized something was wrong. The way her father looked at Jax . . . *He looks at him as if he knows Jax.*

But that wasn't possible, was it?

Sarah kept her chin up and her spine straight as she faced her father. "How have you been?" An innocent question. Amiable. She knew that was the way he liked to start things. As if they were just getting together for a friendly chat. But the truth was that she'd come back to him in the past because she'd tried to learn more about his crimes. About his victims. And each time she visited, he usually revealed one more missing victim to her.

Will the bodies ever stop piling up?

"I can't complain. These years I've spent locked away have passed so fast. Almost like a blink." He inclined his head toward her even as that faint smile still curled his lips. "I have a new lawyer. He thinks that maybe I wasn't given the fairest trial before. He's looking for new evidence. Wants me to talk to some shrink he knows."

She'd heard nothing about a new lawyer. Sarah didn't let her expression change even as fear spread within her.

"But while I've been in prison, I missed so much. So many years with you." He leaned forward. "I've served my time. Maybe it's my turn to be free again."

Sarah shook her head. "The people you killed don't get to be free." Again, no emotion was there. She couldn't allow emotion with him. It would be too dangerous.

"Oh, Sarah . . ." His eyes actually twinkled then. As if she were a funny child who'd just amused him. "Those people deserved exactly what they got. You know that. The world is a better place without them in it."

Her father's twisted logic. He'd always claimed that he was justified in his kills.

Justified in killing young Ryan Klein because the boy had hurt Sarah. He'd made fun of her. The boy was a bully, obviously escalating in his wicked actions. If he hadn't been stopped . . .

"There's no telling what they would have done," her father murmured, "if I hadn't intervened."

Her gaze fell to the table. To his cuffed hands. "You didn't intervene. You killed. There's a huge difference."

"I'm not so sure about that." His voice was warm. "Are *you* so sure, Sarah?"

She looked up at him. She was conscious of Jax moving slightly in his chair, edging toward her. *No, Jax, no!* Her father was so good at reading body language. The man was actually a genius, not that most people realized it. He would have made for a fantastic psychiatrist himself, provided he hadn't been so ass-crazy.

"I'm absolutely certain."

Her father's lips thinned. "I can tell when you lie. You know that."

Enough of his small talk. It was wearing far too thin on her nerves. "I came today because someone is trying to kill me."

Surprise flickered on his face. Surprise, then rage. "*Who?*" It was a low, lethal whisper.

Sarah swallowed. "I don't know. I was hoping you could tell me."

He shot to his feet. His restraints groaned and stretched with his movements. "You think I sent someone after you? Sarah, *no*! Never! You are mine. My flesh and blood and I would protect you . . . always." His eyes glittered down at her. "Always."

She could feel goose bumps rising on her arms. *No, I'm not. I'm not yours and I am nothing like you.* "Do you remember Gwen Guthrie?"

A muscle flexed in his jaw. "You know I can't forget her."

Right. Not Gwen. Because she'd been her father's first.

"Life is funny," Sarah said. "It's filled with all of these chance encounters. Random events that don't seem to make sense."

He slowly lowered back into his seat. The guard who'd stepped forward also eased back.

"Your mother's death wasn't a random event," her father said. "That woman killed her. She almost killed *you*."

And that was the instant her father's life had changed.

Now, with the understanding she'd gained through years of study, she realized that her father had probably managed to control his darker urges. Maybe her mother had even been some sort of anchor for him. True psychopaths didn't form strong connections with others, but it certainly seemed that her father had bonded with her mother.

And with me.

Or, at least, bonded as much as he could.

But when Sarah's mother had died in that accident, her father had lost his anchor. There'd been no more hope for him. There had only been rage.

"She'd been drinking," Sarah explained as she glanced over at Jax. He was silently watching the byplay between her and her father. "Gwen Guthrie had been out partying that night. Mixing drugs and booze, and when she drove away, she never even noticed that the light at the intersection was red."

Gwen had smashed into her mother's side of the vehicle.

It had sounded . . . well, just like a bomb had gone off. Sarah knew she'd never forget that sound. *Boom.* The impact had woken her from sleep in the backseat, and Sarah had screamed and screamed.

Screamed as the glass fell.

Screamed as the seat belt cut into her skin, seeming to burn her.

Screamed . . . screamed while the firemen used the Jaws of Life to cut her mother out of the car.

Her screams had stopped when she realized her mother wasn't moving.

"She laughed," her father said. His gaze seemed to be focused on the past. "The cops were trying to get Gwen Guthrie in the back of their car, and she *laughed* while my Sabrina lay dead on the ground."

Sarah eased out a slow breath. "Gwen was sent to rehab. The judge gave her probation. She was a young, single mother. She had two small children. The judge put them in foster care while she was getting help—"

"She wasn't going to get better, Sarah." Her father's fingers tapped on the table. "When I found her, she was at the liquor store. Such a loving mother."

And Sarah had woken later, to Gwen Guthrie's screams.

I didn't know! I didn't!

"Random events," Sarah murmured. "Guess where I've been? Down in the Big Easy. I'd just finished working a case . . . when a woman named Molly Guthrie went missing."

Her father blinked. That was it . . . the only change in his expression. A slow blink.

"The man who took Molly contacted me. You see, Dad, he knew about you. About your connection to Molly. He told me that Molly would suffer, just like Gwen had, if I didn't find her."

He wasn't tapping his fingers against the table any longer.

"So my team and I started looking, but it was all a trap. For me. For them. The first place he led me to . . . it exploded just when my partner Wade was about to rush inside." Her spine was so stiff that it was starting to ache. "The next time he called me, I managed to keep him on the phone long enough to get a trace—"

"You were always so clever." Pride beamed in those words.

"We tracked him. Found the missing woman, but he'd wired that place, too. If it wasn't for Jax," her gaze darted to him, then back to her father, "I wouldn't have gotten out, and neither would Molly."

Her father's attention shifted to Jax. "You saved Sarah."

"He carried Molly out," Sarah explained. "He—"

Her father's hands slammed into the table. "I don't care about her." He pointed at Jax. "I know what you are. I can see it. I could always see it."

Her father saw his own evil, that was all. Evil tainting everything around him.

"The man wasn't done, even though we got Molly away from him." She waited for her father to look at her again, but he seemed only focused on Jax. "That's when he came after me and my boss. He was following behind us, and he shot at the car."

Her father's head slowly turned back to her.

"The bullets were aimed at Gabe. I think he wanted to take Gabe out so that he could get to me."

"He's a dead man."

Really? Her father was going to make threats? In prison?

"He wants revenge," Sarah said. "Maybe you can understand that. After all, isn't that why you killed Gwen? For revenge?"

"I stopped her from hurting anyone else! From destroying another family!"

"And you were mad because Ryan had been mean to me, so you killed him—"

"He was always going to be bad, Sarah. *Always*."

"You had a reason for them all, didn't you? You could find a reason why every single one of them needed to die. Jonathan Kerns—"

"He'd been selling drugs! He was going to hurt—"

"Eliza Mayo—"

"She was a prostitute, Sarah. She was sick and she was—"

"Jennings White—"

"That bastard was corrupt. He was taking away money that was *mine*—"

"There was always a reason that you could come up with, but the simple truth is that you just wanted to kill. You came up with excuses so you wouldn't have to admit to yourself . . . you're a murderer, Dad. Murphy the Monster. You killed when the urge came to you."

He was silent. A faint line of red stained his cheeks.

Most serial killers had preferred victim types. All blond women with blue eyes. Or college-age girls or—hell, a *type*. But her father had claimed victims of all ages, all races, and all sexes. *That* was one of the reasons he'd been so hard to catch. The cops had thought they were looking for multiple killers.

Not just one man.

"I thought you knew me better than this, Sarah." The beam of pride was gone. He shook his head, disappointment slumping his shoulders. But . . . did he really feel disappointment? Did he really feel anything?

Or was he just pretending?

"Do you love me?" Sarah heard herself ask.

"Of course," he said instantly. "You are the *only* thing that matters to me."

"Then help me." She couldn't look away from him. "This man is coming for me. He wants to hurt me. He knows how to rig bombs and he knows how to fire a gun from a moving vehicle. He's got training—"

"Sounds military," her father said.

Because, yes, he'd been the one to teach her how to profile long before she'd studied psychiatry.

"He's a white male, probably in his thirties, maybe early forties." Because he was fit and strong. "He has blond hair. Blue eyes . . ."

Her father grunted. "Sounds like the guy next to you."

Jax leaned forward and put his hands on the table.

"Nice tats," her father murmured. Sarah shook her head. "Who does this perp match to? Who did you take from him?"

Her father glanced back at her.

"The blond man with military training. I gave you his description, his age. He's in New Orleans now, but he could have been *anywhere* before." And that was key because her father had crossed state lines. Another smart way to avoid detection. When the kills were spaced so far apart, it had been harder for the authorities to connect the dots and find their perp. "You took someone away from him, and now, Dad, he's trying to take me away from you."

Her father's focus shifted to Jax.

"Not him," Sarah said. "Dad, dammit, look at *me*! Tell me! I know there's another victim out there. One that links to the man after me. I need that victim's name. Give me the name, and then I can find this guy.

I can unmask him, and I can stop him!" If her father would just give her a *name*.

"I never forget a face," her father said.

"Dad . . ." He was still staring at Jax.

"I've seen your face, son."

Jax stiffened. "We've never met. I don't think I would forget you." Anger hummed there, slicing in his words. Then Jax reached for Sarah's hand. His fingers squeezed hers.

Sarah had often doubted her father's emotions but when she saw rage burn in his eyes right then—she knew that emotion was real.

"I want you to get away from him, Sarah," her father said in a voice that was low and intense. Then he shouted, "Guards! Guards! Escort my daughter out of here, *now*."

They immediately stepped forward. When the Monster said jump, even the guards moved.

But Sarah didn't.

"You can't trust him," her father said with a slow shake of his head. "Get away. Now. Go back to your LOST friends . . . go back to them, Sarah."

Sarah didn't move. "Jax is with me. I'm—"

"You look a whole lot like him." His cuffed hands pointed to Jax.

Jax was frowning at her father. "Like who?"

"He screamed, in the end. Wanted to die."

Sarah didn't know who he was talking about then, but she wanted to push her father more so she said, "The man after me . . . he told me that he'd make Molly beg for death. He wanted her to beg before she died.

When she didn't beg, he didn't kill her." Her fingers were shaking so she balled them up in her lap. "Remind you of anyone?"

And, just like that, the rage vanished from her father's eyes. All of the emotion just winked away. "If they ask to die, then where's the crime? It's just like putting an animal out of its misery." His head turned, almost snakelike, as he gazed at Jax once more. "Isn't that right, Jax Fontaine?"

Sarah stood up. "You're not going to help me. You're just going to let him keep attacking me. Keep coming until, what? He kills me?" Her hands were fisted at her sides. "Come on, Jax. We're leaving. We're—"

Sarah stopped. She stared down at her father. Jax was rising beside her. Standing so close. Normally, he made her feel warm, but, right then, she was ice cold. "I never told you Jax's last name."

A faint smile curled her father's lips. "I never forget a face . . . or a name."

"You haven't met Jax before." But he'd said . . . *I never forget a face.* She tried to rush through the options in her mind. "You've been keeping tabs on me, haven't you? You sent someone to watch me!"

"From here?" He laughed. "Hardly. My reach isn't that strong, Sarah. But I am flattered you think so."

"How did you know his last name?" Had a guard told him? They'd signed in before and—

"I knew the man who took him, of course. Thought about killing him myself. But then, well, other prey came to my attention." He shrugged, as if none of what they were discussing really mattered.

Shock was rolling through Sarah. Her father was a master manipulator. Was he lying to them? Or was there a grain of truth in his words?

Murphy's eyes turned to slits as her father studied Jax. "Is that why you've taken up with daughter? Because you found out what I did?"

"Wh-What?" Sarah could feel her careful control fracturing.

"My victims deserved to die. They all did. Including your father."

Sarah stumbled against Jax. No, she didn't stumble. He'd just grabbed her and pulled her close. "He's lying," Jax snarled.

She wanted him to be lying.

His father's stare was assessing as it swept over Jax's features. "He had your eyes and your jaw. Your face, but his hair was darker." Her father seemed to consider things. "I think you have your mother's hair."

"You don't know my parents." Jax's voice was ice cold.

"Of course I know them." He shrugged one shoulder. "*Knew* them, rather."

Sarah tried to pull Jax toward the door. Only he wasn't moving.

"After all, I killed them, so I *had* to know them."

SARAH AND JAX had vanished.

He'd been waiting for Jax to return home, but the guy hadn't. Why? Had he decided to slip away with the doctor?

Sarah . . . Sarah Jacobs. *Just like her father.*

His little surprise for Jax could wait only so long.

With every moment that passed, he grew more and more impatient.

Hurry back, Sarah. Hurry the fuck back. And bring Jax!

If she didn't show herself soon, he'd just start killing her friends. Maybe he'd start with the redhead. She hadn't entered the game yet. What was her name . . . ?

Viki . . . Victoria.

She'd been the one in the news, the one who'd been taken on the last big case that LOST handled. Poor Victoria probably thought the danger was over. That she was safe now.

No one was ever really safe. Certainly not Victoria.

And not Sarah.

And sure as fuck not Jax Fontaine. That bastard was going to pay. Before this was over, he'd be the one to suffer the most.

I KILLED THEM.

Murphy's words rang in Jax's ears. He shook his head, denying them, because that sick bastard had to be lying. Just playing another one of his head games. Sarah had warned him about that. She'd told him that her father would try to get in his mind . . .

"Your father had a meth lab. He'd sell that shit to anyone he saw. Your mother . . . hell, he whored her out half the time."

No, this wasn't true.

"It's time to leave, Jax," Sarah said as she pulled on his arm. "Let's go. Now."

But he couldn't move. He couldn't take his eyes off Murphy Jacobs. "You don't know them. You're spouting bullshit."

"It wasn't until I took him that I realized . . . your father was a whole lot more than just a drug dealer." He laughed. "He was running weapons, taking hits, doing anything, if the money was right. A real high opportunity player. He was wanted in four states."

"Jax, Jax, look at me," Sarah said. Her voice was shaking.

"Your mother had been with him since she was fourteen. I don't think she loved him. I think she was too scared to leave him. I tried to get her to leave. She wasn't the one I was after, but she wouldn't go. She screamed and she fought. He'd hooked her on so many drugs, I don't know if she even realized what was happening."

A dull ringing was filling Jax's ears. "Stop it."

"You remember them, right? They had that little house on the edge of town near the South Carolina coast . . ."

"I live in New Orleans." But he hadn't, not always. He'd been in Atlanta when he was with Charlene. Charlene and . . .

"They put you in a closet when they did business. A damn closet. You were quiet as a mouse in there."

It's dark. Let me out! Daddy!

But his dad hadn't come. No, no! Jax violently shook his head. Mitch Fontaine had been the one to put him in a closet. Not his real father.

Right?

"You didn't make a sound, so I didn't know you were in there. Not when I came to take them."

"Please, Jax," Sarah whispered. Her hold on him was fierce. "Just come with me."

He couldn't move.

"I killed him first. He was the fighter, but he didn't last long. Once the pain started, they never do." Murphy leaned forward even more. "Do you have one of those snake tats like he had? It used to wrap all the way around his forearm . . ."

Jax had a flash then. Of a man reaching out to him. A man with a green snake circling his arm. *Stay quiet until I'm done. Then we'll go out . . . we'll go fishing . . .*

He'd . . . liked to fish. But his father had never really taken him.

They never did anything.

"No," Jax rasped as the ghosts of his past started to slip through his mind.

"Your mother . . . I tried to let her go. I didn't think she'd tell anyone about me, and who would believe her? I mean, she was so strung out."

Play with me, Mommy. Play!

But . . . she hadn't. He fucking remembered that—*now.*

"I set that house on fire. Put your father's body inside. She *ran* back in. Just ran in there . . . hell, I didn't know why she was doing that. I left her."

Sarah grabbed the table. "You left her to burn?"

Again, he shrugged. "She's the one who went into the fire. Didn't realize . . . not until I heard the screams . . . that the kid was in there, too."

Jax's skin felt ice cold.

"In the closet . . . that's where they'd put you."

"Stop talking, Dad!" Sarah yelled at him. "Just stop!"

Silence.

Jax stepped forward. Murphy tilted back his head as he gazed up at Jax.

"You really think . . ." Jax rasped, "I'll believe your lies?"

"I think you need to get away from Sarah. I think Sarah now knows *exactly* what you are . . ."

"Sarah has always known what I am." And she didn't care.

Murphy gave a sad shake of his head. "Did he seek you out, Sarah? Start showing an interest after he learned just who *you* are?"

"Jax hasn't—" she began, her voice furious.

"If the man after you has been using fire in his attacks, then you should certainly be looking at the fellow right beside you. Though perhaps he should be more grateful to me. I mean, I am the one who got him out of the fire. His mother didn't make it, but I got him and—"

"No!" Jax roared, and he shoved Sarah out of the way as he leapt across that table. Because suddenly, he could feel flames against his skin. He could hear himself crying out.

Mommy! Mommy! And he could see smoke, coming beneath the closet door.

He tackled Murphy. They hit the ground and he put his hands around the bastard's throat. He squeezed, his fingers tightening and cutting off Murphy's air supply, and Murphy was just smiling, smiling—

"Stop!" Sarah's scream. She was yanking on Jax. So were the guards. It took three guards to pull Jax off Murphy.

Then Murphy growled out, "She sees you now . . ."

Jax's breath heaved out. His head whipped up and he saw Sarah—staring at him with horror in her eyes.

"Come on, buddy," one of the guards said as he pulled Jax to the door. "Don't let him fuck with you any longer."

Jax glared at Murphy. "Bastard, I *will* be seeing you again."

"Stay away from Sarah," Murphy fired back. Two guards were pulling him toward the other exit. "She's not for you!"

A red-haired guard had Jax in the hall. "Calm down, man," he said. "Hell, we probably should have let you kill him. Would have saved us all some pain . . ."

He killed my parents. That bastard just confessed—

"He's a sick sonofabitch," the guard muttered.

Jax stared down at his hands.

And he wanted to *kill.*

"STOP," SARAH WHISPERED.

The guards didn't hear her.

"Stop!" she yelled.

Her father looked back at her. The guards stilled, but they didn't loosen their grip on him.

"You . . . you never killed two people at once."

He shrugged. "Didn't mean to kill the mother. Charlene shouldn't have run back to the fire."

Charlene.

"You're a liar, Dad."

"No, sweetheart. He is. That man out there . . . he's as dark and twisted on the inside as I am. You need to stay away from him."

"How'd you know his last name was Fontaine?"

"Figured . . . had to be . . . I got the kid out and I left him with Mitch Fontaine. The guy was a mechanic—worked with the boy's father—I figured leaving the kid with him would be better than nothing."

"He hurt him, Dad. That man abused Jax."

His eyes hardened.

Sarah swallowed to ease the lump in her throat. "And I don't think Charlene died that night." Jax had told her that a woman named Charlene raised him. That she'd even been there to help him get rid of the body years later.

Jax's mother had never gone looking for him because she'd been there with him, the whole time.

"Why would you lie and tell him that?" Sarah asked.

The guards were staring at Murphy and Sarah with a kind of sick curiosity. She got that. She felt rather sick herself.

"I watched," Murphy said simply. "I watched her. The woman she'd been died that night. She became someone new. I killed what she'd been."

Sarah was trying to make sense of this madness. Trying to look through her father's lies and riddles and understand the truth. "She ran away with Jax because she was scared of you. You didn't give Jax to that man—Mitch. *She* took Jax and went to him, didn't she?"

His eyes crinkled at the corners, as if he were fighting a smile. Was he proud because she'd caught his lie? His twist on the truth? "I guess she thought the mechanic would keep her safe from me," he murmured.

"But you were never going after her."

"Maybe, maybe not . . ."

She walked closer to him. The guards stiffened.

"Why?" Sarah asked him, hurt and desperate. "Why did you tell Jax all of this?" He'd destroyed Jax in that room, and she'd been helpless to stop Jax's pain.

"A man with blond hair . . . a man with blue eyes . . . a man who wants vengeance . . . sweetheart, didn't you see he was right in front of you? And he used fire . . . *fire*." He shook his head. "I was pushing him because you needed to see past the mask he was showing you. He's the one messing with your head. He's the one trying to kill you."

"No, he was there with me when Molly Guthrie vanished. He was—"

"He knew I didn't kill his mother. He *knew* it. *Think about it.* He lived with her his whole life. She told him about me. And he found out about you. Now he's trying to get his payback. He wants to hurt you, he wants to *wreck* you because of what I did." His shackled hands lifted, as if he'd touch her. "But you're my one good thing. Even I . . . I couldn't destroy you. I couldn't make you . . . like me."

He was still lying about Jax. He *had* to be lying.

"Run from him. Get away fast. Because that man out there, he will shatter you. And when you're gone, he knows that I'll be . . ." His words trailed away. "There will be nothing for me then."

His hands were between then. Once, she'd always linked her fingers with his. He'd tucked her in. He'd hugged her when she was scared.

"Nobody hurts my baby girl," he said, his expression hard. "I knew when I saw him . . . *he's the one . . . I have to protect you from him.*"

Sarah backed away from him.

His hands fell.

And Sarah became very, very cold.

"I need a name," Sarah told him. "If you really killed Jax's biological father, then tell me his name." So she could check out this story. Find out if it was bullshit or the truth.

Her father's head cocked to the right as he studied her. "Carl Winston."

The guards led him away. The clang of that door shutting behind her father seemed incredibly loud. Sarah reached down for her phone, but then she remembered it was gone. She'd had to turn in her phone and keys and everything else she carried when she entered the prison. She couldn't call Gabe or Victoria right then, but, God, she needed them.

Because for the first time in years, Sarah was lost.

Chapter 15

HE WAS WAITING FOR SARAH OUTSIDE THE prison. Jax had been pacing, anger pumping through his blood, but when he saw Sarah, he stopped.

She hesitated, just for an instant, then she came toward him. Her steps were slow, almost hesitant.

"Did you know?" Jax demanded. Everywhere he looked, Jax could have sworn that he saw red. He couldn't breathe because the rage was choking him. For so long, he'd thought he hadn't been wanted, but now . . .

They couldn't come for me because that bastard in there killed them! He wrecked my life. Took away everything from me!

"No," Sarah said softly. "He . . . I still don't know all of his victims. That's why I have to keep coming back. If I come back, he tells me a little more." Sarah was standing a few feet away from him and her gaze as it slid over him—was that fear in her eyes?

For an instant, he didn't care that she was afraid. "Your father killed my family."

"Jax . . ."

He stalked toward her. Grabbed her shoulders. Held her tight. "He killed them!" And his head seemed to be about to burst. His temples were pounding. The memories were erupting from the recesses of his mind, like Murphy had unlocked some sick, twisted door in his head. "I was in the closet—I could smell the smoke! The fucking smoke!" His hold tightened on her. "Your father! He did this! He—"

He let her go. Stared at Sarah in shock. He'd been about to shake her. What if he'd hurt her? *Sarah?*

"I don't know what's true," Sarah said. His voice had been sharp with fury. Hers was soft with sadness. "Not yet. I have to call my team. We'll find out what's really happening."

Jax rubbed his head. The pounding felt as if his head were exploding then. And he kept hearing a voice, a voice saying . . .

If I'm dead, he won't search for us. You have to forget who we were. Do you understand? Forget! Forget for Mommy . . .

He drove the balls of his hands into his eyes. "No."

Forget . . . Mommy . . .

"No!" Jax roared as his hands jerked down.

Sarah backed up.

Fear was on her face. Guards were running up behind her. "Is there a problem here?" one of them demanded.

Jax glared at them. "Let's go, Sarah." They needed to be alone. He had to figure out what was happening. He needed to know—

"You go, Jax." She tossed the rental keys to him. "I'll find my own way back."

His fingers fisted around the key. "Sarah?"

"Go," she said again, sounding sad and so very . . . certain.

The fog of fury began to clear from his mind.

She sees you for what you are.

Sarah was edging closer to the guards.

And staring at him as if she'd never seen him before. Not until that moment. But, no, Sarah understood him. Sarah had always understood.

That was before you nearly choked a man in front of her. A man who's her father.

"I'm sorry," he whispered.

"So am I," Sarah said. It sounded as if she was fighting tears. "Please . . . *go.*"

Because she was afraid of him? Right then, he was almost afraid of himself. Jax turned and he . . . left her.

I'm sorry, Sarah. Every step that he took away from her seemed to rip into his heart.

GABE HAD POWERFUL friends. When Sarah called him and dropped her cluster-fuck bombshell on him, he reached out to one of those friends and got her a ride back to New Orleans on a private jet.

Sarah's stomach had knotted by the time she landed. And she kept seeing Jax's face in her mind . . . a face that had been twisted with so much rage and hatred.

When she left the plane, Wade and Victoria were waiting for her. One look at their expressions, and she knew that Gabe had briefed them.

Victoria stared at her a moment. There was sympathy on Victoria's face. Sympathy, not pity. Sarah knew the difference.

Wade took her bag.

"Jax may be trying to kill me," Sarah said. He certainly had the power to do it. To stage everything so that she'd fall right into his web, like a lost, desperate fly. "And I think . . . I think I was falling in love with him."

"Oh, Sarah." Victoria wrapped her arms around Sarah and pulled her close in a tight hug. "We're going to figure this out. You'll see."

"I knew I should have decked the guy," Wade muttered. "Sarah, don't you worry. Viki's right. We're going to take care of this. LOST sticks together, you know that. You mess with one of us . . ."

Sarah's head lifted. She stared at her friends.

"Then you are damn well going to battle us all," Wade finished, his eyes and voice grim.

But Sarah didn't want a battle. She wanted . . .

Jax.

A man who may have lied to her. Played her.

And tried to kill her.

"IT FITS," WADE said, pacing around the hotel room. Sarah's room. "I mean, think about it . . . if Murphy's story is actually true . . ." Wade tapped his chin. "Then Jax would sure have one strong motive for vengeance."

"But *is* Murphy's story true?" Victoria asked. She was sitting on the couch beside Sarah. "It's not like that guy is the most reliable source." Her worried stare darted to Sarah. "We all know just what a great liar your father truly is."

Yes, they did. "We've got people digging into the records in South Carolina." Assistants from LOST who were checking on old arsons and fire-related deaths. If her father had killed Carl Winston, then they'd find a record of the man's life . . . and death.

"I *know* Jax." It was Emma who spoke up now. Emma who was glaring at them all as she stood next to Dean. "He wouldn't do this." She pointed at Sarah. "And you should know better."

Dean turned toward her. "You always defend him. Look, I get that he helped you when you were alone, but do you even know all of his secrets?"

Her gaze fell. "No one knows all of his secrets," Emma murmured.

Sarah had thought that she was close. She'd thought that she *knew* him.

She still did. That was the part that hurt. She still thought she knew . . . "He could be innocent."

"Love is so fucking blind." Wade gave a sad shake of his head. "Blind as a bat and I hope I can always keep seeing."

Sarah frowned at him.

"Sarah . . ." Now Gabe was sighing her name. "The guy had means and plenty of motive."

She wasn't so sure about means. "He was with me when Molly vanished. He was—"

"His guards have been following you for days," Victoria reminded her. "How hard would it have been for one of those guys to swipe Molly?"

"His guards don't have blond hair and blue eyes."

"Maybe one does," Victoria told her. "And you just haven't met him yet."

Sarah's fingers twisted in her lap. "He's the one who helped me get Molly out of that building. He wouldn't do that, unless—"

"Sarah." Gabe's voice was quiet. "Profile him. You tell us why the perp would help to rescue her."

She didn't want to profile Jax. She'd never wanted to . . . "To throw me off. To establish trust. To make me think that he was someone I could . . ." *Love.*

No, she wouldn't say those words. Wade had been mocking a few moments ago. He had no clue just how deeply she had actually fallen for Jax. "A perp would do that," she continued, clearing her throat, "so that when he did go in for the kill, that final act would be all the more painful because of the lies and betrayal."

The room was quiet. So quiet she could hear the faint ticking of Wade's watch.

"We found out something while you were out of town." Wade glanced at Gabe. Gabe nodded, and Wade said, "That building that nearly blew you and me to hell and back? The one wired with all the cameras? It belongs to Jax Fontaine."

Instinctively, Sarah shook her head, denying his words.

"We had to pry through a paper trail about fifty miles long," Wade continued, "but we tracked the place back to him."

If Jax had owned the place, he would have told her . . . right?

"You know that Jax Fontaine is capable of murder." Those soft words came from Victoria.

She did. She knew he could kill but . . .

Sarah stood. "It's wrong." *I won't let this doubt eat me alive. I have to trust someone!*

And that someone wasn't going to be her father.

"Jax was enraged when my father made his big revelation." She'd never forget the sight of him going across that table. "He didn't know until that moment." His reaction couldn't have been fake.

"Are you sure?" Victoria asked.

Trust . . . trust . . . Jax's face flashed in her mind. She remembered the way he'd held her when she'd woken after her nightmare. The way he'd rushed into that fire even when she screamed for him to leave.

He could've rushed in because he knew he was safe. Because he'd told one of his men just where and how to attack in order to set off the explosives.

Sarah gave a hard, negative shake of her head. "He didn't know," she said again. "My father knew, and Charlene knew."

"Charlene?" Emma stepped forward. "The woman who raised Jax? How did she knew his real parents—"

"She *was* his real mother." And Sarah hadn't told Jax that. Because he'd already been hurting enough. To find out that his real mother had committed suicide, that she'd been the one abused with him for so many years . . . "It's possible she told someone else. Or that Mitch Fontaine told somebody. Someone knows about Jax's past, and that person is using it against him." She rubbed her temples. "Using it to set him up."

"Maybe the guy is just fucked in the head," Wade offered with an exasperated wave of his hand. "Maybe he's—"

"He's more than you think." She rose from the couch. Paced to the window. Stared out. "There is more going on here than we see. The perp out there . . . I still think he's using Jax. I think he wants to destroy Jax just as much, if not more than he wants to destroy me."

She put her hand on the glass. It was slightly cool to the touch. The city was a hum of activity below her.

"Is that why you called us in?" Gabe asked as he paced toward her. "Because you thought Jax might be in danger and you wanted to put some distance between the two of you? The same way you tried to ditch all of us?"

"I just want you all safe." She wanted to protect them all.

"Yeah, we figured out why you were trying to ditch us," Gabe added.

Sarah glanced over at him. Eve was beside him. Her eyes were worried. "You were shot," Sarah said to Gabe. "Eve wasn't exactly going to forgive me if something else happened to you."

Gabe threaded his fingers with Eve's. "Do you think I'd forgive myself if something happened to you?" Gabe asked her. "We're a team, Sarah. And we stick together."

Yes, they did. She knew they would have her back, but . . . who would be watching Jax's back?

JAX TURNED OFF the alarm at his house. He stood there a moment, just inside the doorway. The place was big and empty and dark, dark even with the faint sunlight streaming through the windows.

I lost Sarah.

After all the shit that had gone down in the last twenty-four hours, that was the part that jarred him the most. Sarah. She'd been afraid when she looked at him.

Emma had been afraid of him, too. She'd run.

Charlene had been afraid. She'd died.

Everyone who feared him . . . they left.

Sarah was gone now, too.

Fucking . . . *Sarah.*

He slammed the door shut behind him. He looked up at that staircase, but, no, he didn't want to go upstairs. If he did, he'd just see Sarah there. In his bed. He'd smell her scent in the air. Sweet vanilla and—

There *was* a scent in the air. Only it wasn't sweet and it sure as shit wasn't vanilla. His nose burned as he stepped forward.

It was heavy, rank . . .

Jax started climbing the stairs. The scent deepened. It was definitely stronger up above.

He stopped at the landing. The smell so strong up there. But it wasn't coming from his bedroom. The bedroom was empty. He glanced around.

The bathroom door was ajar. He pushed it open a little more. The rancid smell was thick enough to choke him.

He wasn't really surprised when he saw the body. After all, that particular scent was pretty damn unmistakable.

The body was spread on his bathroom floor. It looked

like the man had been shot in the shoulder and his throat had been cut.

From ear to ear.

The man's bald head gleamed.

"Sonofabitch."

Ron Tate was dead on his bathroom floor.

Jax just stared at that body a minute. "I told you to run fast," he muttered. But Ron had obviously thought Jax was the only one after him. And the cops were going to think he was the one who'd gone after Ron, too. He'd already been booked for assaulting the man once.

Now the guy was dead, in his house.

Jax backed out of the room. He tried not to touch anything, but, hell, it was his house. His fingerprints were going to be everywhere.

He went back down the stairs. Out the door. He hit the remote to open his gate—

And he saw Brent West standing there.

"Have a good trip out of town?" the detective asked. Brent took a step toward him. His hand went to the butt of his weapon. "Because I just got the most interesting tip about you."

Jax lifted his hands. "It's not what you think . . ."

Brent glanced over at Jax's house. "I can't help you anymore, man. I just . . . can't."

Jax knew he was well and truly fucked.

The sonofabitch out there had set him up, and he'd played right into the guy's hands by letting his emotions rage out of control.

GABE'S PHONE RANG.

Sarah glanced over, wondering if one of their assistants had already struck pay dirt in South Carolina . . .

He frowned at the screen, then put the phone to his ear. "Spencer," he said. His face tightened. "What the hell?" he demanded.

Sarah tensed.

"And why would I do that?" His gaze slanted toward Sarah. "That could be straight bullshit."

Then his lips clamped together.

"I will destroy you if you've been playing us," he promised.

Sarah had no clue what was happening.

Gabe lifted his phone and offered it to her. "It's Jax."

Her heart slammed into her chest. She took the phone, far too conscious of everyone staring at her. "H-Hello?"

"Sarah . . ." Jax said her name with longing, with need, and she ached.

"Why did you call Gabe?" she asked him, trying to calm her frantically racing heartbeat.

"Because I think you've switched phones a dozen times in the last few days. I don't have your current number . . . and I figured you'd be with him."

"Jax—"

"I don't have long to talk, so just listen, okay?"

She could hear voices in the background. A siren?

"I'm using up my last favor, but I needed you to know . . . I'm sorry, Sarah."

Her hold tightened on that phone.

"I was out of control at that prison. I never wanted

you to see me that way, but hell, maybe I wasn't hiding from you. I was hiding from myself."

"What's happening?"

"I'm going to jail. This kill wasn't mine, but the body was in my place."

What?

"Ron Tate. Shot in the shoulder . . ."

The shoulder . . . the shoulder . . .

"And with his throat slit. The cops are going to say I was enraged at him. I made the threats in front of everyone—"

Her mind spun. "I shot the man who—who came after Gabe and me—I shot him in the shoulder."

Jax's laughter was bitter. "Then maybe the cops will say I thought Ron was the one who's been hunting you. That he was the one who took Molly. I wanted to stop him, so I did. I killed him."

"Jax, please, don't say anything else." Because she *had* heard a siren in the background. If the cops were there, they would be paying careful attention to every word that he said.

And they'd use those words against him later.

"Fuck them, Sarah, I need you to know, I didn't do this. I didn't kill him. I didn't use you. *I won't hurt you.* You got to me, pretty Sarah. Know that. You made me want . . . so much."

She had to swallow to clear the lump from her throat. "Jax, what can I do?"

"Watch your back. Because he's out there, and he's taking me away from you."

She couldn't suck in a deep enough breath. "I'm coming to the police station. We'll fix this. Victoria is here. She can examine the body. She'll find proof that you didn't so this!"

"Sarah, there's something you should know . . ."

"Jax, I didn't know what my father had done!" The words were torn from her, tumbling out so fast. "I didn't know, and *I'm* sorry." She hadn't been able to look at him without guilt eating her alive. He'd lost everything because of her father. Because—

"I love you," he told her.

Then he hung up.

Sarah gazed down at the phone. She could hear the erratic sound of her own breathing. Could feel her too fast heartbeat shaking her chest.

This wasn't right. It wasn't—

He shouldn't love me.

She'd wrecked him. She'd destroyed his life—her *father* had taken everything from him.

"Sarah?" Victoria said her name softly. She touched her shoulder.

Sarah jerked. "They're arresting Jax." She grabbed for Victoria's hand. "They found a body at his house. I'm going to need your help, Viki, *please*."

Victoria nodded. "Always."

"YOUR LAWYER ISN'T going to be able to get you out of this one," Cross said as he closed in on Jax. Yeah, it figured that guy would be there. Like a shark, smelling blood in the water. He'd just pulled up at Jax's house. "Your ass is going down. You're going to rot in jail, and that's just where you belong. Locked up for the rest of your life."

Murphy Jacobs was locked up. Locked up and still laughing.

"Did you enjoy hitting that girl?" Jax asked Cross.

Brent was a few feet away, watching them warily.

Two uniforms stood by their car.

No one had cuffed Jax yet. Their mistake.

"What girl?" Cross demanded as his chin jutted into the air.

"The nineteen-year-old stripper at Lucky Lady. She wouldn't give you a private dance—oh, sorry, I mean a private fuck for free—so you broke her nose. Made it so that she couldn't get any money. That's what you told her, right? 'If you can't fuck me, then I'll make sure no one fucks you.' "

Cross flushed and glanced toward Brent. "That's a lie! That's—"

"I know what you did. She told me. And now . . . it's your turn to get broken." He drove his fist into Cross's face. Hell, he was already going down, so why not enjoy the hell out of his last bit of freedom?

He heard the crunch of bones as Cross yelled.

Then the dirty cop was attacking him. The other cops closed in, and Jax just punched Cross even harder.

"You shouldn't hit women," Jax told him. "Because it just pisses me off."

Brent grabbed his arms. So Jax used his legs to fight. He slammed them into Cross's stomach. The guy grunted and then he collapsed. He fell in a heap on the ground.

"Payback," Jax told him. "It's a real sonofabitch—"

His house exploded.

HE SMILED AS he watched the fire. Jax Fontaine had just flown through the air. He'd slammed into the side of a police car, and the guy wasn't getting up now. Maybe he'd broken some bones. Maybe his damn neck.

The cops weren't moving. They'd been knocked back by the blast.

Chunks of debris were littering the street. And that house—the house that Jax had been so very proud of—was nothing but fire right then.

He headed across the street. Kicked a groaning cop out of his way.

Then he reached down and put his gun under Jax's chin. "Hey, asshole," he said. "Want to live or die?"

Jax's eyes slowly opened. He saw the flash of surprise there as Jax stared at him. Yeah, the fool had never seen him coming.

"'Cause I can shoot you right here . . . or you can drag your ass into my car and live just a little longer."

"Fuck . . . off," Jax said. He was bleeding from a huge gash near his forehead.

"That's not the right answer." He slammed the gun into the side of Jax's head. He hit *hard,* and Jax's eyes rolled back into his head. "Guess I get to drag you." He started hauling the guy with him, humming as he walked.

"*Stop!*"

He didn't.

"*Stop or I'll shoot you!*"

It was the detective—the one who was so freaking chummy with Jax. Detective Brent West. Sighing, he stopped and turned to look at the guy. West was on his stomach, trying to crawl toward him. All of those cops were still alive. Groaning, hurt, but breathing.

Why?

He fired at West. The guy cried out and fell back. Then he shot at Cross. A bullet to the head. He took care of the two uniforms in seconds.

Now when help finally came, people would wonder . . . had Jax attacked them all and escaped? Set the bomb to try and cover his tracks?

People in this town always suspected Jax.

He was such a good villain.

But I'm better. So much better.

JAX DIDN'T MAKE it to the New Orleans PD. And neither did Sarah. Gabe got the call about the fire at Jax's place while they were racing across town. They spun around and headed hell fast for his house.

When they got there, the street had already been blocked off. The fire—a sight that Sarah had become far too familiar with—was lighting the sky. There were ambulances in the street and . . . body bags.

Jax. No, not Jax. No!

Sarah leapt out of the car and ran ahead. She shoved people out of her way, people who'd just gathered to watch the carnage. She was counting those body bags and not even breathing. *One. Two. Three . . .*

"Jax!" Sarah screamed. Because he couldn't be dead. He couldn't.

She saw a stretcher being loaded into the back of an ambulance. And—Brent was on it. Strapped down, covered in blood, but still alive. "Brent!" She ducked under the police tape. "Brent!"

A cop grabbed her arm and tried to shove her back.

Wade caught the cop's hand. "You don't want to do that, buddy," Wade told him, voice flat. "Trust me."

The uniformed cop's jaw dropped. "This is a crime scene, bozo! Get your ass back—"

Sarah slipped away from him and ran to Brent. His head had turned. He was staring blearily at her.

"Brent, what happened?"

"Jax . . ."

Jax hadn't done this. She knew it. *I love you.* His words were cutting into her. "Where is he?"

"Ma'am, you need to step back," one of the EMTs told her.

Sarah stepped closer. "Where is he, Brent?"

His chest was covered in blood.

"T-Taken . . ."

No. "Who took him?"

"*Ma'am, get back!*" The EMT pushed her. Sarah pushed right back.

"Brent, please!"

But his eyes were sagging closed. And more cops had closed in on her. They grabbed Sarah and carried her back. Her gaze darted frantically around the scene. One of the body bags was partially open. She could see—

Detective Cross.

The other bags were zipped up. Smoke filled the air. Sirens were screaming.

And Jax was *gone.*

"Stay here!" The cop told her when he shoved Sarah beneath the police tape. She almost ran right back under, but Victoria caught her hand.

"He's not dead, Sarah!" Victoria's hold tightened on her. "I talked to the ME. Cops . . . the three dead are cops. Detective Cross and two uniformed officers. Jax isn't here."

She sucked in a deep breath, but her heartbeat wouldn't slow down. It felt as if her heart would leap right out of her chest at any moment. "Where is he, Viki?"

Victoria shook her head. "I don't know." She nodded. "But we'll find him, Sarah. You can count on it. We'll find him."

Sarah looked at the chaos around her. So many cops. So much fire.

The house Jax had loved was gone. Nearly obliterated. But he wasn't dead. He was still alive.

"I'm coming, Jax," Sarah whispered. She wasn't going to just let him vanish. She'd tear this city apart if she had to do it, but Sarah *would* find him.

BY NOW, SARAH would know that Jax was gone.

She'd be looking for her lover. Worried. Afraid.

In the hours to come, her fear would just get worse. Fear was such a powerful weapon. He knew that. Murphy had taught him that.

Jax was out cold. Maybe he'd hit him too hard with the gun, but he didn't really care. The guy would die in the end, so it didn't matter if he'd cracked Jax's skull or not. He just needed him alive long enough to speak a few words.

Molly had been good bait.

Jax was even better.

He'd bound the guy's hands behind him. Tied his legs to the chair. They were in an old empty house, a house that sat alone on a dead-end street. Once upon a time, the place had probably been nice—now it was just crumbling ruins. Why the hell Jax bought places like that he didn't know. But at least Jax's property had sure made things easier for him . . .

In this area, there was no one to watch. No one to hear the screams. And before he was done, there would be plenty of screams.

Jax groaned.

Ah, so he was coming around. Good. It was almost time to make a little phone call. He'd already taken Jax's phone. Soon, they'd be contacting sweet Sarah. Inviting her to join their little party.

And when Sarah got there, that was when the real fun would begin.

"F-Fucking . . . bastard," Jax muttered.

He took his knife and sliced down Jax's arm, cutting right through the tattoos.

Jax's eyes opened. They were bleary, but rage was already starting to burn there.

"Guess what happens next?" he asked Jax.

Jax didn't answer. The guy just glared at him.

"It's your turn to die . . ."

Chapter 16

THE POLICE STATION WAS A FRENZY OF ACTIVITY. When three officers were killed and another was sent to intensive care, the brothers-in-blue went into serious attack mode. They were combing the streets then. Talking to witnesses. Flashing photos of Jax to the media.

Sarah and Emma were at the station, trying to keep tabs on all the chaos so they could catch any leads that the police might get.

Gabe was in the captain's office, making deals, as usual, to keep LOST fully in the loop.

Dean was at the hospital, waiting for Brent to get out of surgery so that he could find out what else the guy might know. Brent was their best bet right then. Their main chance of getting a lead on the bastard who'd taken Jax.

"He's alive, right, Sarah?"

She turned at Emma's soft question.

"The guy wouldn't take him to just . . . just kill him right away. Jax is still alive." But her words sounded more like a question than anything else.

Sarah nodded. “He’s alive.” And she was going to find him. She wouldn’t give up on Jax. Because he wouldn’t give up on her.

I love you.

Her gaze slid around the station. So much chaos. Tips were coming in, but, so far, those tips weren’t panning out at all.

“Your father didn’t know who we’re after?” Emma asked her.

Sarah’s lips thinned. “All my father wanted to do was tell me to get the hell away from Jax. He thought Jax was the threat.”

“Jax isn’t!” Emma’s denial was immediate. “I know his past is dark. He’s done things that crossed the line, but I swear, he’s good inside, Sarah. He’s—”

“You don’t have to convince me,” Sarah told her softly. “I know exactly what he is.”

Emma swallowed. Her arms wrapped around her stomach.

“And we’re going to find him, Emma. We are.” If she said those words enough, Sarah knew they had to be true. She knew—

My father wanted me away from Jax. He wanted me to stay with LOST. He’d been intent on driving Sarah away from Jax. But if Jax *wasn’t* the threat, and if her father had known that . . .

Then my dad thought the killer was coming for Jax. He thought I could be in danger, just because I was near him.

“Emma, you didn’t know about Jax’s childhood, did you?”

Emma shook her head. "Not until Dean told me. Jax was always so private. He never talked about what his life was like when he was a kid. Jax didn't share his secrets with anyone."

He'd shared them with Sarah.

Look at this all again. You're missing something. Think!

"If Jax were going to tell someone, who would it be?" Sarah asked. "His closest friend? Who's that, Emma? Who is it?"

"Carlos," Emma whispered. "They've been tight for years. Ever since Jax found Carlos in an alley. Two jerks were cutting him, holding him down, and Jax stopped them."

Carlos. "Where is Carlos now?" Because he wasn't being her shadow any longer. Actually, she hadn't seen Carlos since she'd returned to New Orleans.

But, before then, the guy had been her guard. Hanging in the shadows, watching her, watching the LOST agents . . . he would have been aware of every move that they made.

"It's night now, so he's probably at the bar. He may not even know that Jax is missing."

If he'd turned on a TV or radio, he'd know. Sarah nodded. "I need to speak with him. Now."

Emma's face tightened. "Carlos isn't involved."

Maybe. Maybe not.

"Molly said a blond man lured her away. Carlos isn't blond, and the guy's scar is pretty hard to miss. If she'd seen him, Molly would have—"

"We don't know that the killer is working alone."

Because she'd seen partnerships in the past. And when those partnerships were formed, they were the deadliest combination she'd ever witnessed. "I need to see him."

Emma stepped closer. "I'm coming with you."

She'd been hoping Emma would say that. Emma knew the city better than anyone else in LOST, and she was well-acquainted with the darkness that surrounded Jax's life.

Emma pulled out her phone. "I'll tell Dean where we're headed. Viki and Wade can take over here."

Sarah sucked in a deep breath. She could feel her control fraying. She'd always tried to be so careful on her cases. She'd played by the rules. Done everything *right.*

Only now, everything was horribly wrong. Jax was gone. He could be hurt, dying, and she had to find him.

Sarah knew it was time for her to let go. To stop holding back. It was time for the world to see her as she truly was.

Time for the bastard who'd taken Jax to realize . . . Sarah was her father's daughter.

And she had a monster inside, too.

Sarah slipped away while Emma made her phone call. She'd been watching the detectives, and she'd seen one guy put his gun in his desk. The guy hadn't even bothered to lock that desk drawer. Sarah took the gun and slipped it under the hem of her shirt.

I'm coming, Jax. Wait for me.

SHADE WAS PACKED. Men and women were drinking, dancing, and damn near fucking in the middle of the bar. Voices filled the air and Sarah had to shove gyrating bodies out of her way. She didn't see Carlos. Not—

"There!" Emma grabbed her arm. "He just slipped behind the bar."

Sarah pushed toward the bar, and there was Carlos. He was smiling. He had a tequila bottle in one hand and a glass in the other.

Smiling.

Sarah could feel heat spreading up the sides of her face. She stalked toward that bar. "Carlos!"

His head whipped toward her. His smile dipped.

She put her hands on the bar. The people around her were too damn loud. "Where is he?"

Carlos glanced at the folks shoving against the bar. Then he motioned toward Sarah and Emma. He gave a quick curl of his finger as he headed away from the bar and toward the door marked PRIVATE.

The door opened. Carlos walked inside, strolling slowly. "Look . . ." It was quieter in there, so she could hear him easily. "Jax told me to pull the guard on you. I get that you two are done, but you need to let go—"

She wasn't letting go of anything. Sarah grabbed him by the shirtfront and pushed him against the nearest wall.

Carlos blinked at her.

"Jax is missing, my control is *gone,* so don't even think of feeding me bullshit."

Emma shut the door behind them, then she took up a position right next to Sarah.

"Missing?" Carlos's scar twisted even more as his brows shot up. "What the hell are you talking about?" His gaze jumped from Sarah to Emma. "Em?"

"His house is ashes," Sarah told him. She was screaming on the inside, but when she spoke, her voice was flat. Almost calm. *Such a lie.* "Three cops were killed there and Jax was taken. Then I come in here and find you having a good old time with your tequila in his bar—"

"*My* bar!" Carlos snapped. "Jax gave it to me. Signed it over right before he flew off with you . . . said he was looking to make some changes."

What?

"I thought that meant he was going to try and live on the right side of the law. For you." Fear flashed in his eyes. "But he's . . . gone?"

"You haven't watched the news," Emma muttered. "You should really turn on a TV sometimes."

"I never watched the damn news!" Carlos shouted. "When? When was he taken?"

"Two hours ago." Hours that were eating at Sarah's soul.

"No." Carlos jerked away from her. "Liar. You're lying!"

Emma was right beside Sarah. "Two hours ago," she said.

Carlos pulled out his phone. "He texted me!"

Sarah snatched that phone from his hand. Her fingers slid over the screen as she pulled up the texts and sure enough, there was a note from Jax.

It's Jax. Pull off detail on Sarah. We're done.

Goose bumps rose on her arms. She shook her head. "This isn't Jax's number."

"The guy keeps burner phones. With our lives, it pays to have a few of those." He shrugged, but his eyes were darting nervously between her and Emma. "I didn't . . . didn't even question him."

You should have. "Jax and I aren't done." Her chin lifted. "That text came in an hour ago."

She heard Emma's hard inhale.

"He wants me unprotected," Sarah said. "The perp wants to make sure that no one follows me . . ."

So he'd texted Carlos. Gotten the guy to back off. "But I've got you," Sarah whispered. She called Gabe. He answered on the second ring. "I have a number I need you to monitor. If we can find this phone, then we can find Jax."

JAX JERKED AGAINST the ropes that bound him. They were cutting into his wrists, slicing his skin. He could feel the blood dripping down his hands. The bastard had tied him up tight.

The *dead* bastard.

Or, rather, the man who was supposed to be dead.

"You can pull against those ropes all night long," Mitch Fontaine told him with a cold smile. "It won't do you any good. You're not going anywhere."

"How the *fuck* are you still alive?" Jax demanded. The guy's neck had broken. He'd been *dead*.

"I guess it takes a lot to kill me." Mitch strolled toward him. Moving like he didn't have a care in the world and taking his sweet-ass time. The knife in his hand glinted. "Let's see how much it takes to kill you." Then he drove the knife into Jax's side. The burn of that blade was white-hot as it sliced into him. And it went deep, shoving until the hilt hit him. "This is the start," Mitch said, "of the payback I owe you."

Jax slammed his head into the guy's chest, and Mitch stumbled back. He yanked the knife out of Jax as he fell back.

"You going to kill me?" Jax locked his jaw against the pain and snapped, "Then do it!"

Mitch shook his head. Mitch . . . *Mitch.* The bastard even looked the same. Same dirty blond hair. Same eyes—eyes that were darker than Jax's. He and Mitch kind of looked alike—that was why everyone had believed that Mitch was Jax's father. *But he wasn't!*

Mitch's hair was longer and stubble covered his jaw, but it was as if all of those years hadn't passed. Jax was staring at the man who'd made his life hell.

The man who wanted to slice him apart.

"You and that bitch dumped my body. You left me in that stinking field to rot."

"You were my first dead body," Jax muttered as he bled out. "Sorry if I didn't do shit right."

Mitch laughed. Laughed. "Here's a tip. Make the fuck sure the victim is dead!"

Charlene had been the one who told Jax that he was dead. She was the one who said they had to leave his body out there. Then get away, get out of town as fast as they could. She'd . . . "She knew," Jax realized. "Charlene knew you weren't dead!" And she'd wanted Jax to get away from him because she'd been afraid that Jax *would* kill Mitch.

A muscle jerked in Mitch's jaw. "After all I did for her . . . she left me in that field and chose you."

He yanked harder at the ropes. He shoved against the chair.

"She thought that was her chance to be free." Mitch raised the knife. Stared at the blood that dripped off the blade. "It took me some time, because the two of you had fucked me up so bad . . . had to stay in a hospital for months after that farmer pulled me out of his field, but, eventually, I found her."

Jax struggled even harder. "No!" He shook his head. "No, you—"

"I didn't realize how much I liked killing back then. I mean, I was mostly worried about getting caught. So I just made it look like she'd killed herself. Shoved those pills right down her throat. Made her *choke* on them." He smiled. "Then I watched her. I watched all that life bleed right out of her eyes, and I finally understood just why he'd done it."

"You *killed* Charlene!"

He shrugged. "I've killed a lot of people. More than him . . . and I haven't been caught."

"Who are you talking about?" Mitch was insane!

"You know, he laughed at me the first time we met. He brought Charlene and your bratty ass to me. Told me I had to take care of you or he'd come back to slice me apart, just like he'd done to your dad." His eyes turned to slits. "Who the hell was he to talk to me like that?"

Murphy.

"I ran because hell was breaking lose in that city. Took you and Charlene, but you two never appreciated a damn thing I'd done."

No, they hadn't appreciated the beatings or the drugs or the shit.

"Then I realized . . . he wasn't coming after me. I could do anything I wanted."

And Jax remembered that Mitch had become even more violent. That last night . . . *when I pushed him down the stairs, he was about to kill Charlene.*

"But you thought you were the one in charge. You shoved me down those stairs. I was in a hospital for all those long months! Trapped in that damn bed! Barely able to move!" Spittle flew from his mouth. "When I got out, I killed that bitch. Then I was gonna kill you but . . ." He shook his head. "I wound up in fucking jail . . . got sent—" Mitch broke off, his lips clamping together.

But the way the guy was raging . . . Jax could put the pieces together, and as he did, shock rolled through him. "You were at the same prison with Murphy." *Sonofabitch.* Fate could sure be a twisted bitch.

All that time, he'd thought Mitch was long gone, but the guy had been alive. Alive—and what? Getting kill lessons from Murphy the Monster?

After Charlene had died, Jax had left town—moving again—and he'd never looked back. Jax had been on the streets, moving fast and just trying to stay alive. He'd wound up in New Orleans. He'd never even thought about searching for Mitch. Why would he? The guy had been a dead man.

"When they locked me up, that bastard recognized me. The guards were all scared of him. Let the fool do whatever the hell he wanted." Mitch yanked up his shirt.

Jax saw the slashes across his skin. "He used his shiv on me within forty-eight hours of my check-in. But he didn't want to kill me. That wasn't what he did. He just wanted to make me beg. To show me that he had the power."

Fuck, fuck, *fuck*!

"I know about the power rush that comes from death. I felt that power when I took Charlene's life . . . and after a while, after all of his twisted torture games, Murphy realized we were more alike than he'd thought. He told me things . . . showed me so much . . ." His words trailed away. "I survived by playing him. Then one day, I was free and he was still rotting on the inside."

"That's when you came down here."

"I was just gonna kill you, then I saw Sarah. Beautiful Sarah." His hand slid over the scars on his chest. "I couldn't think of a more fitting payback for Murphy."

Jax shook his head. *No.* "You aren't killing her."

"You aren't going to be able to stop me." Mitch smiled and lifted the phone to his ear. He hummed then, a light tune . . .

A tune that Jax had heard Sarah hum, when they'd been in that little motel near the prison.

"Hello, Sarah . . ." Mitch murmured into the phone as he kept his eyes on Jax. "Are you ready to come and find your lover?"

"I'M READY," SARAH said. She was more than ready. Gabe could track the phone, just like he'd done before, and they'd have—

"You're not tracing the call this time. I learn from my mistakes."

She wasn't so sure he did. "Proof of life," Sarah demanded.

He laughed. "Screw that. You know you want him either way."

"*Sarah!*"

She tensed. She'd heard Jax's shout. Heard it so clearly.

"*Stay away, Sarah! He wasn't dead! Stay—*"

"Come find him," the bastard taunted. The line went dead.

Sarah looked up. Emma was on the phone with Gabe. They'd been waiting for this, hoping to get the lock when the call came through.

Emma shook her head.

No.

"Where is he?" Carlos asked as he paced in that narrow room. "*Where is he?*"

VICTORIA STARED DOWN at the bulletin she'd just gotten. Well, it was a bulletin that the desk sergeant had received, but since her current job was to monitor the intel that came through the police station and report back to Gabe, she'd made a point of snagging that bulletin.

She read it three times to make sure there wasn't a mistake.

Four.

Then she ran toward Wade and Gabe.

"We didn't get him," she heard Gabe snap to Wade. They were behind a group of cops, all leaning over a computer. "The techs didn't have time to locate the phone—"

Victoria cleared her throat. "Gabe."

He glanced over at her.

"We need to talk. Now." Her hand fisted on the paper. "Come on." Because the cops hadn't made the connection with the bulletin, not yet. After all, why pay that much attention to a bulletin that had come in from so far away?

She hurried toward the first empty office she could spot. Gabe and Wade followed her inside.

"Viki, what is it?" Wade said. "We need to be out with—"

She lifted the paper. "Murphy Jacobs escaped from prison."

"*Fucking, no,*" Gabe said, his eyes widening as he snatched that paper from her.

"He was in the infirmary because of—of some accident that had happened . . ." An accident that seemed to have occurred when Sarah was visiting with him. Only Sarah hadn't mentioned an accident to Viki. "He was cuffed, the guard had just cuffed him—but Murphy had a key. He got free and he killed the guard on his way out."

"Sonofabitch." Wade looked shell-shocked. Victoria felt the same way.

"He's been missing since then. The cops are searching everywhere, but if anyone can vanish . . ."

"It will be Murphy," Gabe finished.

She nodded.

Wade took the paper from Gabe. "He's not vanishing."

He already *had* vanished! Slipped out of a maximum security prison and gone—

"He stayed in jail for eleven years." Wade's eyes burned with gold fire. "He got out now for one reason."

Gabe's brow furrowed. "Sarah went up there because she wanted him to tell her who the perp is. Sarah thought Murphy knew the guy's identity."

"And the bastard *did* know," Wade said. "But he wasn't going to let Sarah be threatened. The perp had gone after the one person Murphy cares about. So now Murphy is out—"

Victoria backed up a step. Murphy Jacobs terrified her. "You think he's coming here?" No, that wasn't possible. New Orleans was too far away from his prison. He'd have to get transportation. Not a plane, no way would he risk that kind of exposure. But he could hitchhike. And, hell, so many big rigs traveled down to the Crescent City. If he'd gotten a ride from one of those drivers . . .

He could already be in the city.

"I think he's coming to protect Sarah. I think he's going to kill whoever tried to hurt her. Because that's what Murphy does best . . ."

Kill.

Gabe already had his phone out. "We have to call Sarah. *Now.*"

"HE'S NOT DEAD," Sarah repeated. Jax's words kept replaying in her head. He'd told her those words for a reason.

Eddie Guthrie was dead. She knew that. Victoria had gone down to the police station and confirmed the guy's cause of death. The three cops were dead—they'd been loaded into the body bags and driven away from Jax's burning house.

Brent West was still in the hospital.

Who isn't dead?

"How many people has Jax killed?" It was a question that she had to ask.

Emma's mouth dropped open in shock. "What? Look, right now isn't the time—"

"Jax isn't a murderer," Carlos said, throwing back his shoulders "No matter what you might think. Why the guy was so crazy about you I don't—"

"Mitch Fontaine."

Carlos clamped his lips together.

"You knew about him, didn't you, Carlos?"

Carlos looked away.

Emma was staring at Sarah in confusion. "He . . . he killed—?"

"He's not dead," Sarah repeated Jax's words. Jax wouldn't have said that unless he thought she'd make the connection to the killer. But there was only *one* man Jax had confessed to killing. The man who'd beat him and Charlene. She lunged for Carlos and grabbed him again.

"Stop doing that!" he snapped.

"What did Mitch look like?"

Carlos glared.

"Do *not* push me!" Sarah yelled at him. "I don't have time for that crap. Jax needs me, and I'll be damned if I let him down." She shook the guy. So what if he was a foot taller and probably seventy pounds heavier? She was going to make him talk. "Did you ever see a picture of Mitch? Did you—"

"Blond, like Jax. About his size." His words were grudging. "Darker eyes . . . saw a picture just once. Jax burned that shit after that."

"Mitch Fontaine," Sarah whispered. She fumbled and had her phone out again. She—

The phone rang. She nearly dropped it. Her fingers swiped across the screen. "Hello?" Sarah answered, voice scared and tense.

"Sarah!" Gabe's voice was just as tense. "You need to come into the station. Right now. Come in."

"No, no, Gabe, listen." She started walking around that little room. "I've got a lead that I need you to follow. A guy named Mitch Fontaine. He was Jax's—" Hell, she didn't know how to explain this. "Stepfather. He disappeared years ago, but I think . . . I think he's in New Orleans. I think he has Jax and—"

"And I think *your* father is in town, Sarah!"

Once again, the phone nearly slipped from her fingers.

"He busted out after you left. The guards took him to the infirmary . . ."

Because he'd pushed Jax into attacking him. Choking him.

"He was cuffed, but he managed to get a key from the guards . . ."

When they'd swarmed him and pulled Jax away. It had just been a pile of bodies for a moment. They'd all been so close. It would have been incredibly easy to take the key from a guard then.

"He killed a guard and vanished. Murphy is out, Sarah. You need to get back here. We need—"

"I need to find Jax." He was the only thing that could

matter right then. "Please, Gabe, just send me everything the cops have on Mitch Fontaine. Send me everything that LOST has. I need it now."

"Sarah . . ."

"My father isn't going to hurt me."

"You put a gun to his head," he reminded her.

She didn't need the reminder. "I need to know about Mitch Fontaine."

A pause, then . . . "Give me five minutes."

She hung up the phone. Emma and Carlos were both watching her. Sarah put her hand to her temple. Rubbed. Tried to figure out just what this perp would do. "You wouldn't go back to the riverfront . . . you already had a victim there. This is your endgame, so you'd want to go to a place where you felt like you had the most control. A place that you'd been using . . . this whole time."

"Uh, Sarah," Emma began.

"Mitch, Mitch . . . Jax tried to kill you, so you want him to pay just as much as you want Murphy to pay. If this is about Jax, if he's what first pulled you to the city, then you studied him." Her temples were pounding as she kept trying to get into the mindset of this killer. "I was a bonus. You found me, through Jax. And you decided it was time to act. You've been here, though, biding your time. Jax drew you. He took what was yours. So you . . ."

"Does she always do this?" Carlos asked.

Sarah's hand dropped to her side. "You take what belongs to Jax." She whirled toward Carlos and Emma. "Mitch framed him because he wanted to make sure everyone thought Jax was a killer. He destroyed Jax's home because he wanted to take it away from him." Her gaze flew to the door. "We should get everyone out of here. If he wants to hurt Jax, he'll take this place, too—"

"It's *my* bar now," Carlos reminded her as he stepped in front of that door, barring her path. "And, hell, Jax has plenty of property in this town. If the guy wants to take things away from Jax, he's got tons of options."

A cold fist had closed around Sarah's heart. "A building that's secluded. No close neighbors. One that wouldn't attract attention."

Carlos nodded. "Yeah, yeah . . . there's a place like that in the Quarter. On Tibideaux Street. He buys houses, fixes them up. He's always trying to fix things . . ."

To make up for his past.

"But he hadn't started on this one yet. He met you and everything else fell away." He shook his head. "He's got that one . . . and another, closer to Slidell. An antebellum place in the swamp. Guy thought he could turn that snake hole into something special."

Her phone was ringing again. She shoved it to her ear. "Gabe, what did you find out?"

"Mitch Fontaine did two tours of duty in the military. Want to know his specialty back then?"

"Explosives," Sarah whispered.

"He got out, had scrapes with the law, and vanished for a long time."

Yes, she was sure he had.

"But then he turned up years ago, got busted for assault and drug running. He wound up in Biton Penitentiary—"

Biton? "With Murphy." And it all made sense.

"The guy went dark after he got out. Slipped parole and no one has seen him since. According to the report, his parole officer figured he was dead."

"I think that happened a lot." She shoved back her hair when it tried to fall forward. "Look, Jax has two houses that are sitting empty right now. We need to check them out."

"You think the perp is keeping Jax at his own place?"

"Why not? He wants to hurt Jax . . . why not kill him in his own home?"

Gabe swore. "All right, let's hit them."

"Emma and I will go to the one in the Quarter," Sarah said, thinking quickly.

"I'm coming!" Carlos said immediately. "There is no damn way you're leaving me behind. If Jax is in danger, I'm there."

Her gaze met his. She read the steely determination in his stare. "Carlos is coming with us." They might need him because Sarah had no idea what they'd find when they arrived.

Carlos's shoulders straightened. "Damn straight I am. Jax is my friend. I owe him."

"Carlos, give me the addresses for the two houses."

He rattled them off and she immediately told Gabe the locations "You take a team to the house near the swamp, and I'll cover the one on Tibideaux Street. We split up and we find him faster . . ."

"No, Sarah," Gabe argued, "we need to stick together. With your father on the loose—"

"I told you, Jax is my priority." Not her father. "I need your help, Gabe. I need the team."

"Dammit . . ." His rough sigh carried over the line. "Get Dean. You and Emma need more backup and that guy will *kill* me if Emma rushes into danger without him at her side."

Sarah slanted a glance over at Emma. The other woman was already on the phone. "He'll be there with us," Sarah said.

"Be careful," Gabe told her.

"You too," Sarah whispered. The gun was a cold weight against her.

HE SAW SARAH rush from the bar. Run as if she were escaping hell.

Or rushing straight into the fire.

Two others were with her—a man and a dark-haired woman.

Sarah didn't even bother to glance around before she jumped into the car and sped away.

He shook his head. He'd taught her so much better than that. Sarah was taking too many risks. Risks for no reason. "I told you, Sarah," Murphy whispered, "you should stay away from him." But Sarah hadn't listened. He'd been afraid of that. Especially when he saw the way she looked at Jax Fontaine.

Did Sarah even realize all that she'd given away to him during that little visit at the prison? She used to control her emotions so much better.

If he'd realized her weakness, then others would, too.

Like the bastard who was trying to hurt his baby girl.

Your mistake.

He cranked his car. The car he'd stolen twenty minutes ago. Then he pulled onto the street. It was rather good to be back in action again.

Now, if he could just get his hands on a really sharp knife . . .

Chapter 17

"I CAN'T BELIEVE YOU FUCKED HER," MITCH SAID. He'd wiped the blood off the knife. Now he held that gleaming edge up, letting the light from the lanterns bounce off it. There was no electricity in the old home, because Jax hadn't connected the power yet.

Jax recognized the house. He'd had plans for this place. Those plans sure hadn't included *dying* there.

"I mean, I get that Sarah is hot. A nice piece of ass, but you knew who she was." He laughed then. "Oh, wait, you didn't know everything about her father, did you? You didn't know that he was the one who—"

"I know he killed my parents," Jax rasped. "He told me."

Mitch looked momentarily surprised. "You . . . talked to Murphy?" What could have been fear cracked in his voice. The emotion was mirrored in the flash of his eyes.

I guess we're all afraid of something . . . or someone. "That's where Sarah and I went . . . you know, when you were busy dropping a body in my house."

Mitch smiled. "Did you nearly shit a brick when you

saw him? That one was too good. I almost didn't blow the house because it was such a good way to tie you to old Ron's murder . . . but then I realized, hey, his DNA will still be there. The cops will find *some* pieces of him left. And you got to lose out on that fancy-ass house that you *never* should've had." Mitch stalked toward him, that knife gripped tightly in his left hand. "I like the fire. It's a pretty bitch when it burns."

Mitch was insane. He'd always been, Jax just knew it now.

Mitch leaned toward him. "Murphy lied to you."

Jax tilted his head back as he stared up at the guy.

"Oh, he killed your old man, all right . . . sliced him apart. But he didn't kill your mother. Your mother, sweet, stupid Charlene, was with you all along."

"No," Jax said. That wasn't possible. The guy was jerking him around. Playing mind games, just like Murphy.

"*I* killed her." Mitch smiled.

"You're fucking lying! Charlene wasn't—"

"She was so afraid Murphy would come after her. She dyed her hair, changed her whole life . . . said that the woman she'd been died. That she was someone new." His laughter was mocking. "She even used to tell you that she was someone new, that she was different. Made you repeat that shit with her over and over again." His eyes gleamed. "In case you didn't know it, your mom was crazy. Murphy's attack did that to her . . . she never got over it."

Your old life is over . . . He could see Charlene in his mind. Staring at him, with tears in her eyes. *But I promise, I'll protect you. I'll be with you. It won't be like it was before.*

"No," Jax said once more. Forcing that word out. Mitch was just screwing with him. It couldn't be true . . .

I love you. Charlene's words whispered through his mind. *But you can't ever go home. You have to stay with me.*

"I killed your bitch of a mother. Just like I'm gonna kill Sarah, and then I'm gonna kill you."

Something seemed to switch off inside Jax. He wasn't afraid. Wasn't angry. He wasn't anything at all. "You won't hurt Sarah."

"You're tied up, and I'm about to slash your veins wide open. All you'll be able to do is bleed and watch." He seemed to consider that. "I wonder which one of you will go out first. Do you want Sarah to die first? I mean, the expression is . . . ladies first, right?"

"I'm going to break your neck," Jax told him softly. "I'll do it with my bare hands this time. There won't be any doubt that you're dead when you hit the floor."

Mitch's hold tightened on the knife.

"I loved my mother," Jax said. "She loved me." Charlene's tear-filled gaze flashed in his mind.

Mitch didn't move.

"And I love Sarah." He yanked hard against those ropes and felt the thick hemp slice even deeper into his wrists. He didn't even mind the pain.

"You think Sarah loves you? She's like Murphy, she can't love, she can't—"

"Like you fucking can."

Mitch looked at the knife, then he drove it into Jax's arm.

"DEAN IS ON the way," Emma said as she put down her phone. Emma was in the front of the car and Carlos was leaning forward from the backseat. "We'll beat him there, but he wants us to wait—"

Carlos lunged forward, grabbed Emma's head, and slammed it into the passenger side window.

Sarah screamed.

Carlos pressed a knife against her side. "Just drive."

The knife sliced into her.

"Drive the damn car. Keep going just like you'd planned."

When she'd gotten in the vehicle, Sarah had put her gun in the glove box. Dammit. She needed that weapon! She cast a fast glance over at Emma. Blood trickled from her head, and Emma's eyes were closed.

"She's still alive," Carlos muttered. "And if you keep driving, you will be, too."

He pulled out his phone.

"You're working with Mitch," Sarah realized.

The knife sliced deeper.

"I've got her," Carlos said into his phone. "I'll leave her with you, and then I'm out. Got it? Whatever you're doing, I don't want to see that shit."

He put the phone back down. She could feel his eyes on her. "I thought you were Jax's friend," Sarah said.

"No, you didn't. Not really. That's why you came to the bar tonight, all ready to rip into me. You thought I'd betrayed him. Well, guess what? I had."

"He gave you the bar—"

"I don't want to be second place to Jax Fontaine. He's run this town too long. It's time for some new blood to take over."

He was still leaning in close. He didn't have his seat belt on, and Sarah thought about wrecking the car. Just driving it straight into the nearest pole. He'd fly forward. Probably slam his head into the windshield. Then she wouldn't have to worry about him but . . .

Emma could be hurt even worse. Dean loved Emma. So Sarah had to protect her. She kept driving.

"He went soft for you. Forgetting everything else, everything but you. I knew it was time then. Time to make my move. I'd held back, looking for this moment. Then when Mitch approached me, offering me cash if I just kept him in the loop about Jax's comings and goings . . . how could I pass up that chance? I knew he wanted to take out Jax, and I thought, hell, yeah, and this way—"

"You thought you wouldn't have to get your hands dirty."

"If he hadn't gone soft," Carlos said, "then he would have seen the threat coming."

"No, he just trusted you, and that's why he never realized the danger was closing in." But the danger had been there all along, and Carlos had set them up so perfectly—getting Sarah and Emma in the car with him. Insisting that he had to go along with them . . .

"You saved me before . . ." Sarah reminded him. "At the first fire, you saved me and Wade." *Now* he was turning on them?

Carlos gave a bitter laugh. "Had to do it. Others were with me. Nate and George. They always looked out for Jax. Couldn't turn with them there."

So he'd played the hero? The friend?

"Not that they matter now, especially Nate." His voice sharpened. "The dead don't matter."

"Were you ever his friend?" Sarah asked, needing desperately to break through to him.

"Just drive the damn car."

"SARAH'S COMING. LOOKS like she found you, with a little help." Mitch had left the knife sticking out of Jax's arm. "Want to know who's bringing her in to me? You'll like this part. Ready? Carlos."

The guy was lying. Carlos was as close to a brother as he'd ever had.

"Did you ever wonder why those men were beating the hell out of him in that alley? I did some checking. Turns out Carlos was in their gang. They'd made a heist and, during the middle of that robbery, Carlos had left two guys behind. He wasn't exactly the kind of guy that could be trusted."

But Jax had trusted him. Carlos had been at his side for years—

"All it took was a little cash, and he told me everything he could about you." Mitch sighed. "Of course, I did also have to promise to kill you so that Carlos could step out of your shadow. But I'd planned to do that anyway so it was all good for me." Mitch yanked the knife out. Blood poured down Jax's arm. He ignored the pain and kept pulling his wrists againsts the rope. All the blood had really slickened his hands.

He was *almost* free.

"He's bringing Sarah to me, and I'll start using my knife on her. How long do you think it will be before she starts to beg?"

SARAH BRAKED IN front of the house on Tibideaux Street. Emma was still out cold. "She needs a doctor," Sarah said. She unhooked her seat belt, ignoring the sting of that blade, and she leaned over Emma as if she were reaching out to help her. But Sarah's fingers slid toward the glove compartment. *I've got to grab the gun—*

Carlos rammed her head into the steering wheel. The horn sounded, a long, desperate cry.

"Crazy bitch. I *saw* you put the gun in there." Then he was climbing out of the car and dragging Sarah with him. Blood trickled from her lip. "Now I need to drop your ass off and get the hell out of here." He headed for the door. Kept his grip on her. His hand lifted, and he pounded, hard.

"He'll kill you," Sarah said. "Don't you see? Mitch will . . . turn on you . . ."

"Nah. I've never done anything to him. I'm the one who helped him." His head lowered toward her ear. "You're the one he wants to cut into pieces. Turns out, your old man really screwed him over."

The door opened. A tall, blond man was there. Had to be Mitch Fontaine. He was grinning at her. He yanked her from Carlos's arms and—

Mitch drove his knife right into Carlos's throat.

Carlos tried to cry out, but only a gurgle escaped him as he sagged to his knees, with the knife still lodged in him.

"Keep that one," Mitch told him with a sneer. "I've got another knife. By the way, you aren't getting paid." He dragged Sarah fully into the house and slammed the old door shut behind him.

HE DIDN'T SEE Sarah. Murphy parked the car well down the overgrown road, not wanting the sound of his engine to alert the people who were waiting in the old house. He walked down that lane, keeping to the shadows.

Sarah's car was parked near the house. Someone was in that car. A woman, slumped over. He opened the passenger side door, and she fell into his arms. Her black hair was matted with blood. A pretty woman. His hand touched her throat. Her pulse was strong, but the wound on her head was bleeding a little too heavily.

He eased her back into her seat. That woman's phone was ringing, again and again. He turned the phone off. Then he searched the car's interior. When he opened the glove box, Murphy smiled. Ah, Sarah had come ready for battle.

But what good would the gun do if it was still in the car? He tucked it into his waistband. Then he made his way to the house's front door. The body was there. A man with a slashing scar. The man who'd gotten into the car with Sarah. That guy had been in the backseat. Murphy frowned and looked back at the vehicle.

The attractive but unconscious woman was in the front passenger side, and based on the location of her injury . . . He knelt down next to the man. Saw the faint rise and fall of his chest. He wasn't dead yet, either.

Murphy's fingers closed around the knife. The guy's eyes flew open.

"You'll stay alive," Murphy said, keeping his voice whisper soft, "unless the knife gets pulled out. When it comes out, you'll die."

He could just make out the man's face in that darkness. Light spilled from inside the house, maybe from candles? Lanterns?

"You hurt the woman. And don't lie, because lies just piss me off."

The man nodded.

"Did you hurt Sarah?"

Again . . . a nod.

He yanked out the knife. Then Murphy rose and pushed open the door of that house.

JAX HAD ONE hand free. He just had to get the other out of the ropes, then he could untie his legs—

"There he is, Sarah, all tied up and waiting."

Jax stopped struggling. He looked up and his gaze locked on Sarah. Her eyes had never looked darker. She was afraid, he could see it on her face. He didn't want Sarah to be afraid.

"I found you," Sarah whispered.

Mitch had the knife at her throat. "Where should we start first?" He yanked up her arm. Shoved the sleeve away from her wrist. "How about right here, a nice long swipe across your— Oh, Sarah . . . someone's already cut this vein once."

Sarah was still staring at Jax. She smiled. "Help's coming."

Jax slammed back against the chair, trying to break those chair legs. Once. Twice. Three times. Again and again.

"Help won't arrive in time." Mitch seemed so certain of that. "I've got this place wired. If anyone gets too close . . . *boom*!"

Jax felt the give of the rope around his legs.

"I always loved the fire," Mitch said. "Your father used to let me set some fires for him, Jax. When he needed to make evidence disappear. That's why when his place burned, I was more than ready to clear out with Charlene. Figured the cops would try to pin that fire on me." He yanked on Sarah's hair, tipping her head back. "'Cause no one knew about her freak of a father back then."

"Let her go," Jax shouted.

"I want to hear her scream." Then Mitch grabbed for Sarah's right wrist. "No mark here . . . let's give you a matched set."

Sarah shoved against him, but he sliced open her wrist. Her blood dripped down her fingers, coming in a long stream.

"*No!*" Jax bellowed. "Fuck it, stop!! Don't hurt her! You want some payback, then hurt *me*!"

Mitch shrugged. "But it does hurt you when I hurt her."

He put the bloody knife back against Sarah's throat.

"Sarah," Jax whispered. "I'm sorry." Sorry for everything. Sorry for being a fool when they'd been at the prison. Sorry for scaring her. Sorry for not telling her how much he loved her until it had been too late.

Because he'd loved her from nearly the beginning. When he'd looked into a pair of dark eyes and actually seen . . . hope. Something more. A future that he'd never thought to have. He'd loved her, and he would do *anything* for Sarah.

Mitch let the edge of the blade trail over Sarah's collarbone, then down to her chest, resting that tip right between her breasts. "Are you scared, Sarah?" Mitch asked her.

Sarah didn't answer.

He sliced through her shirt. "Are you going to beg?" Mitch demanded. "Beg me to let you live?"

She shook her head.

"You will!" Mitch swore. "You will—"

Her head turned toward him. "You're going to die soon." Her voice was cold and flat. "You won't get out of this house."

Mitch hesitated.

"You should have never come after me or Jax. It'll be your own fault when you die."

"I'm not dying!" Mitch yelled. "You are!" And he drove his fist into Sarah's jaw.

"*No!*" Jax roared. He yanked at the last of those ropes. They tore free and he kicked out of the chair, fighting to untie his legs. Fighting to get to Sarah. But Mitch was over her with that knife. Right over her heart. "*Stop!* You want someone to beg, then I'll beg! Don't kill Sarah! Please, don't!"

Mitch kept that knife right at her heart. His head turned and he smiled at Jax. "Beg again . . ."

Jax was on his feet now. He wanted to run at the bastard, but he needed the man to get away from Sarah. "Mitch, don't—"

The blade sank into Sarah's chest.

"*No! Please, fucking no!*" And Jax launched his body at the other man. He slammed into him because if he didn't do something, Sarah was dead. Jax knew it. She was dead.

He couldn't let that happen. No matter what else happened, he needed Sarah to live.

He grabbed for the knife. There was so much blood on Sarah. And she hadn't made a sound. No screams. No cries of pain. Not even when the knife had gone into her.

"She's gonna die, and so are you!" Mitch swung that knife at Jax.

Jax caught his wrist, stopping the knife inches from his throat.

Mitch snarled.

Jax tightened his grip. He kept tightening it and tightening it until . . .

Snap.

The knife hit the floor.

"Not your neck this time," Jax said, "but I'll work my way up there."

Mitch head-butted him. Jax fell back, but then he launched forward again, adrenaline and fury giving him strength. He had to get Mitch away from Sarah. Had to take him out. He drove his fist into the man's face. Again and again and again.

Mitch just . . . laughed. "Bitch is . . . dying."

Jax stopped, his hand poised to slam into Mitch again. "Sarah!" Jax shouted.

She didn't answer.

Mitch was sprawled beneath him, not fighting. Jax glanced over at Sarah. She wasn't moving. *So much blood.* "Sarah?" Jax called once more, fear breaking in her name. "Sarah, no!"

He jumped off Mitch.

And Mitch surged forward, grabbing for the knife. Swearing, Jax dove for it, too. He caught it right before Mitch could get it. Then Jax drove his foot into Mitch's side, sending the man rolling back.

Jax ran to Sarah. The knife was still in his right hand. His left reached down and touched her cheek. "Sarah . . . princess, look at me."

Her head turned. Sarah smiled at him. "I would . . . always . . . find you."

Fear clawed in his chest. "I'm going to get you out of here." He leaned over her. "Sarah, I'm going to—"

Gunfire blasted. At first, Jax didn't even realize that he'd been hit. He didn't feel the pain because he was staring into Sarah's eyes. Sarah's beautiful eyes. But then he heard her screaming.

She hadn't made a sound before, but she was screaming as if in agony now. Over and over and she was screaming—

His name.

Jax looked down at his chest. Blood. *But I still don't feel the pain.*

"*No one hurts Sarah!*" It was a roar that came from just a few feet away. A roar that had come from Murphy Jacobs. "I told you to stay away from her!"

Sarah was trying to reach out to Jax. Her fingers

were nearly touching him. She was crying. He hated for Sarah to be in pain.

"I . . . love you," Sarah whispered.

He wanted to tell her that he loved her, too. He wanted to say that everything was going to be all right. But his body was slumping, and even though he tried to touch Sarah, he couldn't. He couldn't do anything . . . but fall.

I love you, Sarah.

DEAN SLAMMED ON his brakes when he reached the house at the end of Tibideaux Street. He jumped out of his car, checked his weapon, and ran forward. Another vehicle had been parked a few yards back, but it had been empty. Now he could see Sarah's rental car up ahead and—

It wasn't empty.

Dean staggered to a stop. Right then, his whole life seemed to stop. He hurried to the car and yanked open the passenger door. He'd been calling Emma, over and over, but she hadn't answered. Now he knew why.

She sagged against her seat belt, slumping toward him.

"Baby?" he whispered. She had a huge knot on her head and blood had streamed over the right side of her face. She was breathing—thank Christ. "Baby, please, look at me."

Her eyelashes fluttered.

His heart started beating again.

"Th-Thought you were . . . the other one . . ." Emma whispered.

The light from the interior of the car was making

them a target. He lifted her into his arms. Shut that door. Plunged them back into darkness.

"Man . . . came before . . . went after Carlos and Sarah . . ."

He carried her back to his car. He needed to find Sarah. She was his teammate, but Emma—Emma was his whole fucking life. He had to make sure she was all right. He eased her down behind his car. Dean pulled out his phone. Dialed Gabe as fast as he could. "Screw the house in the bayou, get to Tibideaux Street. *Now.*" Then he put his gun in Emma's hands. "I have to check on Sarah." He tightened his grip around her. "You keep this, and if anyone comes at you . . . baby, you shoot, do you understand?"

Emma gave a faint nod.

He leaned forward and kissed her.

Then he heard the screams.

SARAH COULDN'T STOP screaming. Jax had been there, reaching for her one moment, then he'd been shot the next. She rolled, *crawled* to him. Her chest hurt. She hurt, and Jax was too still.

"He won't hurt you again."

She knew that voice. It was her father's voice.

Sarah touched Jax's chest. The bullet had gone in, blasting fast and deep. "What did you do?"

"He won't hurt you." The wood creaked beneath his footsteps. "Not ever again."

Sarah's shaking fingers touched Jax's face. "I love him."

"Wh-What?"

"He never hurt me." Jax's eyes were open and on hers. "He was protecting me."

"Sarah . . ." Jax whispered. "Please, go . . ."

"Not without you." Her fingers squeezed his. "I came for you and I won't leave without you."

"*Fucking bastard!*"

That yell had Sarah's head whipping up and she saw Mitch pushing to his feet. He was glaring at Murphy, hate twisting his face. "You're not getting out . . . you're *not*!" Then he pulled a phone from his pocket. No, not a phone exactly . . . "*No one is getting out!*"

Mitch smiled and pressed a button.

Sarah felt the whole house shake when the bomb went off. She threw her body over Jax's, trying to protect him as best she could. Then she felt the rush of fire . . . all around her. "I love you," she whispered.

DEAN WAS RUNNING toward the house—and it exploded. Fire burst from the front door, sending that wood flying back and into him. Dean was thrown to the ground. He shoved the door off him, stared at the fire, and bellowed, "*Sarah!*"

Chapter 18

SOMEONE WAS HUMMING. SARAH OPENED HER eyes, coughed, choked, and tasted . . . smoke?

And someone was humming . . . she could hear the tune even above the crackle of the flames. Sarah sat up, shoving aside a chunk of wood that had fallen on her. Fire was streaking up the wall, but she wasn't burned. She wasn't, and—

"Jax!" He was beside her, his hand reaching out, as if he'd touch her. She grabbed his hand, holding tightly to him. "Jax, please!"

His eyes opened. "Sarah . . ."

Her breath heaved out. *He's still alive!*

"Was dreaming of you . . ." Jax said. "We were on an island . . . the beach was so hot, it burned you when we walked . . . I picked you up . . ." His fingers tightened on hers. "I took you away . . ."

"Jax, we have to get out of here." The smoke was so thick and—where was her father? Was he the one humming?

Or was that Mitch?

Didn't matter. Jax was the reason she was there.

"My heart's . . . still beating . . ."

Her father hadn't shot him in the heart. She'd realized that. The entry wound was too low, but it could still be a shot that would kill him, if Jax didn't get help soon.

"We're going to stand up, and we're getting out of here." Even if they had to walk through the fire. "Do this for me, Jax. For me."

His gaze held hers. "I'd do anything . . . for you, Sarah." Then he pushed up. He moved slowly, and she knew every moment was agony for him. But he rose, and she slid her shoulder under his arm. They started heading for the door. For the flames.

"*You aren't getting away!*"

And Mitch was there. Appearing out of that smoke. Blocking their path. And he still had that trigger in his hand. "That was just the start . . ." He laughed. "That one sealed off the exit downstairs . . . there's more . . . more . . ." He was about to press that trigger again.

Her father appeared behind him. Murphy had a knife in his hand and he just slipped that knife right up to Mitch's throat. In a flash, he'd cut Mitch's throat. From ear to ear.

Mitch gurgled . . . then fell. The trigger dropped from his hands.

And her father started humming again.

Jax pushed Sarah behind him. "Stay away . . . from her . . ."

Murphy shook his head. "You're a dead man walking. You won't get out. You'll just slow my daughter down."

That humming . . . such a familiar song . . .

She could almost hear him sing . . .

Hush little Sarah, don't say a word. Papa's gonna buy you a mockingbird.

If that mockingbird won't sing . . . Papa's gonna buy you a diamond ring.

He'd sung his slightly altered version of that song to her for years . . . then he'd started humming it, humming it whenever he seemed stressed. Humming it . . .

Hush little Sarah, don't say a word. Papa's gonna teach you to hunt and kill.

By the time we're done, the bodies will be still.

The lyrics had twisted over the years, just as he'd become twisted and evil. He'd stopped being her father and become . . .

The Monster.

And I'm like him.

"Will you . . . let Sarah pass?" Jax asked.

Mitch was still moving, grabbing at his throat. With all the smoke, she couldn't tell how deeply her father had cut him.

"I'm here to save Sarah," Murphy said. "I love her."

The fire crackled louder.

"So . . . do I . . ." And Jax stepped aside. "Go . . . Sarah . . ." He pushed her toward the door. Toward Murphy.

Sarah grabbed Jax. "I'm not leaving you!" The smoke thickened even more. She coughed, but clutched tightly to him. "I won't!" There was no way she'd leave him to the fire.

Her father locked his hand around her arm. "There's

no time, Sarah! Go out the window! Climb down—" He coughed, too. "Go!"

She shoved him away. Held tighter to Jax. "*I love him!*"

Jax kissed her. "You were . . . the best thing . . . to ever happen to me . . ."

He felt so cold against her. In a room that was burning hot, Jax shouldn't be cold, but he was.

"Don't do this," Sarah begged. For him, she'd beg. For him, she'd kill. For him, she'd do anything.

I just can't leave him.

"Go . . ." He pushed her. Her father was pulling her and . . .

Mitch was reaching for the trigger he'd dropped. Her father hadn't cut him deeply enough!

"No!" Sarah lunged for the trigger. She knocked it out of Mitch's reach.

Her father grabbed Mitch, jerking him up. "Stay away from her!"

Then the gun went off.

Even in the midst of the fire, Sarah froze. She looked over. Mitch was in front of her father . . . and he had a gun in his hand. She didn't know where he'd gotten the weapon. But he'd just shot her dad. And that shot—it had been fired point-blank into her father.

Murphy looked down at the wound. Then he . . . laughed. And he drove his knife into Mitch. Mitch staggered back and fell.

So did Murphy.

Her father . . . her father *fell.*

Sarah dropped to her knees beside him. "Daddy?"

And for that one instant, he was just . . . her daddy again.

He turned toward her. "Sweetheart . . ."

Sarah felt a scream building in her throat. He was dying, she knew it. Jax—Jax had slumped against the wall. The fire was spreading and she was trapped there.

"Go . . . out the window . . ." her dad said.

Sarah shook her head. "You . . . you're here and Jax . . ."

"Go . . ." And his eyes closed. His breath sighed out.

No. Not like that. He couldn't just *die* that fast. He couldn't . . .

Jax needs me.

"Sleep tight," Sarah heard herself whisper. *You're safe tonight.* She pressed a kiss to her father's forehead.

She pushed to her feet. Mitch was still not moving. Her father had finished him. She put her arm under Jax's shoulder once more. They couldn't go through the door. The fire was too strong. Her father had been right. She steered Jax toward the window. They were on the second floor, but they would have to take that jump. Broken bones—fine. They'd be *alive.*

She kicked out the old window. Fresh air blew inside and she gulped it in greedily.

"*Sarah!*"

Dean was down below, waving to her.

"Jump, Sarah," Jax said, his voice low and rough. "Go . . ."

Her father had been trying to push her, too. Trying to make her leave, but she hadn't. Didn't Jax get it?

"Not without you." She wasn't going anyplace without Jax.

He shook his head. "I'm . . . already . . . d—"

"No!" She locked her fingers with his. "This is how—" She choked on the stupid smoke. "It works. Either we both go . . ." Another cough. " . . . or we both stay."

Because she wasn't leaving him to the fire.

Jax stared into her eyes. "You . . . love me?"

"Yes." She kissed him. Fast and hard. "Now let's go, let's—"

Something was moving in the fire. Mitch? Still not dead. No, no that wasn't possible! Why wouldn't he just stay down! And he had the gun . . . he was lifting it. Aiming it—

Jax wrapped his arms around Sarah, shielding her with his body.

And they jumped.

HE FUCKING HURT.

There wasn't a single part of Jax that didn't ache or burn, but that was okay with him. If he hurt, then it meant he was still alive.

"S-Sarah . . ." Talking was one hell of a lot harder than it should have been. Jax felt like he'd swallowed glass.

Or been trapped in a fire.

"I'm here." Soft fingers brushed over his cheek. He felt his body being lifted. He should open his eyes, but that seemed to require a whole lot of effort.

"H-Hurt?" Jax managed to ask. Had Sarah been hurt when they jumped? Mitch had been firing and Jax had tried to protect Sarah with his body. He thought he might have been shot again, but as long as Sarah was safe . . .

"You saved me," she told him.

Jax shook his head. No, he hadn't. Sarah had saved him, from the very beginning. "Love . . ."

"I love you, too," Sarah whispered. Her lips pressed to his.

"Ma'am, we have to take him to the hospital," Jax heard a voice say. "He's losing blood too fast."

"I'm coming with you, Jax," Sarah told him. "From now on, I'll always be with you."

And he smiled.

The pain didn't matter.

Sarah was safe. Sarah mattered.

GABE SPENCER STARED at the burning house. He'd just been pulling up to the scene when Jax and Sarah had burst out of the window. Jax had broken his leg when he hit the ground. Broken his arm. But Sarah . . . Jax had held tight to her. She'd been safe.

"They were the only ones to come out," Victoria said from beside him. Her gaze was on the house. On the wreckage. Firefighters were battling the flames. The house was so old, the wood so rotten, that the fire had spread too quickly for them to easily control it.

"Sarah said Mitch was still alive when they jumped," she added.

Gabe kept his gaze on the fire. "He's not alive now." Not Mitch. Not Murphy. They were gone. "No one's alive in there now."

Victoria was silent. Then, after a long moment, she asked, "Why did Murphy come down here?"

"Because he knew the man who was after Sarah. He had to stop him."

"Why? He killed so many people . . . Sarah's said herself that he's a psychopath." There was confusion in Victoria's voice, and Gabe knew she wasn't just thinking of Sarah's father, she was thinking of her own.

Victoria's father hadn't killed dozens of people. He hadn't been a slick serial killer who'd eluded capture for years.

Instead, Victoria's father had struck out at the people closest to him. He'd killed Victoria's mother. No one had believed Victoria when she tried to tell the cops . . . not at first.

That's why Viki always speaks for the dead.

"Did he . . . love her?"

The smoke blended with the darkness of the night.

"I figure he did, as much as he could love anyone."

Gabe turned away. Victoria kept watching the fire. He'd taken two steps when she said, "Do you hear that?"

Gabe looked back. Victoria was still staring at the fire.

"I could have sworn," she murmured, "that I heard someone humming."

JAX OPENED HIS eyes. He wasn't particularly surprised to find himself in a hospital room. He remembered doctors peering at him. Men and women in green masks. There had been lots of bright lights and pain. Surgery.

He'd kept asking for Sarah. She hadn't been there then and now—

He turned his head.

Brent stared back at him.

"Aw, fuck," Jax muttered. Yeah, it still felt as if he'd swallowed glass when he spoke.

Brent's lips quirked. "Expecting someone else?"

"Sarah." He needed to see her.

"She's been at your side for the last twenty-four hours. While the docs were saving your sorry ass in surgery, she got herself stitched up. She hasn't left since then."

She wasn't there now. And he needed to see her. To make sure she was all right. He started to push up from the bed.

"If I weren't dragging around an IV bag and feeling like shit, I'd shove you back into the bed myself," Brent told him gruffly. "But since you've got a broken leg . . ."

Hell, he *did* have a broken leg. The cast was stretched up and hanging in the air.

"I figure you can't go far." Brent rolled back his shoulders. The guy was wearing a white hospital gown. So was Jax. "Relax. Sarah just stepped out to talk with your docs. She's literally on the other side of that door."

The room's door opened. Sarah was there. Shadows were under her beautiful eyes. Scratches were on her cheeks.

She was perfect.

When she saw him, her lips curled—a fast, brilliant, beautiful smile. She ran across the room. "Are you with me this time?" Her fingers slid carefully over his face. "Truly with me?"

He lifted his hand. His damn fingers were shaking. He touched her. *Real.* Sarah was in front of him. Real and safe and alive.

"I should go get your doctors," she said. "They were briefing me and I need to let them know you're back—"

He caught her hand. "Don't go." He needed her close.

Sarah's face softened as she stared at him.

"Don't ever go, Sarah." He knew they had a ton of shit to work through. Her past. His. But the past . . . the past didn't matter right then. He wanted the present, with her. The future . . . with her. Anything that she could give to him, he wanted. "Stay with me."

Sarah leaned forward and kissed him. Light and sweet. The best kiss of his entire life. "Always," Sarah promised him. When she looked up at him, Jax saw the truth in her eyes. Sarah loved him. Him.

He knew he was the luckiest bastard on earth.

Jax pulled Sarah closer—with his left hand because his right arm was in a cast, too. And he just . . . held her.

He'd found what had been missing from his life for all of those long years. The other part of his soul. And, yeah, he knew that probably would sound corny as shit if he ever told anyone but . . .

"I love you," Sarah whispered.

But it's the truth.

He kissed her cheek. "Forever, Sarah. Forever."

EPILOGUE

Victoria hurried out of the morgue. She was practically running, but she didn't care. She had to get to Gabe. Fast. She rushed up the stairs and then threw open the door to his makeshift office.

Gabe spun around. Wade glanced over at her, frowning.

"Viki?" Gabe stepped toward her. "Is everything all right?"

No, no, things were definitely not all right.

They'd stayed in New Orleans for a few extra days. Everyone had needed time to recover, and since Viki was one of the few who'd actually remained injury free on this particular case, she'd volunteered her services to the PD.

She'd been working in the morgue, going over the remains recovered from the fire at Tibideaux Street. But the news she had . . . it wasn't good.

Not good at all.

"He wasn't there," Viki said. Her words quavered.

"Who wasn't?" Wade asked as he, too, crept closer.

"They brought the bodies in. Three bodies," Viki said.

Gabe nodded. "Right. Carlos, Mitch Fontaine, and Murphy Jacobs—"

"No." That was the problem. "Carlos." She nodded. "Mitch Fontaine." They'd identified them both very quickly. "Not Murphy Jacobs."

Gabe's eyes widened. "What?"

"The remains for the third victim . . . we just identified them. They didn't belong to Murphy. They belonged to a guy named Nate Tremaine. He—he worked for Jax. I don't know how he wound up there . . . maybe he was selling Jax out, too, just like Carlos. Or maybe Mitch was torturing the guy to get information, but his body was there. It was recovered. Him, not Murphy."

Wade's face had gone slack with shock. "So where is Murphy Jacobs?"

Victoria shook her head. "I don't know. Sarah said that he'd been shot, but the firefighters didn't find his remains."

"Maybe there just weren't enough remains left." Gabe's voice was grim.

"No. There should have been something."

"They just haven't found him yet." Wade straightened. "That's all. They got the three bodies, so they slowed down the search. We'll call them and let them know another body has to be there. Remains, something—"

He broke off and they all looked at one another.

"Murphy Jacobs *is* dead," Wade said.

Victoria wasn't so sure.

"He is," Wade said again, but he sounded as if . . . as if he were trying to convince himself.

And Victoria remembered the faint humming she'd heard, the sound blending with the fire . . .

That humming had been oddly familiar, a tune that she'd heard before . . .

Hush little baby, don't say a word . . .

Have you read the first two sexy and suspenseful novels

featuring the LOST team

from *New York Times* best-selling author

CYNTHIA EDEN?

Don't miss

BROKEN

and

TWISTED

Available now from Avon Books!

Read on for excerpts . . .

PROLOGUE

SHE COULD SMELL THE OCEAN AND HEAR THE pounding of the surf. She could see the sky above her, so very blue and clear, but she couldn't move at all.

Her body had gone numb hours ago. At first the numbness had been a blessing. She'd just wanted the pain to stop, and it had. She didn't even scream any longer. What would be the point? There was no one around to hear her. No one was coming to help her.

Seagulls cried out, circling above her. She didn't want them to fly down. What if they started to peck at her? *Please, leave me alone.*

Her mouth was dry, filled with bits of sand. Tears had dried on her cheeks.

"Why are you still alive?" The curious voice came from beside her because he was there, watching, as he'd watched for hours. "Why don't you give in? You know you want to just close your eyes and let go."

She did. She wanted to close her eyes and pretend that she was just having a bad dream. A nightmare.

When her eyes opened again, she'd be someplace different. Someplace without monsters.

He came closer to her, and she felt something sharp slide into the sand with her. A knife. He liked to use his knife. It pricked her skin, but then he lifted the knife and pressed the blade against her throat.

"I can end this for you. Do it now. Just tell me . . ." His words were dark. Tempting. "Tell me that you want to die."

The surf was so close. She'd always loved the ocean. But she'd never expected to die like this. She didn't *want* to die like this. She realized the tears weren't dry on her face.

She was still crying. Her cheeks were wet with tears and blood.

"Tell me," he demanded. *"Tell me that you want to die."*

She shook her head. Because death wasn't what she wanted. Even after all he'd done, she didn't want to stop living.

She didn't want to give up.

The knife sliced against her neck. A hoarse moan came from her lips. Her voice had broken when she screamed and screamed. She should have known better than to scream.

That was what he'd told her. *You should know better, sweetheart. It's just you and me. Until your last breath.*

Her blood mixed with the sand. He was angry again. Or . . . no, he'd always been angry. She just hadn't seen the rage, not until it was too late. Now she couldn't look at him at all. No matter what he did to her, she *wouldn't* look at him.

She didn't want to remember him this way. Actually, she didn't want to remember him at all.

Her gaze lifted to the blue sky. To those circling seagulls.

I want to fly, Daddy. She'd been six the first time she'd come to the island and seen the gulls. *I want to fly like them.*

Her father had laughed and told her that it looked like she'd lost her wings.

She'd lost more than that.

"I want to fly," she whispered.

"Too bad, because you're not flying anywhere. You're going to die here."

But there was no death for her yet, and she wasn't begging.

The gulls were blurry now, because of her tears.

He'd buried her in the sand, covering her wounds and packing the sand in tightly around her. Only her head and some of her neck remained uncovered. Her hands were bound, or so he thought.

But she'd been working beneath the sand. Working even as the moments ticked so slowly past, and he kept taunting her.

He had taken his time with this little game. Tried to break her in those endless hours.

She wouldn't be broken.

Her hands were free. If he'd just move that knife away from her neck . . .

He lifted the knife and stabbed it into the sand—into the sand right over her left shoulder. She choked out a cry as the sharp pain pierced her precious numbness.

"You'll beg soon," he told her. Then he was on his feet. Stalking away from her. "They all do."

He'd left the knife in her shoulder and made the mistake of turning his back on her.

She'd lived this long . . . if she was going out, she'd fight until her last breath.

Her fingers were free. She just had to escape the sand. The heavy sand that he'd packed and packed around her.

Burying me.

She could feel the faint cracks start to slip across the sand as she shifted. Her strength was almost gone, but she could do this. She *had* to do it. If she didn't, she was dead.

PROLOGUE

WHAT DO YOU SEE FOR MY FUTURE?"

Emma Castille slowly glanced up from the cards that were spread on the table before her. The young girl who sat across from Emma appeared to be barely sixteen. Her blond hair was secured in a haphazard knot at the nape of her neck, her clothes were faded, and her blue eyes were wide with a fear that couldn't be controlled.

Emma didn't reach for the cards on her table. She just stared at the girl, and said, "I see a family that's waiting for you. You need to go home to them."

The girl's chin jerked. "Wh-what if they won't have me?"

"You'd be surprised at what they'd have." Darkness was coming, the night slowly creeping to take over the day. Emma knew that she would have to leave Jackson Square soon. Her time was almost up.

The others around her were already packing up their booths for the day. Psychics. Artists. Musicians. They were a mixed group, one that assembled every day as the sun came out, to capture the attention of the tourists in New Orleans.

Emma wasn't psychic. She wasn't gifted when it came to music or art. But she did have one talent that she used to keep her alive and well fed—Emma had a talent for reading people.

For noticing what others would too easily miss. Too easily *ignore*.

"You're running from someone," Emma said flatly. The girl had already glanced over her left shoulder at least four times while they'd been talking. Fear was a living, breathing thing, clinging to the girl like a shroud.

Emma knew what it was like to run. Sometimes, it seemed as if she'd always been running from someone or something.

"Will he find me?" the girl asked as she leaned forward.

Emma almost reached for the girl's hand because she wanted to comfort her. Almost. "Go back to your family." The girl was a runaway. She'd bet her life on it.

The young blond blanched. "What if it's the family you fear?"

At those words, Emma stiffened.

"Aren't you supposed to tell me that everything will be all right?" the girl asked. She stood then, and her voice rose, breaking with fear. "Aren't you supposed to tell me that I'll go to college, marry my dream man, and live happily ever after?"

Others turned their way because the girl was nearly shouting.

"Aren't you?" the girl demanded.

Emma shook her head. She didn't believe in happily ever after. "Go to the police." She said this softly, her words a direct contrast to the girl's angry tone. "You're in danger." There were bruises on the girl's wrists, bruises peeking out from beneath the long sleeves of her shirt. A long-sleeved shirt in August, in New Orleans? Oh, no, that wasn't right. *What other bruises are you trying to hide?*

The girl stumbled back. "Help me." Now her voice was a desperate whisper.

Emma stood, as well. "I'll go with you—" Emma began.

But the girl had glanced over her shoulder once more. The blonde's too-thin body stiffened, and she gasped. Then she was turning and running away. Shoving through the tourists crowding the busy square. Running as if her very life depended on it.

Because maybe, just maybe, it did.

Emma called out after her, but the girl didn't stop.

Let her go, let her go.

But Emma found herself rushing after the girl, going as fast as she could. But New Orleans, oh, New Orleans, it could be such a tricky bitch, with its narrow streets and secret paths. Emma couldn't find the blonde. She turned to the left and to the right, and she just saw men and women laughing, celebrating. Voices were all around her. So many people.

And there was no sign of the terrified blond girl.

Emma paused, and pressed her hand to the brick wall on her right as she fought to catch her breath.

But the wall was . . . wet. She lifted her hand, and in the faint light, she could see the red stain that covered her palm. A red that was—

Blood.